By Christopher Dow

Fiction
Effigy
  Book I: Stroud
  Book II: Oakdale
The Books of Bob
  Devil of a Time
  Jumping Jehovah
The Clay Guthrie Mysteries
  The Dead Detective
  Landscape with Beast
  The Texas Troll Unlimited
  Darkness Insatiable
Roadkill
The Werewolf and Tide, and other Compulsions

Nonfiction
Lord of the Loincloth (nonfiction novel)
Book of Curiosities: Adventures in the Paranormal
Occasional Pilgrimage: Essays on Film, Literature, and Other Matters
Living the Story: The Meandering, True, and Sometimes Strange
         Adventures of an Unknown Writer
  Vol.I: Growing Up Takes a Long Time
  Vol. II: Growing Old Takes Longer

Martial Arts
The Wellspring: An Inquiry into the Nature of Chi
Circling the Square: Observations on the Dynamics of Tai Chi Chuan
Elements of Power: Essays on the Art and Practice of Tai Chi Chuan
Alchemy of Breath: An Introduction to Chi Kung
Leaves on the Wind: A Survey of Martial Arts Literature (Vol. I–VI)

Poetry
City of Dreams
The Trip Out
Texas White Line Fever
Networks
A Dilapidation of Machinery
Puzzle Pieces: Selected Poems

Editor
The Abby Stone: The Poetry of Bartholo Dias
The Best of Phosphene
The Best of Dialog

THE TEXAS TROLL UNLIMITED

THE TEXAS TROLL UNLIMITED

CHRISTOPHER ROW

Phosphene Publishing Company
Temple, Texas

The Texas Troll Unlimited

© 2022 by Christopher Dow
ISBN 13: 978-1-7369307-1-7

Published by:
Phosphene Publishing Company
Temple, Texas, USA
phosphenepublishing.com

2.1

For Julie

It is not just night-crowing cocks who end up dead when violence is the only way for the dominant order to protect itself.

—Lewis Hyde
Trickster Makes This World

THE TEXAS TROLL
UNLIMITED

1

"IT WAS A NICE WEDDING. Congratulations, again, and thanks for inviting me."

"No," Howard Graham said. "Thank you, Clay, for being my best man. Besides, it never would have happened without you. God knows where we'd be now if you hadn't helped us."

"Dead, probably," Diane Graham, nee Weston, affirmed, her pretty face darkening. "Or worse."

They remembered too well the worse: watching living things, including humans, melt and twist into horrid parodies of life.

"We're all here and safe now," Guthrie said, wiping away the memory. "And moving forward. Diane told me your career is rebounding."

"I managed to mend a few fences," Howard said. "Or, rather, Diane did." He looked at his new wife, long face sheepish. "I finished the portrait of that banker I stiffed gratis, and thanks to the ability I got from Adriana," Graham winced as he said the name, "he was really pleased with the result. He was mollified enough that he recommended me to some of his friends."

"Howard's being too modest," Diane said. "The portraits are doing very well, but his landscapes are what we sell here at the Zephyr Gallery, and they're going like hotcakes. People say they're like windows on real scenes."

They all laughed, though the laughter was tempered with caution and hesitancy and tinged with apprehension. That case hadn't been easy on the body, nerves, or soul.

"Little do they know," Howard said, suddenly sober.

"I think we should all forget what happened," Diane said. "The real windows are closed now, and the future beckons."

"Absolutely," Guthrie said, raising his glass of ginger ale. "Here's to a strong art market and the success of the Zephyr Gallery in its new and improved location." He waved around them. "And to Howard's soon-to-be artistic world renown."

Howard and Diane lifted their glasses of wine, and after the glasses clinked, everyone sipped.

"Speaking of new and improved locations," Diane said. "How are you doing in your hunt for a new office?"

Office City, a cluster of three office buildings where Guthrie had a small suite, had recently been torn down and replaced with a string of fast-food joints. Apparently filling bellies was more profitable than filling desks. For the past six months, Guthrie had been working out of his house in Park Place, but he knew he couldn't procrastinate much longer. Clients needing a detective were not impressed, and the watchdog that Tereba had installed on the premises tended to gum up the works when upset or potentially violent clients approached the front door unannounced.

"I know I have to find a place," he said, "but there aren't a lot of options inside the Loop on my side of town. There are a handful of office buildings a little farther out the Gulf Freeway I need to check out." He chuckled. "When I get the time between cases."

"What have you been working on?" Howard asked.

"Recently, I looked into thefts from a large machine shop, and right after that I helped a local restaurant owner who was being pressured for protection money by a Vietnamese gang that has a strong presence in my area."

"That sounds dangerous," Diane said.

"It could have been if I'd tried to confront the gang directly. Instead, I looked into their activities, found some serious dirt, and turned the evidence over to the police anonymously. At present, the gang members are too busy defending themselves from the charges filed against them to bother with the restaurant owner."

"Clever," Diane said. "I wish what you did for us was so easy."

"I guess not everything is simple," Guthrie said. "Besides, I earned a couple of good friends." Friends he needed.

They all raised their glasses again, but Guthrie had only barely set his down again when his phone chirped.

"Sorry," he said as he pulled it out of his pocket and glanced at the the number on the caller ID. He didn't recognize it, but that didn't mean he wasn't going to answer it. "Duty calls," he said apologetically and thumbed the answer button, hoping he wasn't opening himself to a sales pitch or a scam. "Clay Guthrie speaking."

"Hello. My name is Gilbert Espinoza. I think I need a detective to look into something."

Despite the surname, the voice held no trace of a Hispanic lilt, but it did sound strained and tense.

"All right," Guthrie replied. "What sort of thing?"

"I guess you'd call it a disappearance."

"Does this concern a family member?"

"No," came the hesitant reply. "A friend. A coworker."

"What about the police? Have you gone to them."

"I can't."

Can't, or won't, Guthrie wondered.

"Why not?"

"I don't think I can explain over the phone. Can we meet in person?"

"May I ask why you chose me?"

"Some older black guy named Mr. Terry recommended you," Espinoza responded.

"How did you meet him?" Guthrie asked.

"Do you know him?"

"I know him."

"Well, I was in a bar, trying to drown my sorrows not to mention calm my nerves. I mean, what I saw was…. Well, it was pretty bad. Mr. Terry sat down next to me at the bar, and we had a drink together. He seemed like a pretty friendly and open guy, so I guess I just started talking to him. He listened a little while, then he said he had to go, but he gave me your card and told me to look you up. Said you might be able to help."

Guthrie was silent for a moment. Tereba. Directing another case his way. And carrying Guthrie's business card, no less. Why couldn't it have been something easy like dealing with a Vietnamese gang? He glanced at Diane and Howard, thinking of the last case Tereba directed his way, and cringed inside.

"Are you there, Mr. Guthrie?" Espinoza sounded lost and frightened, as if Guthrie might be his only lifeline. Maybe he was, and if Tereba was involved, it might be he was lifeline for a whole lot more.

"I'm here, Mr. Espinoza. All right, I'll meet you."

"Want me to come to your office?"

"Let's make it a more neutral place. What part of town do you live in?"

"East Houston, off the northeast corner of the Loop."

"I know it's a bit of a drive, but can you meet me at Dot Coffee Shop? It's at the Woodridge exit off the Gulf Freeway south, just outside the Loop."

"That'a not far. What time?"

"What time's convenient for you?"

"I work nights, so mornings are best. I sleep during the afternoon and early evening."

"Nine or ten?"

"Nine sounds good." The voice held the first hint of humor that Guthrie had yet heard. "That's dinnertime for me."

"All right, Mr. Espinoza. I'll see you at nine at Dot. They know me, so just ask for me at the counter."

Guthrie thumbed off the phone and looked up at his friends.

"I guess I'd better hurry up and find an office, otherwise, folks'll think I'm hustling for Dot."

They all laughed, but Diane wasn't taken in by Guthrie's attempt at humor.

"That was something about Tereba, wasn't it?"

"How could you tell?"

"You could laugh about dealing with a Vietnamese gang, but something about that call changed your whole demeanor."

"Yeah, it was about Tereba. Or rather, a case Tereba sent my way."

"That can't be good," Howard commented, scratching an eyebrow.

"Probably not, but for the same reason, I don't think I can say no."

"Well," Diane said dolefully. "I just hope it isn't as scary as the case I brought you."

"If it involves Tereba, it's bound to be scary," Guthrie replied, feeling the truth of that deep in his bones.

His friends nodded in sober agreement.

2

GUTHRIE ARRIVED AT DOT COFFEE Shop about 8:15. He wanted to have a chance to eat before Gilbert Espinoza showed up at nine. The hostess knew him well since he ate there several times a week when he was too busy to cook, which was often these days.

"Does Kay have an open booth?" he asked.

The hostess leaned forward, scanning the length of the restaurant.

"She does. Follow me."

Menu in hand, she led Guthrie to a booth along the glass front wall, near the back. He slid onto the bench seat on the side of the table where he could watch the front windows and door, and the hostess set the menu on the table in front of him.

"I'm expecting company in about half an hour," he told her. "He doesn't know me, so if he asks, send him my way."

"Sure," she said, then she headed back to the front, leaving him to the ministrations of the waitress.

"Hi, Mr. G," Kay said, setting a cup of black coffee next to the menu. She was a big, homely woman with a nice personality, and Guthrie knew she had three children in middle and high school and a husband who was nowhere to be found. She also tended to work double-shifts to make ends meet. He always tipped her well.

"Hi, Kay," he replied, handing her the menu without looking at it. "I'll have a number two with sausage, grits, and whole wheat toast."

"You got it," she said.

Guthrie sipped his coffee and absently watched her heavy-bodied walk as she went toward the kitchen.

He'd finished his breakfast and was nursing a second cup of coffee when an average-looking Hispanic man with close-cropped hair walked around the corner from the side parking lot and came inside. He went up to the front counter and said something, and the hostess pointed toward Guthrie. The man glanced at Guthrie, said something else to the hostess that looked like a thank you then walked toward Guthrie's table.

As he approached, Guthrie made him out to be around six feet, in his mid to late thirties, and in pretty good shape. He was wearing jeans, boots, and a button-down shirt in a dark blue plaid. Guthrie waved to him, and his pace quickened slightly.

"Mr. Guthrie?" he asked when he got there.

"Mr. Espinoza." Guthrie gestured to the bench seat on the other side of the table, and Espinoza slid into it.

He seemed to be simultaneously relieved and nervous.

"Thanks for seeing me."

"My pleasure," Guthrie said, wondering just how much of a pleasure it was going to be. "What do you do for a living, Mr. Espinoza?"

"Please, call me Gil. Mr. Espinoza sounds too formal."

"Okay. My name's Clay."

"Thanks. I'm a railroad safety and compliance officer for Union Pacific Railroad. I work out of the Englewood Yard—that's the big rail yard just inside the northeast corner of the 610 Loop."

"Near where you live?"

"Not far."

Kay came over to the table with a menu, and Espinoza ordered a chicken-fried steak, vegetables, and ice tea.

So, Guthrie mused. Gil was nervous and upset, but not too much to eat. That said something about either the strenuousness of his job or an ability to absorb stress and deal with it. Maybe both.

"You married?"

"No, but I have a steady girlfriend," Espinoza said, perking up a little. He smiled. "If it gets any more serious, we'll have to make it official. How about you?"

"Used to be. If it got any more serious, one of us would be in jail."

Espinoza laughed, and it was good to see something on his face besides trepidation.

"What does a safety and compliance officer do?" Guthrie asked.

"A lot of things. Mostly we inspect railcars and cargo. You know those warning signs on freight cars and tankers? The ones for hazardous chemicals and such? We're supposed to make sure those are correct and in place. We also inspect cars for damage, and the same with rail lines. Anything that has to do with the safety of the line, passengers, personnel, rolling stock, the goods we transport, and so forth."

"Sounds like it's a pretty meaningful and secure job," Guthrie said. "We're always going to be using trains to move stuff around."

"Meaningful, maybe," Espinoza said. "But that doesn't mean I'm secure." He looked at the tabletop and said, "Most likely I'm going to be fired soon. Maybe worse."

"Mind telling me why?" Guthrie asked, wondering about the "worse" part.

Kay brought Espinoza's ice tea and he waited until she left to answer. He took a sip then looked at Guthrie.

"I do mind," he said, lowering his voice and leaning across the table. "I'll only sound crazy. But I'll tell you anyway. That's why I'm here, talking to you. Besides, I got to tell somebody, or I'll really go crazy." He paused reflectively. "That Mr. Terry said something that really hit home. He said it's easy to tell your secrets to complete strangers because they don't know you, and you can just walk away afterwards."

"Sure," Guthrie responded. "It's like that. Mr. Terry sent you my way because I can deal with things that sound crazy. Tell me what's on your mind."

Espinoza peered at him for a moment, then nodded.

"Okay. So here's what happened two nights ago."

Espinoza told Guthrie that he'd been working in the southern part of the rail yard, inspecting a line of well cars holding double-stacks.

"Sorry," Espinoza said, seeing Guthrie's puzzled look. "Well cars are like flatbeds but with short side walls. They're designed to hold intermodal containers. Those big metal shipping containers. The side walls keep the containers firmly in place.They hold two containers, one stacked on top of the other. That's a double-stack. In cases like that, the containers are not only fastened to the car but to each other with big clamps. This particular lineup had maybe fifty double-stacks. That's what I was doing out there, inspecting all the clamps since the lineup was due to be entrained and ship out first thing in the morning."

He'd finished with a little more than a dozen cars when another yard worker, Buddy Horton, came by, headed for a switching unit at the far end of the yard. Horton paused to make some neighborly comments since the two of them were on friendly terms, and they chatted for a few moments before splitting up.

Horton walked off down the track toward the end of the train while Espinoza went back to his own task. He finished with the well car he was inspecting and was moving on to the next when he heard frantic yelling from down the track. There was a slight curve there, so he couldn't see what was going on, but he recognized Horton's voice, so he raced in that direction, thinking Horton might have encountered vandals or thieves.

As he rounded the curve, dimly ahead he could see the tail end of the train, where a dozen or so boxcars were coupled behind the line of double-stacks. It looked like the door of the last boxcar was open, but he couldn't see the interior because the angle was wrong.

But he could see Buddy Horton. He was standing in front of the open door, struggling to pull away from something that Espinoza couldn't see. As Espinoza ran toward him, Horton, screaming, was lifted off the ground and brutally yanked out of sight, into the boxcar. Just as Espinoza skidded to a stop in front of the door, Horton screamed again, but the scream was abruptly cut off by a loud, wet, crunching sound.

Espinoza shone his flashlight inside the boxcar, horrified at what he saw. In the space in the front half of the boxcar squatted a monstrosity. It was holding Horton—or what was left of him—in a giant, hairy, horny-nailed hand.

"The fucking thing had eaten off Buddy's head and one of his arms." Gil was whispering now, though he stared intently at Guthrie with an expression that mixed terror with a fear for his own sanity. "It looked like that famous painting by Goya, where the god is eating his son."

"I know it."

"Yeah, only this one was real. And it was a lot uglier. A whole lot uglier." His eyes lowered, unfocused. "I don't know what it was. It was like some giant, hairy, butt-ugly man. It had the ugliest goddamn face I've ever seen." He shuddered then looked up at Guthrie, resignation in his eyes. "Hell, I even sound crazy to my own self."

"I'm still listening," Guthrie said blandly, and he took a sip of coffee.

"You mean you believe me?"

"Let's not go that far, yet. But keep talking."

Kay returned with Espinoza's food, and he waited for her to leave to continue, ignoring the food cooling on the plate.

"Okay," he went on uncomfortably. "Well, it jerked back from the glare of my flashlight. It seemed like it didn't like the light. But then the fucking thing just sat there and grinned. It was horrible. Buddy's blood was all around its mouth and oozing down its chin and beard. Then it took another bite, and Buddy's other arm just fell onto the floor. I nearly puked, but then it made a grab for me with its free hand. I just instinctively jumped back, otherwise it might have got me, and I'd be just like Buddy."

"Obviously it didn't."

"No, man. It was like its leg was chained to something. It couldn't get out of the boxcar. But you know what's really weird? Somebody was in there with it. Some guy. He was standing in the space in the other side of the car. He was just as close as Buddy had been, but the thing wasn't trying to eat him."

"Interesting. Did you get a good look at him?"

"It all happened so fast, and it was dark in there," Gil said, shaking his head. "I just glimpsed him out of the corner of my eye. He was standing there, watching that thing eat Buddy with absolutely no reaction. But I couldn't look right at him. Not with that monster right there. Then it grabbed for me, and I ran."

"Did you go back to the office and report it?"

"As quick as my feet could carry me. Funny, but I was so scared I didn't even think of using my walkie-talkie. Fuck, I just wanted to get away from there as quick as I could and inside someplace safe. I kept looking back over my shoulder, expecting it to come out and chase me, but it never did. And the guy in there with it didn't, either.

"Hardly anybody was in the office when I got there. It was the night shift, you understand. We haven't got a lot of people on staff at night." He snorted a bitter laugh. "Like I said. I sound crazy to myself. How could I expect them to believe me? They just laughed it off, thinking Buddy and I were making some practical joke. It wasn't a joke. Not for Buddy."

Espinoza paused, and Guthrie could see he was getting hold of himself and pushing down dark memories. He even managed to begin eating his meal.

"I wanted to call in the cops," Espinoza went on around a mouthful of steak. "I know what I saw, and nobody can tell me I didn't." He shrugged. "But my supervisor—that's Dan Beaman—said, no. He made me stay in his office while he sent his assistant, Ray Hudson, down there to check it out and all the other guys to look around the rest of the yard to see if Buddy was somewhere else, maybe the north yard. That's on the other side of the Loop. Ray was gone a long time, and when he came back, he said he looked everywhere but hadn't found anything suspicious.

"But I kept on complaining, and I guess I sounded frantic enough that they had to think something was up. Plus, obviously, Buddy never did come back. So everybody got together and went down to the end of the train." Espinoza shook his head. "The boxcar's doors were shut and locked, but Ray climbed up and cut the lock off with some bolt cutters he'd brought along. I was ready to run, but it was filled with about a million cases of canned dog food, not a monster."

"You sure you had the right boxcar?"

"I couldn't swear it was the same one. I never got a look at any serial numbers. It was the same as the one Buddy got dragged into, and it was at the end of the same train. But it was dark and everything happened so fast." He shrugged. "Besides, who could move it? Everybody was busy, and any movement on the tracks registers on the control board in the office.

"I swore to god I'd seen it, but by then, everybody thought I was crazy or on drugs. Dan Beaman sent me home to cool off and get my head back on straight, but in the end, they couldn't ignore the fact that Buddy was just gone. They finally called in the authorities, which means the feds because of interstate commerce laws and such. Naturally I was the main suspect in his disappearance. I was the last to see him, and I had this wild story about a monster in a boxcar eating him. But there wasn't any evidence of foul play, so all they had was that Buddy vanished. Dan said he thought Buddy was having trouble at home, and he just ran off."

"You think there's anything to that?"

"Well, Buddy had been pretty half-assed at work for the last few months. I even caught him sleeping on the job a couple of times, but he never said anything about it, and I never asked. But even if I hadn't seen him get killed, I'd know he didn't just run off."

"How?"

"Because I saw his car in the parking lot when I left."

"You're sure?"

"Absolutely. I checked. He always parked in the same place, and his car was there. So he didn't just drive off. So far, I still have a job, but that's only because the union says I have to be prosecuted and found guilty before the company can fire me. And that depends on the findings of the investigation, which so far hasn't turned up anything suspicious that points to me except that Buddy disappeared right after I saw him. But even if they never find anything, my name is mud at work." He paused, staring at Guthrie. "I can tell you, it hasn't been easy there. My coworkers all think I'm crazy or a murderer. Or both. So here I am, telling my crazy story to a stranger. Want me to get up and walk away?"

"No," Guthrie said. "You haven't finished eating." He waved at Kay for the check. "I'll get your meal," he told Gil when she came over. He handed her two twenties and told her to keep the change.

"You mean you'll take the case?" Espinoza asked as she headed toward the cash register, a hesitant look in his eyes.

"I'm sure you're wondering what it's going to cost you."

"Was it that obvious?"

"No, just usual. Don't worry. Any work that Mr. Terry sends my way I do pro bono."

"That doesn't sound right."

"Let's just say that Mr. Terry and I have an arrangement. I'll look into it for you and see where it leads, but there are no guarantees."

"After seeing that monster, I'll never believe in guarantees again."

Guthrie gave a faint smile and nodded.

"I hear that. I'd like to look at the place where the incident occurred."

"That's going to be tough. The area is restricted to rail employees. But since I work nights, I can probably sneak you in. Give me a couple of days to arrange it."

"I look forward to it," Guthrie said, standing. "Enjoy your meal. We'll be in touch."

He headed for the door and a moment later was out in the warm sunshine, wondering how long *that* would last.

3

THE NEXT MORNING, GUTHRIE SAT in a chair on the porch over-looking the wide paved area behind the privacy fence and in front of his new two-car garage. The weather had turned, if not exactly cool, then at least cooler as the year eased into fall. He tried not to look at the drifts of pecan leaves piling up against the low chainlink fence separating the driveway from the backyard, knowing he'd have to do something about them.

He was waiting for Li Wu to show up for one of their twice-weekly tai chi session. Turning his attention from the leaves, Guthrie thought about what Gilbert Espinoza had told him: A monster in a boxcar ate his coworker. On the surface, it didn't seem credible, but during the two cases Guthrie had worked on Tereba's behalf, he'd seen and experienced things just as strange or stranger. If Es-pinoza's story was true, there were only two real questions: What had been inside the boxcar, and where was it now?

Three. Assuming he found it, how would he deal with it?

The sound of Wu's car pulling into the driveway and its door opening and closing interrupted Guthrie's chain of thought, and a moment later, Wu came through the gate. He was about Guthrie's age, average height, and weight, but he was much stronger, more powerful, and far more deadly. Guthrie didn't like to think about what he'd done to Craig Stanton in the alley behind the strip mall where Tereba's door was sometimes located. Not that Guthrie had any sympathy for Stanton, who'd been there to kill Guthrie, and al-most had before Wu intervened.

After they greeted each other, they settled into their practice rou-tine. Wu watched while Guthrie went through the tai chi form—the sequence of movements that was tai chi's catalog of methods and techniques. When Guthrie finished, Wu gave him some corrections and pointers, and they worked on those for another twenty minutes, Wu demonstrating how they could be used in combat.

Then it was time for push hands—tai chi's basic two-person self-defense exercise—followed by light free sparring. Wu always went easy on Guthrie during the push hands, concentrating on several established patterns designed to teach one to sense how an opponent's energy was moving and, more important, to allow one to feel one's own deficiencies and excesses in balance and movement.

Wu was no bully. He gave Guthrie openings to let his pupil actively engage, but he always managed to slip free and counter when Guthrie least expected it. With gentle nudges here and slight pulls there, he helped Guthrie see where he was erring, but he didn't try to take advantage. If he had, Guthrie would have been staggering back, lurching forward, slamming down, or finding himself in a painful joint lock every time Wu touched him. Guthrie appreciated Wu's restraint because it gave him many chances to improve without deadening frustration. It was, Guthrie thought, the mark of an excellent teacher who also was highly skilled.

The sparring and applications practice was more energetic, but thankfully Wu still held back. Most of the time, Guthrie felt like a child being tossed around and poked and prodded by an adult, but Wu did his best to refrain from hurting him, though that occasionally happened. Over the past couple of years, their sparring routine had become more vigorous as Guthrie's skill improved. He knew he'd never match Wu's expertise, but he longed for the day when he could actually make at least one real score against him.

"You're getting much better," Wu said when they finished and were sitting on the porch, cooling off.

"You could have fooled me," Guthrie said.

"No, seriously. I have to work much harder to mess you around."

"But mess me around you still do."

"True, but only because I'm more experienced. Have you had to use tai chi against anyone lately in the course of your job?"

"A little."

"Pay attention the next time you do, I think you'll be surprised. Tai chi development is kind of like climbing a hill. All the while, you're so concentrated on the climbing, which seems never ending, that you don't look back to see how far you've come. When we skirmish, I am the hill in front of you. But if you fight someone of lesser skill, they will be on the slope beneath you."

"I hope so since there's every chance I'll need to use it soon. You probably know Tereba's got me on a new case."

"He told me."

"I need to talk to him about it. Give him a call, will you? I don't want to drive all the way across town only to discover his door isn't there."

Wu chuckled and nodded before pulling out his phone and punching in a number from memory. Tereba's contact information was too sensitive to entrust it to a phone's contact log.

"Clay wants to talk to you about his new case," he said after a moment. "Okay, I'll tell him." Wu thumbed off the phone and looked at Guthrie. "He says to come by at two this afternoon. Maybe we need to put off our practice for a time?"

"Yeah," Guthrie said. He hated the idea since not only was Wu his tai chi instructor, he was the only person, aside from the Grahams, who he considered a friend. "I guess so. I'll call you when it's all over."

If I can, he thought.

After Wu left, Guthrie logged-on to the Houston Police Department servers. His connection wasn't exactly legal. He'd established it while he'd been on medical leave after the shooting that pushed him off the police force and nearly destroyed him. The shame of his perfidy still haunted him, but he knew he was coming to terms with it, thanks to Tereba. Who, he suspected, had a hand in keeping Guthrie's police logon active despite its illegality.

Once in the HPD system, he did a background check on Gilbert Espinoza. After that first case with Tereba, he knew it was smart to know as much about a client as he could. But in this instance, there wasn't much besides a straightforward and innocent bio. Following high school, Espinoza enlisted in the U.S. Army and served two tours in Afghanistan, the second as a demolitions expert defusing IEDs. That took nerve. No wonder he'd been able to eat his chicken-fried steak while telling Guthrie how a monster ate his coworker.

After that, Espinoza had gone to the University of Houston and emerged with a BS in environmental science and a MS in environmental engineering. Union Pacific hired him soon after, and he'd been with the rail company ever since. He paid his bills on time and owned his own home. He had no police record, not even a speeding ticket. He seemed like just what he presented: a solid, hardworking citizen who lived a non-controversial and upwardly mobile life.

Only now there was a monster in it. Or so he said.

Guthrie shut down the computer, ate a quick lunch, then got in his car and drove toward Bellaire.

The entrance to Tereba's home was located in the wall of the service alley behind a large strip mall off Bellaire Boulevard. But there was a rub. The door wasn't always there, and Tereba's home did not exist inside any of the mall's stores. Guthrie knew because he'd checked. He also knew that if he just showed up, the door might not be present, but that didn't make it, or Tereba's home, any less real. Guthrie had been inside several times, and the view from its windows showed a bucolic countryside that couldn't exist anywhere in Houston—or for thousands of miles in any direction. Guthrie had been told that when the door wasn't in the service alley, it was somewhere else. Or one of multiple somewhere elses.

This time, as he steered his Xterra around the end of the mall and into the alley, the door was there. He parked along the wall nearby and went up to it. Like the door to Guthrie's home, Tereba's door had an arcane symbol on it. But unlike the symbol Tereba had painted on Guthrie's door, this one was more elaborate and artfully carved into the thick, dark wood. The symbol on Guthrie's door was what had installed his watchdog—some sort of spirit that guarded the property from malevolent intent. Guthrie pushed the door open and stepped inside.

As always, it opened into Tereba's apothecary shop. The usual—or unusual—assortment of herbs, dried plants, fungi, and unidentifiable substances filled jars on shelves lining the wall behind the counter, and the dark parquet floor in front of the counter was as worn—and well swept—as ever.

Tereba's slender but supple form was perched on a stool behind the counter. He was writing something in a ledger, and he looked up as Guthrie entered, a seemingly genuine and gleaming smile breaking on his almost-handsome, dark-complected features. But Guthrie never could tell what was genuine when it came to the old man. What he did know was that Tereba might look to be sixty-five or seventy, but he really was many centuries old, at least, and wielded mysterious power. Using both his experience and his power, he could toss Guthrie around mentally and emotionally—and psychically—as easily as Wu could toss him physically. Consequently, Guthrie always remained cautious when he was around Tereba. Not that caution would do him a bit of good if Tereba turned on him.

"Well, Mr. Guthrie," the old man said, laying down his pen. Guthrie noted that it was a cheap ballpoint stick pen.

"I'd have thought you'd be using a quill and ink." He gestured to the pen.

Tereba chuckled.

"When you write as much as I do," he said, "you develop a certain contempt for fancy writing instruments. Fancy pens say more about their owners than anything the owners might write with them. They aren't used to write, they are used to impress." He gestured toward a stool standing in the corner. "Pull that over and make yourself comfortable."

Guthrie carried the stool over to the counter and sat across from Tereba. He couldn't say he was exactly comfortable.

"What is it you'd like to discuss?"

"Gilbert Espinoza and a monster in a boxcar. He saw it eat a coworker."

"A monster? No wonder he was so upset when I spoke to him in the bar," Tereba said. "You think there's anything to it?"

"Maybe, but how am I supposed to trace a boxcar? And what's that thing inside?"

"Both questions are excellent," the old man said. "Perhaps Mr. Espinoza might be able to help trace the boxcar. As for the monster," he shrugged slightly. "I have no idea."

"Something caused you to approach Espinoza. You must know something."

"As with your last case, I merely sensed a breach of our reality," the old man said. "Mr. Espinoza was not at the center of it, but he was, shall we say, tainted by proximity. It was pure chance that I encountered him. I was in the bar for a different reason, and there he was, the aura of something very wrong clinging to him."

Guthrie doubted that Tereba meeting Espinoza was pure chance. He didn't think Tereba even knew what pure chance might be. But there was no use pressing the point.

"And when I find this monster?"

"Who knows? Perhaps you will need to eliminate it. Perhaps something else. How can I tell without more information? I might know many things, Mr. Guthrie, but I do not know either everything or the future."

"Well, at least give me something to go on before I start. Is there anything you can tell me?"

"It seems that you have started already. As usual, I am depending on you to discover what I need to know and to resolve any issues that you can."

"I appreciate your confidence," Guthrie replied, unable to keep the sarcasm out of his voice. "As usual."

Tereba smiled. "Would you care for a cup of tea or coffee?" he asked. "I'm sure Cindy and Mary would be happy to make some for you."

Cindy and Mary were Tereba's…, well, it was hard to know exactly what their relationship to the old man actually was. Guthrie tended to think of them as his granddaughters, but that close a relationship would be stretching the point considering the fact that they were in their twenties. Guthrie liked both the young women fine, but now was not the time to dawdle over coffee and enigmatic small talk.

"Another time," he said, rising. "But tell them hi for me."

"Keep me apprised, won't you?" Tereba queried as Guthrie walked to the door.

"When possible."

Moments later, he was in his Xterra, and the door he'd just come through had already evaporated.

4

ON HIS WAY HOME FROM his visit with Tereba, Guthrie called Gilbert Espinoza's number. Because Espinoza worked nights and slept in the afternoon, Guthrie didn't expect him to answer. But he wanted to know as soon as possible how to get to the rail yard office and hoped his client would notice the message when he woke.

Expecting to work late, Guthrie spent the rest of the afternoon fixing dinner and eating. After that, it was just a waiting game until Espinoza called just after seven.

"Thanks for getting back to me," Guthrie said. "I want to talk to your supervisor. Daniel Beaman, right?"

"Yeah, but I wish you wouldn't. He'll only get more pissed at me than he already is."

"Don't worry. I'll work another angle and won't bring you into it."

"Okay. Well the yard office is on Grand Street, but you have to get to the end of that off Wallisville Road. If you're coming around the Loop from the south, take the Wallisville exit, turn left, and go about two miles. You'll see a sign that reads Englewood Yard Signal Depot. Turn right, and the office is about half a mile down on the right."

"What would be a good time?"

"Any time after eleven, but it's hard to say if Dan'll be in the office or not. He might be out on the yard somewhere. But if you ask for him, they'll call him in."

"All right."

"Say, I'm sorry I haven't gotten back to you about looking at where it happened," Espinoza said. "That was in the south yard, and Dan's had me working the north yard since I talked to you. That's on the north side of the Loop. I think he's trying to separate me from the rest of the crew, but I'll be back in the south yard on Wednesday night. We can meet then.

"What time?"

"Let's make it late," Espinoza said. "For you. Is one AM okay."

"I'll be there."

"Good. When you drive over, go a little past the turn for Grand, and down on the left you'll see a little all-night convenience store. You can park there on the side where nobody will question why your car is there, and it's close enough to where that monster ate Buddy. Call me, and I'll direct you from there, but try not to let anybody see you go into the rail yard. It's a restricted area."

"I'll let you know how things go with Beaman when I see you."

"Wednesday night, then."

Guthrie hung up and consulted his map app to get his bearings.

That evening at eleven, he drove to the Union Pacific office where Beaman worked and went into the low metal building. The reception room inside had two chairs flanking a low end table in the back left corner, but most of the space between the door and the counter, which was about one-quarter of the room, was open. A pair of desks sat behind the counter, one occupied by a dark-haired man, average-sized and in his forties but going to seed, working on a computer terminal. He looked up when Guthrie came in, surprised at seeing a stranger in the office this late.

"We're closed right now," he said, rising and stepping toward the counter. "You'll have to come back tomorrow during regular business hours."

"I'm not here on railroad business," Guthrie said. "I'd like to speak with Daniel Beaman. I understand he's the supervisor on this shift."

"That's right," the man said. "What is it you need to talk to him about?"

"Are you Mr. Beaman?"

"No."

"I'll save it for him then."

"He's not in the office right now," the man said, obviously miffed at Guthrie's response. He wasn't going to be helpful, it seemed.

"Can you call him, and let him know I'm here and need to talk to him?"

"I'm not sure I...."

"Look," Guthrie interrupted, turning on his cop voice. "You can call him or not, but I'm here on a legal matter, so I suggest you don't obstruct me, and make the call."

The man behind the counter bristled, and for a moment Guthrie thought his bluff might not work. But then the man went back to his desk and picked up a walkie-talkie.

"Dan," he said into the mic. "You out there? Come in."

"What is it, Ray?" came the crackled reply.

"Some guy here in the office wants to talk to you?"

"Who is it? What about?"

"He won't say."

"All right. I'll be there in ten minutes."

Ray. Ray Hudson, Guthrie surmised. Beaman's second in command. Hudson set the walkie on the desk and looked at Guthrie.

"You heard." When Guthrie nodded, Hudson gestured toward the two chairs in the corner. "Might as well sit down."

Taking his own advice, he reoccupied the seat behind his desk and turned his attention back to his screen, though he kept glancing sidelong at Guthrie.

Guthrie sat, and the ten minutes turned into fifteen before the door opened and a balding man in his mid-fifties and carrying too much gut pushed through. The eyes in his blunt features immediately sought the chairs in the corner.

"I'm Dan Beaman," he said. "Something I can help you with?"

"It's a personal matter concerning one of your employees," Guthrie said, standing. "Is there somewhere we can talk privately?"

"Sure," Beaman said, a puzzled frown crossing his face. "My office. Come on back."

Guthrie went around the end of the counter and followed Beaman down a short hall to one of the offices at the end. Beaman ushered Guthrie inside but didn't bother to shut the door.

"Have a seat." Beaman gestured to a chair in front of the desk. The desktop was cluttered with papers and folders and a tier of four plastic paper trays, all the slots partially filled. Toward the front sat a nameplate that read, "D. Beaman," and next to it was a plastic business card holder filled with business cards.

Guthrie sat while Beaman went around to his own chair, helping himself to several of the business cards while the man's back was turned. He'd barely pocketed them when Beaman sat down and leaned across the desk.

"So, what's this about one of my employees?"

"My name is Clay Guthrie. I'm a licensed private investigator." He showed Beaman his credentials. "I've been hired by a law firm in Philadelphia to locate Mr. Benjamin Horton. Only when I tried to contact him at home, I discovered that he's missing."

"Buddy." Beaman said, eyes hooding. "We called him Buddy."

Called, Guthrie noted. As far as Beaman was concerned, Buddy was past tense.

"I see. Well, I can tell you that Mr. Horton's uncle died and named Buddy as his sole heir. As you can imagine, the law firm I represent is reluctant to make a payout to a man who is missing."

"So, you're here to find out about Buddy being missing."

"That's right."

"It's kind of funny you're looking to ask Buddy about something right after he disappeared." Beaman tried to sound merely curious, but he sounded suspicious instead.

"Yes," Guthrie countered. "It is peculiar that Mr. Horton disappeared right before he was due to receive a substantial inheritance, isn't it? But the fact is, the ticket to find Mr. Horton was issued a couple of weeks ago."

"And you're only now getting around to it?"

"You know how those legal office bureaucrats are," Guthrie said. "It can take them forever to get things done. I was hired only a couple of days ago."

Guthrie wasn't sure if Beaman really bought that, but the man nodded appreciatively.

"Tell me about it," he said.

"I understand that Mr. Horton disappeared while here at work."

"That's right. He just walked off the job one night and never came back."

"Just like that?" Guthrie asked, putting a touch of amazement in his voice. "No words to anybody? No forewarning?"

"Not to anyone here," Beaman said.

"How long had he worked here?"

"I'd have to check personnel records. But I don't think...."

"Roughly," Guthrie said. "I don't need exact dates."

"Well, maybe ten, twelve years."

"That's a long time to just up and quit without a word to anybody."

"People do strange things," Beaman said impatiently.

"That's for sure," Guthrie admitted. "But come on. There has to be more than that. The case is still open, and I gotta give my client something. How was his work ethic?"

"Good enough. He's never been written up for anything. But he's changed lately."

"How so?"

"By all reports, he's gotten lazy and his work is sloppy. He's also been absentee a few times over the past month. Maybe he was making arrangements for dropping out of sight."

"What motive could he have for doing that?"

"I got hints that things weren't going well at home."

"Oh? Such as?"

Beaman's manner grew confidential.

"Nothing specific. But Buddy had become grumpy, and I know for a fact he was spending as much time away from home as he was there."

"How do you know that?"

"I had to call him up a few times to verify something or other. Like I said, he'd gotten sloppy. He was never there. His wife would just say he was out, and she didn't know when he'd be home. She always sounded stressed on the phone, so I assumed that Buddy and her were having troubles. Maybe he was drinking, maybe he had another woman on the side." Beaman shrugged. "Wasn't my place to ask."

"Even though it was affecting his behavior at work?" Beaman made no reply to that, so Guthrie said, "I read the police report made the night he disappeared. It said another of your employees, a Mr. Gilbert Espinoza, claimed Buddy was killed by some sort of wild animal out in the train yard."

"Yeah, that's what Gil said," Beaman replied, shaking his head, his face a sad frown. "It's completely crazy. I had all the men on the shift search the yard, and nobody saw either Buddy or a wild animal capable of harming a full-grown man. And there was no blood or any other signs of violence."

"So you don't give any credence to Mr. Espinoza's account?"

"A wild animal killing someone on the yard? Isn't anything in Houston that can do that outside the zoo." Beaman laughed, though it didn't sound sincere, and furtiveness pooled the backs of his eyes.

"Any chance I can talk to Mr. Espinoza?"

"I'm afraid not. Fact is, Gil is under investigation himself into Buddy's disappearance, and maybe more."

"Want to fill me in on that?"

"Some of us speculate that Gil was in on some sort of smuggling operation. He's a safety and compliance officer, and he could pass any load, even if it was packed full of drugs. It's possible Buddy found out about it, and Gil or his associates killed him to keep him quiet."

"Is that the official take on it? Any proof?"

"Can't say. All that's above my pay grade, and probably above yours."

"You'd be surprised."

"Maybe, but all I can do is relay what's filtering down from above. I'm not in on the investigation."

"So, you think this Espinoza fellow is lying?" Guthrie asked, thinking it was Beaman doing the lying. Truth tellers don't rely on damaging, unfounded gossip to dissuade legitimate inquiry, and then claim the information is from an unequivocal higher source for which they cannot answer. Besides, if Buddy ran off with another woman, then what was this about smugglers wanting to kill him?

Guthrie wanted to laugh in Beaman's face at the absurdity of either story. What he did know was that liars often accuse others of the very sort of malfeasance they, themselves, engage in, and then confuse themselves with their own prevarications.

"That's about the size of it. The front office, the local cops, and the feds are all looking at that angle."

"But why would Espinoza concoct such a harebrained story about Mr. Horton being attacked by a wild animal? He or his associates could have just killed Horton, taken his body, and said nothing. Or killed him elsewhere. Then there'd be no suspicions about him vanishing on the job, and nobody would have been the wiser. Instead, this Espinoza fellow gets the whole workforce out there searching for a victim that didn't have to be there. It doesn't make sense."

"You got me," Beaman said, his features hardening. "I guess he thought he was being clever."

Somebody thinks he's being clever, Guthrie mused.

"I see. Well." He stood. "Thanks for your time, Mr. Beaman."

"Hope you find your man," Beaman said. He didn't rise or offer his hand.

"I can find my way out."

He left the office, and as soon as he had, he heard a phone ring in the front room. When he got there, Ray Hudson was listening to the handset as he watched Guthrie walk through the reception area and out into the night.

5

AFTER BREAKFAST, GUTHRIE DID A background check on Buddy Horton. Horton had two speeding tickets and a citation for parking at an expired meter—all recent—but otherwise seemed to be clean. That didn't mean he was at peace with the world. His credit score, never too high to begin with, had tanked over the past four months. He was still keeping up with the payments on his house, but he'd had to surrender a couple of credit cards, and both he and his wife, Emily, were driving old cars.

That reminded Guthrie to check something Espinoza had told him. A quick scan of the police report showed that the investigating officers had gone through the parking lot at the Englewood Yard but hadn't found Buddy's ten-year-old Toyota. It was discovered the next morning near the bus depot downtown. The report said there was no evidence or video surveillance footage of him parking the car, walking near the bus station, or buying a ticket. Somebody had moved the Toyota, and it hadn't been Buddy.

The information Guthrie had on Horton was too sketchy. He needed something more up-close and personal given Beaman's implication that Buddy had home-life troubles and decided to just skip out, forsaking not only his family, but his job and his identity. Guthrie left home and drove to Horton's house.

It was located in a neighborhood not far from Espinoza's, which made sense since both were relatively close to the Englewood Yard. But Espinoza's neighborhood was several steps above the one where Buddy lived.

Had lived, maybe.

Guthrie got out of the Xterra, went up the cement steps to the wood-frame house's small front porch and pushed the bell button. Listening, he heard no answering chime, so figuring the bell no longer functioned, he knocked on the screenless door.

An older woman in her mid to late sixties opened the door and peered out. She did not look well. Her shoulders drooped, and so did every feature on her colorless face except for the crow's feet at the corners of her eyes. Those were taut.

"May I help you?" she asked, staring up at Guthrie with dull eyes.

"I'm looking for Emily Horton," Guthrie said.

"Are you from the police?" the woman asked. There was suspicion in her voice, but resignation, too.

"No. I'm an investigator working in conjunction with Union Pacific. Is Mrs. Horton home? I just need a few minutes of her time."

"Who is it, Mama?" came a voice from behind the woman.

The older woman stepped aside to let a younger one take her place. Emily Horton was slender and medium height, with shoulder-length mousy brown hair that needed brushing. She looked tired as she finished wiping her hands on a dish towel. Her face bore the careworn look of years of hardship and recent tragedy. Guthrie winced inside, knowing there was more to come for her.

"Hello, Mrs. Horton. My name is Clay Guthrie. I'm an investigator looking into your husband's disappearance. I'd like to talk to you for a few minutes, if that's okay."

"I already talked to the police and the FBI," she said.

"I'm sure. But I'd like to get my own perspective."

"All right," she said after a moment's hesitation. She opened the door. "Come in. We can talk in here."

She gestured toward the living room off to the right. The curtains were open, and it was brightly lit, highlighting the toys strewn all around and the cheapness of the worn furniture.

"Sorry for the mess," she said as she cleared a couple of dolls off an easy chair that had seen better days.

"No, no," Guthrie said. "Forgive me for dropping in unannounced."

As he sat, Emily and her mother settled onto the sofa. Guthrie saw pain pinch the older woman's face as she lowered herself carefully to the cushion. He also noticed a stack of neatly folded bedclothes on a nearby end table. Somebody was sleeping on the sofa.

"How many kids do you have?"

"Three. Two girls and a boy. They're in school right now."

Her voice held love but also relief. Three kids, a sick mother, a missing husband, and almost no money. No wonder she was thankful the kids were at school.

"How long have you and Mr. Horton lived here?" he asked.

"Eleven years," she said. "We moved in right after Ginger was born. She's our oldest."

"I know you're going through a rough time," Guthrie said. "And I'm sorry to have to ask these questions, but we all want to find out where Buddy went and why."

"I wish I knew," Emily said. "It isn't like him to just run off."

"So you weren't experiencing any difficulties at home?"

"Oh, we have plenty of trouble," she said, "but not like you mean. The police asked that, too. No, there's nothing like that." She shook her head. "Buddy is a loving husband and a good father."

"Money troubles?"

She nodded then looked askance of her mother. The older woman shrugged.

"You can tell him. Don't make no difference, anyhow. Won't make me sicker or well."

"My mother moved in with us about five months ago. She's been diagnosed with liver cancer."

"I'm sorry to hear that," Guthrie said sincerely, looking at the older woman. "What's the prognosis, if I might ask?"

"Not much," the older woman replied flatly.

"Don't say that, Mama," Emily said then turned to Guthrie. "She's undergoing treatment at UT Cancer Institute. The doctors are hopeful, and so are we. Aren't we, Mama?"

The older woman snorted.

"The longer you live," she said, "the less time you have. I have to be realistic."

"All that must be putting a strain on things around here," Guthrie said.

"Not really," Emily said, the lines on her face saying her words were untrue. "We had to move Jesse out of his room to give Mama a room of her own, but otherwise things are fine."

"Not fine," her mother said. "Buddy was having to work a second job to help make ends meet and take care of me. I'm nothing but a drain on him. If he ran off, it's because of me."

"Don't say that, Mama," Emily said. "Buddy loves you and wants to take care of you. You can't blame yourself." She looked at Guthrie. "It's true that Buddy's tired all the time and a little edgy, but he's a strong man. He wouldn't just up and leave us without anything. Without a word."

"Where might he go? Any friends who might put him up?"

"We don't have many friends, and all of them know Buddy's gone. They'd have told me if they knew where he is."

"How about Gilbert Espinoza?"

"Buddy and Gil are friends, I guess. They're saying Gil had something to do with Buddy's disappearance. Is that true?"

"It might be true that people are talking, but it's not true that Mr. Espinoza had anything to do with Buddy's disappearance. I know that for a fact." He paused. "This is a sensitive subject, but I have to ask if Buddy has made any withdrawals in the last few days?"

"The FBI asked that, too," Emily said. "No, what little we have is still in the bank. They also asked about credit cards, but we only have one now, and he hasn't used it."

Hard for a man to run if he has no place to go or money to go with.

"I think that's all for now," Guthrie told her. "Thanks for your time. I might get in touch with you later if I find I have more questions. If it's all right."

"That's okay," she said. "As long as it helps bring Buddy back."

Guthrie rose and went to the door, and Emily followed, but her mother remained on the sofa.

"Did you bring the stuff from his locker?" Emily asked as Guthrie opened the door.

"No, sorry. That hasn't been returned?"

She shook her head. "Not yet."

"I'll see what I can do, Mrs. Horton," Guthrie said. "I'm sure we'll find out what's going on soon. Thanks for talking to me."

"Wait. Will you let me know when you find him?"

"Of course. I promise."

As Guthrie drove out of the neighborhood, he thought about what he'd learned. The presence of another woman was highly unlikely. Horton was in financial difficulties, but they were family related and not connected to anyone who might want to harm him. And while they were severe, Guthrie didn't think they were enough to make Horton give up his entire life. Not voluntarily.

From what he'd learned in the Horton household, the story that Espinoza told him still held, while Beaman's finger-pointing and rationalization about Espinoza's potential involvement in a smuggling operation were looking more bogus than they had at first. And they'd definitely stunk from the moment Beaman opened his mouth.

Guthrie drove home.

GUTHRIE FOUND THE CONVENIENCE STORE and parked next to the building on the left side as Espinoza suggested. Glancing out across the rail yard, which was well lit by area lights on poles jutting here and there above the railcars, he pulled out his phone and keyed in Espinoza's number from the call list.

"It's Guthrie," he said. "I'm at the convenience store. Now what?"

"Look across the street. See that big gray electrical box?"

"I see it."

"Go around it. There's a line of nine grain cars on the second track over. Go between the two cars right behind the circuit box, and wait for me there. Remember, try not to let anybody see you cross the street and enter the yard."

Guthrie hung up, got out of his truck, and walked to the corner. The electrical box was right across the street, but the corner was lit by a street light. He strode down the sidewalk in front of the store, noting the two cars parked in front. They were empty, their drivers inside. He could see a man at the counter, paying for something, and another in front of the coolers at the back.

A telephone pole stood off the right corner of the parking lot, but it didn't have a street light, though the next one did. That was about the darkest spot around, so Guthrie looked up and down the street. The closest cars were about half a mile away, but only one was coming his direction. With a last glance at the convenience store to make sure that the customer and clerk still occupied each other's attention, he dashed across the street, over the curb, and up the low gravel berm to the first set of tracks.

As Espinoza said, the second tracks held a row of nine grain cars. Keeping in the narrow band of shadow running alongside them, he hurried toward the car that was even with the electrical box. There, he crouched beneath the coupling just as the automobile that had been approaching passed. He stayed low for another minute while the convenience store customer emerged, got into his car, pulled out of the lot, and drove down the side street, into the neighborhood behind.

Guthrie ducked beneath the coupling, to the opposite side of the cars from the street. Keeping in the shadows of the cars, he straightened and surveyed the part of the yard that lay before him. He hadn't spotted Espinoza yet, but there was no telling where he'd been, and Guthrie figured it might take him a few minutes to arrive. After two long minutes, Guthrie saw him walking down the side of the line of grain cars, feet crunching on the gravel.

Guthrie stepped out of the shadows so Espinoza could see him, and the man quickened his pace until he was standing close. He was carrying a big flashlight, though it was turned off.

"I guess you must believe me, seeing as how you're here," Espinoza said softly, relief showing in his tone.

"Let's say I'm closer," Guthrie said. "I talked to Beaman, but his story that Buddy just ran off doesn't add up for me. Nor did his attempts to finger you as a drug smuggler and Buddy's murderer."

"No shit? That son of a bitch...."

"Relax. I know it's bullshit. I talked to Buddy's wife and mother-in-law. Did you know that the mother-in-law has cancer, and Buddy was working two jobs to help her out?"

"I didn't. No wonder he was slacking off around here."

"Buddy doesn't seem the type to throw away everything, and his wife doesn't think so, either. What do you think?"

"No. Buddy didn't have much, but he valued what he had. He wasn't that type."

"Shall we?" Guthrie gestured toward the interior of the rail yard.

"We have to be careful. I saw Ray Hudson not far from where we're going. Dan sends him out to check on me, no matter where I am. He's done that every night since it happened. Come on."

Keeping in the narrow shadow cast by the line of grain cars, Espinoza hurried up the tracks, which split just a few cars up, with the one they were following and the one next to it running into more junctions to the right, along Wallisville Road. The track on the left angled off to run parallel to another cluster of tracks, deeper in the yard. Guthrie couldn't tell how many tracks were over that way because several were filled with lines of cars, and all rounded a gentle curve toward the northwest.

Between the first and second clusters of tracks lay a narrow wedge of ground maybe six hundred feet long and forty at the widest. Its greasy ground was barren of anything but a few scraggly weeds and a scattering of puddles miring the lowest spots. In the middle of the widest, driest area sat an open-sided metal shed and two small metal structures for electrical circuitry. Beyond were several lines of cars on parallel tracks.

The line of grain cars they were following ended.

"We have to get over there," Espinoza whispered, gesturing toward the ends of the lines of cars across the narrow wedge of dirt. "Once we're there, I think we'll be okay. I'll go first just in case Ray's around. When I know it's clear, I'll signal for you to follow."

Guthrie nodded and watched Espinoza saunter away from the grain car, across the dirt margin between the two clusters of sidings. He disappeared into the shadows of several tankers attached to the end of the nearest line of cars. Two or three minutes passed before he was back, waving.

Guthrie hurried from the cover of the grain car, across the gravelly dirt. In seconds, he was beside Espinoza.

"I didn't see Ray," Espinoza warned in a whisper, "but he could be anywhere around here, so stay quiet. The boxcar with the monster was over there." He gestured. "Come on."

Guthrie followed Espinoza past four tank cars, where the trainman ducked beneath the coupling and looked up and down the tracks.

"Ray can't go anywhere in the yard without his flashlight on," Espinoza chuckled. "If he comes up, we ought to be able to spot him a long way off."

They went across to the next track, where a line of tank cars stood.

"This is where it happened," Espinoza said. "This tanker is right about where the boxcar with the monster was."

Guthrie pulled a small flashlight from his pocket and switched it on, aiming its small beam at the ground.

"Careful," Espinoza warned. "Ray might see it."

"I have to examine the scene," Guthrie said. "No point in me being here if I can't."

"Okay, but do it quick."

"Hmm."

"What?" Espinoza asked.

"All the gravel around here is dirty and oily, but this patch here," Guthrie pointed, "looks newer."

"Yeah, you're right. Maybe they covered something up."

Guthrie squatted by the lighter-colored patch and scuffled through it with his free hand. Beneath the top layer was one that was darker than even the surrounding greasy and dirty gravel. He picked up a piece and dropped it into one of the baggies he'd brought along.

"You gonna analyze that?" Ray asked.

"Someone will," Guthrie said, standing.

As he did, Espinoza touched him on the shoulder.

"Ray," he hissed.

Guthrie glanced up the track. A flashlight was swinging from side to side in short arcs as it approached along the narrow gap between the rows of cars.

"Better get back over there," Espinoza said, pointing to the line of tankers they'd come through.

Guthrie stepped across the space between the two lines of cars, ducked beneath the coupling, and crouched behind the tanker's wheel. Hudson came up to Espinoza, feet scuffling across the gravel, and stopped a few feet away.

"Saw your flashlight. Looking for monsters?" he asked, tone sarcastic. "I don't think you'll find any here tonight." He chuckled appreciatively at his own joke.

"Does that mean I might find one on another night?"

Despite the dim light, Guthrie saw Hudson stiffen.

"You won't find none any night," he snapped. "What the hell you doing over here, anyhow?"

"I have a job to do, Ray. That's what I'm doing over here."

"I thought you was checking out those covered hoppers down the line on Track 16."

"Done with those. Now I'm inspecting these tankers."

"But they're empty," Hudson said, suspicion in his voice.

"Can you think of a better time to make sure they're sound?"

"Can't say no to that," Hudson admitted grudgingly.

"All right, then. If it's okay with you, I'll get back to it."

"Go right ahead. I ain't your supervisor."

"You're right, there, Ray."

Without saying anything more, Hudson walked back the way he'd come, flashlight beam swinging in small, stiff arcs across the ground in front of him.

While Espinoza dealt with Hudson, Guthrie had crouched behind the tanker's wheel, his attention on the conversation. But after a few moments, he detected a foul stench of offal rising somewhere behind him. Even before Hudson was out of sight, Guthrie cautiously walked around, scanning the ground with his small flashlight. This was where the long wedge of ground between the two clusters of tracks narrowed into a lane about fifteen feet wide, the center filled with a large, shallow puddle. He'd just paused beside it when Espinoza came up behind him.

"What are you doing over here?" he hissed. "Ray's gone. Let's go back to where the boxcar was."

"Wait. Smell that?"

"Yeah. Jeez. What is it? We got some stinks around here, but I never smelled any like that."

"Any of you guys take a crap out here in the yard?"

"Not me. I'll take a leak if I have to, but never a crap. I can't vouch for the others."

Guthrie skirted the puddle, keeping his small flashlight beam on the ground in front of him. Then there it was, half in and half out of the puddle. It was reddish brown in color and looked like a pile of cow dung magnified ten times. But it reeked like no cow dung ever had.

"Any idea what this is?" Guthrie asked.

"None at all," Espinoza said, shining his own light on the pile. "What the fuck is it?"

"It's really nasty is about all I can say," Guthrie said, fishing another baggie out of his pocket and bending over.

"You're not really going to collect some of that, are you?" Espinoza asked with disgust.

"Can't say that I want to, but, yes."

Wrinkling his nose and using the baggie like a doggie poop bag, Guthrie pinched up some of the offal then sealed the bag, being careful not to smear any of it onto the outside or on himself. He put the baggie inside another one, but he still wasn't about to put that mess into his pocket, so he held it between his thumb and forefinger. Delicately.

"You going to have that analyzed, too?"

"I am." Guthrie glanced up and down the tracks. "I'm wondering if someone could have moved the boxcar, leaving the one with the dog food at the end of the line."

"I don't know about that." Espinoza sounded skeptical. "Either one's possible, I suppose. Like I said, it was a long line of cars, and I wasn't counting when we all went back and opened the one with the dog food. Heck, I sure wasn't counting when I ran down there while Buddy was being attacked. We were just going to the last car in line. There's a switch just down the line, back even with where you came into the yard. That's where Buddy was going when that thing got him. I guess someone could have moved the car. Damn, I didn't even think about that."

"Why would you?" Guthrie asked. "Nobody would expect someone to move it." His eyes narrowed. "Maybe it was that guy you saw in the car with the monster. Maybe he figured you'd be back, and he moved the car."

Espinoza shook his head.

"He couldn't have done it alone, even if he was a trainman," he said. "It would take a railcar mover, and even then, he'd have to throw the switch. All that would register on the board in the office."

"Who would have noticed?"

"Dan Beaman. He was the only one in the office besides me after he sent everybody else out to look for Buddy." He paused thoughtfully. "You know, he made me wait in his office with the door closed, so I couldn't see the board. No telling what went on while I was shut in there."

"And Beaman's already lied to me about Buddy. And you."

"You think he's in on it?"

"You said Ray was gone a long time. Could he and Beaman have been working together?"

"Maybe. They're pretty tight." Espinoza nodded and was quiet for a few moments, thinking. "You know, come to think of it, Dan was on his phone when I busted into his office to tell him about Buddy, and he was looking pretty nervous. Pale, even. It was right after that he sent everybody else in opposite directions from the boxcar—most of them up to the north yard. He told them to look for Buddy, but it could have been to give Ray and the guy in the car time to move the car. With nobody else in the office, only Dan would have noticed movement on the tracks or that the switch had been operated. Right after that, Dan sent me home, and that could have been when they brought the car back to the line."

"So," Guthrie said. "It looks like there might be some experienced trainmen on the other side of the equation."

"I guess it does."

"In that case," Guthrie replied, "I'll probably need your help. Is it possible to check the manifests for that train? Find out where it was going and where it was making stops?"

"I can do that, but it'll take a little time since I have to be careful Dan doesn't find out what I'm doing."

"One more thing. What about Buddy's locker? His wife wanted to know if its contents can be returned to her."

"I don't know. I'll check that, too."

"Okay. Call me when you have something. Until then, be careful."

"I will," Espinoza said as Guthrie turned and headed back across the rail yard to his Xterra.

7

WHEN GUTHRIE GOT HOME, HE punched in Li Wu's number.

"I didn't think I'd hear from you so soon. Have you solved the case already?"

"Just getting started," Guthrie replied. "I have a couple of pieces of evidence I need analyzed. I'm sure Tereba has the connections to do something like that."

"I'm sure he does. Can it wait until morning? I'm on another assignment for him right now."

"Yeah, morning's fine. Maybe we can get in a short practice session while you're here."

"I look forward to it."

They disconnected, and since it was close to midnight, Guthrie went into his bedroom to get ready for bed. Hours later, he was awakened by a profound sense of unease. It was still dark outside, but he knew instantly what had disturbed his sleep. His watchdog.

The watchdog wasn't an animal. Guthrie didn't know what it was, but he liked having it around. Like a canine, it was a sort of intelligence that hovered around his house and protected it and Guthrie from harm. A person with innocent intentions who approached the house would have no problem with it, but any sort of negativity toward Guthrie or his home would activate it, causing the interloper to experience a profound and debilitating sense of dread, weakness, and nausea. Guthrie knew from personal experience just how debilitating a watchdog could be.

His watchdog had come courtesy of Tereba during the first case Guthrie worked for him. It was, he guessed, some sort of spell, and it was tied to the glyph the old man had painted onto Guthrie's front door. Guthrie called it Fred after a deceased neighbor whose passion had been acting as the neighborhood watchdog.

The fact that Fred had awakened Guthrie at—he glanced at the bedside clock and saw it read a few minutes before four—was a serious cause for concern. He rose, quickly slipped on his pants and shoes and picked up his carry pistol: a S&W M&P compact 9mm. Without turning on any lights, he went into his office and glanced at his surveillance video screen.

He had five cameras planted around the property: one each at the front and back doors, one overlooking the front yard and driveway, one the back yard, and one the side patio in front of the garage where he and Wu practiced tai chi. Occasionally, he watched some of the footage of Wu tossing him around, partly to study what Wu had done to him and partly for the amusement value of seeing himself taking pratfalls.

At first, he didn't see anything unusual, which was usual. But after a couple of minutes, a medium-sized, dark-haired man in dark clothes climbed over the wooden fence that ran down the right side of the deep backyard, separating it from the parking lot for the two-story apartment building that overlooked the rear of Guthrie's property. The man dropped into the yard then quickly rounded the freestanding garage and approached the back of the house. Fred's effects reached about sixty feet beyond the outer walls, and sure enough, that margin was about where the man stopped and swayed uncertainly. But he pressed on, moving closer to the house, seeming to struggle to walk.

He's really determined, Guthrie thought, wondering how close he'd be able to get before he was too stunned to move.

"Fred. Let him get closer," Guthrie said aloud in a quiet voice.

As the watchdog slackened its effects, the approaching man straightened, shook his head, and moved stealthily toward the back door. The image from the camera there showed he was carrying a pistol with a silencer. He pulled out a pair of lock picks and worked on the door latches for a moment before they opened.

By now, Guthrie could hear what was going on from his office. As soon as the man's quiet footsteps began to pad across the kitchen floor, he said to the watchdog, "Fred. Stop him now."

A sick grunt and a retching sound came from the kitchen, followed by the clatter of the gun on the tiles and a loud thump as the man collapsed, still retching.

Guthrie took a pair of handcuffs and a roll of duct tape from his desk drawer then walked to the office door. Keeping his own pistol at low ready, he eased down the hall and into the kitchen. The man was lying on the floor, balled up and heaving, a puddle of vomit nearby. Guthrie picked up the gun—a SIG P250—uncocked it and set it and his own pistol on the counter. By now, the man was so depleted that Guthrie had no trouble cuffing his hands behind his back and duct taping his ankles and knees together. Then he searched his pockets, finding only a set of car keys, a second magazine for the gun, and a cheap phone.

"Okay, Fred," he said. "You can let him go now."

With a sigh of relief, the man on the floor relaxed and glared up at Guthrie, anger and defeat in his eyes.

"Look," Guthrie waved at the floor next to him. "Who's going to clean up all that mess?"

"I don't know how you did that," the man said, "and I don't care. When I get loose, I'm going to take you apart before I kill you." His English was heavily tinged with an Italian accent.

"Good thing you aren't getting loose then," Guthrie replied blandly. He stepped forward, grabbed the back of the man's collar, hauled him upright, and propped him against the lower cabinet doors. "You going to tell me who you are?"

The man just snorted.

"That's okay. I'll find out soon enough." Guthrie straightened, picked up the SIG, and turned it over in his hands. "Nice gun. Silenced, too. Obviously you're here to kill me. Who sent you?"

A glare was his only reply.

"Have it your way."

Guthrie put the gun back onto the counter, shoved the man prone on the floor, and started winding duct tape around his torso and arms. At first the guy struggled, but when Guthrie told Fred to subdue him and he started retching again.

"Okay, okay," he managed to gasp.

Guthrie told Fred to let up, and the man stopped struggling and allowed Guthrie to finish the taping.

"You have some kind of unholy magic," the man ground out when Guthrie rolled him over. "You truly are a minion of the Dark Lord."

"And you aren't?" Guthrie responded. "I guess sneaking into the home of a man you don't even know in the middle of the night with the intention of murdering him is purely God's work?"

"You wouldn't know God's work," the man spat.

"That makes two of us," Guthrie said.

He stuck his own pistol into the back of his belt then took the hitman's SIG and the now depleted roll of duct tape into his office.

"Do you mind waiting here for a few minutes?" he asked when he returned to the kitchen. "There's something I have to check." The man just glowered. "Fred," Guthrie went on, "if he moves, incapacitate him." To the man, he said, "My unholy magic will really screw with you if you do anything but lie here quietly. I don't think you want that."

There was no response, so Guthrie just went out the back door and opened his garage. There, he got out his extension ladder and carried it outside and over to the fence. Pulling the ladder apart into two ladders, he made a stile over the fence, climbed it, and stood for a moment in the apartment parking lot, glancing around. At this early hour, no one was stirring. Guthrie thumbed the lock button on the key fob. About sixty feet away, a dark blue, late-model compact Chevy beeped, and its lights flashed briefly.

Guthrie went through the car's interior but found nothing, which was suspicious in itself. After noting the license plate number, he went back to his stile, climbed over it into his own yard, then pulled the ladder propped on the parking lot side of the fence into his own yard. He left both pieces lying beside the fence for the time being. He'd come back later to collect and store them.

Inside the house, the man was again retching. Unproductively, Guthrie noted with gratitude.

"You can let him go, now, Fred," Guthrie said. To the man, he said. "I warned you. You can be a good boy, or you can keep dry heaving, it's up to you."

"All right," the man gasped.

"Going to tell me who you are?"

"Not even if you make me puke to death."

"That could be arranged," Guthrie said. "But I'll use less brutal means. Sit tight. I'll be back in a moment."

He went into his office, turned on his computer, and connected to the HPD database, where he ran a check on the assassin's license plate. The owner's name was Thomas Greer—presumably the man in his kitchen. He did a background search, and when Greer's drivers license photo popped up, he saw his prisoner's face staring back at him. Then he checked the number of Greer's phone, did a reverse search, and learned that it was a burner with no registered owner. Only one number was in the phone's contact list, and another reverse search showed that it, too, was a burner.

Also odd was a man named Thomas Greer who spoke with a heavy Italian accent.

"Nothing's ever easy," Guthrie muttered as he punched the burner's call button.

"Is it done?" a man's voice asked without preamble. The voice bore a heavy Scandinavian accent and sounded mighty perky for just after four in the morning, almost like the owner had been waiting up for Santa.

"Depends on what you wanted done," Guthrie said. "If you wanted Greer hogtied on my kitchen floor, then it's done."

"I suggest you let him go."

"Why? So he can try to kill me again? Nothing doing."

"You won't get any information out of him. He'll die before he tells you anything."

"It won't be me he's telling. I have friends who can extract any information out of anybody."

"No matter. He doesn't know anything that will be of use to you."

"Maybe. Only time will tell. But what about you? You want to tell me why you sent him? Maybe we can work out something less drastic than murder."

"This is your only warning, Guthrie," the voice said, turning harsh and ignoring Guthrie's question. "Give up looking for Benjamin Horton or suffer the consequences. Next time, you won't be so lucky."

"Luck favors the prepared mind," Guthrie responded, but the other man had already disconnected.

He went back to the kitchen and dragged Greer over to the door where he'd be out of the way. After cleaning up the mess on the floor, he started a pot of coffee.

"Your boss tells me you won't talk, Thomas," he said to the man as the pot began to drip.

"So you know my name. So what?"

"Do I?" Guthrie mused. "Thomas Greer. Mighty peculiar name for an Italian."

"Who says I'm Italian?"

"You do every time you open your mouth. Being a hitman is a mighty unusual occupation, too, isn't it?"

Greer just glared at him.

"Have it your own way," Guthrie said. "You'll tell what you know sooner or later."

Ignoring the man's icepick stare, Guthrie fixed himself a bowl of cereal and leaned against the counter, perusing his prisoner while he ate.

"What are you going to do with me?" Greer asked as Guthrie rinsed out the bowl in the sink.

"Nothing. My boss is going to do something with you."

"Espinoza?"

"Why?" Guthrie leaned close to his prisoner. "You better hope you haven't done anything to him."

Greer—or whoever he was—just turned away. Guthrie went into his office and punched Espinoza's call button. After a tense couple of rings, Espinoza answered.

"Guthrie? You're up early. What's up?"

"Just checking to make sure you're all right."

"Why? Something happen?"

"I just had an unexpected visitor. I think he probably was going to visit you, too, when he was done with me."

"You mean someone came to kill you?"

"Don't worry. At least not for the moment. He's tied up on my kitchen floor. I'll let you know more about it later, but right now, I have to attend to him."

Guthrie hung up and went back to the kitchen.

"Just for your personal information, Espinoza might be my client, but he's not my boss. He doesn't even know what's going on here. But my boss does. He's a very different sort of man. Talk about unholy magic." He shook his head and smiled. "We're just going to wait here until his assistant arrives to take you to him. After that, it's out of my hands."

Greer didn't seem to like hearing that, but he made no further inquires. Guthrie poured a cup of coffee.

"You just hang out here," Guthrie told him. "I'll be in my office if you need anything. And remember: Fred is watching."

"Fuck you."

Guthrie chuckled then went down the short hall to his office with the coffee and a lot more questions than answers. Like why had an Italian hitman with an English name been sent to kill him, and who, with a Scandinavian accent, had sent him? The computer screen in front of him could give him a lot of answers, but not to the questions he now had. Not until he had more information from other sources.

Wu showed up at eight. When he entered the kitchen, he eyed Greer with amusement.

"I see you have a guest," he said. "I take it we won't be practicing this morning."

"I guess not. Meet Thomas Greer, a man whose accent belies his name and who moonlights as a hitman. He's not talking, so I'd appreciate it if you took him to see if our boss can get anything out of him. But he's not the reason I originally called you."

He picked up a plastic grocery bag cinched at the top and handed it to Wu.

"Inside are a couple of samples I need analyzed. One's a rock with brownish stains that might be blood, and the other is…. Well, let's just say you don't want to open the baggie to examine it yourself."

"Okay. I assume you need this as soon as possible."

"Sooner, if possible."

Wu chuckled, and after that, Guthrie helped him load Greer into the trunk of Wu's Pontiac. He handed Wu the key to the handcuffs and watched as he drove away. Then he went back to his office to figure out what he was going to do next.

8

GUTHRIE HAD JUST FINISHED BREAKFAST the next morning and was sitting at his computer when the phone rang. It was Tereba.

"Hello, Mr. Guthrie. I have news regarding the samples you sent in. The analysts haven't had enough time to run full DNA sequences, but their preliminary findings indicate that the red stains on the gravel are human blood. The blood and the mucky sample in the baggie—excrement—each contain human and bovine DNA. Both human readings are from the same source. If you can provide a known sample, we can see if there's a match. The bovine DNA came from two different sources. The excrement it also contains some odd, unknown DNA type." The old man was silent for a moment before asking, "What do these findings mean?"

"It appears my client is right about someone getting eaten."

"And the unknown DNA?"

"As I said, Gil claims it was some sort of very large and hideous humanoid creature."

And just like that, Guthrie realized he accepted the idea that Buddy Horton hadn't just run off but was killed and eaten by a monster.

"What about the man Wu brought to you? I hope you didn't have to torture him too much."

"Mr. Guthrie," Tereba admonished. "You shame me unnecessarily. You know I have more subtle means to gain access to information than torture, though I admit he was rather resistant at first."

"Sorry. I guess I do. So what about my hitman?"

"Mr. Bertrando Galtero. He's from Rome. He entered the U.S. on a forged Italian passport bearing a phony name, which isn't surprising since he is known to be one of the best hitmen in Europe.

Police there lost track of him about six months ago, and some of them suspect he secretly fled the country."

"Making that possible would cost some bucks. Has he said who he's working for?"

"He says he's employed by a man named Donner Thorvald."

"Sounds Scandinavian," Guthrie said. "I talked to a man on Galtero's burner who spoke with a Scandinavian accent. He knew me but didn't let on who he was. Any word on who this Thorvald might be?"

"I cannot tell you much because Galtero doesn't know much. But he met Thorvald in a most unusual way. Every time Galtero performed his duties as an assassin, he was in the habit of immediately visiting the Archbasilica of Saint John Lateran for confession. Trying to save his unsavable soul, I imagine."

"I take it that's some sort of church."

"It is the oldest and highest-ranking of the four major papal churches in Rome. It is, among other things, the papal seat. Apparently, Galtero was appealing for spiritual mercy from the highest authority he could find. After one of his killings, Galtero went to the basilica as usual, and Thorvald was the priest who heard his confession."

"So Thorvald is a priest?"

"It would seem so. And perhaps with some rank since he has a position at the Vatican. After Thorvald heard Galtero's confession, he told Galtero that he wanted to hire him to kill several people and to travel with him to the United States to help eliminate potential enemies. He told Galtero that all the targets—several of them priests— were enemies of the Church, and since Galtero was propositioned inside a confessional, he took Thorvald at face value. He also was all too happy to escape Europe with a generous open-ended contract, but he says he doesn't know what Thorvald is up to. All he knows is that Thorvald assigns him a hit, and he carries it out.

"During the past year, he killed eight priest for Thorvald, all in Rome. Or rather, he killed three. In each case, he delivered the bodies to Thorvald, though he doesn't know how Thorvald disposed of them. The other five he kidnapped and delivered to Thorvald alive. He didn't know what happened to those five, either, but none of them ever showed up again. According to official channels, all eight priests simply disappeared without a trace. And it seems you're not the first non-priest Thorvald sent him to kill. There were about a dozen others, all in various positions in the transportation industry in Europe, and all after the priests were eliminated. When Galtero could, he delivered the victims alive to Thorvald, and when he couldn't, he delivered their bodies. After the last of these, he was sent to the U. S. You're his first target here, and Mr. Espinoza was to be the second."

"How about Thorvald? Why did he come to the States?"

"Unknown. But if he's here, it isn't under the auspices of the Church. I consulted my contact inside the Galveston-Houston Diocese, and he tells me that Thorvald has never been assigned there. And after he dug a little, he learned that there is some sort of trouble with Thorvald, though exactly what that might be is known only to the upper level of the priesthood at the Vatican. One set of rumors says he's a member of a secret group of Catholic priests and ex-priests attempting to undermine the authority of the Church, and another is that Thorvald is in possession of a fortune he embezzled from the Vatican while working as an accountant there. Perhaps both are true. Perhaps false. Certainly he is on the run."

"No mention of a monster in a boxcar?"

Tereba chuckled. "I'm afraid not."

After Guthrie hung up, he called the Galveston-Houston Diocese to see what they'd say about Thorvald. He realized that Tereba had already made an inquiry through his source in the diocese, but there was something to be said for the blunder-in approach.

"Hello," he said after a woman's voice answered. "I'm hoping you can help me. I'm trying to track down a priest who once helped me out. I lost touch with him a year or so ago, and I want to fill him in on how I've been doing since then."

"Certainly," she said pleasantly. "I'm sure he'd appreciate the update. I can look him up right now. What is his name?"

"Donner Thorvald. I met him at the Vatican, but I understand he recently traveled to the U.S. I thought I might catch him while he's here."

"Let me check...." Her voice dropped off, and in the background, Guthrie could hear the click of fingers on a keyboard.

"Sir," she said after a moment, voice suddenly impersonal. "I'm going to transfer you to someone who can help you."

"Thank you." Guthrie waited while the call was transferred, which took longer than the punching of a few buttons. Most likely the receptionist was having a conversation with someone.

"Hello," a man said a few moments later. "This is Father Graves. I understand that you're trying to locate Father Donner Thorvald."

"That's right." Guthrie repeated his fabricated reason. "I'm hoping you can help put me in touch with him."

"And you knew him from Rome?"

"That's right. I met him at the Vatican while I was on vacation."

"May I ask your name?"

"Jim Bridger." Why not? A detective is a little like a mountain man explorer, facing danger to find the truth of the terrain beyond the easily seen.

"Well, Mr. Bridger, I'm sorry to inform you that Donner Thorvald left the priesthood about six months ago. We have no record of his current location."

"Left the priesthood?" Guthrie said, putting what he hoped was the right amount of consternation into his voice. "That's a shame. And he left no forwarding address?"

"That's correct."

"I guess priests don't get any sort of pension."

"Normally one isn't needed since most priests are with the Church for life."

"You have a point there," Guthrie conceded.

"If there's nothing else...."

"No. Nothing. Thanks for your help."

Guthrie hung up, thinking, thanks for nothing. But there *had* been something. Thorvald was no longer at the Vatican, so he very well could be here in Texas. And apparently the Catholic Church wasn't too pleased with him, so maybe the rumors about him were at least partly true.

The rest of the day was a waiting game until Espinoza called with more information on the train with the boxcar. Guthrie spent some of it doing background checks on Espinoza's boss, Dan Beaman, and Beaman's second-in-charge, Ray Hudson. Both had a few speeding tickets, and Hudson had one for running a stop sign, but for the most part, their records were clean. They both lived a little more extravagantly than their salaries warranted, though that, in itself, wasn't damning. They might be frugal financial geniuses for all Guthrie could prove.

But to his suspicious mind, it indicated the possibility that they were taking bribes for expediting the journeys of clandestine cargo and just being careful about it. One thing Guthrie had learned from observing habitual liars was that they often damn those whom they perceived as threats by leveling accusations that are really descriptions of their own actions and behaviors. Guthrie knew Beaman was a liar, and since he'd accused Espinoza of being a drug smuggler, then most likely it was Beaman and Hudson who were involved in smuggling.

After sitting at his computer for long enough, Guthrie felt the need to move around, so he did a second tai chi practice session then showered. No sooner had he gotten out of the shower than he felt a warning from his watchdog that someone with negative intent was approaching the house. But by the time he'd hurriedly dressed and gone into his office to check the video surveillance monitors, nothing unusual was there and the feeling was gone. Maybe it had just been a salesman or canvasser, both of which types Guthrie had ordered Rover to rebuff gently.

Nevertheless, Guthrie cautiously scanned his surroundings when he went outside to drive to Ninfa's Mexican Restaurant for dinner. He didn't notice any unusual cars or pedestrians, and the drive to Ninfa's, which was just a couple of exits south on the Gulf Freeway, was uneventful.

Inside, the owner, Señor Álvaro, greeted him as the hostess led him to one of the booths in the front. Guthrie had been coming to this Ninfa's for a long time, and in the early years, Álvaro had merely been a waiter. But for a time, the quality of the food had gone down, and Guthrie stopped going. When he finally tried it again a couple of years later, things were different. Álvaro and his son had bought the franchise and turned it around. Guthrie had complimented the waitress on how good the food was, and she pointed out Álvaro as the new owner. On his way out, Guthrie stopped by the man to compliment him, and they'd been friendly ever since.

Guthrie hadn't noticed anyone following him to Ninfa's, but they must have since they were waiting for him in the parking lot when he emerged. Just as he reached his Xterra, they popped up from behind the next car.

"We'd like a word with you, Guthrie," said the shorter of the two. He had a British accent.

Guthrie thought that might be best since both of them held Glocks pointed in his direction. The Brit gestured toward the car they'd hidden behind, and the taller man opened the front passenger door.

"Get in."

"No," Guthrie said.

"If you haven't noticed, we're holding guns, and you're not," the shorter man said.

"There are surveillance cameras all over this parking lot," Guthrie pointed out. "I doubt you'll shoot me here. Besides, if you want me to go somewhere, that means you want information, and I can't give you that if you shoot me."

The Brit glanced at the other man and said, "Get him in the car."

The taller man wisely handed his gun over to the Brit before he advanced on Guthrie. He was a good head taller than Guthrie and probably at least thirty pounds heavier, but it did him no good. As soon as he grabbed for Guthrie, he found himself in a painful arm-lock, his body between Guthrie and the shorter man. Less than a second later, Guthrie's own pistol was in hand, aimed at the shorter man beneath the locked arm of his assailant.

"Shit," the man in the arm lock ground out. "I'm gonna fuck you up when you let go." Unlike his companion, his accent was pure American. To remind him who was the actual threat, Guthrie tightened the arm lock just a bit, and the man grunted in pain.

"What was that?" Guthrie asked.

"Nothing," the man replied, grimacing.

"Toss 'em," Guthrie ordered the man with the British accent. Looking disgruntled, the man bent over and laid both of the Glocks on the pavement. "Now walk over there." He indicated a spot a dozen feet from the guns. Giving the arm of the man he had in the lock a quick squeeze to make him think twice about retaliating, Guthrie released him and shoved him toward his companion. As the man stumbled to a stop, flexing and rubbing his stressed arm, Guthrie stepped to the guns and kicked them under the men's car.

"Toss your wallets over here in front of me."

"I'm not giving you shit," said the American.

Guthrie aimed his pistol at the man's right leg.

"I'll cripple you for life, then I'll take your wallet and find out who you are, anyway. You came up on me with guns drawn. Don't think I'll have mercy if you won't cooperate."

"What about the surveillance cameras?" the Brit asked.

"I'm friends with the owner. He'll give me the recordings if I ask. Now hand over your fucking wallets."

Both men reluctantly pulled out their billfolds and tossed them to Guthrie's feet. Keeping the barrel of his S&W on the Brit, Guthrie squatted and picked them up. The first one belonged to the Brit, whose name was Patrick Croft. The American was Robert Miller. Both carried the IDs of Catholic priests, though they were dressed for night work.

"Okay, Patrick. Why the fuck are two Catholic priests confronting me with guns in front of one of my favorite restaurants? Be truthful. I can check out any part of your story, and if it doesn't jibe, I'm going to be upset."

The two men glanced at each other, and Miller shrugged.

"Might as well tell him. He's got the drop on us."

"All right," Croft said. "You're right. We are Catholic priests...."

"With guns?" Guthrie interrupted.

"Sometimes Satan must be fought with his own tools," Croft replied a little defensively. "The Catholic Church is a worldwide organization with many enemies. Do you really think we don't have an enforcement bureau to deal with problems?"

"I'd have thought that saving souls would be tough enough," Guthrie commented.

"Some souls can't be saved," the priest said.

Guthrie nodded.

"True enough. But why is it that I'm suddenly a problem to the Catholic Church?"

"You called the Galveston-Houston Diocese office and queried about a priest named Donner Thorvald," Miller replied.

A disgruntled feeling settled over Guthrie. If he was going to use a phone to barge into places in the future, he was going to have to start using a burner so he couldn't be traced. Maybe he'd just keep the one he'd taken from Galtero.

"We were sent here to find out what you know about Father Thorvald and why you're interested in him."

"Why are *you* interested in him," Guthrie asked. "Better make it good. If what you say doesn't agree with what I know about him, it won't go well for you."

"We can't tell you that," Croft said.

"You will tell me."

"You won't shoot us," Miller said. "Not in cold blood. Not over that."

"Maybe not, but I know someone who can make your lives pure hell on Earth if I just give him the word. Now tell me."

"There's nothing you can do to us that our boss won't do worse," Miller said, pointing meaningfully downward, past his feet. "Excommunication is the ultimate and eternal punishment leading to the infernal pit."

"Well, I'm in a little different boat," Guthrie said. "Like I told the fellow last night: I didn't have any knowledge of involvement by the Catholic Church in the matter I'm investigating. Before he, then you, showed up, that is."

"Someone came to you last night?" Croft asked.

"Yeah. To kill me. That didn't work out for him. His name is Bertrando Galtero. Ring any bells?"

The blank looks on their faces were convincing enough.

"No? Then you'll probably be interested to learn that I discovered that Galtero is a professional hitman working for Thorvald, and he is responsible for the murders and disappearance of eight Catholic priests in Rome over the past year. I also heard a rumor that Thorvald is a member of a secret group of Catholic priests and ex-priests who are attempting to undermine the authority of the Church."

That gave the two Catholic enforcers pause, and a glance passed between them.

"Okay, Guthrie," Miller said. "We don't know anything about any of that, and we appreciate the tip."

"Look," Guthrie said. "I'm not part of that network. I'm not even a Catholic. I didn't know about Thorvald until Galtero showed up. I'm telling you now in all sincerity that I'm simply on a case that involves a disappearance of someone not connected to the Catholic Church. I have no idea why or how Thorvald is involved. Or even if he's involved. So, now that I've told you about Galtero and the renegade network, why don't you reciprocate and tell me something I don't know."

"Why should we if your case has nothing to do with the Church?" Miller asked.

"Indulge me, especially since *you* think it does and I gave you information you didn't have. Plus, I have you at gunpoint, and you weren't hesitant to ask me something similar but much more rudely."

"All right," Croft said. "The truth is, we don't know anything about any priests disappearing. We were told that Thorvald embezzled a large sum of money from the Vatican and absconded to parts unknown. We're after him only to take him into custody and to recover as much of the money as we can."

"So, you're skip tracers for the Catholic Church?"

Both the men chuckled.

"Yeah," Miller said, face twisting into a sardonic grin. "I guess we are, at least in this instance."

"I'm going to make a deal with you two. I'm going to continue on with my case, and if I run into Thorvald and he's not part of it, I'll let you know where he is. And if he is, I'll let you know that, too. Meanwhile, both of you keep away from me and pursue your own leads. If I see either one of you without calling first, I might forget to share any information I might gather on Thorvald. Deal?"

"We'll abide by that," Croft said, "as long as you're sincere about letting us know Thorvald's whereabouts."

"So far, Thorvald is peripheral to my case. You'll have your man if I run across him. Meanwhile, just stay where you are until I've driven off. Give me a contact number."

Croft handed him a card bearing only a phone number.

"Ask for me," he said.

Guthrie took the card, then went to his car, unlocked it, and got in without holstering his pistol. He backed out of the parking space, and drove off, leaving the two Catholic enforcers in the lot, bending to retrieve their guns from beneath their car. As he drove, he couldn't help but wonder how a group of renegade priests were linked to a monster in a boxcar and a hoard of money missing from the Vatican. And what was the monster, and how and why was it in a boxcar in Houston?

Guthrie intended to answer all of those questions.

9

THE NEXT MORNING, GUTHRIE MET Espinoza at Dot Coffeeshop. Right off, he told his client about the results of the analysis of the sample of blood stains and the muck he'd collected.

"That's great," Espinoza said, then his eyes fell. "I mean…." He paused, turning a bit green, then looked blankly at Guthrie. "I can't believe that was Buddy." He was silent for a few moments while he got hold of himself.

"It's great that we have tentative confirmation of your story, so it's okay to be happy about that," Guthrie soothed.

"Are we going to take it to the police?"

"No so fast. We don't know for certain the human DNA belongs to Buddy. We'll need a sample we know came from him to compare. What about his locker or anything at work? Something in there might yield a DNA sample. Emily Horton said the company hasn't brought his stuff to her."

"Dan cleared out the locker yesterday. Like he knows Buddy isn't coming back."

"Well, maybe we can get something from Emily. But that's not important right now."

"Not important? What could be more important than proving Buddy's dead?"

"All we'd have is evidence that Buddy is dead instead of running off. That looks worse for you since you were on the scene where and when he was killed, and I assure you the cops won't listen to your monster story. It either sounds crazy or like something you're making up to cover guilt. And if Beaman voices his so-called suspicions that you're involved in a smuggling ring, that only looks worse for you. And if he's in on the ring, he can fabricate evidence implicating you. No, we need more to go on. Besides, there's still the monster. That's the real problem. I need to find it."

"So you really believe me?"

"I believe there is a monster, and that it ate Buddy. But that doesn't tell us what it is and where it went."

"I might have something on where it went," Espinoza said. "Or a trail, at least. And there's an odd thing. Usually, railcars are owned by a carrier who charges to transport cargo, but this one is owned by a private company. That makes it harder to track."

"Got a name for this company?"

"I do. It's called Trumpet of Faith."

"Interesting name," Guthrie said, thinking it sounded like something a renegade priest might be involved in. "Ever heard of them?"

"Nope. And here's the other odd thing. It looks to me like the car was expedited, but now there's no sign of it in the computer system. Because it's owned by a private company, that makes it easy to erase from the system."

"How can you tell, then?"

"There is some tangible paperwork if you know what you're looking for. Can't get rid of every paper document and checklist. When I looked at some of that, I could tell the timing was too short. That boxcar was in and out of the port and then the Englewood Yard like a shot. Any regular car would have taken a couple of days at least, not something like twelve hours. And with no computer record. At least, none that still exists."

According to the little paperwork Espinoza managed to track down, the car started in the Port of Houston, supposedly holding cases of olive oil from Italy. After that, it was shuttled to the Englewood Rail Yard, slated for a train being assembled to head out the next morning—the morning after the night Buddy was killed. Instead, as Espinoza also discovered, the train had left only about two hours after Beaman sent him home.

"I checked the manifests, and it wasn't due to roll for another four hours. That kind of thing is practically unheard of. Rail lines have to operate on strict schedules. Besides there's no way they could have finished all the inspections in that amount of time, especially with both me and Buddy absent. Not unless Dan—or someone else—broke all the regulations and protocols."

"Which he would do if he was in a hurry to get that train out of the yard before any sort of investigation happened," Guthrie pointed out.

"A little less than half the train was the lineup of well cars I was inspecting, and the rest was a mix of tankers, boxcars, and a few flatbeds with oil drilling and refining equipment headed for West Texas. Also maybe half-a-dozen auto transporters. No grain or bin cars, though. The tankers were going to several refineries in the Permian Basin to be loaded with petroleum products. The containers were loaded with food and durable goods, and the boxcars were mostly hauling mechanical parts. Supposedly. According to the paperwork, the train had four engines pulling one hundred and twenty cars even, not counting the caboose. That's what the last manual count read, and all the serial numbers on the cars tallied with the manifest."

"Looks like someone hitched the missing boxcar back onto the train."

"They must have done that after Dan ordered me to go home."

"And the train headed west?"

"All the way through Texas on the Southern Route. That runs from Houston, through San Antonio, then to Del Rio and roughly along the Mexican border to El Paso, then farther west. It was due to swap out the full boxcars and containers for empties along the way, with most of the rest of the tankers detraining at the Alfalfa Rail Yard in El Paso."

"I guess I'd better go pack a bag," Guthrie said.

"You going to follow the train?"

"I have to."

"I'm coming with you, then."

Guthrie shook his head.

"Not a good idea. It might be dangerous."

"I saw that monster. If anyone knows the danger, it's me. Besides, you're not a trainman. I am. I can go places and do things around rail lines you can't. You need me."

"Okay. You have a point. But what about your job?"

"I'll figure something out. As a safety and compliance officer, I have some leeway and discretionary action. Right now, they don't want me around the yard, anyway."

Apparently those words were more true than either of them suspected. Around eleven, Guthrie's phone rang. He glanced at the screen. Espinoza. He answered and lifted the phone to his ear.

"Gil. Anything wrong?"

"I'm not sure. As soon as I got to work a couple of hours ago, I told Dan I was still suspicious about that car and wanted to go up the line to look for it. At first, he just shut me down, made fun of my monster, and all that. Told me no. So I went out into the yard to do my job, when half an hour later, he calls me on the walkie and tells me to come to his office. When I get there, he's not exactly all smiles, but he's not up in arms like he was when I last saw him. And he tells me I can go. I'm checking out a HiRail first thing in the morning and heading west. Want to ride along?"

"What's a HiRail?"

"A four-wheel-drive pickup with a set of rail guides that can be lowered so it can ride on tracks. Usually for inspection or maintenance. You've seen them."

"That would certainly aim us straighter at our target," Guthrie said. "But I'm a little concerned about Beaman's sudden reversal. It's suspicious."

"So is him letting me take a HiRail on what he supposedly thinks is a wild goose chase through Texas. But so what? We'll be leaving him behind."

"That makes me wonder what he's sending us toward."

10

ESPINOZA PICKED HIM UP EARLY the next morning. The HiRail was a nearly new Super Duty Ford F-250—the XLT model. The interior was a bit abused but sported all the bells and whistles and featured an extended cab.

"Nice truck," Guthrie said as he tossed his kit bag into the back compartment.

"Yeah, we railroad guys ride in style when we're not laying tracks," Espinoza responded dryly. "Since we have a long way to go, I checked out one of the fancier models."

"You doing okay?" Guthrie asked, settling into his seat, knowing the trainman had just come off a full shift.

"No problem. This is like late afternoon and evening for me. I'll be fine, at least until San Antonio. We can spend the night there." He gave Guthrie an apologetic glance. "It's going to take me a couple of days to get on a daytime schedule."

"Sure. So what's in San Antonio?"

"That's where the train was scheduled to lay over for twenty-four hours while some of the cars were switched out," Espinoza said. "There were no stops between Houston and SA. I have a friend in the Kirby Yard there. He'll help us find out where the monster's boxcar went next. I called him last night, and he'll meet us at the rail yard office when we roll in."

Guthrie was surprised that Espinoza drove the distance to San Antonio on I-10 instead of using the HiRail's ability to drive on tracks.

"Driving the road is quicker," Espinoza explained. "At least between the major cities like Houston, San Antonio, Austin, and DFW.

There's just too much rolling stock on the tracks. We'd do more waiting than driving. But don't be disappointed." He smiled. "We'll take the rails west out of San Antonio."

The three-and-a-half-hour drive to San Antonio was uneventful, but Guthrie learned a little more about his client. He already knew Espinoza's basic background, so he asked him about his time in the army.

"Specialist first class," Espinoza said with a grin that quickly faded. "Afghanistan. I saw some bad shit over there. When I first went, I was right out of high school and needed a job. I even thought I might be able to do some good. That was during my first deployment, so I signed up for a second, but pretty soon after that, I saw that nothing good could be done there. The people don't want our kind of good. They just wanted us out, and I was right with them in wanting that, too."

"What did you do?"

"Infantry, at first. I was in a few firefights, and some of it was pretty intense, but we were mostly just shooting to shoot. They were doing the same thing. Some on both sides would get hit, but a few days later, we were right back at it. Then one day when we were riding three Humvees to some little village, the one in the lead drove over an IED. It took out the whole Hummer and everyone in it. I thought, fuck, that one blast killed more of my buddies than the last two months of shooting matches. And I could have been inside, too. Helpless. So I signed up for demolitions. They trained me in the use of explosives, and I spent my second tour finding and defusing IEDs and blowing up stuff they wanted blown up."

"Damn. Not the kind of work that tolerates mistakes."

"Yeah, but I was careful, and here I am, in one piece. Right after I got out, I went to UH, got a degree in mechanical engineering, and caught a lucky break in getting on with UP. Been with them ever since."

"You said something about a girlfriend."

"Paula. We met a couple of years ago at a party."

"But no ring?"

"If we come back from this, I'm going straight to the jewelers."

They both laughed, but not with much mirth.

"What about you?" Espinoza asked. "How'd you become a detective?"

"It's a long and painful story," Guthrie said. "The short of it is, I was a Houston cop, but I got shot up in a drug raid. My right hip was so damaged that they replaced it with a titanium joint. The truth is, it doesn't bother me much, but I wasn't deemed fit for street duty. I didn't want to just sit at a desk, so I took a disability pension. For about a year, I just sat around on my ass, anyway, getting bored and depressed, then I was offered the job of finding a missing art object. I took it, and that got me started."

"You said you'd been married."

"Yeah. She left while I was in the hospital recovering from the gunshot."

"That must have been tough."

"It was tougher realizing how badly I'd treated her and fallen from grace in the rest of my life."

They were silent for a few minutes.

"I know why I'm out here," Guthrie said at last. "It's my job." My redemption, he thought. "But why you? Why put yourself at risk?"

"Two reasons. For one, my job's on the line, too. This is what I do, and there aren't a hell of a lot of railroad companies to do it for. If my job at UP goes belly up for any questionable reason, so does my whole career. But there's something more important. Buddy. I saw what happened to him, and I want some personal justice for that."

"I hope we get it," Guthrie said. "For you and Emily Horton."

"Yeah, her especially." Espinoza paused and glanced at Guthrie. "What's it with that old man? Mr. Terry? I get the impression you know him pretty well."

"Not a chance." Guthrie laughed, Tereba's dark, inscrutable face popping into his mind. "I don't think anybody really knows Mr. Terry. I doubt there's anyone else like him."

Guthrie wasn't about to tell Espinoza that Tereba might be a thousand years old. That would make *Guthrie* sound crazy. But then again, they were out here looking for a monster Espinoza had seen eating a coworker, so maybe the trainman might be inclined to accept it.

"But you know him well enough for him to send me to you."

"I've done a couple of jobs for him," Guthrie said. "He calls me when there's a special case he wants me to work on."

"Like a monster in a boxcar?"

"Yeah," Guthrie said, this time without humor. "Like that."

When they reached San Antonio, Espinoza drove straight to the office of the Kirby Rail Yard. The yard was much smaller than the Englewood Yard in Houston, and its main office was smaller, too. Espinoza parked on the far side of the lot in front of the building, and Guthrie started to get out, but Espinoza stopped him.

"Let me call my friend," he said. "He'll meet us out here."

"Good idea," Guthrie said.

Espinoza pulled his phone from the case on his belt and quick-dialed a number.

"Frank. Yeah. We're here. A HiRail at the back of the parking lot. Okay." He thumbed off the phone and slipped it back into its case. "He's on his way."

Less than two minutes later, a tall man in jeans and a blue work shirt emerged from the front door, squinted toward the back of the lot until his eyes found the HiRail, then walked purposefully over.

"Hop in," Espinoza said, popping the locks so the man could slide onto the seat in the back of the cab. "Frank, this is Clay Guthrie. Clay, Frank Belton. Frank's another safety and compliance officer. We met in Houston about the time I hired on with UP."

Guthrie twisted awkwardly in his seat and shook Belton's hand.

"What's this all about?" Belton asked, leaning forward expectantly.

"I don't suppose you heard what happened in Houston about ten days ago?"

"No. What?"

"Remember Buddy Horton?"

"Vaguely. He'd just started when I transferred here. Something going on with him?"

"He's dead, Frank."

"Dead? How?"

"Well, he's not officially dead. Officially, he's disappeared. Right off the job in the middle of the night shift."

"If he disappeared, how do you know he's dead?"

"I saw him die."

"But if you saw him die, how can he have disappeared? What happened to him?"

"Let's just say that's something you probably shouldn't know," Guthrie put in.

"Clay's a detective. I hired him to find out what happened to Buddy."

"What about the cops?"

"They don't believe my story about Buddy's death. The Fed's either. They all think I'm crazy, and so does UP. They're looking for an excuse to fire me."

"Why are you here? What's all this have to do with me?"

"Buddy was killed because he saw something he shouldn't have inside a boxcar," Guthrie said. "We know the train carrying it came through here, and we need to know if the car stayed here or went on with the train."

"Can you find that out?" Espinoza asked.

"I can do that. If you find the car, will it save your job?"

"Maybe," Espinoza said. "Maybe not. But it's important we find it, no matter what happens to me."

"But you're not going to tell me any more than that?" Belton looked a bit disgruntled.

"Can't have you thinking I'm crazy, too," Espinoza chuckled.

"Okay," Belton said after a moment's reflection. "I'll do it, but it might take some time."

"By tonight?"

"Morning. I'll give you a call."

"Thanks," Espinoza said as he handed over a slip of paper. "This is the train in question and the boxcar's serial number. The car is owned by a company called Trumpet of Faith. But listen: Any records of it might have been wiped from the computer system. Be sure to check the paper records from the guys in the yard."

"Will do," Belton said. "I'll be in touch."

He got out and headed toward the office.

"Well," Espinoza said. "That's that for now."

"Think he'll find something?"

"If there's something to find."

"Well, since we're going to be here overnight, we ought to grab a bite to eat and find a hotel."

Later, while Guthrie was watching TV in his hotel room, a knock sounded on the door. It was Espinoza.

"I heard from Frank," he said.

"That was quick."

Guthrie invited him in and closed the door.

"He said that the monster's car didn't detrain here, so it must have gone on west, but he only knows that from a paper checklist made by one of the yardmen. So we're right in assuming Dan, or someone else, erased the car from the computer system company-wide. As far as UP is concerned, that boxcar no longer exists."

"Won't that make it difficult to pass on through?"

"Not necessarily. A lot of the yardmen rely on paper records that could have been printed before the car was erased from the computer. Besides, if Dan's in on it, other trainmen might be, too."

"Good thing you got the serial numbers in Houston before Beaman destroyed the records there. Can we still track it?"

"Only by following it. Frank gave me the train's route and its scheduled stops, but he couldn't tell me the boxcar's destination. We'll ride the rails after this. Next stop, Del Rio."

"Sounds like a plan," Guthrie said. "I'll meet you downstairs for breakfast at six, then we'll head out."

11

THE DRIVE FROM SAN ANTONIO to Del Rio took a little more than four hours. Espinoza told Guthrie it would have taken closer to two or less if they didn't have to pull off onto sidings every half hour to let trains rumble by on the main line. Most were freight trains, though the *Sunset Limited* went by, heading east. They even got stuck behind a freight liner on a siding about half way to Del Rio.

"We have an online sat-link to view traffic on the network of tracks," Espinoza explained, pointing to a screen in the HiRail's dashboard. It showed a map with lines that weren't roads running between cities and towns. Red dots crawled down almost all of them, and a readout below gave information in the form of data.

"We can zoom in anywhere we want, but we'll have to pay sharp attention to the line we're on if we don't want to decorate the front of some locomotive. But don't worry. There are plenty of sidings ahead, and if there isn't one when we need it, we can derail the truck just about anywhere."

Del Rio didn't have a full-fledged rail yard, the trainman said.

"It's mostly a loop siding. That's what we call a siding that's connected to the main track at both ends. This siding has a handful of spurs: short or sometimes long dead-end tracks to hold cars that are being loaded or unloaded."

"Could the boxcar have detrained there?"

"It's possible. But if it stayed with the train, it went on farther west since there are no other lines going out of there. Unfortunately, I don't know anybody working here, I'll just have to go into the yard office and ask."

"Won't that look funny?" Guthrie asked. "You're from Houston, and we're a long way from there."

"Like I said, as a safety and compliance officer, I'm not bound to the Houston yard," Espinoza reminded him. "I can legitimately track a car anywhere on the UP system with the approval of my supervisor, and Dan gave me that."

Espinoza was right, beginning with the skimpiness of Del Rio's rail yard. The Union Pacific headquarters was only a couple of hundred feet from the small passenger station, and both fronted the main line, with the loop siding just beyond.

"I'd better go in alone," Espinoza said after he parked in the UP lot, which was across the double tracks from the office—a one-story, dark tan brick building with a beige metal roof. "It might look funny if I bring in a non-railroad worker."

He left the truck, walked across the half-asphalted, half dirt lot, across the tracks, and into the building. While he was inside, Guthrie got out to stretch and walk around a little. He didn't wander far because there wasn't any place to go. Across the adjacent street, empty ground with a dirt road paralleled the tracks to the west for as far as he could see in the dry and diminishing distance. Flanking that, right across the street, was another, smaller parking lot with eight cars and pickups and a van. On the far side of that was a third lot, more ragged than the other two and holding five eighteen-wheeler trailers. To the east, the right-of-way with its dirt road paralleling the tracks ran for about half a mile before ducking beneath a bridge over the tracks and disappearing in the distance. All-in-all, it was a dry, dusty, dreary scene.

Guthrie strolled over to the lot with the trailers, mostly just to walk somewhere. Even before he reached them, he saw by the dust on top of their sagging tires that they'd been there for some time. Their presence didn't seem too unusual for West Texas, where rusting vehicles and equipment and crumbling structures dotted the landscapes around towns, roads, and the railroad. Some of the ruins, he mused, might be worth an archaeological dig.

Espinoza came out of the UP office about ten minutes after Guthrie returned to the HiRail.

"Good news," he said as he slid behind the wheel. "It turns out the train stopped here to take on several cattle cars. The guys in the office took a manual count and have a record of the boxcar's serial number. When the train left, the car was still with it."

"Going west," Guthrie said.

"To El Paso, then on into New Mexico."

"Let's hope we don't have to chase it that far."

"Probably not. I had them call ahead to El Paso. The train stopped there for a couple of days to detrain the tank cars bound for the Permian Basin and pick up a few that were full and bound for destinations to the west. A final count before the train went on into New Mexico showed it was one car short and our boxcar's serial number wasn't on the checklist."

"So it was cut loose somewhere between here and El Paso."

"Looks like it, but no one seems to know for sure where." Espinoza shrugged. "Because the boxcar's been scrubbed from the computer, the company doesn't even acknowledge it exists. They've chalked up everything to a miscount before the train left Houston."

"Does that happen often?"

"Occasionally, but it's pretty rare."

"So, what's next?"

"There must be forty or fifty sidings between here and El Paso. Most are simple loop sidings out in the middle of nowhere to allow trains to pass each other on the fly. No chance to detrain a car on one of those. There'd be no place for it to go. But some have stubs, spurs, or small yards where ranchers from the surrounding area load up cattle. Our boxcar could be cut out on any one of them."

"We'll have to be selective, then. Just where would the people in charge of the car take it? Not likely to a town. Not with a monster in it. They won't want that known."

"Most of those sidings are out in the middle of nowhere," Espinoza said, "and in that country, nowhere is a big and desolate place. In fact, I suggest we stay here tonight and proceed in the morning."

12

THEY ATE A QUICK BREAKFAST at the hotel's continental breakfast bar then headed for the main rail line running west. Espinoza found a spot to maneuver the truck onto the tracks, where he lowered the rail wheels. In a couple of minutes, they were rolling westward down the line. As soon as they'd settled in, Espinoza put the truck on cruise control.

"Once you're on the rails," he said, "you don't have to steer or worry about the accelerator. The only thing you have to worry about is the traffic."

The ride was almost idyllic, with nothing to interfere with the view but the muted, steady rumble of the engine and the metallic rolling sound from the wheels. It wasn't the sort of view you'd ever get from a road or highway. It made Guthrie realize more than ever how much he needed to get out of Houston for a long vacation. The main problem with that was the lack of anyone to vacation with. He hadn't thought about women much since he'd quit brooding over Alice's departure after the close of the first case he'd worked for Tereba, but that had been more nearly five years ago. Maybe it was time to start looking for someone to share time with. If he could remember how to do either.

Not far out of Del Rio, the tracks crossed a trestle over a large body of water.

"Lake Amistad," Espinoza said.

"Yeah. I've seen it from the highway bridge over there." Guthrie pointed to a highway span that paralleled the trestle as the two jumped a narrow spot in the middle of the long lake.

The water was a beautiful clear blue nestling in the dry brown terrain. A few boats floated on its azure surface, some with fishermen, some trailing skiers, and others just skimming along.

Espinoza told Guthrie that the HiRail truck could only go fifty or sixty on the rails. There was a west-bound train due to pass through Del Rio in about an hour, and he wanted to make it to Comstock, which was about twenty miles up the track, where there was a siding. They made it with plenty of time to spare.

"I'll have to throw the switch manually," Espinoza said, stopping the truck.

He got out, threw the lever to let them onto the siding, then got back in and pulled forward before getting out again to return the switch to its original position. Once back in the truck, he pulled forward to the end of the siding and let the truck idle while they waited for the train to pass.

"I guess you've been out this way before." Espinoza said.

"Several times. A couple of camping trips to Big Bend when I was younger, and I drove out to Marfa to see the lights."

"I never thought much of that legend. Did you see them?"

"No, but that doesn't mean they don't exist."

"Yeah, I guess not. Most people wouldn't believe a monster's out here somewhere, riding around in a boxcar."

At last, the train they were waiting for—a combination of tankers, boxcars, bin cars, and flatbeds loaded with various types of equipment and shipping containers—passed. It took a long time.

"Man, I've seen some long trains," Guthrie said, "but this one takes the cake. How long can they get?"

"Most places they're not as long as they are out here in the desolate west. It's a long way across and not much in between, so the rail carriers pack in as much rolling stock as they can. Some of these trains max out at nearly two miles. But that's nothing compared to the record, which was an Australian train that was a little more than four-and-a-half miles long."

"That's unbelievable."

"Yeah, and not to be repeated. Not only did the weight and stress screw up the tracks and car couplings, it took forever to unload."

After the train passed, Espinoza put the truck in gear and followed as the caboose gradually diminished in the distance ahead.

They reached the next siding about an hour later—this one out in the middle of nowhere. It had no spur and was empty.

"We have another hour and a half before the next train," Espinoza said as they cruised on through. "We can easily make the Pumpville siding before then."

"What's in Pumpville?"

"I guess there's a pump," Espinoza chuckled. "The route map doesn't show details like that. But that's the first siding with a stub where they could have detrained the boxcar."

Guthrie pulled out his phone and looked up Pumpville on his map app.

"I don't see a pump," he said, "But there's a church and a scattering of houses in the area, mostly in ruins. Not much else."

"If they detrained the boxcar there, it should still be on the stub" Espinoza said, consulting his onboard computer. "I can't see any record of a pick-up there this last week."

The ride to Pumpville was uneventful except for the trestle over the Pecos River gorge.

"I've driven over the US 90 bridge down that way," Guthrie said, waving toward the south while staring out the window at the river below. "It's higher than this one, but this is still pretty impressive."

"Yeah. You get a great view when you go over trestles in a Hi-Rail. Nothing between you and the river except a few flimsy girders and air."

As if to prove Espinoza's point, a large gray hawk emerged from beneath the trestle on Guthrie's side, its wings motionless as it glided the gorge's air currents upstream.

They arrived at Pumpville about an hour later, but there was no sign of a boxcar—or any other car—on the stub, which was a couple of hundred feet long. Espinoza got out to throw the switch to take them onto the stub, and Guthrie got out with him.

"Show me how to do that," he said. "It'll save time."

Espinoza showed him.

"Throw the switch back after I cross," he said. "We'll wait here for the train."

Guthrie did, and after the HiRail was parked safely on the stub, he walked over to the vehicle.

"I'll be back in a few minutes," he said.

He ambled toward the small church that sat nearby. An even smaller frame house squatted next to it like a young animal hovering next to its mother. The interior of the church was cool and dim, but nobody was in it. Guthrie walked back into the sunshine and over to the small house and knocked on the door. A careworn middle-aged woman with pleasant face answered, looking puzzled.

"Pardon me, ma'am," Guthrie said. "My partner and I are with Union Pacific. We're tracking a boxcar that seems to have been mis-placed, and we're wondering if a west-bound train stopped here sometime in the last week and left one on the siding out there."

"Ain't seen one," the woman said, peering out toward the stub and the HiRail. "And I'd sure have done if one was there. That'd be the most exciting thing to happen here all year." She looked back at Guthrie and smiled. "Since it didn't, I guess that makes you the most exciting thing. We don't see many strangers around here." She laughed. "Heck, we don't see much of anyone. Care to come in for a cup of coffee?"

Guthrie chuckled.

"I appreciate the offer," he said, "but we have to make El Paso by tonight."

He thanked the woman, and returned to the truck.

"It didn't get detrained here according to the minister's wife."

"Well, there's plenty more chances up the way," Espinoza said. "We'll just wait for a clear track. Shouldn't be long."

About fifteen minutes later, the train whooshed down the rails and was soon out of sight. Even before it was, Guthrie threw the switch , and Espinoza pulled back onto the main line.

"How long do we have before we have to pull off again?"

"There's plenty of time to reach the next siding with a stub," Es-pinoza said, consulting his computer. "Maybe twenty-five or thirty miles."

They passed two more long, stubless sidings without pause and finally arrived at the one with the stub. It was even more desolate than the one in Pumpville. Guthrie's map showed that the tiny town of Dryden lay about a mile down the track from the siding, but out where the siding's stub lay, the only sign of humanity was the pres-ence of the seemingly ubiquitous dirt road that paralleled the tracks. In this sort of dry environment, that dirt road would persist for centuries, even if no vehicle ever drove it again.

"This is one of those places where ranchers load cattle cars, but obviously our car isn't here," Espinoza said. "There are two more sidings before Sanderson, and there's a small yard there where we can make inquiries."

They had to divert onto the second siding to let a freight train pass, and not long after, they pulled into the rail yard in Sanderson. It was even smaller than the one in Del Rio.

"Let's get off the main line and the siding," Espinoza suggested. "There's a stub off to the left." He pointed.

After Guthrie had thrown the switches, Espinoza drove onto the stub, pulled up a few hundred feet, and stopped just in front of a small utility engine hooked to three cattle cars. A boxcar also sat on the tracks, a couple of dozen feet behind the last cattle car. The two men glanced at each other, suspicion on their faces.

"Let's look," Guthrie said.

"I can't see them leaving their cargo here," Espinoza said as they walked toward the boxcar. "Or offloading it."

Guthrie kept his hand on the butt of his S&W as they reached the boxcar, but almost immediately it was apparent that either this wasn't the right boxcar or the monster had been taken elsewhere. The door was ajar and the interior empty. It also was unstained. If it had been the right car, there should be significant blood stains on the plywood floor, even if the monster had departed.

"Wrong serial number," Espinoza said. "Pardon me for a moment. Professional curiosity."

He spent a couple of minutes walking around the boxcar and looking up into its chassis.

"Anything wrong?" Guthrie asked as Espinoza straightened.

"Not really. Looks like one of the trucks has a problem. Nothing to concern us." He nodded down the tracks. "Let's walk down the yard."

The yard wasn't large enough for a UP office, though there was a small metal work building with a couple of shipping containers to one side about a thousand feet up the track. Piles of rails and ties lay here and there around the building and containers, and a small crane completed the setup.

"Probably storage for tools and equipment," Espinoza said, gesturing at the shipping containers as they walked by. Nobody was around.

"There'll be a crew here only if there's a problem on the line nearby," Espinoza said. "We'll have to go up to the station to get any information."

He gestured ahead to a small cement-block building about eight by ten, painted off-white, and sitting another a hundred yards ahead.

Even before they reached the station, Guthrie could hear the hum of an AC unit affixed in one wall. He followed Espinoza through the door, into the small, cool interior. A middle-aged man sitting at a tiny desk behind the counter looked up from a paperback novel as they entered, expression puzzled.

"Can I help you gentlemen?" he asked.

Espinoza showed his credentials.

The man chuckled.

"That explains it," he said. "I knew you weren't from around here, and I didn't hear a car drive up."

"We came in on a HiRail."

"I hope you didn't leave it on the main line," the clerk said, a worried look creasing his tanned brow. "We got a freighter coming through in just a few minutes."

"I parked on the stub," Espinoza assured him. "Does it stop here?"

"We're a flag stop, but nobody's getting on or off, today. Unless you fellows want to board."

"Just information," Guthrie said. "We're tracking a misplaced boxcar that was on a train that came through here about a week ago. Anything like that detrained here."

The man frowned, wrinkled his lips, and shook his head.

"Nothing's been cut loose here for at least a month except for the rolling stock you see out on the stub right now. One a them's a boxcar. You can go check it out if you want."

"Thanks," Espinoza said. "We already had a look. Why are they all here?"

"The cattle cars are waiting for stock from the Simpson Ranch later this week. As for the boxcar, some inspector, same kind as you, said there was some sort of problem with the front wheels or something like that. They're sending out a repair crew. They're supposed to be here sometime in the next week or two. Soon as they finish a job up the line." He gestured toward the west.

"Ever hear of a company called Trumpet of Faith?" Guthrie asked.

"No," the man said, shaking his head again. "Can't say as I have. I know most of the places around here, but most are ranches. Your place sounds like a church."

"Any place to eat around here?" Guthrie asked.

The man laughed.

"We only got one restaurant, if you can call it that. It's take-out only, but they got a patio. You can walk there if you've a mind not to unhitch your HiRail."

He gave them directions, and they thanked him and left to find the restaurant. It was a small, pink stucco adobe-style structure with a red metal roof and an awning that covered a patio holding four weathered wooden picnic tables. At the window, they both ordered burgers, then they sat at one of the tables to eat.

"I think we can make Alpine before dark," Espinoza said as he wadded the paper that had held his burger and stuffed it into the sack along with the paper tray that was now empty of French fries. "It's just about the biggest town out here. We can spend the night there and resume our search in the morning."

"Assuming we don't find our car before then."

"Assuming," Espinoza nodded.

They walked back to the HiRail and resumed their journey. From here, the terrain grew ever more desolate, mountainous, and bleak. It was amazing, Guthrie thought, that anything at all could survive out here, but it seemed that life always managed to find a toehold wherever it could, even in places that seemed to be only bare stone and barren dirt.

The drive from Sanderson to Alpine took nearly four hours, at least one of which was occupied by waiting on sidings for trains to pass, going one direction or the other. In that distance, there were six sidings with stubs, but none held any rolling stock, much less the box-car they sought. Nor did the attendants at the tiny station in Marathon have any knowledge of the errant car or the Trumpet of Faith.

"Maybe we'll have more luck in Alpine," Espinoza said. "There's a junction there."

"Let's hope they didn't send the boxcar off along the other line," Guthrie said. "We could be chasing the damn thing all over the state."

Espinoza shook his head.

"That's possible but not likely. If the shippers wanted the boxcar up there, they'd have sent it along the northern route. Quicker that way."

At last, tired after the long drive, they reached Alpine. Espinoza retracted the rail wheels at a street crossing next to the Amtrak station then pulled into the station parking lot. The clerks inside could give them no information about the boxcar, but they did recommend a nearby hotel and place to eat.

Afterwards, while Guthrie lay on the bed in his room, he contemplated the wisdom of their strategy. There seemed to be little else they could do, though, but follow the train's route. They knew the boxcar hadn't made it to El Paso, and it wasn't anywhere behind them. It had to be close. Surely they'd find some trace of it the next day. With that thought, he drifted off to sleep.

13

AFTER BREAKFAST, GUTHRIE AND ESPINOZA got into the HiRail and drove back to the rail crossing next to the station, where Espinoza mounted it on the tracks.

"The next big stop is Sierra Blanca," he said. "Three to four hours away. Between here and there are maybe a dozen sidings. Five with stubs."

"Well, that damn car has to be out here somewhere," Guthrie said. "I hope we find it soon."

"Tired of looking at the scenery?"

"Tired of waiting to see your monster in the flesh."

"I'd laugh," Espinoza said, "but that thing's no laughing matter."

The ride to Sierra Blanca went smoothly enough. Out here, many of the sidings, especially those with stubs, were accompanied by medium to large stock pens to hold cattle prior to loading them into cattle cars. A scattered few ran beside small, dusty towns that made Guthrie wonder just what the people who lived out here did beside ranching to justify settling in these barren reaches. But nowhere did they find the car they sought.

About an hour northwest of Marfa, the rail line diverged from US 90, which it had roughly followed since they'd left Del Rio. The terrain became ever more desolate as they drove, the valleys through which the rails ran flanked by small and low but rugged and arid mountain ranges.

At last, they rolled into Sierra Blanca, passing a true junction angling in from the northeast.

"That's a Santa Fe line," Espinoza said, pointing to the intersecting tracks. "It runs northeast, so our car probably didn't go back up that way. I don't think there's much of a UP facility here, or an Amtrak station, but there is a railroad museum. There must be fifty railroad museums in this state, but this one is truly important because this junction is historically significant. It's where two competing railroads met, creating the second U.S. transcontinental line, now called the Southern Route."

"Maybe they'll know something," Guthrie said as Espinoza found a stub about a hundred yards down the track from the museum.

He parked the truck, and they walked back to the building, which sat about two hundred feet from the main line. The sign read, "Hudspeth County Railroad Depot Museum."

"This was the original depot for the entire county," Espinoza said as they approached.

Indeed, the building looked like an Old West railroad depot, walls painted a dark, dull yellow and the newer metal roof a forest green.

"It's weird it's so far from the tracks," Guthrie said.

"They might have shifted the tracks over time," Espinoza speculated.

Inside, they discovered why. Two women sat at desks behind the counter: a slender forty-something brunette with a short bob, and the other a little older and heavier, with bottle-blonde, neck-length hair. The older one glanced up with curiosity from the book she was reading, while the younger one pulled her attention from her computer screen. She rose and came up to the counter, a smile on her face and the name, "Margaret," on her name tag.

"Welcome to the museum," Margaret said. "Would you like to sign our guestbook?"

She pushed the guest book forward, hopefully.

"We're not here to see the museum," Espinoza said, showing her his credentials.

The woman seemed surprised.

"We're not part of Union Pacific, anymore," she said, a bit flustered.

The older woman lay her book face down on her desk and joined her friend at the counter, the curiosity stronger on her face. Her name tag said she was Janie.

"We're not here about the museum," Espinoza said. "We're looking for a stray boxcar, and since you're close to the rails, we were wondering if you noticed one being left out there in the last week or so. Or any other unusual activity."

"Unusual activity?" Margaret frowned and cocked her head slightly to the right. Then she straightened and shook it. "No, I don't remember anything unusual or any boxcar. But to tell the truth, I hardly pay attention anymore."

"I don't remember anything, either," the older woman said. "The trains come and go, but from here, we can't really see what goes on down on the sidings.

"Who does own the museum?" Guthrie asked.

"It's a project of the Hudspeth County Historical Society," Margaret answered, obviously happy to be on familiar ground. "Janie and I are members."

"In good standing,"Janie assured them.

"In good standing," Margaret repeated. "This building once stood beside the tracks, but when it was decommissioned, it was bought by the society and moved here, right on Sierra Blanca's main street. But," she chuckled, "it isn't really Main Street. You see that dirt road out back, just this side of the tracks?" She laughed again, pointing through the back windows. "Well, that's Main Street. Isn't a thing on it but the dirt it's made of, and it's the most miserable road in a town full of miserable roads. Tell the truth," she leaned forward conspiratorially, "this museum is just about the only thing worth visiting in around here."

"Not unless you count our historic slurry pit," Janie said sarcastically.

"The slurry pit?" Guthrie questioned. "What's that?"

"Was, thank goodness," Janie said. "We made 'em shut it down."

"Who were 'they'?" Guthrie asked.

"New Yorkers," Margaret said. "They bought a tract with a wide, shallow wash not half a mile east." She pointed. "Started trucking in their raw sewage and dumping it right in there."

The older woman shook her head.

"Why they got to dump their…well, their sewage right here, I'll never know."

"I guess they don't have good places for all of it anymore up there in New York," Margaret said. "Especially when they have all them people, and they figure we have all sorts of empty space out here. They might be right about the space, but choosing a place right on the edge of town was just plain dumb."

"The stink got so bad, wouldn't nobody use the city park," Janie said. "It's only about a hundred and fifty yards away. But distance don't really matter when the wind blows the stink all over town."

"Now, Janie," Margaret said, laying a hand on the older woman's arm "Maybe we shouldn't give these gentlemen the impression that Sierra Blanca is a sewage dump, even if it is part of our so-called heritage." To the men, she said, "All that happened twenty years ago. The town took legal action and won, and they shut down. The smell is long gone."

"Maybe they'd like to hear about the time the Army bombed the town," Janie volunteered. "That's part of our heritage, too. Back at the end of World War Two. I wasn't born yet, but I heard the story from everybody who was while I was growing up. They was practice bombs. Five of 'em blew up the train tracks, and one hit the gas station, but it didn't blow up the gas tanks."

"That was lucky," Guthrie said.

"It sure was. Kinda funny, too, the government blowing the main line apart right where the government paid two railroad companies to join it."

"It is," Guthrie agreed with a chuckle.

"At least nobody got hurt," Margaret said. "But it sure gave everyone something to talk about. Even now."

They all laughed at that.

"Say," Guthrie said. "I'm sure you ladies know just about every church around these parts."

The two women exchanged a half-humorous, half-critical glance.

"I'll bet we do," the younger one said.

"My sister heard of a religious group somewhere out this way," Guthrie said. "Seems they operate a spiritual retreat or something like that. Since I'm out here, anyway, she asked me to look into it. It's called Trumpet of Faith."

The women looked quizzically at one another, then turned back to Guthrie, both shaking their heads.

"I never heard of one like that," Janie said. "Maybe it's closer to El Paso or up towards Van Horn. Ain't much south of here but the border, or north, either. Just desert covered by mountains and big ranches up that way." She shook her head apologetically. "Sorry we couldn't help you."

"You still can," Espinoza said. "Can you direct us to the best restaurant in town?"

The two women laughed.

"Aren't but three places to eat in town," Margaret said. "There's a taqueria over by the Americana Inn on I-10, another taqueria over there, on the other side of the tracks," she pointed, "and a regular cafe just down the street." She pointed again.

"It's good. Jerry and I eat at there all the time," Janie volunteered.

"Thanks for your help, ladies," Guthrie said, and he and Espinoza left the museum. The ladies seemed sorry to see them go, and as Guthrie went through the door, he noticed them turning to one another, mouths moving.

Sure enough, the cafe sat about a hundred yards down, on the opposite side of the road. It occupied the east end of Sierra Blanca's only real block of connected brick buildings, and it's big windows overlooked the street and the parking lot to its left. The building just to its right was a small grocery store. The one on the far end was a gun shop, but the three intervening spaces were unoccupied.

The walk wasn't far, but Guthrie relished the brief exercise after sitting in the truck for so long. The cafe accommodated ten or so tables, a lunch counter fronted by eight stools, and five booths beneath a wall of windows overlooking the street. It was cool and quiet and only sparsely occupied. A middle-aged white couple sat in a booth and two Border Patrol agents, both Hispanic, occupied stools at the counter. A sign taped to the back of the cash register read, "Take a Seat."

"Sit anywhere you like," the waitress called from behind the counter. "I'll be right with you."

They chose a booth beside a window overlooking the street and away from the other customers. A moment later, the waitress came over with water, menus, and silverware. She was skinny, with narrow hips behind her short apron, and the lines on her face put her well into her fifties. Her light brown hair was in a mini-bouffant with a bright red barrette fixed to one side. The name tag pinned over her skimpy chest read, "Irene."

"Coffee, gentlemen?" she asked, her face creasing even more in what seemed to be a genuine smile. She gave each one of them a menu.

"Please," Guthrie said.

"Tea for me," Espinoza said. "Unsweet."

"I'll give you a minute to look over the menu," she said, and she went back to the kitchen. She was back in two minutes, and by then, they'd decided. She took their orders and headed to the kitchen.

They didn't say much while they waited. Their food arrived shortly, and they dug in. They left a nice tip, paid their bills at the cash register, then stepped out into the sunshine. The stub where the HiRail was parked was about a fifteen minute walk, and as they traveled the distance, Guthrie took in some of the features of this part of town, which included, in addition to the railroad museum, a fair-sized bank, a post office, and three small motels. Unlike a lot of the businesses along the road that were closed up and desiccating into ruins beneath the unrelenting sun, the bank was new and fancy looking, and the motels, though modest, were in curiously good shape despite their conspicuously empty parking lots.

At last the HiRail came into view, and they could see a second HiRail parked right behind it, a man sitting in the cab. He got out and faced them as they neared.

14

"YOU FELLOWS DRIVING THIS?" THE man asked, gesturing toward their truck.

"I am," Espinoza said. "And you are?"

"Jack Fleming. Safety and compliance officer for UP in El Paso." He flashed his credentials like they were an FBI badge. He was a big man, but approaching middle age and not in the best shape. His thinning brown hair crowned a face that had never been handsome, even in youth.

"Gilbert Espinoza." Espinoza matched Fleming with his own credentials.

"And you?" Fleming turned to Guthrie.

"A licensed private investigator assisting Mr. Espinoza." He held out his PI license so Fleming could see it.

"I see," Fleming said, his tone saying he didn't. He turned to Espinoza. "Mind telling me what a safety and compliance officer out of the Houston office is doing way out here?"

"Simple," Espinoza said. "An unregistered boxcar made it out of the Englewood Yard. We're tracking it to see where it went."

"That would seem more like a job for us in my district."

"Not if the car holds improperly labeled hazardous cargo and shipped out under my watch."

"And this one does?"

"That's right."

"I guess you must be the fellow who called El Paso to see if it went through there."

"Then I guess you must already have know who we were when you asked," Espinoza said.

"And I suppose you're the same fellow who reported that a missing Englewood employee was eaten by a monster living in a boxcar."

Espinoza laughed.

"Is that what they're saying?"

"That's what they're saying."

"Jesus," Espinoza said, shaking his head. "Seriously? I told them he just disappeared off the job. One of them must have made up the monster part. The only monster I know at Englewood is my boss."

Fleming had to chuckle at that, but it sounded hollow.

"And what's your role in this, Mr. Guthrie?"

"I represent individuals with an interest in the car's contents."

"The owners who shipped hazardous cargo?"

"People who are upset UP lost their hazardous cargo. I'm curious. Who told you about Mr. Espinoza and the employee who disappeared?"

"I don't rightly remember," Fleming replied in a tone that said Guthrie had no right to ask. "News travels fast on the rails."

Miraculously fast, Guthrie thought. Just two days before, Espinoza's colleague in San Antonio, Frank Belton, knew nothing about it, and San Antonio was a hell of a lot closer to Houston than El Paso. And Belton had known Horton, so he definitely would have paid attention to any story circulating about him.

"Well, you can forget that," Espinoza said. "We're just tracking a car. Has any news of *it* traveled fast on the rails?"

"Not that I heard of. In fact, the management in El Paso thinks you might have a screw loose."

"More like my boss back in Houston's the one with the loose screw. He's the one responsible for the car not being on the manifest and from being erased from the computer system. That's a privately owned car, so there'll be hell to pay when I make my report to the main office after I get back. I'm sure there'll be an investigation of the computer system, especially since I've noticed some other irregularities. Didn't the train show up in El Paso missing a car?"

"That sort of thing happens," Fleming bristled slightly at the mention of an investigation then shrugged to cover it up.

"Not on my watch. Not when I'm responsible."

"Have it your way," Fleming said.

"You said you came from El Paso?" Guthrie asked.

"Looking for you fellows," Fleming affirmed. "My boss thought I might be able to lend a hand in finding your lost car."

"Is there any place up the line where a car could have been cut loose?" Guthrie asked.

"Several," Fleming said. "But I didn't see a stray boxcar on my way here, and I looked up every stub. Pretty tedious work." He shrugged. "I guess that means you fellows can go back to Houston."

"I guess it does," Guthrie said.

"Maybe I'll see you again if I ever go to El Paso," Espinoza said, with a curious look at Guthrie.

"So, you heading back to Houston?"

"Looks like it," Guthrie said. "I mean, if you didn't see anything on your way here…."

"Nada." Fleming glanced at his truck then looked back at Guthrie and Espinoza. "Well, since we've taken care of everything, I guess I'll get on back to El Paso." He lifted his hand in a mock salute but didn't offer to shake with either of them. "You fellows have a safe trip home."

With that, Fleming strode to his truck, got in, and pulled back onto the main line.

"If he's a safety and compliance officer," Guthrie said dryly as the truck went out of sight around a bend in the westward track, "I'm betting he's heavy on the compliance side."

"Are we really giving up?" Espinoza asked.

"Not a chance. Fleming might have missed something we'll catch. Besides, he seemed a little too anxious to send us home empty handed."

"You think he's in on this thing?"

"Do you really believe that normal railroad gossip would have mentioned anything about a monster this far from Houston or this quickly? Frank Belton didn't know about it."

"Seems kind of unlikely."

"Then how did Fleming know about it?"

"It does seem suspicious."

Guthrie shrugged.

"We already know that Beaman and Hudson are in on it, though how deeply, I'm not sure. If they're part of some large-scale smuggling operation, they won't be the only railroad employees involved. Fleming included." Guthrie waved toward the track. "Do you think he's far enough ahead for us to follow without him seeing us?"

"There's a spur where he can wait a mile and a half ahead, but the next siding is another seven or eight miles past that," Espinoza said. "Maybe we should give it another half hour. Just in case he's waiting at one of them."

Guthrie had been scanning the rail lines ahead on his map app, and he saw that the long spur just ahead lead to a huge, open-pit excavation on the flanks of a mountain about six miles north of town —the very mountain, in fact, for which the town had been named.

"I have a better idea. Let's get off the rails. At least for a little while." He showed Espinoza the map image on his phone. "The spur ahead runs to this mine, here, but there's a big dirt road that runs just east of the tracks, and see here? This small dirt road angles off the service road way before the big road turns off, and it comes out well behind the rail junction. If Fleming's waiting for us at the junction and watching down the tracks, he'll never see us come out behind him. Then we can drive the road all the way to the mine, and he'll be none the wiser. We can check for the boxcar while we drive."

Espinoza nodded and derailed the truck then steered it toward the service road for the westbound lanes of I-10. A mile farther on, they found the dirt road they sought, and Espinoza turned onto it. It was only a ranch track, but it was out of sight of the rail junction nearly a mile farther to the west. Espinoza kept the speed slow, the truck's tires rolling over large rock and through deep ruts as the track crawled across the rugged terrain.

After less than five minutes, the track met the main dirt road running north. Espinoza eased onto the road, and both men turned to stare toward the south. They were only half a mile behind the spur junction and could clearly see that Fleming's HiRail was nowhere in sight.

"Let's go on to the mine," Guthrie said. "Check out the rail line up there."

While Espinoza drove, Guthrie scanned the excavation on the map app. The pair of huge, off-white, open-pit mines carved out of its north and northeast flanks were clearly visible against the surrounding landscape's darker surface. The mountain hadn't been named for the light color of its composition, however. Guthrie learned that in springs past, the slopes had been covered with white flowers. He didn't know if that still happened, and spring was a long time off.

The mine was owned by a company called Texas Ores and Minerals. When he checked the company's website, he learned it was a mining concern that excavated rare earth elements. Rare earth elements had been known of for a long time, he read, but only recently had they found a practical use, being indispensable in the manufacture of computers, cell phones, and a vast array of other electronics and batteries. This particular mining company had a modest share of the American market, but its main competitor was China, which produced ninety-five percent of the world's rare earth elements. He also learned that there was about to be a "white gold rush" by companies seeking to cash in on other deposits throughout the American west.

The drive to the mine was close to ten miles, and Guthrie thought the route was kind of bizarre. They'd emerged onto the main road only half a mile north of I-10, so they hadn't seen any sort of street sign. But the map app identified the road as The Boulevard. It seemed a pretty pretentious name for a dirt road leading out into the desert, but it was a pretty pretentious dirt road, consisting of a divided street with one lane going north and another south, an esplanade between. Both sides were well graded and wide enough for two cars abreast and looked well traveled.

The Boulevard continued north for a couple of miles past the mine. Then, as a regular two-lane dirt road, it angled to the east for another eight miles before looping down and back—now named the Mountain Road—to reconnect with The Boulevard half a mile south of the mine, forming a giant P. To the north and northeast of the place where the loop met the mine excavation was an area that had been laid out in a network of roads, like the circulatory system of a phantom neighborhood whose main artery was named Clubhouse Road. Guthrie couldn't spot a clubhouse on the map app image. Or structures of any sort. With the layout so close to the mine, Guthrie wondered if the mine owners had envisioned a company town right on the outskirts of their operation.

As Espinoza drove north toward the mine, he maintained a relatively sedate pace. Despite The Boulevard's pretentious name, well-graded and maintained surface, and the fact that it was a weekday afternoon, they encountered almost no traffic—only a ten-year-old Ford pickup going the opposite direction. But it was around two-thirty, so the mine shift probably was well underway, and the product wasn't shipped out by truck but via the rail spur that wound across the landscape just to the west of The Boulevard, sometimes out of sight, sometimes close at hand.

"We needed to check it out, anyway," Guthrie said, waving toward the spur.

"No traffic on it," Espinoza said, giving it a glance. "Maybe we'll find something at the end."

"I'm skeptical. If the car was up this way, I'm betting Fleming would be guarding the entrance, and he wasn't. Besides, this spur is too well used. Any stray car would have already attracted attention." He shrugged. "Just the same, we need to leave no stone unturned."

During the rest of the drive, Guthrie sat with the window rolled down, enjoying the fresh, dry breeze and the contemplative landscape they drove through. The road wound for several miles in broad curves across the rugged flatlands east of Sierra Blanca Mountain. About a mile from the mine, it intersected a smaller dirt road. To the left was the entrance road to the mine, and to the right, the terminus of Mountain Road.

"Go on ahead," Guthrie said. "There's a place up there where we can get a good look at the mine."

They didn't have to go that far to see the end of the spur since the road paralleled the tracks until they ended. The rails held a pair of aged locomotives at the head of a train of big bin cars. There looked to be more than sixty of them, about a third of them loaded and covered with dull blue tarps.

"Those are gondola cars," Espinoza told him. "Sometimes we call them covered hoppers."

"Not a boxcar in sight," Guthrie said.

Just beyond the end of the train , the road curved slightly to the left and split, with Clubhouse Road ongoing off to the west and around the northern outskirts of the mine. Guthrie directed Espinoza to stay on The Boulevard for less than a quarter of a mile past the split, where there was a low hillock with a short dirt road to its top. From there, they had an excellent view of the two huge, off-white scars gouged out of the mountain.

Amazingly, there weren't any fences or gates—too much land to fence, and it was too flat for gates alone to do any good. The mine's open pits, crisscrossed with tire tracks, lay beneath a pall of dust churned up by huge excavating and earthmoving and processing equipment. Even here, half a mile from the lower excavation and twice that from the upper one, a subdued roar filled the air.

Most of the actual excavation was taking place at the upper site, and they could see a regular, if spaced-out, procession of dump trucks trundling loads of gray-white dirt down to the lower site, which abutted the tail end of the rail spur.

The lower excavation was nearly flat but was mounded with piles of fine white earth in a seemingly random pattern. It looked to Guthrie as if it had been the original mine, leveled out of Sierra Blanca's foothills, but was now a lot to sort and process the earth from the upper mine prior to loading it into the gondola cars.

"You say that dirt is valuable?" Espinoza asked.

"That's what I read. It wasn't when it was first discovered, but it's gained importance because it's vital to the manufacture of electronics."

Given the proliferation of electronics around the world, Guthrie wondered how much of Sierra Blanca peak was rare earth and how much would be left when the mining company hauled out the last covered hopper. Would the mountain be entirely flattened and re-named Llano Blanco?

They returned to the truck, and another twenty minutes of driving around the mine and the adjacent "neighborhood," was enough. Espinoza turned the HiRail back in the direction of the interstate.

"The next siding isn't far," Espinoza said. "My map shows three sets of rails, so the car could have been left there. Let's see what we find."

"What's that?" Guthrie asked ten minutes later, pointing ahead.

The spot he indicated had a rail berm angling away to the northwest, but no rails ran along it.

"Looks like an old spur or siding where the rails have been removed," Espinoza said, slowing the HiRail so they could take a closer look. "Nothing there now."

As the HiRail moved on, Guthrie watched the defunct rail berm angle across the irregular landscape and spotted an unnaturally straight line atop it before it ran out of sight.

"Looks like some rails are still there, farther up."

"No telling," Espinoza said. "But obviously they didn't cut out the car there."

A few minutes later, they reached the area of the three sidings and saw that, though there wasn't a boxcar, five Union Pacific vehicles were parked on or beside the outside siding. Two were regular pickups, two were HiRail pickups, and one was a larger HiRail truck carrying equipment. Eight workers in hardhats and yellow safety vests were busy laying tracks in front of the larger truck.

"Damn. Is one of those Fleming's HiRail?" Guthrie asked, peering at the vehicles ahead.

"Can't tell. It's too late to back off now. We'll just have to go up and find out."

Espinoza pulled onto the siding and parked behind the other vehicles. As he and Guthrie emerged from the truck, a tall man with a gray mustache and dressed in blue jeans and a red plaid shirt beneath his safety vest detached himself from the others and came over to them. Fleming was nowhere in sight.

"Help you fellows?" he asked.

"Gilbert Espinoza." Espinoza showed him his credentials. "You the foreman?"

"Yep. Jim Edgar."

"What you doing?" Espinoza asked.

"Extending the third loop siding. UP keeps adding cars, so we need to make the siding longer so nothing's sticking its ass out on the main line." He squinted at Espinoza. "Don't see many safety and compliance officers out here. Now I seen two in one day. You come to check our work?"

Espinoza chuckled.

"I'll leave that to the engineers. No, we're tracking a boxcar that might have been left on a siding or stub in this area. Have you seen something like that?"

"Can't say as I have. When would this be?"

"The last week."

"We've only been out here three days," the foreman said, shaking his head.

"You said you saw another safety and compliance officer today?" Guthrie asked.

"I guess that's what he was. I never saw him before, but he was driving a HiRail, and he sure wasn't on a track crew."

"Did you ask him what he was doing out here?"

"Didn't get the chance. He came by early, right after we got here, but he drove on by without stopping. Then he came back through just an hour later, driving like a bat outta hell. He have something to do with your missing car?"

"Not that we know of," Guthrie assured him. "Just curious. How about a company or church called Trumpet of Faith? You ever hear of that?"

"Can't say as I have," Edgar said. "But I'm not from around here."

Espinoza turned to Guthrie.

"I guess we'll just have to go on to Findley. That's the next place with a stub."

"Say, don't forget about the stub right up yonder."

"Up there?" Espinoza asked. "Before Findley?"

"Yeah. Just up there a few miles. Way before Findley. It's an old private line that's been out of service. Somebody fixed it up, but it wasn't us. Maybe it ain't on the map because it's so new or because it's private. Got me. It goes up along the bottom of them mountains over there." He pointed to a low but rugged looking range. It wasn't large, but because it was only a few miles away, it dominated the western horizon.

"What's up there?" Guthrie asked.

"Probably some cattle ranch," Edgar said. "But like I said, I ain't from around here, so I ain't sure." He turned and yelled, "Hey, Donnie! Come on over here for a minute."

As Donnie approached, Edgar said, "Donnie's from Sierra Blanca. Maybe he can tell you. Hey, Donnie. These fellows want to know if you know what's up that way in them mountains."

Donnie was a lean man who looked to be in his late fifties, but his weathered brown skin made it hard to tell for certain. Looking puzzled, he aimed an unshaven chin toward the small range.

"Up there? That's the old Dunton Ranch. They even call them the Dunton Mountains. Old Man Dunton used to live up there, but he died, hell, maybe seventy, eighty years ago."

"Can you tell us anything about the ranch?"

"My uncle worked up there as a hand for a few years. For Dunton's grandson, way after Dunton died. He never talked much about the Duntons. Least not to me. Alls I know is Old Man Dunton was a prospector when he came to these parts. He found himself silver up there, and when that played out, he used the money to start a cattle ranch. He ranched it until he died, then his son and grandson took over. And that one' kids, too. But the kids that come along after didn't want nothing to do with ranching or living around here. It was abandoned for a long time, but I heard they finally sold it." He shook his head. "Don't make much sense anyone buying it. Ranching don't pay much anymore unless you're some really big outfit."

"That's why you're working on the railroad," Edgar said with a grin, slapping Donnie on the shoulder.

"Ain't that the truth," Donnie said, grinning back.

"And there's a rail line going up there?" Espinoza asked.

"Well, yeah," Donnie said, eyes squinting. "Yeah. I remember. This main line ain't the original around here. The old line started back down the tracks the way you come from, then run up that way toward the ranch, then met up with this line just on the north end of the mountains. Maybe seven, eight miles up the line. Couple of miles past the office."

"We have a UP field office up that way we use when we're out here," Edgar said. "We don't stay there, though. UP puts us up at one of the motels in Sierra Blanca." He nodded. "I remember that old line, now. It was abandoned after UP laid these new track we're on. I guess the Duntons musta bought it. The part down there," he waved toward the south, "is long gone, but for sure, they've reconnected it up ahead."

"Must be gonna start up the ranching operation again," Donnie said. "It's supposed to be a working spread, but funny thing is, the day after we stared working here, they was hauling in a bunch of cows instead of hauling 'em out."

"Thanks," Espinoza said. "You guys have been a big help."

Guthrie and Espinoza returned to the HiRail.

"What do you think?" Espinoza asked when they were settled into the seats.

"I think we need to check out the Dunton Ranch."

"You don't plan on just walking in, do you?"

"Not before we scope it out." Guthrie gestured ahead. "Let go on up to the place where the old line has been reconnected and see what we see."

They drove as far as the UP office, which was located on a dirt road that ran along a siding with a stub. It was nothing but a squat, windowless metal building maybe forty feet to a side, and the big rollup door said it was designed to house equipment. Just ahead, the track went into a broad curve, and Guthrie's map app image showed a long straight stretch after that, all the way to the junction with the old line, which he also could see.

From the junction, the Dunton line ran south along the eastern foot of the mountains for roughly a third of the length of the the small range. There, it went into a nearly circular loop a little more than a thousand feet across before meandering for several miles through a series of broad curves toward the south to reconnect to the main line right where they'd noticed the empty rail berm angling away from the main line.

Along the apex of the circular curve were a stock pen and an open area of dirt from which a dirt road took a tortuous route up the eastern flank of the mountains. At the top, the road entered the mountain's central valley through a gap. Another dirt road ran alongside the rails from the corral to the main line, where it met up with the dirt road there.

"Stop here," Guthrie said.

"You want to go into the office and ask more questions? Doesn't look like anybody's home."

"No. Let's check out the track ahead before we expose ourselves."

"You think Fleming might be down there?"

"I think we better check."

"These might help," Espinoza said after he parked on the stub. He reached into a heavy canvas tote on the floor of the cab's back compartment, pulled out a pair of binoculars, and handed them to Guthrie.

They got out and trudged up the track to the curve. Once around it, they could see all the way to the north end of the Dunton Mountains, and even without the binoculars, Guthrie spotted something glittering slightly to the left of the tracks, maybe a mile and a half distant. He raised the binoculars and saw it was a HiRail, though the distance was too great to make out any details. He passed the binoculars to Espinoza, who focused them on the glitter then gave a grunt.

"Do you think that's him?" Espinoza asked.

"Who else?"

"Yeah, it's definitely not good that he came all the way out here to confront us and try to turn us back, then says he's heading home but waits here to see if we complied."

"Like I said, he's a compliance officer," Guthrie commented, and Espinoza chuckled. "One thing's certain," Guthrie went on. "We can't sneak in through the front door."

"What do you suggest? A hike across the desert?"

"Let's try the back door, first."
"You mean the torn-up connection back down the track?"
"That's exactly what I mean."

15

THEY DROVE BACK DOWN THE main line, the work crew staring with curiosity at the passing HiRail. Donnie lifted a hand in a half-hearted wave, and they waved back. They found the place where the old line met the new and surveyed the scene. Since there wasn't a switch or rails for the old line, Espinoza retracted the rail wheels, drove down the gravelly berm to the overgrown right-of-way for the old line, then along it for a couple of hundred feet. There, they found an old set of rails basically intact though severely overgrown, accompanied by an equally overgrown set of dirt tire tracks.

"Are there dirt roads along every rail line in the country?" Guthrie asked as they got out of the truck so Espinoza could inspect the rails and ties.

Espinoza laughed.

"Pretty much. You might be able to drive just about anywhere in the country on them, completely off the grid. And be thankful." He waved toward the rails. "This line is pretty beat up. We might be able to use it for a ways, but for how far? Let's just take the road."

While Espinoza pulled off, Guthrie surveyed the line and the terrain it ran through on his map app. The Dunton Mountains, where the ranch was located, were some five miles distant from where they now were, though the old line's sinuous route probably doubled that in terms of driving. The intervening distance was a rough and rugged steppe that undulated unevenly but did not rise significantly until the terrain hit the shallow foothills of the mountains.

"Not much cover out there," Guthrie said. "If they're watching from the hills, they'll see us coming."

"Fleming's parked at the other end of the line and is watching the wrong direction," Espinoza pointed out. "He also thinks we've gone back to Houston."

"Maybe, maybe not. But he probably doesn't think we'll come in this way. And we don't have much choice." He gestured forward. "Drive on, but go slow so we don't run into any surprises."

Espinoza steered the HiRail along the lumpy, bumpy dirt track, which had seen some minor traffic in the distant past but never a road grader or bulldozer. While he did, Guthrie unholstered his S&W and put a round in the chamber. As he reholstered it, he found himself regretting bringing the 9mm compact instead of his full-size .40.

"How long since these rails have been used, do you think?" he asked.

"Can't say for certain, but probably at least forty years. Maybe a lot longer. The way the rails are fastened to the ties is old school. We have several more efficient methods now."

"I hope they build better bridges, too," Guthrie commented when, after only a little more than a mile, the dirt track dipped down into a shallow but rough arroyo. Next to them, the low bridge that had supported the rails was gone, long washed away, leaving only rotting pilings and detached and twisted rails as testimony to its existence.

"Good thing we're on the ground and not the line," Espinoza said. "We'll probably see more bridges like that."

A few minutes past the wash, they encountered a pair of dry washes a hundred yards apart, running north and also missing bridges. A quarter of a mile farther on was another, then another. By the time they reached the area where the mountains began to rise, they'd crossed a dozen more washes of varying sizes.

All those arroyos collected run-off rain from the eastern slopes of the mountains and the rugged plains just to the east and gradually converged in a major dry wash that arced around the north end of the small range. From there, the wash turned due south to empty some ten or fifteen miles farther on into the Rio Grande. The big wash might have been a major tributary for this region, but only when it rained. Otherwise, it and its feeders were bone dry.

Their cautious speed and all the arroyos and ruts and bumps conspired to turn the five-mile jaunt into a nearly hour-long trek. At the last dry wash, which was the largest they'd encountered, Guthrie told Espinoza to halt.

"We have to make a decision. The rail line takes a big loop near-ly a mile up there," he gestured. "Then it runs to meet the main line at the north end of the mountains. At the apex of the loop is a small depot, with a stock corral and and open area that has two roads leading away from it. One goes alongside the ranch line to its junction with the main line. The other runs two or three miles up the side of the mountains and over a pass into a small valley just behind that ridge." He pointed. "You can't see the road from here, but you can see where the pass is. We can either leave the truck here and walk, or we can drive on and take our chances."

"We're taking chances with or without the truck," Espinoza said. "But no point in sneaking in a backdoor if you're going to shout that you just did. I'm for checking things out on foot."

"A man after my own heart," Guthrie said with a smile and nod. "Let get going."

Espinoza turned the HiRail around in case they needed to make a quick getaway.

"Are you armed?" Guthrie asked.

Without answering, Espinoza reached into his kit bag where it sat on the floor of the extended cab, right behind the driver's seat, pulled out a holstered 9mm Glock, and clipped it to his belt.

"I am now. Don't worry. I have a concealed carry license."

"I'm not worried, even if you don't."

The two men set off along the dirt track, and thanks to the more severe undulations of the terrain this close to the mountains, they sneaked within a hundred yards of the loop and the ranch de-pot. They couldn't see the depot yet, but they could spot sections of the ranch line's rails and the dirt road that paralleled them as they ran toward the junction with the main line. Even here, Guthrie could tell that the road ahead was better kept than it was back the way they'd come. And apparently the rails and bridges on the northern section of the old track had been repaired. Just as they crept into an arroyo and were coming out of it, they saw a HiRail approaching the depot from the upstream rail line and quickly dropped back into the gully.

"Do you think he saw us?" Espinoza asked.

"I don't know. Let's find out."

They watched the HiRail approach through the north half of the rail loop, but then it disappeared behind a low rise. While it was out of sight, Guthrie and Espinoza, crouching, dashed forward to another arroyo just ahead. They made it just before the truck reappeared, and they peered over the dirt lip while the HiRail drove over a bridge where the rails ran across the same arroyo downstream from where they hid.

Then the HiRail disappeared again as it dipped into a shallow right-of-way cut into the lower edge of the gradually rising terrain where it met the foot of the mountains. From where they crouched, Guthrie still couldn't see the ranch depot, but he calculated that if Fleming passed that by and drove down the track toward them, it would take him less than five minutes. But Fleming's truck didn't reappear, so Guthrie climbed out of the arroyo and up the low ridge above the tracks to survey what lay ahead. Espinoza followed.

From there, they saw that the dirt road snaking up the side of the mountains to the pass was fairly well maintained. At the foot of the road, where it met the apex of the loop in the tracks, lay an open area about the size of a basketball arena. The left half of the space was occupied by the corral, which included a stock chute but no cattle. A dually Ford pickup with a gooseneck trailer was parked along the corral fence, and next to it sat a black Chevy Suburban.

Fleming's truck sat on the tracks next to the open area, and just in front of it, a boxcar rested on the rails at the apex of the loop. Its door was closed.The front of the boxcar was attached to some sort of small tractor engine.

"I'm betting we found our car," Guthrie said. "Is that little engine strong enough to pull it?"

"Hand me those." Guthrie gave Espinoza the binoculars, and he trained them on the boxcar and engine. At last he lowered the glasses.

"That's a Trackmobile TM 95 railcar mover. It's old, but it has enough power to pull several cars like that just about anywhere, though not fast. Mostly used to haul rolling stock around yards. Like our HiRail, it can be derailed and driven on the ground, though not very fast."

Three armed men in addition to Fleming stood around. With camo uniforms that were a little too tidy and complete—and not exactly uniform among them—they appeared to be weekend warriors who'd never had a violent confrontation outside of a video game or riddling paper targets. The poor physical condition of a couple of them reinforced the impression.

They were too far away for Guthrie to hear anything but a murmur of their conversation, but he did notice that there wasn't much camaraderie or joviality among them.

"I wonder if the monster is still in there," Espinoza hissed. "You think they already moved it somewhere?"

"No," Guthrie said. "If they had, why the guards?"

Guthrie had another reason for believing that Espinoza's monster was still in the boxcar. The protective talisman Tereba had tattooed on his belly was itching. Monster or not, something outré was close.

"What now?" Espinoza asked.

"We have to look inside."

"I'm not sure I want to go up and do that."

"Me, either, but that's what we came for."

"What about those guys?" Espinoza gestured toward the men around the car. "They're all carrying assault rifles."

"We'll wait for dark," Guthrie said. "That should make them think we've given up and help cover our approach."

16

GUTHRIE AND ESPINOZA WAITED IN the arroyo as the afternoon progressed from full sunlight to a quick and prolonged dusk when the sun fell behind the rim of the mountains but not beyond the curve of Earth. That sort of false twilight would last four or five hours this close to the base of the mountains.

About an hour before true sunset, Fleming turned his HiRail around and headed toward the main line. Soon after, a second black Suburban rolled down from the mountains. Guthrie noted that it took about ten minutes to arrive—useful information. Three fresh guards emerged, and after a brief soiree with them, two of the three who were relieved of duty drove up the mountainside in the first Suburban, the third following in the dually pickup pulling the trailer.

"I saw on my map app that there's a house up there," Guthrie said as he and Espinoza watched from behind their outcropping of rock. "I guess it was where the Duntons lived. There are three outbuildings near the house, one pretty large with a corral next to it. It's probably a barn. One might be a bunkhouse, and the other some kind of small work shed."

"I wish we knew how many of them there are," Espinoza said. "At least eight, not counting Fleming."

"Right now, we can look at it as just three," Guthrie said.

After that, there wasn't much more to say, so they just made themselves as comfortable as possible and waited for dark.

Guthrie noted throughout the afternoon that none of three guards ever left the immediate vicinity of the boxcar except when they went to find a place to relieve themselves. That was poor judgement on their part. Even if Fleming believed that Guthrie and

Espinoza had returned to Houston, surely he'd have warned the others of the potential threat. At least one of them should have been on short-range patrol.

But from what Guthrie had seen, all the guards might be wearing paramilitary uniforms, and their weapons might be tricked out with all sorts of doodads affixed to the picatinny rails, but there was no precision or professionalism in their actions. They should have been more on their toes. And in better shape. The night crew were, if anything, worse than the daytime one. Even before darkness fell, they switched on a pair of electric lanterns on tripods that threw lopsided ovals of light on the ground in front of the boxcar's door.

"How considerate," Guthrie muttered, watching the guards hover in the light, yet continually throw nervous glances at the boxcar's too-close door. "Now they're blind to anything outside of that light."

"What are we going to do about them?" Espinoza asked.

"They're obviously not expecting anyone way out here," Guthrie said. "Otherwise, they wouldn't have lit those lanterns. If I can sneak up and disarm one, the other two might capitulate."

"And if they don't? They look pretty antsy to me."

"They also look amateur." Guthrie shrugged. "I'd hate to have to shoot them. Come on."

Espinoza was silent as he crept after Guthrie toward a gully not fifty feet from the boxcar. This close to the car, Guthrie's protective talisman was squirming beneath the skin, warning of some outré danger very nearby.

"Okay," he muttered, rubbing it into submission. "I hear you. Calm down." The itching subsided but didn't completely disappear.

"We'll give them a little longer to let them settle in and get bored and complacent," Guthrie whispered after he and Espinoza slipped into the gully.

It didn't take long before one of the guards said to his companions, "I gotta take a piss."

"Well, hurry up," one of the other guards said. "The boss'll be down before long, and we gotta open that thing up." He jerked his head toward the boxcar.

The guard who needed to relieve himself followed the glow of the tactical flashlight mounted on his rifle, into the darkness.

"Wait here," Guthrie whispered as he melted into the night.

He worked his way around to the left, trying not to make any sounds on the rough ground. On the way, he picked up a baseball-sized stone. Just ahead, some fifty feet from the boxcar, the guard stopped, cradled his AR-15 with its light shining on the ground in front of him, and unzipped. He'd barely started to urinate when Guthrie popped up behind him and smacked the rock against the back of his head. Guthrie couldn't completely catch him as he went down, but at least the man's fall didn't make much noise. Guthrie relieved him of his AR and a Glock sidearm. He considered binding the man's wrists, but there was no point. He was out cold, and Guthrie needed to act fast. If the man was gone too long, his companions would grow suspicious.

Guthrie hefted the assault rifle and saw it was a fully automatic model. He made sure it was charged then walked toward the boxcar, aiming the light straight ahead, right into the eyes of the other guards.

"Fuck, Lyle," one of them said, blinking and lifting a hand to shield his eyes. "Get that fucking thing outta my face."

"Drop your guns and raise your hands," Guthrie ordered as he stepped into the circle of light cast by the lantern.

"What the fuck!" the other guard snarled, and he started to level his own rifle, but Guthrie aimed at his chest, and he stopped moving.

"Drop 'em, or I'll kill you," Guthrie ordered again, and both men dropped them.

"You must be one of the guys Fleming was talking about," said the guard who'd first spoken.

"I'm the guy with the gun," Guthrie said, then he called out, "Come on up."

"Where's Lyle," the first guard asked as Espinoza joined Guthrie, pistol in hand.

"Napping." He handed the rifle to Espinoza and said, "Watch them. Shoot them if they move."

"I shot the enemy in Afghanistan," Espinoza whispered, leaning close to Guthrie, "but I'm not interested in shooting these guys if I don't absolutely have to."

"They don't know that," Guthrie whispered back.

He collected their weapons and piled them behind Espinoza, out of the ovals of light.

"I'll get the other one."

He went back to where he'd cold-cocked the third guard and found him groggily coming to. He prodded the man to his feet and followed him back to the boxcar.

"Lie down," Guthrie ordered, and the men reluctantly did as they were told. "Take out your bootlaces."

"Why?" This from Lyle, who'd regained a sense of belligerence along with his few other senses.

"Because I'll shoot you if you don't. And your belt." He glanced at the others. "All of you."

Angrily, Lyle complied, and Guthrie used the bootlaces to tie his wrists behind his back and the belt to bind his ankles. He quickly did that to the others, then went to collect an AR of his own.

"Time to open it up," he said to Espinoza.

"No fucking way you should do that," Lyle said, looking as if Guthrie had just poised him, teetering, on the upper ledge of a tall building. "Not til Mr. Thorvald and Mr. Moran get here. You don't know what's in there."

"I have a pretty good idea." Espinoza reached for the latch handle.

"Fuck," the first guard said. "If you're going to open it, at least drag us away from the door."

"So you know what's in there, too."

"Yeah, and I hope you get close enough to find out yourself."

Guthrie and Espinoza dragged the guards to the periphery of the lamp light, then they went up to the boxcar's door.

"You ready for this?" Guthrie asked.

"Hell no," Espinoza said.

"Open it up."

Guthrie readied the AR as Espinoza grabbed the door handle, gave it a jerk to unlatch it, then dragged the door open and quickly jumped back.

It was well he did. The head and shoulders of a manlike giant loomed into the combined light of the lanterns and the flashlights on the ARs. Its forward-inclined torso was supported by muscular arms and huge, bony, horny-knuckled, gray-taloned hands that rested on the floor of the boxcar. Its skin was a pasty greenish tan, and long but meager orange hair sprouted from its scalp. Despite thinking himself prepared for the sight, Guthrie found he was moderately shocked.

"It's about fucking time!" the thing blared from a wide, thin-lipped mouth, spewing a brutal cloud of halitosis along with the words. "Where's my fucking cow?"

Suddenly it saw the reality of the scene in front of the open boxcar. Its already ugly face distorted into a leer, and a huge arm snatched out, barely missing Espinoza.

"Damn!" Guthrie involuntarily stepped back and his finger tightened on the trigger, sending a three-shot burst into the thing's chest. The monster snatched at him, too, missing by inches.

"Ooh, that tickled!" the thing said in a sarcastic voice.

Despite its grab for Guthrie, the monster didn't emerge from the car but merely leaned forward on its elbows, face and shoulders in the doorway. It looked at Espinoza.

"I remember you," it said. "You were the reason we had problems in Houston. Espinoza, isn't it?" It laughed, spewing foul breath. "I think I'll call you Expinoza since that's what you'll soon be." It laughed again.

"Maybe we should run," Espinoza suggested. He looked scared, but also calculating.

"Yes, you should," the monster said, leaning suddenly forward and giving a threatening grimace that displayed its teeth. Ragged and jagged and yellow, they lined grayish gums beneath the thin lips. They didn't appear to be broken, only made for savagely ripping and tearing, and they looked more than serviceable.

The thing's heavy, coarse, and gravelly English bore a Scandinavian accent. Espinoza had said it looked like an impossibly huge, butt-ugly man, so Guthrie wasn't too surprised to see the thing in the flesh. Espinoza's meager description didn't do the thing justice. It was maybe twenty feet tall, though it was difficult to tell since it was lying prone and slightly curled on what appeared to be a large dais of stone that rested on four wooden pallets. Considering its looks, Guthrie was surprised that it spoke intelligently.

Roughly hewn and ugly to a serious degree, the giant had a long nose that began narrowly but terminated bulbously beneath eyes far too closely set and beady for so wide a skull. But its skull was wide only at the face and was shallow and narrow at the rear. The orange hair on top of its head was brushed back in an oversized ducktail, with a huge wave on top that descended the back of its head. There, the orange hair turned a dirty yellow as it sprouted in profusion all the way down its spine. It wore a full but thin beard that thankfully masked part of its face and powerful jaw. More coarse orange hair covered its shoulders and muscular arms, ringed its bare and grossly bulging pot belly, and continued down the outsides of the legs. Curiously, no navel marred the smooth hemisphere of the thing's gut.

Shining his light into the boxcar and down the length of the giant's reclined body, Guthrie saw that one of its hairy legs seemed to be stuck at the ankle in a crack in the slab of rock it lay on. The approximately eight-by-eight-foot slab was a couple of feet thick, and its irregular angles showed it had been crudely removed from wherever it originated. Thankfully, it acted like an anchor, keeping the thing inside the boxcar. Weirdly, a Mac laptop, open and powered-on, sat on the slab right next to the imprisoning crack. An electric lantern hung from a hook fastened to the boxcar's ceiling.

The monster looked at Guthrie. "And you are?" It put a questioning finger to its lips then suddenly brightened. "Oh, wait. Don't tell me. Don't tell me. I know. Just a second, and I'll have it. Yes, yes." Then suddenly it stopped its posturing and started intently at him for a moment. "Guthrie. That's your name, isn't it?"

"If you say so."

"Not me. The good Father Thorvald." It chucked, as if at some obscure joke, releasing another foul cloud of breath.

"I'm not as shy as you," the monster said. "My name is Halvor." You must be wondering what I am." It chuckled again, accompanied by more oral brutality. "Well, believe it or not, I'm a troll."

"A troll," Guthrie said, shaking his head in amazement.

"You don't seem shocked by my presence," the troll said. "Not like your friend. Expinoza."

It nodded toward Espinoza, who was hanging back, rifle raised and obviously freaked out by the creature.

"A little," Guthrie said. "But not much, so don't flatter yourself."

The troll gave a raucous laughed, emitting more foul odor.

"I like you," Halvor said. "So far, my human companions have been lost in their fear of me, yet even more lost in their fantasies of power and ruination. Take Father Thorvald. He thinks my existence will prove the Christian god to be a false god." The troll laughed again, and Guthrie tried to breathe through his mouth.

"You don't believe that will happen?" he asked.

"Not likely. When I get free to rampage across the countryside, killing and consuming the inhabitants, they won't ask the hard questions. They never do. They'll just think I'm an aberration, which frankly I am, and hunt me down and kill me."

"Why bother with the rampage, then," Guthrie said. "Just go off into some deep forest where there's plenty of wildlife, and do your rampaging where you can be safe."

"Can't." Halvor shook his head. "That's not what being a troll is all about. We're created to rampage across human spaces, wreaking havoc, then be hunted to death. It's our fate and joy. Animals can sustain us, and these modern cows and pigs I've been eating are pretty tasty, but I can tell you I really hate chicken. A whole one is nothing but a chicken tender to me, and it takes forever to pick the feathers out of my teeth. But humans," it smacked its lips. "Ah, we crave human flesh above all others. Such ambrosia." The troll kissed its fingertips then grinned hideously. "In fact, I can't wait to eat as many of you as I can before you take me down."

"And the hunting to death?"

"Oh, that's nothing." Halvor gave an offhand wave. "Merely a temporary discomfort. Trolls live forever. When I'm killed in this world, my spirit just merges into the background noise of reality, waiting for the chance to reemerge. And there's always some fool or ignoramus willing to oblige and reincarnate me and my brethren for their own purposes. But they never realize that they don't control me. I control them."

"I guess that means you have your own fantasies of power and ruination."

"Most certainly. My power and the ruination of others. You have no idea how satisfying it is to rampage across the countryside, snatching up adult humans to take home for dinner and snacking on their children along the way to my den—usually some dank cave in a mountain somewhere north of…well, north of everything human."

"I thought trolls live under bridges," Guthrie said. "Like the story of Billy Goat Gruff."

The troll grunted unpleasantly.

"Most encounters would not go so well for the goat. And bridges are just incidental.We're often under them because we're stuck under them until we can get free."

"Speaking of getting free, that slab of rock your leg is trapped in must be quite an impediment to all that rampaging."

"Yes. Kind of like my ball and chain at the moment. Or perhaps block and leg is more apt. But you have it wrong. My leg isn't stuck in the crack. I'm emerging from it. You see, trolls are birthed like this, not by some bitch in heat." It gestured toward the crack. "Kinda looks like a cunt, though, doesn't it? That's the key. Gotta have a special crack like this if you're a troll trying to emerge into this layer of reality."

"Looks more like an asshole to me," Guthrie said flatly.

"Are you condescending to me, Guthrie?"

"You're so damned warped, it's hard not to."

The thing gave a hideous grin, its eyes angry and teeth grinding together audibly.

"You are a most unpleasant human."

"And you are unpleasant and not even human."

Suddenly the troll's anger dissipated, and it laughed.

"You're right, if course, but it's the nature of trolls to be unpleasant."

"Is that your computer?" Guthrie pointed at the laptop.

The creature glanced at the computer then back at Guthrie. "It certainly is."

"I wouldn't think a troll could operate a computer. Big clumsy fingers, and all."

"Thank goodness for Siri," the troll said, then it gave an ironic moue. "Well, maybe not goodness. But thanks to your digital age, I now know more about humans than I ever did, even after many sporadic lifetimes trapped beneath primitive Scandinavian bridges. It's been a long time since I've been out, and things certainly have changed. There's a whole world of possibilities out there that I never knew could exist, and I intend to take every advantage of them."

"So tell me more about this crack you're crawling out of."

"Oh, we don't crawl out," the troll corrected. "We ooze through."

"Ooze." Guthrie turned the word over in his mouth, and it left a sour taste.

"You see," the troll went on, "it takes a very special kind of crack to give birth to someone like me. It's a troll cunt and it's almost always found under a bridge or in a cave, though they have been known to exist in deep crevasses where the sun doesn't shine. Do you know what that means? Early people lived in caves, and there are no bridges without people. What are the common denominators? People and cracked stone in shadows. Without that combination, no trolls. Know why that is? It's because trolls are half human, so they didn't exist until there were people. Some guy traveling along gets horny and sneaks under a bridge or into some hole in the ground to whack off in private. Under there, he sees a crack that reminds him of a cunt, and when he comes, some of his jism gets into the crack, and voila! Troll."

"Sounds like artificial insemination," Guthrie said. "And not exactly natural, either."

"I suppose not. It's a very, very narrow crack. At its bottom, it cannot pass even one single atom of matter."

"But you got through."

"I am not the same here as I am on the other side." Its eyes once again glanced toward its nether reaches. "The crack cannot pass matter, but it can pass spirit. It can pass an idea."

"So you're an ideopath?"

"A what?"

"Something arising from unknown origins."

"Yes, I like that. You are a wealth of information, Guthrie, even if you are unpleasant. Ideopath. Yes, I suppose you could say that I came through as an idea. Is the idea so shocking?" It gave a wry smile. On the huge, snaggletoothed mouth, it looked demented.

"Once the odor of jism led me to the crack, I was able to pass the idea of myself through to this side and use the jism to produce a polyp and begin building a tangible life. Of course, you have to consume a lot to get to that point, and food is pretty scarce when you're stuck under a bridge or in a cave, so it can take a really long time to get enough food to fully develop and get free. The more food, the less time it takes for a troll to completely ooze through and free itself. Until then, it remains trapped by its attachment to the crack in the rock.

"That's the reason you often hear of trolls living beneath bridges who don't come out but must entice their prey to come within their grasp. And if it takes too long to get free, chances are somebody will figure out you're under there and come to do something about it. But Daddy has been most accommodating. He's managed to provide plenty of food to keep me going and growing. Sometimes even humans. And there are unexpected morsels." It looked at Espinoza. "Like your coworker." It turned back to Guthrie. "But even if cattle and other creatures are not exactly my preference, they are sufficient to empower my growth."

"Food provided by Father Thorvald."

"I admit that I'm lucky," the troll replied. "Daddy wasn't a wham-bam-thank-you-ma'am kind of guy. He actually cares about me." It laughed. "He not only inseminated me and fed me when I was but a wee bud, he's kept me safe. And now," it gestured toward the crack in the slab of stone, "as you can see, I'm almost free. Almost free," it finished with a grating hiss.

"And when you are, you'll do all that rampaging across the countryside and eating people?"

"Can't wait."

"Sounds like a pretty severe mindset," Guthrie commented. "Why are you trolls so violent?"

"Look at me," Halvor said, leaning back and spreading its legs. The outsides were hairy, but the insides showed smooth, leathery skin. Its crotch was an unbroken juncture of legs like a cartoon character. "Do you see a cock and balls? No. We trolls don't have them. That's why we need a human father."

"I already noticed you don't have a navel," Guthrie said.

"Even if we don't have the equipment," the troll went on, ignoring Guthrie's comment, "we have a huge and obviously unfulfillable sex drive. Man, you have no idea what kind of hormonal hell that wreaks on our emotions. Pissed off all the time doesn't half cover it, let me tell you...."

"Spare me your incel angst," Guthrie said.

"Spare you?" The troll laughed. "I think not. Your mommy was the first person to touch you, and I'll be the last. And you'll be crying for her the whole time."

"Hey," Espinoza called out. "We have company."

He pointed toward the mountain pass. Just below the gap, two pairs of headlights were bobbing down through the darkness.

"Damn," Guthrie muttered. He'd hoped to have enough time with the troll to learn more about it and maybe how to kill it. He's shot it in the chest with the AR, and all it had done was laugh, so he knew small arms wouldn't do the trick.

"Reinforcements coming?" the troll asked. "That will be Moran and maybe Daddy. It's dinner time, so I suppose our conversation will be cut short. What a pity."

"We'll be back," Guthrie assured it.

"I'm counting on it," the troll said, running its tongue over its thin lips.

Guthrie and Espinoza turned to make their way back to the Hi-Rail, but the troll stopped them.

"Hey," it said. "Before you go, would you mind dragging those guards over here? I'm sure all Daddy is bringing is another cow, and I haven't had a taste of human since Houston."

Guthrie glanced at the three men trussed up at the edge of the light.

"Please, mister," Lyle begged. "Not that."

Guthrie just turned away and disappeared with Espinoza into the night.

From behind them, the thing bellowed.

"I'll get you, Guthrie. You and Expinoza, both. If you come back, I'll get you!"

17

"I CAN'T BELIEVE YOU JUST stood there and talked to that thing," Espinoza said.

They'd retreated to the main line, and the HiRail now sat on the siding where the workers they'd met earlier had been, though the workers were gone for the night.

"Wasn't much else to do at the moment," Guthrie responded. "But we learned a couple of important facts. First, the troll admitted it can be killed. But not with small arms. Not if an AR-15 can't do more than tickle it, though I think the rounds hurt it more than it admitted."

"What about something bigger?" Espinoza asked. "Like a bomb?"

"Probably effective," Guthrie said. "But unavailable, at least short notice." He rubbed his chin.

"Maybe not."

"Yes?"

"A couple of cases of dynamite will blow that thing to kingdom come." Espinoza's hands flicked up in a mock explosion.

"You can get dynamite?"

"Remember, I'm trained by the U. S. Army and certified by UP. I can get it, but I'll have to go back to Del Rio."

"We have to act fast now that the opposition knows we're here or before the troll frees itself from that rock."

Since Espinoza was the one with credentials and knowledge, he had to be the one to go after the dynamite.

"We can't let the troll escape or have them move it some place we don't know," Guthrie said. "I'll stay here to keep an eye on things."

"What are you going to do if it escapes?" Espinoza asked. "You can't do it much damage with that rifle."

"As long as it's stuck to that rock, I don't need to do anything but wait for you to bring the dynamite. Then we can blow that whole boxcar to hell and back. Just leave me a couple of bottles of water."

"You want me to drive you up there?"

"I can walk from here just about as quickly as we can drive, and they might see your headlights. Plus, I don't want to hold you up. How long do you think it'll take?"

"I have no idea. Two days, at least, maybe more."

"Well, leave me all the food, too, then," Guthrie chuckled.

Espinoza reached behind his seat and grabbed a plastic grocery sack holding three bottles of water, half a dozen energy bars, and a package of mini sugared donuts.

Guthrie held up the donuts, a wry smile on his face.

Espinoza returned the smile and shrugged.

"I have a sweet tooth." He gestured toward the sack. "That's not enough supplies for two or three days."

"I'll hitch a ride to Sierra Blanca with that rail crew if I get desperate. Mind if I take these?" He held up the binoculars.

"Take this, too." Espinoza twisted in his seat again and rummaging in a bin in the back of the cab. He came up with a boonie hat that he handed to Guthrie.

"This should help when the sun comes up."

"Thanks." Guthrie slapped the hat on his head then got out of the HiRail. "Good hunting. Call if something comes up."

He shut the door and watched the HiRail take off. After its taillights disappeared into the darkness, he turned and headed across the desert, toward the ranch depot. And the troll.

18

THE MOON WAS WAXING, BUT it was only slightly more than half full and barely illuminated the desert landscape. Using his small flashlight sparingly, Guthrie picked his way across the uneven, scrubby terrain, pausing now and again to listen for any sounds of human presence. At last he heard them: a faint buzz of voices, with one louder than the rest barking commands.

When he came within sight of the ranch depot, he saw ten armed guards swarming the area, their shadows flickering in the light from half a dozen electric lanterns arranged on tripods around the boxcar and Trackmobile. By now, Guthrie recognized several of them.

Most of the guards were sweeping the barrels of their rifles in short arcs out into the darkness, but Guthrie knew that the flash-lights' dimmer bulbs, washed out by the larger lights, couldn't reveal anything past a few feet.

The glare clearly showed something else, strengthening Guthrie's earlier estimation of the the guards' basic lack of compe-tence now that he saw so many of them together and active. The hodgepodge look of their uniforms and their too-fancy rifles rein-forced the idea that they were weekend militia—wannabe warriors eaten alive inside by a desire to attach themselves to some danger-ous and deadly cause where they could live fire their weapons at the enemy. Some enemy. Any enemy. Preferable unarmed enemy.

The dually Ford was now parked beside the boxcar, with the trailer positioned directly beneath the door, though there was noth-ing in the trailer bed. The boxcar's open door revealed the dismem-bered body of a cow lying on the floor just inside the doorway. Every few minutes, the troll's hands reached out to tear off more of the carcass and lift the dripping flesh to its mouth or toss a bone out onto the growing pile on the ground.

In the open area adjacent to the boxcar, corral, and junction of the dirt road up the mountainside, sat the two black Suburbans, a Mercedes sedan parked next to them. The distance was too far and the light too uncertain for Guthrie to make out the model, but it looked like an expensive one.

Two other men stood conversing near the Mercedes. Both were tall and imposing but as different as night and day. The slightly taller of the two looked to be in his fifties and had close-cropped iron-gray hair topping an angular face. In addition to military-style desert fatigues, he wore an expression that was equally dour and sour, but his attitude and movements showed he probably was very competent, both as a leader and as a warrior. A lot more competent than the camo-clad men around the site. He didn't carry a rifle, though a heavy sidearm hung on his belt.

The other man was a little older and had a spare tire instead of a gun slung at his waist. Although he was dressed casually in tan slacks and a white polo shirt, he bore an air of dignity and authority. But that, in turn, was hollowed out by obvious pomposity. His Scandinavian features were Saturnine and florid. Above them was reddish-blond but graying and thinning hair carefully coifed into a wave on top of his head that reminded Guthrie of Halvor's duck-tail. That has to be Thorvald, Guthrie thought. Or as, the troll referred to him, Father Thorvald. Or Daddy. The family resemblance was unmistakable.

With that many guards and so much light, there was no way Guthrie could get close, but he could circle up the slope and around behind the depot. He'd spent all day out here, scoping out the terrain, and he knew a gully drained the low mountains above him and skirted the depot as it ran toward the large dry creek that bordered the east side of the mountains. After he reached the gully, he crept down it until the boxcar was about a hundred feet away and slightly below him. At that distance, he could hear the men talking but couldn't make out exactly what they were saying. They weren't talking much, anyway, as they patrolled the area immediately around the boxcar and up and down the line. As he expected, they ignored the slope behind them.

Not half an hour later, a pair of headlights came down the ranch's rail line from the north, swung through the loop, and stopped behind the boxcar. The two men conversing near the Mercedes walked toward the vehicle, and the other guards, drawn like moths to light, also began to converge on the truck. Taking advantage of the momentary distraction, Guthrie edged farther down the gully until he was within earshot. Just as he settled in, one of the guards who seemed more competent than the rest, barked a command, and the rest of them returned to their former positions.

The lights belonged to a HiRail, and Fleming emerged to meet the two men who approached.

"They're not anywhere around here," Fleming told the orange-haired man. "I was almost to El Paso when you called. They weren't anywhere along the line coming back, and I checked east for sixty miles. There's no sign of them. Maybe they gave up."

"They followed us all the way out here and saw Halvor and talked to him," said the man, his Scandinavian accent confirming Guthrie's assumption that he was Thorvald. "They will not simply go away."

"I don't know what you want me to do about it," Fleming groused. "They're not on the line anywhere between El Paso and sixty miles east of here. Can't do anything about them if I can't find them or they're not around. They could even have gone up the Santa Fe line."

"We can't afford any more interference," Thorvald said, turning to the man who'd come up with him. "Me must move Halvor to the mine tonight." Thorvald gestured vaguely toward the road up the mountainside. "I don't want anything to go wrong. Are the preparations complete, Mr. Moran?"

"They finished stringing the lights this afternoon," Moran said in a midwestern American accent. "There should be no problem with the move."

"Excellent." Turning back to Fleming, he said, "I want you at the rail junction tonight. If they return, capture them and bring them to me. But don't kill them. I want to learn what they know about us and if others know, too. If they haven't appeared by first light, come back." To Moran, he said, "I'm going to have a word with Halvor before we take him up to the mine. In the meantime, make certain your men understand the consequences of failure."

Then Thorvald strode away, toward the boxcar. That was too far for Guthrie to hear his conversation with the troll, but there was plenty happening closer by.

"Better get going," Moran told Fleming.

"Fuck," Fleming said. I've been out there all day and night without food and hardly any water. Or sleep. Why the fuck do I have to go back out there now?"

"Because I'm telling you to," Moran said in a harsh voice. He gestured toward the Suburbans. "There's some food and water in one of those. Take what you need, but get the hell back to the junction. And don't fall asleep on the job."

Fleming looked like he was going to say something else, but he simply turned and strode, stiff-backed, toward the Suburbans.

"Kelly!" Moran called out, ignoring the retreating Fleming. The man who'd earlier ordered the other guards back into position hurried over. "Assemble the men."

By the time Fleming was on his way down the tracks, Kelly had the others lined up in the glare of the lights, Moran stood in front of them, Kelly at his side.

"I want to make this perfectly clear," he said in a level but penetrating voice. "We have active enemy on site. You are to watch for them, and if you have the opportunity to capture them, you will do so. But do not kill them. Mr. Thorvald wants them taken alive. You may wound them if necessary. Kelly's in charge. I want one man on the boxcar at all times, two up the line, two down, and three patrolling the perimeter to the east." He turned to Kelly. "You maintain a flex position with one other." Kelly nodded, and Moran looked around at the assembled men. "Don't let yourselves get out of sight of at least one other." To Kelly, he added, "Radio checks every five minutes."

"Roger," Kelly said.

"All right," Moran said, straightening. "Attention!"

His crew snapped to, and it looked brisk enough to Guthrie despite their off-the-shelf garb and arms. Sincerity can sometimes overcome inexperience.

"Who are we?" Kelly barked.

"The Bugle Boys!" the assembled guards barked back in unison.

"What is the oath we keep?"

"To faithfully serve!"

"Who do we serve?"

"The Trumpet of Faith!"

"And how do we serve?"

"We blow the Trumpet with hearts, souls, faith, and guns!"

"All right, at ease." The troops relaxed.

"Men," Moran said. "Tonight is a critical stage of our plan. We're moving Halvor up to the mine. This is going to take some finesse, and I don't have to warn you not to get too close to him. He's promised not to harm any of you, but it's better to be safe than sorry. But," he went on sternly, "that doesn't give you license to slack. All right, take your positions."

As the Bugle Boys dispersed, Moran beckoned Kelly aside.

Guthrie shrank into the gully as the two men stepped dangerously close, laying his finger alongside the AR's trigger guard.

"I know you've been here all day," Moran told Kelly, "but I need you to keep guarding the area until the move. Only a couple of hours more. Once he's in the mine, we'll all rest easier. But right now, I'm counting on you to keep those guys in line." Moran gestured toward the grouped Bugle Boys and shook his head. "They're nothing but a bunch of construction workers who like to play militia. They'll follow our lead, but they can't think for themselves. They're not pros like we are. You listen to me, and when we're finished here, we'll be rich and powerful men. You just keep those guys in line and on their toes, and we'll make out like bandits."

"I can handle them well enough, boss, but that troll freaks the hell outta me."

"Don't you worry about that. Think of it like this." Moran tapped Kelly's AR-15. "It's a weapon, nothing more. Like an artillery piece. It's not dangerous unless you stand right in front of it."

In the background, Thorvald strode away from the boxcar, toward Moran and Kelly.

"You go on, now," Moran told Kelly. "Keep them on their toes."

Kelly nodded and went over to the Bugle Boys while Thorvald joined Moran.

"I want to inspect the mine before we move him," Thorvald told Moran.

Moran nodded, and the two men went to the Mercedes and got in, Moran at the wheel. In a moment, the car was headed up the dirt road to the pass, taillights occasionally disappearing into dips and behind obstructions.

Meanwhile, the guards had dispersed, and Guthrie crouched into the gully as the beam of one of their flashlights strayed across the ground in front of him. But they all were paying attention to the tracks and the terrain spreading to the east, not the steepening slope at their backs, and none came near. Settling into a nook in the rocks, he wished he could grab a few winks, but obviously something was in the offing, and he wanted to stay alert.

The next thing he knew, he was waking, stiff and chilled, by shouts and the sounds of metal clanking. He peered over the rim of the gully and saw that the Mercedes had returned and was sitting at the edge of a hubbub of activity. The two Suburbans were nearby. Guthrie also counted twelve Bugle Boys, including Moran and Kelly. That had to be Thorvald's entire contingent.

Moran stood aside with Thorvald, watching Kelly supervise the operation at the boxcar. One of the Bugle Boys was at the wheel of the Ford pickup, which was still positioned with the trailer beneath the boxcar's door. The rest of the Bugles Boys stood well back, many with their rifles raised defensively across their chests.

A loud dragging sound issued from the boxcar, and a moment later, the troll's back loomed in the light, dragging the slab that trapped its foot to the doorway. There, it clumsily climbed its free leg out onto the trailer, and a moment later, half dragged and half heaved the slab out of the boxcar, onto the trailer bed. With a crashing sound, the trailer sagged on its wheels, and the strain of the maneuver showed clearly on the troll's face, but Guthrie was impressed with the monster's strength. That slab had to weigh a ton, and probably more. And Halvor had implied that it wasn't yet fully grown. During the entire operation, the troll had remained silent except to grunt heavily as it transferred the slab from the boxcar to the trailer.

Only two of the Bugle Boys stayed behind to guard the boxcar and railcar mover. The rest piled into the two Suburbans. With the Mercedes leading the way, the small caravan started up the steepening road to the pass, the truck pulling the trailer next, followed by the two Suburbans. Just before the second Chevy dipped out of sight behind the first rise, it stopped, and one of the men got out and hid behind an outcropping of rock on the high side of the road.

The two Bugle Boys who stayed behind resumed patrolling. Guthrie could tell that, even though they were tired, they also were less ill-at-ease—and sloppier—now that the troll was no longer in proximity or their responsibility and Moran was out of sight.

Guthrie needed to follow the boxcar, but walking up the dirt road was out. He surveyed the terrain on his map app and saw a steep runoff channel that descended between two toes of the mountain about half a mile behind him. It looked passable, and if he could climb it, it would lead him up into the shallow valley that occupied the middle of the small mountain range. The valley where the ranch compound sat at the end of the dirt road.

It was only a little after one a.m., but the waxing moon, now high, lent a dim glow to the desert landscape. He didn't really want to be hiking around in the dark, but he had to get into the valley as soon as possible.

Keeping low and making judicious use of his small flashlight, he made his way up the gully then over a ridge. Now out of sight of the men at the depot, he could relax and more readily use his flashlight as he essayed the slope. It was a steep scramble that took the better part of an hour, but at last, panting, he climbed through a low spot between two ridges and stared at the panorama before him.

The rim of the mountains on the other side of the valley were a darker shadow against the night sky, and even with the moonlight, the valley was a trough of darkness. He had no idea what lay below him or how to maneuver across it, so he decided to wait where he was until dawn came. As the hours passed, he managed to make out some of the valley's features in the dim moonlight, and when the sun finally began to light the sky behind him, those features became obvious.

The valley was only about a mile across and five miles long, descending from a cluster of five small but rugged peaks at the southern end to a series of lower but still-rugged hills and ridges in the central region. He couldn't see beyond that from where he stood, but he knew from looking at the satellite images that, just past the hills, the valley flattened as it descended toward its northern end. Nor, from his position, could he see the ranch house or mine, both of which lay on the far side, out of sight behind the central hills.

There were plenty of large rocks and irregularities in the downslope that could serve as cover, but not much foliage. The peaks and hills were mostly barren of vegetable life taller than a foot, but the vales and open areas between the rises were tufted with sparse grass, scrubby brush, and assorted cacti. Donnie, the railroad man, had said this was once a working ranch, but Guthrie was surprised anyone could ranch cattle up here. Apparently they still could, at least to a small extent. Using the binoculars, he could see a few cattle strewn over the valley floor, either munching the sparse grasses or meandering from one place to another.

There must be some sort of water, some spring, Guthrie thought as he scanned the landscape below for a way down and a good path across the valley floor. In one of the low areas, he spotted a windmill turning slowly in the desultory breeze, and below it was the dull gray of a galvanized steel water tank.

Staring across the lightening valley, he wondered where the tiny caravan had deposited its noxious load.

Only one way to find out, he thought, and after taking a swig of water, he began his descent.

19

GUTHRIE DIDN'T WORRY ABOUT BEING spotted as he made his way across the valley. It was too rough and convoluted, with many hillocks, gullies, and dry washes for concealment. Besides, it looked like Thorvald's entire contingent was either at the ranch compound or down at the ranch depot. It was unlikely any of them expected an incursion from this direction.

He hurried across the rugged terrain until he was within a quarter of a mile of the ranch compound, and then slowed. A few minutes later, he climbed a ridge, peered over the top, lifted the binoculars, and took stock of the scene before him.

Directly beneath him was a narrow vale, the far side of which rose to the range's western rim. This consisted of six windswept ridges that were only about half the height of the more-rugged peaks that formed the eastern side of the range. Their outer, western flanks descended to the desert floor in relatively gentle grades, but the sides facing the interior of the valley were steeper, scree-covered, and more collapsed, and each ridge was crowned with a low escarpment. They almost looked like giant, motionless waves frozen in stone as they were breaking over the interior of the valley. Since the valley was much higher than the surrounding desert, the western ridges rose only about two hundred vertical feet from its floor—if you could call such a ruggedly cluttered place a floor.

These outer ridges grew progressively higher and longer as they marched to the north. Guthrie was positioned across the vale and roughly between the fourth and fifth, both of which were about half a mile long. They and their siblings to the south were fairly straight and aligned, but the sixth ridge, the last one to the north, jutted into the valley in a huge irregular curve that was more than a mile at its base. The curving wall of the mountainous ridge and the last cluster of hills of the central region blocked Guthrie's view of the northern end of the valley.

He knew, though, that all the creeks and dry washes down that way carried runoff water toward the north. There, they met the major wash that drained the network of arroyos and gullies on the east side of the range before circling around its northern end and heading south along the base of the western slopes to the Rio Grande.

Here in the valley's middle section and in the highlands to the south, the creeks and washes didn't flow that far down the valley, but ran instead to, and then along, the base of the western ridges. The two longest of the straighter ridges met directly across the shallow vale from Guthrie's position, but the join was complete enough that the channel between them simply drained into the valley and ran toward the north.

But the gaps at either end were more pronounced. Between the ridges to Guthrie's left, a creek cut through, draining the southern highlands. To his right, at the far end of the ridge, was the shoulder of the mountain where the mine lay, rounded by a large wash that drained the less-rugged central valley. Both creeks were fairly large, and from studying the satellite and topo maps, he knew they converged about a mile down the outer western slopes and, soon after, emptied into the big dry wash to the west.

From Guthrie's vantage, the ranch house and other structures were clearly visible in a roughly diamond-shaped plot of land oriented north–south. It looked to be about the length of a football field, and somewhat less in width. All the sides of the diamond were delineated by dry creek beds.

Just below Guthrie, the beginning of a small wash that helped drain the central valley into the main creek served as the diamond's southeast leg. Both western legs were the small, shallow arroyo that drained the inside western slopes, with an elbow caused by a kink in the terrain along the base of the ridge. This gully emptied into the big creek right at the shoulder of the mountain. The final leg was the big creek itself, which came from the east to curve around the shoulder of the mountain, right in front of the mine.

The southwestern channel was closest to the ranch house and clear, but after the elbow, the northwestern gully was clogged with piles of rotting lumber and rusting ranching equipment and mining machinery. Right in the elbow between the two was an unnaturally lush patch of scrub brush above which stood a couple of stunted trees. Either an unexpected spring or a cesspool. Guthrie bet the latter.

At the diamond's southern end, almost right below Guthrie, a divide of higher ground something less than a hundred feet across separated the two creeks forming the compound's northeastern and northwestern sides. From there, the land sloped gently down toward the northern tip of the diamond, which pointed in the direction of the mine. The compound was accessed by a dirt road that was graded for much of its length across the valley, but its last hundred yards simply followed the gravelly and mostly flat major creek bed. A road cut off at the corral and ran behind the barn to provide access to the ranch house and other structures, leaving the creek to continue on down to the mine and around the mountain.

The ranch house sat near the southern end of the diamond, just in front of the flat divide between the two creeks, right on the edge of the wash that drained the western ridge. The original Dunton had situated it in the lee of the western ridge to help shield it from the frequent and frigid northers that swept across this land every winter. It's frame structure wore a ten-foot-deep veranda across the front, but its plank walls were devoid of paint, and the tin roof was mottled with rust. It looked like it might hold three small bedrooms, two of which had clearly been added onto the rear of the original structure at some fairly remote time in the past.

At a slight angle next to the house was a smaller house of similar vintage. The two Suburbans and the dually with trailer were parked in front. The trailer was empty. The smaller structure looked like a bunkhouse, maybe the one where Donnie's uncle had lived when he'd been a hand at the ranch. Behind the two buildings sat an array of solar panels, right next to which stood a cellphone tower. Neither had been on the the map app image and would have taken some bucks to build, Guthrie mused. Big bucks. Stolen Vatican bucks?

About sixty feet from the bunkhouse and occupying the area inside the eastern point of the diamond was the small barn, its corral built off the northern side. A dozen cows in the corral munched on bales of hay and drank from a big metal tank. Just beyond the corral, a four-foot-square structure squatted near a couple of more scrubby trees and some relatively lusher scrub growth. When

Guthrie originally examined the compound on the map app, he'd taken it for a shed of some sort, but a collapsing wooden windmill missing half its blades hovering above said the little structure was a pump house for a well.

The most interesting feature, however, was something Guthrie couldn't see, though he knew it was there, just around the northern end of the ridge and slightly above the major creek. On the map app, all he could see of it was a dark splotch with mounds of spoils lying on either side and much more piled down the western slope and creek bed. Donnie said that old man Dunton had discovered a silver mine up here and worked it until it played out. And Thorvald had asked Moran about preparations for it. The dark splotch had to be the entrance—presumably where the troll now was.

It wasn't a difficult assumption to make. Two men stood guard near the bend concealing the mine entrance, and four other Bugle Boys were scattered around the compound.

Guthrie watched the Bugle Boys for a time and sipped a little water. He glanced at the dwindling supply in the bottle, which was his last one. With nothing left to do, he settled in to wait for darkness and tried to ignore the grumbling of his stomach as he munched the last of Espinoza's donuts. Knowing he was in for a long wait in the sun, he was grateful for the boonie hat the trainman had given him. At least it was early fall, not the dead of summer, otherwise he'd literally bake out here.

At last, the sun dropped behind the western ridge, though true night wouldn't set for another couple of hours. During that time, two of the Bugle Boys retreated to the bunkhouse, leaving the two men guarding the mine and two more patrolling the compound.

Guthrie pulled out his phone, intending to take advantage of the ranch's cell tower to let Espinoza know where he and the troll were, but by now, the battery was drained. He returned the phone to his pocket and resumed his surveillance until true twilight began to fall.

Over the course of the next hour, Guthrie descended the ridge's eastern flank to its end, where the major creek wound by. He wanted to get close to the mine entrance to make certain the troll was in there and ascertain its status. Keeping low beneath the cover of the deepening shadows, he sneaked to the back of the barn. A door in the wall beckoned, and Guthrie gave it a tentative tug. It was unlocked, but he had to ease it open to keep the rusty hinges from squealing. After he edged inside, he dashed to the opposite side to the big barn doors. A personnel door was set in the wall next to the big rolling door, and he opened it a crack and peered through.

The mine entrance was about a hundred feet away. Probably feeling safe with the troll in the mine and still fastened to its rock, the two Bugle Boys guarding it had grown lax. One stood about ten feet in front of the shoulder of the steep rocky slope, smoking a cigarette. He was one of the two Guthrie and Espinoza had gotten the drop on after cold-cocking Lyle. The other was Lyle. Lyle sat propped against the rocks making up the foot of the mountain. Neither he nor the smoker was paying much attention to anything, and both looked a little worse for the wear—probably doing double guard duty as punishment for their failure down at the depot.

Wanting to get closer, Guthrie exited the rear of the barn and crept down the back of the corral to the main creek bed. Using its banks, scrub brush, and the failing light, he managed to crawl to a clump of rock within forty feet of the entrance without either Bugle Boy spotting him. He could see the adit now, the opening curtained by a large tarp.

Nothing happened for many minutes, but the wait terminated when Thorvald and Moran emerged from the house, followed by two more Bugle Boys who lit the way with the flashlights on their carbines. They walked down to the mine, surprising the two lounging guards.

"Do you think this is a game, you slugs?" Moran yelled, shocking Lyle and the smoker to attention. "You're in the Bugle Boys, now," he said, voice just under a snarl, "not some simpleminded militia. This is your second offense. I better not catch either of you fucking off again."

"No, Sir," the two guards responded simultaneously.

"Go down to the corral and bring back a cow."

"Us?" Lyle asked. "I don't know nothing about cows."

"You get a rope. You put the rope around the cow's neck. You drag the fucking cow up here. Is that too complicated for you boys?"

"No, sir."

"Then get to it."

The two left, heading toward the barn door. Guthrie shrank into the angle of the creek bank as they passed above him.

"I don't know why we gotta get the fucking cow," Lyle groused under his breath.

A few moments later, Guthrie heard the barn door open, but from his concealment, he couldn't see what was going on there. Then he heard cows bleating fearfully, the stamp of hooves, and considerable cursing. At last, after several minutes during which Thorvald and Moran waited impatiently, Lyle and the smoker reappeared, half leading, half dragging a cow by ropes around its neck, one on either side. As they approached the mine, the cow jerked nervously and tried to shy away, but the Bugle Boys wrestled it back in line. They dragged it forward far enough that they could fasten the free ends of the ropes to the chassis of an overturned and rusting mine car that was barely visible close to the entrance then backed off. The cow, bleating and grunting, pulled frantically at the ropes but when it realized it couldn't get away, it just stood stoically. Even in the dim light, Guthrie could see it quivering in terror.

Almost immediately, Halvor pulled back the tarp and appeared in the opening. It was still attached to its slab, which apparently was too heavy or cumbersome to drag deeper into the mine. But it could drag the slab a little closer to the mine entrance, the rock screeching like a banshee on the set of mine rails leading down into the darkness.

The bovine panicked, its frantic bawls sounding like screams as it stumbled back as far as the ropes allowed. That wasn't far enough. The troll's long arm reached out, the groping hand found one of the ropes, and it grabbed it with a twist that broke it like a thread. The monster hauled the cow toward the door, breaking the second rope, the beast panting, kicking, and screaming. All that ended in a second as Halvor grabbed it up and bit through its neck with a sickening crunch.

Lyle and the smoker turned from the gory scene, but Thorvald, Moran, and the other two Bugle Boys watched impassively as the troll consumed the cow, tossing the bones out onto the ground after it finished sucking all the meat from them.

The troll had grown considerably, even in the short time since Guthrie had last seen it. Untrammeled but trammeling freedom suited it , and it now loomed in the mine opening. After it finished eating, Thorvald told it he'd be back later.

"You'll be relieved at midnight," Moran instructed Lyle and the smoker. "Don't let me catch you napping."

Then he and Thorvald returned to the house. Guthrie noticed that neither Lyle nor the smoker ventured very close to the adit.

"I don't know why the fuck we have to pull double-duty when the rest of the guys are in there, eating," Lyle said. "I'm fucking starving. We haven't had a decent meal all day."

"Relax, Lyle," the smoker said. "We eat when they tell us to eat. Wanna smoke?"

"How can I fucking relax," Lyle snarled, "when I got a massive headache from that guy hitting me." He reached tentative fingers to the back of his skull then peered closely at them in the near darkness. "Fuck, it's still bleeding." He shook his head. "I want a fucking steak, that's what I want. That thing," he jerked a thumb toward the troll, where it crouched in the mine shaft on its slab of rock, "gets all the beef it wants, and I want mine, too." The thumb poked his own chest. "Hell. We come out here to help Thorvald rebuild his spread, and now we're roped into babysitting a fucking freak monster like that. How did that happen?"

"Money," the smoker said laconically. "When this is all over, we're going to be fucking rich. Hell, we're already rich."

A heavy, coarse, and snide chuckle gurgled from the troll's throat, and after that, the two Bugle Boys were silent. They resumed their desultory guard duty, though now with frequent sidelong glances at the troll, which just sat there, watching them with flat eyes. More time passed, and finally many of the lights in the house and bunkhouse went out as activity on the ranch quieted.

Guthrie wished he could do something about the troll, but at the moment, all he could really do was wait until Espinoza returned with the explosives. So, having ascertained the troll's location, the layout of the ranch compound, and the forces guarding it, Guthrie began crawling backwards, intending to make his way toward the corral and the rear of the barn, and from there, back the way he'd come. After that, he needed to get in touch with Espinoza, and the most direct way to do that now that his cell phone was dead was to try to connect with the rail repair crew over on the main line first thing in the morning.

He didn't get nearly that far. Not even to the corner of the corral.

"Fe, fi, fo, fum," the troll's boomed from the mine. "I smell the blood of an Englishman."

Abandoning caution, Guthrie stood and raced for the corner of the barn, where a figure stepped out of the shadows.

"That's far enough, Guthrie."

It was Moran. The Glock .45 in his hand didn't waver.

"Drop the weapons."

Guthrie did, annoyed with himself that he'd let Moran get the drop on him.

"Nice to meet you, at last, Guthrie. Brian Moran at your service. You're a persistent fucker, aren't you? I had a feeling you were around. Where's your buddy?"

"Gone back to Houston," Guthrie said.

"Sure." Moran said flatly as he pushed Guthrie forward. "You came here to see Halvor. Well, let's go see him. March."

By now, Lyle and the smoker had run up, weapons at the ready, but Moran just gave them a jaundiced look and waved them off. Guthrie stopped a comfortable distance from the adit, and Moran chuckled as he held back.

"Don't worry, Guthrie. Thorvald will want to talk to you first."

"Well, Guthrie," the troll chortled, showing too many of its snaggled teeth for comfort. "Maybe we'll have another chance to chat before they serve you to me. Our last talk was very productive and gave me new ideas. I think you'll make a much better conversationalist than Fleming. Conversation—aperitif, so to speak—not only whets the appetite, but ads savor to the meal. But make no mistake: Serve you, they will. They'll do anything I want." It smacked its lips. "I hope you're afraid. Very afraid. All those fearomones saturating the flesh make it pliable and tender." It sucked air noisily through its ragged teeth and grinned. "I think I'll nibble you slowly from the feet up. That way I can make you last a very long time and use your leg bones for toothpicks while you're still alive." The sucking sound through its teeth turned nasty.

"Fleming was the one in the boxcar with your butt ugly self back in Houston?" Guthrie asked the monster.

"That was him," the troll answered.

"How come you didn't eat him?"

"I admit I was sorely tempted a number of times. It's hard to buck one's nature. But I needed him." The troll edged closer to the opening. "I'm not all impulse, you know. We got to know each other quite well. He taught me how to operate the computer, but beyond that, he's such a dull fellow. If I could exchange him for a more interesting companion such as you," it groped toward Guthrie, grinning, "I'd eat him for sure. And do you know why?"

Guthrie didn't answer, and the troll snickered.

"It's because I *want* to. I'm a creature of the night, Guthrie. I guess you realize that. A creature of darkness." It chuckled nastily. "And you know what? I like it!"

Guthrie wished he could run, but Moran and the Bugle Boys surrounding him had other ideas.

"Let's go," Moran said, leaving Guthrie's detention to the Bugle Boys and leading the way toward the house.

"See you soon, Guthrie," the troll called out, its laugh booming in the dark air.

20

THEY DIDN'T TAKE GUTHRIE TO the house or bunkhouse but to the wood-plank barn. Before they shoved him inside, they stripped him of his possessions, including his boonie hat, though they missed his watch. Then he was prodded through a dark doorway near the horse stalls. In the few moments the interior of the little room beyond was lit by the guards' flashlights, he could see a roughly eight-by-eight-foot space, windowless and barren except for empty rough shelving fastened to the long back wall. Then the interior collapsed into pitch darkness as the guards slammed the door and locked it.

Guthrie had to chuckle at the lock. He guessed that it was a symbolic statement since he could have kicked his way through the old, dried-out wood of the door or any of the walls in about two seconds. Only the continued presence of the guards outside prevented him from doing it.

The night was long and uncomfortable. He tried to sleep but only managed a light doze, propped in one of the corners.

When three Bugle Boys came for him well after the sun was up, his ass was sore from sitting on the bare wooden floor. The guards marched him to the house. In the daylight, the house wasn't much —little more than the size of a three-bedroom bungalow built out of planks that might once have been painted white but had long since weathered to silver-gray. Half a dozen Bugle Boys scattered around the compound watched with curiosity as the men accompanying Guthrie prodded him up the three steps to the porch, through the door, and into a living room. It was set up as an office, and

Thorvald sat behind the desk at the righthand end of the modest-sized space. Moran stood just behind his right shoulder.

The guards pushed Guthrie toward a black folding metal chair in front of the desk, and Guthrie took it and looked at Thorvald. Two of the guards settled in beside him, and the third stood behind.

"There's no use in dissembling, Guthrie," Thorvald said, his accent lilting in the way of a Scandinavian speaking English. "I know who you are and that you've been tracking me."

"I wasn't tracking you," Guthrie said, jerking his thumb over his right shoulder in the general direction of the mine. "I was following that thing you've got out there."

"Yes. You've been following 'that thing,' as you call it. What I mean, is why? Why have you been following? Who asked you to follow?"

"You said you know all about me," Guthrie said. "So you know I'm a private investigator. I was hired to follow."

Thorvald glanced up at the guard to Guthrie's right and nodded. The guard spun and slugged Guthrie on the side of his face. The blow knocked Guthrie out of his chair, though he didn't go completely down but ended up in a crouch. The guard on the other side prodded him sharply with the muzzle of his AR-15.

"Back in the chair," he ordered.

"Do I need to ask again who hired you?" Thorvald asked as Guthrie regained his seat.

"You can, but I'm not saying. Professional ethics forbids it."

Thorvald nodded again to the guard, but this time, Guthrie was ready. As the man drew his punch, Guthrie leaned to the left, cocked his right knee, and chopped outward with the edge of his foot. The unexpected blow caught the guard just below the knee of his supporting leg, and the joint snapped loudly. Screaming at the flaring pain, the Bugle Boy collapsed, clutching his leg.

The other two Bugle Boys stepped forward, aggressively jabbing their assault rifles, but Moran raised a hand to stop them from riddling Guthrie with lead. The guards stepped back but didn't relax the aim of their weapons on Guthrie's chest. At the same moment, three more guards burst into the room.

"If you do that again, I won't stop them from killing you," Moran warned Guthrie. "Stay in your seat." Then he looked at the new entries and gestured to the injured man. "Get him out of here, and have Fleming take him to the hospital."

Two Bugle Boys helped the injured man to his feet and half-carried him out the front door. Thorvald, ignoring them, directed his attention to Guthrie, eyes hard

"Let's try this another way," he said, leaning over his desk, forearms on the top. "Are you an agent of the Vatican?"

"Hell," Guthrie laughed. "I'm not even a Catholic." He peered at Thorvald, eyes narrowing. "How about you?"

Thorvald didn't say anything as he looked at Moran.

Moran shook his head.

"I don't think so. He doesn't have the look."

Guthrie could see relief in Thorvald's eyes as he sat back.

"I told you," Guthrie said. "I'm a private investigator, and I'm not working for the Vatican and never have." He failed to mention he had been contacted by agents of the Vatican and promised to turn Thorvald over to them if he found him.

"Your client?"

"Forget it."

"No matter," Thorvald waved it off. "We know it must be the man who was with you."

"Him?" Guthrie shook his head. "He's just a railroad employee I coerced into helping me, that's all."

"Ah, so." It was Thorvald's turn to laugh. "That's not what Mr. Beaman tells me. He says the man is Gilbert Espinoza. The very one who saw Halvor in the rail yard in Houston. Halvor recognized him, too."

"When Halvor ate Buddy Horton, you mean?" Guthrie intended it as a dig, but it dug into nothing resembling remorse.

"Just so. I asked Mr. Beaman to give Espinoza leeway to investigate, hoping he'd find his way here so Mr. Moran could deal with him. To our surprise, he brought you with him, and now he's gone and you're here. What am I to make of that?"

"He's back in Houston."

"Not according to Mr. Beaman."

"It's a big state. Give him another day or so." Guthrie sure wasn't going to tell Thorvald that Espinoza was off seeking dynamite.

"And why did you stay behind? What did you intend to do?" Thorvald cocked his head. "What *could* you do?"

"I don't know," Guthrie admitted. "But somebody has to do something."

"Yes," Thorvald said. "Somebody has to do something. But what if it is you who are doing the wrong thing? Perhaps it is I who hold the power of true righteous action in my hands and will turn it against the powerful who would enslave us with false doctrines."

"Nice words, but the actions I've seen you take belie them."

"If you only knew the truth, you would support me."

"It's kind of hard to support somebody who creates a monster to murder his enemies."

"You think what Halvor has done—what I've done—is murder? This is war, and in war, there are casualties."

"So, in this war, you're on one side, but who's on the other?"

"The Church, of course. And the establishment that perpetuates its falsehoods for personal gain. And anyone else who supports it."

"The Catholic Church?" No wonder the Vatican thugs had come after Guthrie. "Why, pray tell?"

"It's evil. It's all evil."

"I'm tempted to agree with you, but give me your specific reasons."

"I will, but I tell you only to help you see the righteousness of my cause."

"I guess this is where you tell me your story," Guthrie said.

Thorvald smiled a faint smile.

"You needn't be so cavalier about my life."

"Says the man who's threatening mine."

"It needn't be as harsh as that. After you know more about my situation, perhaps you'll be more kindly disposed toward me."

"Perhaps," Guthrie said, though he doubted it. But the longer Guthrie let a psychopathic egomaniac like Thorvald try to justify acting on his worst impulses, the longer he'd stay alive. Plus, he was curious, and certainly Tereba would want details later. If there was a later for Guthrie.

"Will there be a point?" he asked.

"That's for you to decide," Moran said, though not threateningly.

"Okay. Mind if I eat and drink something while I'm listening?"

"Not at all," Thorvald said and glanced at Moran, who gave a curt gesture to one of the two remaining Bugle Boys.

"Go make him a sandwich, Paige," he said.

"Why do I have to serve this guy? He just broke Willis's leg. Fuck him. We should just shoot him and be done with it."

Moran's features hardened.

"I'm not going to repeat myself. And make it a good one." He jerked his chin toward a door through which a kitchen could be seen.

"Fuck," Paige spat, but he turned and slouched toward the kitchen.

"Hold the mayo," Guthrie called after him.

"Fuck you," Paige muttered without turning as he went into the kitchen.

"You trying to piss him off?" Moran asked.

"Isn't taking much."

Moran didn't answer with words, but the look he shot at the kitchen door said he agreed.

"As you can see, we need cool, experienced heads," Thorvald said, "and you've proved resourceful. Perhaps when you've learned more, you might consider joining me as Mr. Moran and his men have done."

"You're trying to hire me?" Guthrie almost laughed. He shook his head. "Sorry, but I'm not sure I can work with these boys." Guthrie glanced apologetically up at the remaining Bugle Boy. He was a big boy, dark-haired and beefy without being particularly muscular, His gut said the only weights he like to lift were cans of beer. "No insult intended."

The man just stared back, eyes flat, but the tendons beneath his unshaven jaw twitched.

"Because you've proved yourself so capable," Thorvald said, "I'm willing to offer you a higher position. Right under Mr. Moran and Mr. Kelly."

"How about it, Moran?" Guthrie asked. "You up for that?"

Moran's mouth smiled, but his eyes didn't. Guthrie had met psychopaths before, but it was unusual to find them in a subordinate position. Thorvald must be the psychopath's psychopath to command Moran's loyalty. Or maybe the only thing that kept Moran subordinate was simply that Thorvald could help satisfy Moran's own hunger for wealth and power.

"I make you for a stand-up guy," Moran said. "You say you throw in with us, I'll take you at your word."

Like hell you will, Guthrie thought.

"I threw in with my current boss, so what does it say about me if I turn from him to you?"

"It says that you're someone who makes wise decisions," Moran replied.

"Things have changed, Mr. Guthrie," Thorvald said. "Reality is different—or at least, it soon will be. Surely you can see that."

"I can," Guthrie said. "Halvor's pretty obvious."

Thorvald laughed, and even Moran joined in.

"He is, isn't he?" The renegade priest said. "My boy." This last held a touch of pride.

"Don't bother with the baby pictures," Guthrie said.

Paige brought him the sandwich on a paper plate and handed him a bottle of water. As ordered, he'd made a good one, with ham, Swiss cheese, lettuce, and tomato on whole wheat. Guthrie could only hope he hadn't spit in it, but his growling stomach overruled his caution, and he took a big bite and started chewing.

"All right," he said around the mouthful. "Give me the pitch."

21

"As you wish," Thorvald began. "I was born in Kristiansand, which is the fifth largest city in Norway. As I grew up, I discovered in myself a natural capacity for numbers, so I studied accounting. You might think that with that kind of background, I would have turned myself to mundane matters, but the call of God was strong within me. I gravitated toward Catholicism. I don't know why. Maybe it was the ritual, which, to my younger self, seemed filled with holy spirit, dignity, and purpose.

"After I took orders, I was assigned as an assistant bookkeeper for the Diocese of Oslo. I served there for six years, rising during that time to head bookkeeper. Then in my eighth year, I was reassigned to the Institute for the Works of Religion, which is the fancy name for the Vatican bank. Initially, I felt honored to serve the Holy See directly, and I fervently poured myself into my work. Learning the ins and outs of my assignment took the better part of two years.

"The only problem was my direct supervisor, Father Tobias. My nemesis. Call it professional jealousy, authority wielded corruptly, or even some sort of natural, inborn antipathy, but that bastard hated me from the moment I entered the office. He rode me mercilessly for years. Assigned me the most demeaning of tasks. I was at the top of my class in my field at the university and had previously excelled in intricate financial planning for the Church while I was in Oslo. But Father Tobias had me crunching the kind of numbers that any accountant can do, and worse, he assigned me to do the routine maintenance on our office servers. He was overly demanding and all-too-ready and happy to wield his power over me.

"I put up with it for as long as I could, hoping his disposition toward me would mellow over time. But it didn't. It just settled into a rut that was unpleasant, impossible to get out of, and seemingly eternal. I suppose I could have requested a transfer, but the opportunity to serve the Holy See directly was too strong a lure, and it kept me there even as Father Tobias made my life…. Well, not hell, perhaps, but harsh enough.

"Finally, I felt I could take no more, and I lodged complaints with his superiors, only to be accused of being a chronic complainer with unsupported allegations. Tobias was reliable and ensconced in his position, so perhaps the biases were, after all, mine, not his. The upshot was that my complaints spurred Father Tobias to hate and abuse me even more.

"But it was that hatred that was his undoing. That and the fact that I had, thanks to him, intimate knowledge of our servers. Blocked by the Church authorities from confronting the problem with the Church hierarchy, as should have happened, I was forced to take matters into my own hands and find some reason to get Father Tobias reassigned or removed from the priesthood. I began observing him closely. I'd long noticed that each day, he locked the door to his office at the same time for about an hour. He didn't just close it, he locked it. It was like clockwork. And now I grew curious."

"He was doing something he didn't want anyone to know about," Guthrie said.

Thorvald nodded.

"I grew suspicious precisely because he himself acted suspiciously just before and after that time. It was nothing obvious, you understand, but over a period of months of close observation, I noticed subtle changes in his behavior. I knew something was going on. He could have been making phone calls. There was no way I could be sure about that, but I listened at his door and heard no talking. That made me believe he was online, and I *could* do something about that since I controlled our servers.

"First, I attempted to trace his electronic footprint. That did not go well. I could access most of the server files, but there was a cluster of encrypted files I couldn't get into. I might have known how to manage the server, but I'm no hacker. And I couldn't get into his email accounts, either. But then I had what I like to think of as a keystroke of genius, and it hinged on Tobias's demeaning regard of me. His computer was always password protected when he was out of the office for any length of time—for meetings and lunch and such. But his bowel movement was as periodic as his locking the office door. Everyday at around ten-thirty, he'd leave the office for fifteen minutes, and during that time, his office and his computer were accessible."

"Convenient."

"Yes. And very regular." Thorvald smiled. "One morning while he was at his constitutional, I availed myself of his computer and installed keystroke-tracking software that I could access through the server on the terminal in my own office. Within a week, I had knowledge of several important facts. Foremost among them, Tobias was a member of a secret cabal within the Church that was using the Vatican accounts to launder huge sums of corrupt money. Money from drug deals, prostitution, arms sales, smuggling, political corruption. You name it. Worldwide.

"The cabal was nothing but a huge criminal syndicate masked by religion and using the Church funds as its own bank. I discovered who Tobias's principal associates were, and a frightening number of them were in the higher echelons of the clergy. No wonder I'd gotten nowhere with formal complaints. I also learned all of the websites he visited and all of his pertinent passwords. Some of those sites were what you might call off-shore banks holding billions of dollars in illegal funds across dozens of accounts."

"So, you learned that the Church is big business, and people with that kind of power often can't help but engage in corruption."

Thorvald blinked, then his lips tightened.

"Corruption," he agreed. "On a massive scale. You think that trivial?"

"No, but it surprised you? Shocked you? The Catholic Church has long proved itself as corrupt as any criminal organization. Just give a gander at its history."

"That wasn't how I'd seen it. Not until then. I was faithful, you understand. So very faithful. And righteous. I believed fully and completely. There was an eternal war between good and evil, and the Church was on the side of good. I was on the side of good. But all that was erased the instant I discovered that a cabal of some of the highest-ranking Church officials was using the Church as a front to support their corrupt lifestyles. And they cared nothing about how they did it. They exploited whole cultures and ruined nations for profit."

"So you decided to do something about it."

"For me, the Church had been the salvation of humankind, but now I saw that it was just another criminal enterprise that not only trafficked in illegal activities but corruptly and hypocritically exploited the fears and hopes of people the world over for personal ends. What I learned destroyed my faith. Totally. My life. And they'd exploited *me* in the process, getting me to assist them in doing their dirty work without my knowledge or consent. In doing that, they transformed my pure faith into pure guilt and my sense of honor into hatred and a desire for revenge."

Guthrie washed the last of the sandwich down with a swig of water and handed the paper plate to Paige, who gave him an evil look but took the plate and went to the kitchen.

"It's not everybody in the Church, I presume," Guthrie said as Paige returned. "You could have alerted somebody."

Thorvald gave a snort of a laugh that sounded almost like a snarl.

"The Church authorities *were* the criminals. *They* were in control. Or at least very powerful. They were the very people who had blocked me from lodging a complaint against Father Tobias. They even had a lot of Italian law enforcement and government officials under their sway. I was afraid. I didn't know where to turn. National governments have no control over the Church. It's like its own country, though one without borders.

"Because I didn't know what to do, I did the obvious: I roamed around inside the Vatican Archive. Scholars from around the world are granted limited access, but my newfound status as a high-level priest in a security sensitive position afforded me almost unlimited access. That included a portion of the archive that is normally off limits to most, where they keep three major types of records and documents: financial records, personnel files, and manuscripts deemed too dangerous for public revelation but too important to destroy.

"Initially, I just used the financial records in these archives for research for my job or to satisfy my personal curiosity, but once I was aware of the cabal, I began searching them for potentially incriminating evidence to back up my discoveries of the cabal's corruption. It didn't take long to find, and I began to develop a dossier. I had no idea what I might do with such a document. Who could I turn to when simple possession of it might be a death warrant if I told the wrong person. Excommunication isn't the only punishment the Church metes out to traitors."

As Guthrie had discovered.

"So you decided to create a test case," he said.

"Exactly. Very good, Mr. Guthrie." Thorvald nodded. "An experiment in cultural self-correction, so to speak, to find out just how high and how deep the corruption went." The corners of his mouth curled in a faint smile, and his eyes went blank for a moment.

"You framed Father Tobias."

"Very good, Mr. Guthrie. Yes, I framed him, though it took the better part of a year. I set up a handful of dummy companies that could be traced back to Tobias and bled off more than ten million dollars of cabal funds into them. It was pretty good work, and had I wanted, no one would have been the wiser, including Tobias. But then I ratted on him anonymously to someone I knew was part of the cabal. To seal the deal, I planted a copy of the dossier I'd amassed on his computer, in a file that he wasn't aware of but that the cabal's hackers surely would discover. I thought it all would be enough to get Tobias removed, at the very least. It was, but not in the way I expected."

"They killed him."

"Assassinated. I'm sure of it. But most skillfully. It was made to look like a mugging gone wrong in a bad area of Rome rife with social problems and a very high crime rate."

"But you didn't buy it," Guthrie said. "Kind of strange for muggers to attack and kill a priest since priests aren't known for carrying much money on them. Perhaps he was ministering to someone there, and someone took exception."

"Yes. Normally a mugging would be odd. In the case of Father Tobias, someone taking exception to his ministering was unlikely. I'd worked for him for years, and I knew he wasn't ministering to anybody. Tobias wasn't the ministering sort. In any way at all. He was a priest, but he had no heart or conscience. To him, the Church was strictly a business, and that business was to enrich the cabal's coffers, not minister to the sick and poor or to bring light into the world. He didn't even participate in hearing confessions."

"So what was he doing there?"

"I don't think he was doing anything at all. I suspected foul play of another sort, and I'm sure his body was dumped."

"But the police didn't think that?"

"The police. Bah! They were paid off."

"And now you knew the consequences of crossing this cabal."

"I was nervous at first. Maybe the cabal would suspect me. They even sent a priest named Father Danby to question me. Interrogate me. But he had to do it without revealing the reason behind his questions. And I played dumb. Who was I but a lowly accountant? A number cruncher. If they suspected me, it wasn't for long. I'd covered my tracks well. I even removed the keystroke-tracking software from Tobias's computer as soon as I learned he was dead.

"I prayed they'd promote me to Tobias's position, but those prayers went unanswered, too. I was an outsider, and there was no way they were going to let their financial secrets be controlled by someone who wasn't already part of their conspiracy. So they brought in another of their cabal to run the office. Father Innocenzio, who was about as innocent as the Serpent in Eden.

"Father Innocenzio was very watchful after the Tobias incident, but he was a guard dog brought in after the fox has raided the henhouse. While I was framing Tobias, I also spent time setting up similar accounts in hundreds of banks all around the world, to which only I have access. Initially, I left the accounts nearly empty, so that there was no clear sign of theft from the cabal's coffers. But I could perform the theft in a matter of minutes, delivering about half of the cabal's resources into my own hands almost at a keystroke."

"That was enough? Being able to steal from the thieves but not actually doing it?"

"Oh, I meant to do it, and eventually, I did. But loosing the money wasn't punishment enough. That's why I waited. I now dearly wanted to reveal irrevocably the hollowness of the Church and, by extension, the Christian faith. I figured that the advent of aliens on Earth might do the trick." He smiled. "That was wishful thinking, of course, but maybe there was something I *could* do to punish the Church's corruption. I just had to find it."

"It would have to be pretty big to top the Church's own historical evils," Guthrie said. "The Crusades, Dark Ages, the Inquisition, the genocide of Central and South American indigenous peoples, and turning a blind eye to the Holocaust are all pretty damning, yet well known and nobody seems to give a damn."

"That's because people find it simpler to ignore the evils around them in an attempt to ignore their own evil. You can't destroy a religion by pointing out that its adherents are hypocrites, but you can destroy it by exhibiting the kind of proof that cuts it to the core and proves it toothless and hollow."

"And you think that thing out there is proof?" Guthrie asked. "What the fuck *is* it, anyway. It says it's a troll."

"It *is* a troll," came the reply.

Guthrie couldn't say no to that. The thing in the boxcar was definitely a troll.

22

"As I said," Thorvald went on. "I had the proverbial smoking gun to prove the corruption of the cabal and the Church it was using to enrich and empower itself, but there was nothing I could do with it but shoot myself. It was driving me mad. And so was life as an accountant priest in the Vatican, which can be a tedious chore if one is not allowed to fulfill one's potential. For me, it was even worse.

"Can you imagine tabulating and recording numbers representing vast sums of wealth, much of which had been stolen or co-opted in some corrupt way, all day long, then having to spend many of your off-hours hearing confessions from the little people? Can you imagine how boring their confessions can be? Endless illicit and guilt-ridden encounters between sweaty loins. Theft. Spousal abuse. Vandalism. Pointless lies. Occasional murder.

"The litany was stultifying, petty, and repetitive after even a short time. And when I thought about how the Church—upon which all of those same parishioners are emotionally dependent and to which they tithe more than they can afford—had become corrupt, I was disgusted with my own complicity and hypocrisy every time I ordered so many Hail Marys or rosary counts.

"After a time, I found sleep difficult as visions of numbers crippled by human frailties swirled through my dreams. Maybe more important, the Church was no longer a refuge and haven. I now saw it for what it was: a nexus of evil. All the while during those years, I was growing more and more disgusted at the Church's brazen display of Mammon worship, but I was at a loss what to do about it. Too many enemies were arrayed around me, and those who weren't and might believe me were too inured in the fiction to see past it to the reality. Or perhaps they were just afraid.

"Naturally, I was, too. I became truly paranoid of every priest and nun I encountered. There was no telling who was involved in the cabal. It was like a cancer with shoots infecting the entire body and soul of the Church. But then I realized that perhaps there was a way to find allies, and it pivoted on the fact that I'd spent so much time in the archive that the priests in charge knew me and never questioned why I was there or what I was doing. Apparently the powers that be had no idea that an accountant might be interested in something more arcane than numbers. But now I was interested in names. To accomplish my goal of bringing the Church and the cabal to their knees, I needed my own counter-cabal."

"The Trumpet of Faith?" Guthrie asked, and Thorvald looked surprised.

"Again, Mr. Guthrie, you prove your value. Yes, I changed my focus from the financial records and began searching the personnel databases, looking for misfits among the priesthood—priests who'd committed offenses against the Church but who were still involved. I was daunted at first. It's not easy recruiting strangers into a clandestine organization. You never know who to trust, or how deeply, or for how long. And I needed the right misfits. But the task of finding confederates proved simpler than I'd anticipated. There are plenty of malcontents within the Church ranks.

"I stayed away from pedophiles and thieves, but over time, I discovered a number of priests who were being disciplined for various heresies and political activism. Some of them were in Rome, or nearby, and over time, I made contact with them and recruited eight of them to my cause. Gradually, I revealed to them the existence of the criminal cabal, and once I had, they were as outraged as I. It was a purely intellectual exercise at first. I never let on to any of them my plan to drain as much of the cabal's coffers as I could, so I felt I could trust the ones I eventually let in on my plan."

"Making a troll?"

"Not then. I didn't know such a thing was possible. At first, we just met informally and clandestinely to discuss options for attacking the cabal. Though I hadn't told them I could readily relieve the cabal of a huge sum, I knew the money was available at a moment's notice once we had a plan in place. It was the plan that was lacking. We needed something irrevocable and highly public, not something banal like financial crimes that could easily be covered up by an organization beholden to no government and with many law enforcement, government officials, and politicians around the world in its pocket. And with its own enforcement arm.

"Then one of my counter-cabal, Father Stephen, made a suggestion that trumped them all. I've mentioned that the secure area of the archive held financial and personnel records, but they also held something else: a door that opened into a world of possibilities. Next to the secure area were the forbidden stacks where the Church keeps its collection of suppressed manuscripts. I'd always wanted to gain access, but the main entrance, which lay at the far end of the archive, was heavily regulated, and I didn't have the proper authorization. However, Father Stephen told me that there was a back entrance to the forbidden archive in the very area where I often worked, used by library staff. It was protected by a keypad security lock and was unlabeled."

"What would they label it with?" Guthrie asked. "Super-secret and dangerous documents. Do not enter?"

Moran gave a faint chuckle, but Thorvald remained serious.

"Precisely. The door was so innocuous that I must have passed it hundreds of times without noticing it. I always thought it was a storage or utility closet. I suppose the security keypad should have alerted me that more than brooms and mops lay behind it. But once I understood where the door led, I realized that if the Vatican Archives held incriminating evidence, it would be in those stacks. Besides," Thorvald shrugged, "since my investigation was going nowhere without a plan, I needed something to fill the empty time, and a whole world of reading—intriguingly dangerous and potentially damning reading—lay behind that locked door.

"The allure was too great to ignore. Father Stephen didn't know the combination for the keypad, but that was the least of my problems. I simply hid a small surveillance camera on a nearby bookshelf and aimed it at the door. Within a week, I had the combination.

"The forbidden stacks were quite large but largely empty of people. In the time I spent learning something of their contents, I saw only three others. Or rather, I saw two but only heard the third. The two I saw—at different times—were guards of some sort, wearing uniforms and carrying guns. The third, I don't know. Luckily, I saw the guards before they saw me, and I was always careful when moving around in there.

"I'd never had a bent for history, but I found myself now turning to it in an effort to bring myself back to some sort of equanimity as much as to find incriminating evidence. Maybe I was seeking solace in the old and familiar to ease my own guilt at having wasted my life— my soul and spirit—in support of corruption. And the more disenchanted I became with the Church, the more enamored I grew of the golden traditions of my homeland, of the clean and clear lines of its Arctic landscapes and the Aryan purity of its people—a spiritual purity that had been sullied by the Church and Christianity.

'With that in mind, while looking for evidence of Church corruption, I also began researching the Church's influence on my Scandinavian homeland. In the course of that, I happened upon a manuscript on the Christianization of Norway. That subject didn't seem especially scandalous, so I was curious why this particular manuscript was locked away and became immediately interested in it. I didn't expect to find evidence of corruption there that would carry water today, and there wasn't. At least nothing that could have a major effect at this late stage, particularly since the material concerned Church activities in a remote area at a remote time. But there was something better, and the absurdity of it made me laugh.

"I took the manuscript out of the archives and back to my quarters, where I studied it carefully over the next few days. What I'd found was a lengthy letter—a report, really—to the pope from an eleventh-century monk, Brother Fidelio, who was proselytizing God's word among the so-called heathens of Norway. It's a little difficult to tell which pope actually received it since there were six popes between January 1045 and August 1048, roughly the same period of time Fidelio was in Norway.

"The letter was a report on the monk's successes and problems, at the end of which he asked for assistance in devising a method to eliminate trolls and troll creators. It seemed that there was, at that very moment, a troll rampaging the countryside, and the monk bore some guilt for its presence, for he was partly responsible for bringing it into existence, and prayer didn't seem to affect it in the least.

"You've met Halvor, so you know already that his existence is genuine. But reading Brother Fidelio's manuscript, I had no such assurances. His words might just has well have been the ravings of a lunatic. But there was something genuine about what he wrote. Remember, he was writing to the Supreme Pontiff. It seemed unlikely he would deliberately concoct fantastic drivel.

"When I examined the rest of the document, most of which concerned his dealings with Vikings, which was the initial subject that drew me to the manuscript, I saw that nothing else in it was at all strange or objectionable, and that everything was sanely stated in rational terms. In fact, the document would be of value to anyone studying the history of Scandinavia and really should have been in the regular archives. But here it was, hidden away among the records of irredeemable acts and negative statements involving the Church. That fact alone gave the part about the creation of the troll some... well, if not validity, then cachet.

"Since the episode related by the monk had relatively public results, I wondered if there might be any record of it back in Norway. So, on my next vacation, I announced I was going home for a visit, but the truth is, I did very little visiting with relatives and old friends. Most of my two weeks was spent researching local records and archives held by churches, town halls, museums, and families of ancient lineage. Being a priest aided my search immensely. Even the non-religious generally trust priests. I targeted, of course, the region where Brother Fidelio claimed that the troll had attacked several farmsteads and destroyed one small village.

"What the citizenry didn't know was that Fidelio had actually witnessed the creation of the troll by a local shaman of the old pagan ways. The two had gotten into a theological argument about which version of the supreme deity was more true: God or Woden. The shaman argued that the Christian concept of faith was weak in the face of definite knowledge. He said he could prove tangibly and beyond any doubt that his religion was superior and that Woden was supreme. Confident in his God, Fidelio agreed to observe, if only to be able to show the shaman wrong when he failed to prove his claim. But he didn't get the opportunity because he saw the shaman create a troll.

"Then the troll broke free and ravaged the countryside and ate several people before the citizens of the region banded together, searched it out, and killed it, losing nine men in the process. The people then told Fidelio that no troll had been seen in that area for many generations, but that an outbreak of nearly a dozen had rampaged over the whole region a little more than a century earlier.

"Fidelio reported that the shaman intended to kill the troll before it broke free but, for some reason, was unable to. Fearing death at the hands of the locals if it became known he was responsible for the troll, the shaman extracted a promise from Fidelio not to reveal the truth, and Fidelio kept his word, though not in a way the shaman expected. I could not find the pope's reply to the monk regarding the troll, but soon after, Fidelio instituted a pogrom that eliminated every shaman he could find who had knowledge of how to create a troll—beginning with the one who'd proved the reality of trolls to him. And so the method of creating trolls was lost to the Scandinavians. Cementing matters, the personnel records showed that Brother Fidelio resigned the priesthood soon after ending his pogrom against the shamans. After that, he vanished from the historical record."

"Not so fidelio," Guthrie commented.

"Perhaps, like me, his fidelity was to a truth more true and real than the Church," Thorvald replied, then he shrugged. "Naturally, I didn't believe a word. After all, trolls are mythical and impossible creatures. But the more I reread the report, the more my skepticism mutated into…well, not belief. Call it curiosity. Mixed, I'm willing to admit, with cynicism. But Fidelio was deadly sincere, and he was writing directly to the pope, himself. There was little chance he would lie about anything like that to the pontiff.

"By way of proof of such an outlandish claim, Fidelio included the secret of creating a troll. I suppose he hoped the perverse sexuality as well as the pagan connection would help convince the pope to act. And perhaps they did. Certainly Fidelio would not have slaughtered all those shamans without orders from above.

"On my flight back to Rome, I had a revelation. If a troll could actually be created, I could use the same method that the shaman had used to convince Fidelio. But I would not convince one man. I would convince the whole world. Wouldn't it be something: to create a living spawn of an entirely pagan and essentially dead religion? Paganism made flesh. If a pagan religion could be shown to be more obviously real and truthful than Christianity, the Christian faith might just crumble. Certainly the Church would, especially after I also exposed its corruption to the world at large. And what could be more obvious than a pagan troll rampaging across the countryside, eating people and livestock by the fistful?"

"I see what you mean," Guthrie said. "But having the ability to spawn a monstrosity isn't an uncommon feature of many religions, so you have no weight there. And killing all those innocent people just so you can prove a point...." He shook his head. "Sounds pretty drastic, and it would transform a legitimate crusade into terrorism."

"We both agree that the Church's depredations over the centuries are well known and, if not tolerated, then ignored."

"That's pretty much the case."

"Then I submit that if society willfully turns a blind eye to systemic corruption, it is as guilty as the perpetrators. Therefore, there are no innocent people, only those who need to be punished or to have their systems shocked from their complacency."

"A troll rampaging across the countryside ought to do the trick," Guthrie agreed.

"Don't you want to know how I made Halvor?"

"I hate to spoil your fun, but Halvor already told me. You're right, it's kind of perverse."

"The alternative might be even more so," Thorvald said. "Really, can you imagine two trolls copulating?" He shuddered. "The image is beyond sanity."

"You could make a fortune showing it on the Internet."

Thorvald actually laughed.

23

"BEFORE THE METHOD WAS DISCOVERED," Thorvald continued, "trolls were rare and usually solitary, but once the method was understood, there were several large-scale spates of troll activity deliberately caused by men, often out of revenge or dissatisfaction with their lot. I suppose they were the mass shooters of their day. Most of that ended many centuries ago when the method for creating trolls was lost thanks to Brother Fidelio."

Not that Thorvald believed it would actually work. Not at first. Not without a test. On a day off, he drove out into the Italian countryside, found a suitable obscure old bridge and, beneath it, a crack in the stone similar to the one described in Fidelio's report. He nervously masturbated into the crack, expecting someone to stop at any moment to see why his car was parked on the side of the road above. Finished, he quickly backed off and tucked himself away. He half expected a troll to rip open the crack from within and pop out like a manic jack-in-the-box, but nothing happened. All he saw was the crack, dripping with his semen.

"I was disappointed, of course, but what did I really expect? An actual troll? Chiding myself, I drove back to the Vatican, vowing to keep my mind on the mundane matters of stealing from the cabal and cultivating my own group of dissenters. But I couldn't stop pondering what might have gone wrong. I read the report again. Maybe the crack wasn't the right kind. Maybe my sperm hadn't gone deep enough.

"More likely, I was just crazy to think this whole troll business could have any basis in reality. But maybe I wasn't crazy. I knew I had to go back out there to try again. On my next day off, I did just that. I parked, scrambled beneath the bridge, intending to look for a more suitable crack. But my eyes fell on the one I'd inseminated the week before, and I saw some sort of polyp growing out of it. 'What could this be?' I wondered, peering closer. To my astonishment, the polyp had a face—a small and wizened troll face. And a voice.

"'You must be my father,' he peeped to me in antiquated Norse I could barely understand. 'I'm hungry. Bring me food. Lots of food.'

"So I brought him food and, over the ensuing months, watched him grow. All the while, I taught him modern Norwegian and English. He was a quick learner. I believe he was never an infant, at least not in the way we understand it. He might have been small in the beginning, but he was always old. Ancient, even. And very intelligent and canny. He quickly absorbed what I had to teach him and wanted more."

"So you gave it a laptop."

"You noticed that? He has an insatiable appetite not just for food, but for information about this world."

Or information about how to destroy the world, Guthrie thought.

Thorvald was faced with a dilemma: If he left the troll under the bridge, eventually it would work its way free of the crack.

"Imagine that," Thorvald chuckled. "A Scandinavian troll rampaging across the Italian countryside."

"Shades of *20 Million Miles to Earth.*"

"What?"

"Never mind."

"The problem was that if Halvor escaped, I couldn't control his rampage."

"Do you really think you could ever do that?"

"Perhaps not, but I could better direct it. I wanted to cause the most damage and have the greatest public impact. For that, the best target is the United States, where the terror and publicity will be greatest. Americans are used to living in fear and trauma. I believe they even love it. If something were to truly shake them up, it would have to be huge. My boy is that. It was quite a balancing act, letting him grow but keeping him from completely emerging before we arrived here."

"Now that you've got it here," Guthrie asked. "What do you intend to do with it?"

"I'm thinking of letting him loose in the Mall of America where he can rampage through the heart of the American dream. But I knew it wouldn't be easy removing Halvor and transporting him across Europe and over the Atlantic to a place where I could house him in secret and feed and nurture him, too.

"There were several problems, foremost of which, of course, was the matter of revealing the troll to my associates in the Trumpet of Faith. A certain number of them had to know about him. And so would a limited number of secular people who might come into contact with him during transportation. Gradually, I introduced my proposed upper echelon to the troll. All were shocked, horrified, amazed. Only three of the eight demurred."

"How did you ensure their silence?"

"I fed their bodies to Halvor. I have to admit, he complained about them already being dead. He will eat livestock all day long, but what he really craves is fresh human flesh." Thorvald's eyes grew vacant for a moment. "How I'd like to feed Father Innocenzio to him. Perhaps I shall."

To fund the enterprise, Thorvald went on, was simple. He used the cabal's own money against itself.

"They stole most of it, anyway, or got it through corrupt or criminal means. I'm just putting it to better use. I channeled about a third into my own accounts and another third into the accounts of thousands of charities around the world. I did that partly to obscure my own trail, but that's where the money should have gone anyway. I had to leave a third in place, though. Certain accounts had to remain intact, for a time, otherwise the cabal would have been onto my plan—at least the part of it that entailed stealing their money— if I acted too soon or too thoroughly. In other words, I have almost unlimited funds at my disposal. Of course, I also kept Brother Fidelio's manuscript. Would you like to see it?"

Without waiting for an answer, Thorvald opened one of the desk drawers and pulled out a large, manilla bubble-wrap envelope from which he drew a file folder. He lay the folder on the desk and opened it so Guthrie could see the contents. It was an old manuscript, all right, tight, ancient Latin lettering covering many sheets of what looked like velum.

"I don't read Latin," Guthrie said, "but I'll take your word that this is the real deal."

"As real as my son."

The troll cemented the plan, and the money made its execution possible. But a necessary piece of the puzzle was missing. Thorvald knew a lot about bookkeeping and finances but absolutely nothing about being a criminal—especially a criminal on the scale he planned.

"With my troll, I could prove my point," Thorvald said, "But to get that far, I needed more than my little priestly cabal. I needed someone who knew about criminal behavior and wasn't afraid to do the dirty work necessary for my plan to succeed."

"You mean a hitman. That wouldn't have been Bertrando Galtero, would it?"

Thorvald looked astonished.

"You truly are an excellent detective, Mr. Guthrie. Since I have yet to hear from him, I simply assumed he tried to do his duty, and you killed him, but it seems I assumed incorrectly. How did you learn his real name? He would have died before he divulged that."

"I have my detective ways," Guthrie said. "He also divulged your name. He's how I knew about you at all."

Thorvald laughed—a little too loudly. Guthrie figured he was trying to cover up momentary consternation.

"You refer to Mr. Galtero in the past tense," Thorvald said. "Does that mean you did kill him?"

"He's not dead," Guthrie said. "Let's just say he's in a safe place. What I want to know is how a priest came into contact with an internationally wanted assassin?"

"Being a priest actually facilitated the process. Galtero was notorious in the Italian underworld, and to many others, including the police, knew who he was but could never gather enough evidence to prosecute him. I, myself, was unaware of him or his profession until one day when he came to the Church for confession. I was talking with another priest, who stopped our conversation to point him out across the nave. 'That's Galtero,' he told me. 'He's a hitman.' I was astonished. How did my companion know that? 'Almost all of us who listen to confessions here have listened to his sins often enough.' He sighed and said, 'They are very grave.' I asked what they were, but my companion wouldn't tell me, saying he wasn't comfortable repeating them especially since they'd been divulged during confession. That would be a sin of its own.

"Intrigued, I contrived to be in the confessional the next time Galtero made an appearance, and he confessed to me that he'd just murdered a man and his wife on the orders of a Mafia capo. He was seeking forgiveness. 'I cannot give you that, Mr. Galtero,' I told him. 'No man can. But I can give you purpose and opportunity. What would you say if I told you that I want to hire you on a full-time basis?'

"'I'd say you were no ordinary priest,' he replied. I heard a metallic clicking sound as he cocked a pistol, and I half expected him to shoot me right there through the partition. But he didn't. That would have been the end of confession for him, and confession was all he had left after his many crimes. 'I'm deadly serious,' I told him. 'I am very expensive,' he said, and I replied, 'I am very wealthy. Meet me later to discuss it. Wherever and whenever you want. I promise you won't be disappointed.'"

Thus began Thorvald's association with Galtero, who helped open a number of underworld connections. But the main transportation wasn't part of that. For that, Thorvald only had to consult his own dossier on the cabal to discover who their major smuggling contacts were. Beaman and his associates in Houston, for example, were part of a long-established smuggling and criminal organization that had been used occasionally by the cabal to move illicit goods. Unbeknownst to the cabal, Thorvald used bribery, extortion, and occasional murder as well as generous payment to get the smugglers to do his bidding.

Brian Moran came in via another route. He'd been a top level enforcer for the Church cabal, though he was unaware of the cabal's true nature, believing that he was simply working for the Vatican. Thorvald boldly visited him in his quarters and proved to him that the last three people he'd been sent to kill—two men and a woman —were on the verge of cooperating with the authorities on cases involving aspects of the cabal's illegal activities. Then he made a better offer: Eliminate the true enemy of the Church—the Church itself—and subsequently take control of worldly wealth and power.

Moran had been pondering the woman he'd just killed. She'd seemed just like a housewife, not some enemy of the Church. Indeed, she hadn't been, but her husband was beginning to be troublesome, so in the view of the cabal, she had to go, too.

Moran didn't have great feelings for the woman, but he resented being used as a lackey to satisfy the greed of hidden men—especially if his own greed wasn't being satisfied in return. So he joined Thorvald's Trumpet of Faith, bringing in a handful of his experienced soldiers and recruiting a more ragtag bunch from the construction trades to join the Bugle Boy army. They needed construction workers with various skills to renovate he ranch buildings and improve the mine, and they weren't hard to recruit. A guy who makes twenty dollars an hour is going to jump at the chance to make millions for a few months' work, some of which was playing militiaman and maybe even getting to shoot someone.

The first task of the Trumpet of Faith was to transport Halvor to the United States, and concurrent with that was the need for a place to transport it to. But before any of that could be accomplished, Thorvald had to remove the stone surrounding the crack from which the troll was emerging. He couldn't hire a construction crew to jackhammer out the stone since the workers would learn about the troll, so Moran brought in Kelly and another of his top boys to aid Thorvald's cabal. Dressed in road crew garb, they and the priests managed to roughly hew the slab from beneath the bridge and, using a forklift, maneuver it into a box truck for transportation the the rail line.

After that, it was up to Moran and the smuggling network to transport the troll to Texas. The troll and its slab were loaded into a shipping container on a truck trailer and driven to the train depot. There, the container was transported to the nearest port, where it was shipped to the U.S. All along the way, Thorvald and his growing army of minions—the smuggling ring as well as the Bugle Boys—greased palms, engaged in subterfuge, and even resorted to nearly a dozen murders and disappearances—most carried out by Galtero—to avoid scrutiny by authorities or anyone else.

Once the container reached the Port of Houston, the Bugle Boys transferred the troll to a boxcar Thorvald had purchased because the container had become too confining and suffocating for the troll's comfort and safety.

From the port, the boxcar was taken to the Englewood Yard to be added to a train going west. The only glitch in the plan had been at the rail yard, when Buddy Horton happened on the boxcar, which was open at the time because Halvor had told Jack Fleming it needed some fresh air. Being at the wrong place and time was just bad luck on Buddy's part. Gilbert Espinoza witnessing the incident had nearly derailed Thorvald's plan, but luckily Fleming had been there to contact Beaman when the troll ate Horton. Beaman sent Ray

Hudson to help Fleming move the boxcar to a different track. After Beaman sent Espinoza home, they simply returned the car to the line, so things had worked out, despite the glitch. After that, Halvor was on his way west, to the place chosen to raise up baby. And now it was here on the ranch, safe and secure.

"But why here?" Guthrie asked. "Out in nowhere West Texas."

"That was precisely the point," Thorvald said, giving an offhand gesture. "Even discounting his size, raising a troll is no small thing. You can't have close neighbors wondering about what's going on, and you need a steady supply of livestock to feed him. And there is the need to keep him in check. He knows that there isn't significant shade for farther than…." Thorvald caught himself then continued. "Let's just say he likes caves, and I have a very nice one for him here at the ranch. Anyway, for my purposes, this is not the middle of nowhere. It is the nexus of the web. Once Halvor is free from his stone and grown to full size, I can ship him anywhere in the country within three days." He leaned back and smiled. "However, I'm debating now whether the Mall of America is the proper target. There are so many good ones. But taking down the Mall of America still has a great deal of appeal."

"How did you choose this place? The Dunton Ranch, isn't it?"

Thorvald smiled appreciatively.

"I knew I was right about you, Mr. Guthrie. You would be a valuable addition…."

"I'm not Catholic. But while I dislike Catholicism and almost all other religions, I don't dislike them enough to employ mass murder as a tool to destroy them. They've already done that themselves, and nothing changed."

"No, I suppose not." Thorvald shrugged. "It would take a dedicated sort such as me. No one is more bitter than the idealist whose faith has been destroyed."

Thorvald sat for a moment, eyes downcast, lips pursed in thought. Then he looked up at Guthrie and continued his story.

"The current owner of the ranch was old and didn't even live on the property. His children didn't want the trouble of managing the ranch and preferred urban living. So the ranch went on the market. I was looking for such a place and bought it through an agent. The mine was the final selling point. I could have built some sort of building on an out-of-the-way property to house Halvor, but he'll feel much more at home in the mine."

The setup was perfect for Thorvald. The ranch had been a running operation, though relatively modest, and it could support enough cows to feed the troll, whose size and appetite were both growing fast. Plus, the ranch had the private rail spur, so the boxcar could be taken right onto the property—and off again at the appropriate time.

"But now there is you, Mr. Guthrie. And the man who hired you. You say he's gone back to Houston?"

"That's what I said."

"Just tell us where he is, Guthrie, and things will go easier for you," Moran said.

Guthrie looked him in the eyes and said, "As the stand-up guy you think I am, I'm telling you I saw Espinoza head back toward Houston." That was true enough. "For all I know, he's there by now." That also was true.

Moran's eyes bored into his for a moment, and Guthrie had the impression he was having a stare-down with a snake. Then Moran nodded, though he didn't quite smile.

"And what does he know."

"That a monster ate his friend. That everyone thinks he's crazy."

"Is he likely to talk?"

"To whom? He's already told the authorities, and they don't believe him. What's he going to do. What can he do? If he keeps it up, he'll lose his job. He needed to go back to work, so he decided to forget what happened and left."

"But you stayed," Thorvald said.

"Let's just say it's my job to deal with situations like this. With people like you."

"With a monster who eats people?" Thorvald asked.

"I've seen worse. Much worse. You say your monster is ancient, but it's really nothing but an overgrown brat."

Thorvald laughed.

"Yes, he can be difficult and impulsive, but he's really quite interesting and charismatic once you get to know him." Thorvald leaned back in his chair. "I will have to ponder what to do with you. The simplest thing would be to feed you to Halvor. But I'll give you a chance to reconsider my offer to join my organization."

"Okay. I'd like to sleep on it, anyway. There will be serious ramifications if I leave my current employer."

"I'd expect no less," Thorvald said.

"Keep him in the small bedroom," Moran told Paige. "But don't hurt him unless he resists or tries to escape."

"Why do I gotta babysit this fuck?" Paige demanded.

"Because I told you to," Moran said.

A sullen look on his face, Paige prodded Guthrie with the muzzle of his carbine.

"Move," he commanded.

Paige took Guthrie down a short hall and into a ten-by-ten-foot room that held three cots. Scattered between the cots were duffel bags and personal items.

"Over there, by the wall," Paige commanded.

"I'm not sitting on a bare wooden floor," Guthrie declared. "I did that last night."

He dragged one of the cots over to where Paige had indicated while Paige, face apoplectic, raised his rifle.

"I think that if you shoot me," Guthrie said, not looking at his guard but arranging the blankets and pillow, "your next experience will be as troll food. Moran already has you in his sights."

"Get on that fucking cot," Paige snarled, pointing at the cot with his rifle, and Guthrie complied. "I'll kill you in a second if you fuck around."

In response, Guthrie lay back on the cot and tried to nap. It had been a long night and day. He slept only fitfully, though, and periodically watched the sky outside the window turn from blue to gray to black.

About eleven o'clock, the screaming started.

24

GUTHRIE STOOD AS PAIGE STEPPED quickly to the window and peered through the glass. It was too dark to see anything clearly, and anyway, the window faced the wrong side of the house. A scatter of gunfire sounded from close by, and some of the voices outside grew more panicked.

"Stop firing!" Moran yelled. "Don't fire!"

Guthrie couldn't see him, but his voice sounded like it came from the front porch.

Paige turned to Guthrie, leveling his rifle.

"I gotta go out there," he said. "Stay here. If I see you outside, I'll shoot you, no matter what the boss says."

Then he was gone, slamming the door behind him.

Guthrie moved to the window. Two guards had been visible through the glass all day, but now they were gone. More screaming and yelling sounded from the far side of the house, then someone turned on some kind of extremely powerful light. And a second. Guthrie couldn't see the sources, but their glares splayed brightly across the rocky ground, starkly highlighting every feature. Every few seconds an elongated, distorted human shadow dashed across the ground. The shouting stopped, but the screaming continued intermittently and from farther away. Then everything went suddenly quiet.

Guthrie went to the door and tried it. It was unlocked, so he left the room and cautiously moved down the hall to the front room where he'd talked with Thorvald. No one was in it, but through the open front door, he could see Thorvald standing on the porch, flanked by Moran and Paige. Thorvald and Moran each wielded a large and extremely powerful flashlight whose beams swept over the compound. Beyond them, two men dashed across the lit ground, away from the direction of the mine, and the screaming started again.

Just as the two men disappeared at the left side of the door frame, Thorvald, Moran, and Paige shied back. A second later, Halvor, now freed from his rock, lumbered across the frame. It was obviously headed for the mine and had a man gripped in each hand —Lyle from one, the smoker from the other. Lyle dangled lifelessly, but the smoker kicked, struggled, and screamed until Halvor casually bashed his brains out on the ground. A moment later, the monster disappeared around the shoulder of the mountain that hid the mine's adit.

Guthrie was thankful it was night, the monochrome moonlight hiding the gruesome details. At that moment, Paige noticed him and started to swing his weapon around. Thorvald turned to see what the Bugle Boy was aiming at, and pushed the rifle down.

"It's all right, Mr. Paige," he said. "Ah. Mr. Guthrie. I'm glad you've joined us." He actually smiled as he waved Guthrie onto the porch. "Now you see firsthand how effective my weapon is."

"You certain that thing is *your* weapon? It just killed two of your own troops."

"If they can't get out of the way," the renegade priest said, "they aren't of much use to me. As for Halvor, don't worry. I've chosen my location well. He can leave the mine if he chooses, but it would be impossible for him to find adequate shelter before daybreak without being seen. I have him trapped here. He's at my mercy, and he knows it."

"The captor is himself a captive," Guthrie said.

"Perhaps," Thorvald said, giving Guthrie an appraising look. "But in my case, I get two for one: you as well as Halvor." He jerked his head toward Paige. "Take him back to his room and watch him. I might need him."

As Paige shoved Guthrie toward the door, Moran stepped off the porch and yelled at several men hiding behind what cover they'd found—none of it adequate. Not against a troll. A tank might do, but little else would besides distance.

Guthrie walked across the front room to the hall entrance, Paige jabbing the muzzle of his AR into the small of his back. When they entered the room, Paige shoved Guthrie toward the cot.

"Sit down, you fuck. If you get up, I'll shoot you, and Thorvald won't be here to stop me."

"Do I have to explain again that if you shoot me, Thorvald will feed you to Halvor?" Guthrie asked blandly and saw the blood leave Paige's face. "Besides, I gotta take a piss."

"You can hold it til you bust, for all I care."

In answer, Guthrie strode to another of the cots, this one piled with Bugle Boy kits, and started to unzip.

"What the fuck are you doing?" Paige yelled, waving his rifle threateningly.

"I told you I gotta piss," Guthrie said. "This looks like a convenient place where it won't run all over."

"Stop! Stop! Okay, I'll take you to the bathroom."

The trip to the john was short but unpleasant since Paige kept poking Guthrie painfully with the AR. With Paige observing, Guthrie relieved himself and zipped up.

"Ain't you gonna flush it?" Paige demanded as Guthrie turned toward the door.

"Normally I would, but for you boys, I'll make an exception. You're lucky I didn't piss on the seat,"

Paige snarled and made as if he was going to shoot Guthrie, but Guthrie just shook his head, shouldered past the Bugle Boy, and left the room. Paige was right on his heels, the sound of the toilet flushing in the background.

"I need some water," Guthrie said.

"So you can make me flush your piss again? Fuck that."

Instead of answering, Guthrie turned into the kitchen, which lay on the other side of the bathroom.

"Get back here!" Paige ordered.

Ignoring him. Guthrie went to the refrigerator, opened it, and pulled out a bottle of water. He opened it, took a big swig, then grabbed a couple of energy bars off the counter. He tore one open and quickly ate it, chasing it with another gulp of water. It helped top him off food-wise after the sandwich earlier.

"Okay," he told Paige.

In the room, Guthrie looked out the window and saw that the two guards who'd been outside before Halvor freed itself from the slab had been replaced by a single man.

"Back on the cot," Paige ordered, but Guthrie ignored him.

Paige was the sort who could be needled, and the sort who would react to needling with carelessness. But he also would be too fearful of reprisals to hurt or kill Guthrie as long as Guthrie didn't give him an overt excuse. With nothing much else to do at the moment, Guthrie was only too happy to wield the pin.

So far, Halvor had killed and eaten at least two of Thorvald's men, and Guthrie wondered how many more it would take before the rest of the Bugle Boys fled in terror. Truth was, Guthrie wished he could flee, too, now that he'd seen what Halvor could do to a man. And he'd seen the pile of offal back in Houston that had been Buddy Horton. No way he wanted that for himself. But there also was no way he was going to let down Tereba. He owed the old man too much, and he'd sent Guthrie to take care of this situation personally, and that was what he was going to do. If Halvor or the Bugle Boys didn't get him first.

Things outside quieted a lot in the next hour, and ignoring the angry heat emanating from Paige, Guthrie lay down on the cot and tried to sleep. He actually managed to doze for a few hours, mostly because he was too tired to let his brain keep running over the situation. He needed to recharge, and he did feel better when he woke an hour or so before dawn light broke over the mountains' eastern ridge.

Paige didn't look so chipper after staying awake all night, watching a sleeping man.

"I gotta use the bathroom again," Guthrie said as he got up and went to the door.

This time, Paige didn't argue or threaten, but his eyes held hatred for Guthrie—for his lack of control over Guthrie. Or maybe he'd been holding his own piss all night. Soon after, another guard replaced Paige. This one wasn't as belligerent as Paige, but he was more taciturn, evading all of Guthrie's attempts at conversation. At last, Guthrie quit trying and just sat there and waited.

It wasn't until well after noon when the door opened and Paige and a second Bugle Boy ushered him to the front room, the room guard following. Thorvald was behind his desk, Moran standing nearby. The renegade priest looked up as Guthrie entered.

"I've been down into the mine," he said. "I had to ascertain what Halvor is doing down there."

"I don't imagine there's much *to* do down an empty mine shaft."

"For us, maybe," Thorvald chuckled. "But he's a sort of rock creature. I found him making a thorough inventory of the place."

"Looking for a back entrance or a way to dig himself deeper?"

Thorvald shrugged.

"He's a troll. Who can fathom what goes on in the mind of such a creature?"

"Oh, I think it's pretty forthcoming about what's on its mind," Guthrie said. "It's just pretty disagreeable stuff."

"The better for my purposes," Thorvald replied. "He knows what I want of him, and he's agreed to do his part."

"You trust it to support your idiotic plan to let it loose in the Mall of America? That would be suicide."

"Not really. Trolls expect to die for their rampages. And they have no fear of death, since they don't actually die but simply revert to their unmanifested shadow existence, waiting for the chance to reemerge and do it all over again. And he knows I will immediately aid him in returning as soon as he dies. I'll even use the same crack since I have it in my possession. The Mall of America offers him a rare opportunity to claim as many victims as possible. Besides, What choice does he have? He can rampage around out here and be destroyed by the military without claiming many victims besides cattle. I offer him apotheosis with repeat performances."

"So you're going to just keep it down there in the mine, feeding it, until you're ready to launch your attack?"

"I wish you would stop referring to Halvor as 'it.' He's a sentient being like you and me."

"Not quite like us," Guthrie reminded him. "Halvor showed me that it is effectively genderless."

"All right. Have it your way. It changes nothing. We will remain here, nicely and quietly, until the week before Christmas, when the shopping season is in full swing. Don't you think it appropriate that I intend to destroy Christianity on the eve of the birthday of its founder?"

"Clever."

"By Christmas, Halvor should be full size and far more powerful than he now is. We'll ship him to Minnesota in the boxcar then deliver him to the mall in a rental truck. He can sneak in through the loading docks, and once he's inside the mall, well...."

"And you have no compunction about the deaths of all those innocent people? I agree that Christianity is a pretty limited and hypocritical religion, but if you're going to kill a bunch of people because of that, you might as well try to kill the whole world."

"You are, of course, correct. But one could legitimately argue that there are no innocent people or that innocents always pay the price for war. And this is war, Mr. Guthrie. A war for the soul of humanity."

"Religious wars for the soul of humanity are always the most corrupt," Guthrie said, looking Thorvald in the eye. "But you didn't bring me out here to chat ethics, since you clearly have none."

"Perhaps my ethics are beyond you," Thorvald said, stiffening. "But you're right when you say I didn't bring you out to chat. Have you thought about my offer of employment?"

"Before I answer, tell me about your accomplices in your own cabal. The priests. You said there were eight of them and you fed the three dissenters to Halvor. Where are the other five? Why aren't any of them here?"

"They are elsewhere, performing other necessary tasks."

"Pushing up daisies from piles of troll shit?"

"You don't know what you're talking about. They simply went into hiding, just like me."

"That's not what Bertrando Galtero says."

"Bah. You're putting words in his mouth."

"Not at all. He admits to killing three priests in Italy and disposing of the bodies by giving them to you. Who conveniently has a body disposal device. They must have been those first three who couldn't stomach an alliance with a monster. So what about the other five Galtero brought you. Alive."

Thorvald shrugged dispassionately.

"Halvor required high-quality food for his overseas trip. Food that didn't need much feeding itself and didn't take up much space."

"Itself," Guthrie repeated then glanced at Moran. "What do you think about the longevity of Thorvald's accomplices? Aren't you an accomplice, too?"

"Sometimes you have to get rid of dead weight," Moran said in a monotone. "They were weak."

"Mr. Moran has nothing to worry about," Thorvald said. "He has ongoing and perpetual worth. The utility of my cabal had ended, and they knew too much. Sooner or later, the Church authorities would put two and two together and come up with at least one of them. I simply became another of them. One of the disappeared."

"Yeah," Guthrie said, shaking his head, thinking, you wish. "You see, I have problems with that. Loyalty needs to go both ways. Up and down the chain of command. I don't see that here, so I'll have to decline. Besides, you can't pay me more than my current employer does, because he pays me in something more valuable than money and power. And he's a lot scarier than you'll ever be, even with Halvor at your side. Plus, I don't like you, and I...." Guthrie paused reflectively, then shrugged. "I respect him."

"You were going to say 'like,' weren't you?" Thorvald asked.

Guthrie said nothing.

"Interesting," Thorvald went on. "You respect him, but you don't like him. You also fear him."

"I didn't say that."

"You didn't have to. He must be quite an individual. I'd like to meet him one day."

"No, you wouldn't," Guthrie said with a twisted smile.

"No matter," Thorvald said with a wave of his hand. "You won't be the one to introduce us." He nodded his head toward the door. "Since you won't join us, Halvor wants me to take you to him, and that's what I'm going to do." He turned to Moran. "We're taking him into the mine. If he resists, you have my permission to hurt him, but don't kill him. Halvor prefers his meat fresh."

"Okay," Moran said, then he jabbed a finger at Paige. "You're with me."

Paige shied back.

"I'm not going in there," he said. "You saw what it did to Lyle and Joe. It's just as likely to snatch me as well as him." He jabbed the barrel of his rifle toward Guthrie.

"I'm getting sick of your whining, Paige," Moran said harshly. "You'll do as you're told, Here, take one of these." He opened a cardboard box sitting on the floor beside the desk, pulled out another of the large, powerful flashlights, and held it out to Paige.

"Just stay away from Halvor," he said. "If you think you're in danger, you can shine this in his face. It has a hundred thousand lumens, so careful. It'll burn your skin or fry your eyeballs up close."

"The light isn't powerful enough to freeze him," Thorvald soothed, "but it'll stiffen him up where it hits and slow him down. But he won't hurt you. He wants him." He indicated Guthrie.

Paige seemed unconvinced, but he took the flashlight. Moran gave a second to Thorvald and kept a third for himself.

"Don't I get one?" Guthrie asked. "I'm not sure Paige can handle something that size."

Paige slammed him on the upper right back with the butt of his rifle. Guthrie staggered, then he turned and stared hard at the Bugle Boy. The man, fear in the back of his eyes, raised his rifle muzzle toward Guthrie, but Moran pushed it aside.

"Paige!" Moran's command wasn't loud, but it was sharp.

"Sorry, boss," Paige said, his tone not at all apologetic. "I just hate fuckers like him. They think they own you."

"Stay focused," Moran said, and Paige nodded stiffly.

"Better to watch Halvor take care of him," Thorvald said as he rounded the desk, walked to the door, and opened it.

"Yeah," Paige said to Guthrie, a smirk crawling across his mouth. "Better. Hope you have a nice dinner date with that monster, motherfucker."

"Mr. Paige," Thorvald admonished. "Please don't refer to Halvor as a monster."

"Pardon me, Mr. Thorvald, but you treat that thing like kin. All I see is a fucking giant that killed Lyle and Joe right in front of me and took them into that mine to eat them. I'm telling you, I ain't gonna be next."

"Calm down, Paige. The only person who is 'next' is Guthrie. So get yourself together." Thorvald turned to Moran. "Bring him along."

Without waiting to see if Moran complied, Thorvald went through the door and across the porch. By the time he'd gotten less than twenty feet from the house, Moran and Paige had caught up, pushing Guthrie ahead of them. Paige carried his AR, but Moran was armed only with his sidearm. He was smart enough to know that the carbine was useless against the troll. It might temporarily hurt the thing, but it wouldn't stop it from slaughtering you.

The sun was about three hours past its zenith as Guthrie and his captors's shadows marched with them along the gently sloping ground, toward the shoulder of the mountain around which the mine entrance lay. Along the ground in front of them stretched a heavy-gauge electrical cable that trailed like a long, skinny, orange snake toward the mine.

"Why is it hiding in there?" Guthrie asked as they led him down the slope toward the adit. "What happened to all that rampaging across the countryside? Isn't that what it's supposed to do? Isn't that what you wanted?"

"Shut up," Moran snarled.

Born under a bridge. Only seen outside its boxcar at night. Hiding in the mine. In the darkness. Stiffens under the glare of powerful flashlights and freezes in the sun. It didn't take a logician—or a detective—to figure that one out. The troll was allergic to sunlight—at least to the direct rays of the sun. Figures, Guthrie thought. It might take that powerful and potent a cleansing agent to eradicate a moral stain like a troll.

They passed by the barn and corral, and the electrical cable they'd been following split, with the secondary line running toward the pump house beneath the rickety windmill. A thick hum emanated from the structure.

Inside of two minutes, they'd rounded the mountain's rocky shoulder, and Guthrie could see the adit some fifty feet away. The canvas tarp that had protected the opening from the sun during the day was gone, revealing a squarish oval opening, about ten feet tall and eight wide, the edges flaring out into the surrounding rock. It didn't go straight into the mountainside but angled in at about forty-five degrees, with a slight downward slope.

A rusted old narrow-gauge rail line led into the tunnel, tracks littered with chunks of rock, whether fallen from the hillside above the opening or discarded after being hauled up out of the shaft, he couldn't tell. About ten feet from the opening, lay the overturned iron mine cart that Lyle and the smoker had tied the cow to. It was on its side, wheels and undercarriage rusting past usability even in the dry air. The orange electrical cable continued down the passage between the set of mine rails. There was no sign of Halvor's slab.

Paige shoved Guthrie ahead, into the darkness beyond.

25

ONCE GUTHRIE WAS OUT OF the sunlight and into the mine, the shaft wasn't as dark as it had seemed from the bright outside. The electrical cable fed a string of scattered light bulbs that stretched down the tunnel, dimly lighting its length.

The ceiling was supported by timber bridges every ten or fifteen feet. From what Guthrie could see in the light from the string of bulbs, the ceiling was mostly solid slabs, with the bridges spanning the frequent cracks between them.

"How deep is this hole you all crawled out of?" Guthrie asked, only to receive another blow from Paige.

"Mr. Moran told you to shut up."

I guess I'll just have to wait to see, Guthrie thought, as his captors forced him ahead of them, deeper into the mine.

At about a hundred and fifty feet, the rails ended and the tunnel narrowed to a more angular shape, though it remained wide enough for two men to walk abreast. The sides of the tunnel became rougher and more irregular, and the passage began sloping more steeply down and sharply to the left, deeper into the heart of the mountain.

As they went, the temperature gradually dropped a few degrees. They descended for a minute longer, still angling to the left, when Thorvald stopped them.

"Slow now, Guthrie. We're almost there."

"Is that Daddy I hear?" a large voice rumbled from below. "Did you bring me a snack?"

Guthrie eased forward, rounded a sharp corner supported by beams, and saw a large space open before him. It was dimly lit by electric bulbs and was like a rough, ill-shaped pocket in the heart of the mountain, about fifty feet across in any direction. The ragged ceiling angled up at one point to about twenty feet toward the back, but mostly it was about ten to fifteen feet high. Chunks of rock rubble fallen from the ceiling lay strewn across the cave's floor.

Halvor reclined against the far wall, roughly beneath the ceiling's high point. Propped against the wall to its left was the slab holding the crack it had oozed out of. Off to its right sat a pile of bones, some animal, some human, and some with meat and tissue still clinging. A scattering of more bones littered the floor around the pile, and an intact body lay on top of the heap. It was Joe, the smoker. Except for his brains, which were scattered over the ground outside. There was no sign of Lyle. Or maybe some of those bones....

"Remarkable, isn't it?" Thorvald said, thankfully interrupting Guthrie's train of thought. "It seemed that Mr. Dunton unwittingly tunneled along a crack and right into a natural cave. The deed states that it was formed by an ancient earthquake. It makes a fine room for my boy. Isn't that right, Halvor?"

He stepped toward the troll, Moran following.

"Move," Paige ordered, jabbing Guthrie in the lower back with his gun. Guthrie stepped forward, noticing that Paige carefully kept him between the troll and himself.

"Well, hello, Guthrie," the troll said, ignoring the renegade priest. "You'll pardon me if I don't stand to greet you. As you can see, the ceiling is a little low for me."

"You're fine right there," Guthrie said. He looked around the space then back at the troll. "I see you brought your slab down here."

The troll glanced at the slab.

"But of course. It is dear old Mom, after all." The troll gave a wistful chuckle. "How convenient when your only portrait of your mom *is* your mom."

"What are you doing down in this hole?" Guthrie asked. "What happened to rampaging across the countryside, eating everyone you come into contact with?"

"Daddy assures me that there just aren't enough people out here in West Texas to make it worthwhile. And I wouldn't want to get caught out in the open in this barren countryside."

"Bad for the complexion, I hear."

Halvor chuckled.

"That's what I like about you, Guthrie. You treat me like just one of the fellows. And as one fellow to another, I'll confess that I've given the matter a lot of thought since my journey here from the Old World. And I have to say that this," it raised up its laptop, which looked like a toy in its huge, gnarled fist, "has been of tremendous assistance. And you, too, have helped open my vistas. I now realized that rampaging across the countryside is the old way. Obsolete. I have a new idea for the New World: rampaging through cities. Through whole societies."

"How's that going to work when you keep eating all the Bugle Boys?" Guthrie asked.

"Halvor has promised not to eat any more of Mr. Moran's men," Thorvald said. "Thanks to your interference, he understands how valuable they are to our effort."

"Is that right, Halvor?" Guthrie asked. "You're now going to be a good little troll and not eat any more Bugle Boys?"

Halvor laughed.

"I like you, Guthrie. I really do. Too bad you're not a troll. You'd make a good one." It laughed again. "Or even better, a really bad one." It stared appraisingly at him.

"Of course," Thorvald went on, "if you'd severely wounded one of them, well…." He shrugged. "Human flesh is best for a troll, isn't that right, my boy?"

"That's right, Daddy."

"Is that right, Moran?" Guthrie asked.

"The men know the score."

"So," Guthrie said to Halvor. "You'd eat this cretin behind me?" He jerked a thumb back over his shoulder at Paige.

"Enough of this shit," Paige snarled. "Eat this bastard, and be done with it."

"Yes," Halvor grinned and licked its lips. "Let's eat."

"Time for dinner, Guthrie," Paige ground out, and the sound of sudden motion came from behind Guthrie as the Bugle Boy stepped forward, slamming the butt of his rifle at the back of Guthrie's head.

He wasn't expecting Guthrie to crouch and spin, rolling back beneath the rifle butt, snaking his right arm around Paige's right arm, and entangling it. Instantly, he twisted Paige around, between himself and the troll. As the man rotated, confused expression quickly turning to anger, Guthrie grabbed the carbine's butt and forward grip and gave a quick twist, ripping the gun from Paige's hands. With the man off balance, Guthrie's sudden surge forward with a two-handed push slammed the rifle into his chest, sending him stumbling backward, straight at the troll. Paige twisted and lifted his arms to stave off immanent impact with the creature, a scream growing in his throat. If he thought any of that might help him, he was mistaken. One of Halvor's hands snatched out with lightning speed and grabbed him.

"Not him!" Thorvald shrieked. "Guthrie! Take Guthrie!"

He was too late. Maybe with the troll, he'd always be too late. In a second, Paige's terrified scream was cut off by a hideous wet crunching as the troll bit off his head and tucked it into its cheek. This was followed by a thick slurping sound as the troll's mouth enveloped the stump of Paige's neck and sucked the blood as it spurted out.

Even before it had, Guthrie, made the most of the confusion by whirling behind Thorvald, keeping the renegade priest between him and Moran, who, after his initial shock, had drawn his sidearm.

"Drop it," Guthrie said, jamming the AR's barrel into Thorvald's jawline hard enough to make the renegade priest cry out.

Moran didn't drop it, but he didn't shoot. Not with Thorvald between Guthrie and his muzzle.

"Or what? You'll never get out of here alive."

"That wasn't going to happen anyway, so that's no threat," Guthrie said. "But if I don't get to the entrance alive and unmolested, your meal ticket here doesn't, either." He turned to the troll, who was sucking Paige's body dry of blood, calmly watching what occurred. "Hear that, Halvor? What's going to happen to you if you don't have your Daddy's financial backing? Somehow, I don't think you'll want to spend the rest of your existence in this cave, feeding on wild cattle and unable to go anywhere to do any real rampaging."

Halvor lowered Paige's body then crunched up and swallowed the head that had been tucked into its cheek.

"One hole is as good as another," it snarled.

"Maybe, but you're already complaining about having to eat cows all the time. Before long, you won't be unable to resist picking off a human here and a human there. The pickings around here will be sparse, and that'll be a disadvantage. People go missing in a place like this, somebody will start looking for the reason. When they find you, it won't be long before the military comes in and blasts you to bits. What happens to all your big plans, then? Hell, you'll never get out of this barren county alive, much less rampage across the countryside or any city."

The troll belched then callously tossed the corpse onto a the growing charnel pit at the back of the cavern.

"Sorry, Daddy," it said to Thorvald. "I just couldn't help myself. Human flesh is just too tasty to let it go. It's my entire raison d'être. You know that." It smiled, bloody drool running from the corners of its mouth. Then it looked at Guthrie. "Strangely enough, failure tastes best. Thank you for that tasty snack. Now, down to business. You have a temporary advantage, it appears. Very well. We will not pursue."

"Put it down," Guthrie ordered Moran again.

Moran still hesitated.

"Give him what he wants, Brian," Thorvald said. "How far can he go, anyway?"

Moran grudgingly lowered his pistol and bent to lay it on the cavern floor.

"Not there," Guthrie said. "Throw it over here." Moran complied, and Guthrie picked up the .45 and jammed it beneath his belt.

"Phone, too."

Moran tossed the phone over, and Guthrie crushed it beneath his heel.

"Backup," he ordered.

Moran hesitated, and Guthrie snorted.

"A man like you always carries a backup. You can toss it over, or I can kill you. Your choice."

Looking sour, Moran bent and carefully pulled a pistol from an ankle holster and tossed it to Guthrie. His expression said he'd kill Guthrie the first chance he got. Guthrie felt the same way and wanted to follow through now, but he didn't want to provoke an attack by the troll.

Keeping the AR pressed into Thorvald's neck, Guthrie picked up the pistol—a subcompact Glock .380—and stuck it in his waistband, too, wishing he could loosen his belt a notch and momentarily thankful for not eating as much as usual the last few days. His stomached suddenly growled at the thought of food.

"Phone," he hissed in Thorvald's ear.

The priest handed Guthrie his phone, and it went the way of Moran's.

"What now?" Moran snapped.

"Over there. Beside Halvor."

Moran glanced at the troll, dripping gore, a paranoid look in his normally steely eyes. He hesitated.

"Move," Guthrie barked.

"Don't worry, Brian," the troll said, picking at its teeth with a dirty fingernail. "I won't hurt you. We have to work together to rescue Daddy."

"So much for your monster's promise not to eat any more of your men," Guthrie said to Thorvald. To Moran, he said, I'm taking Thorvald to the opening. If I hear the slightest whisper of sound of pursuit, he's dead. Give me the flashlight," Guthrie ordered Thorvald and practically snatched the flashlight out of the renegade priest's hand. "You fuck with me for one second," Guthrie hissed in Thorvald's ear, "and I'll kill you. Then where will your boy be? Controlled by Moran? Dead inside a week?"

"I understand." The renegade priest nodded. "What are you going to do?" His voice shook.

In answer, Guthrie switched on the flashlight and twitched it up to shine in the monster's face for a second, then turned the beam to the floor. Halvor growled and shied back, a forearm shielding its face, its already horrible features disfigured with rage and frustration.

"I see you don't like the light," Guthrie said to Halvor when he was done.

"Who says I don't?" the troll snarled, but the words came out oddly, like those spoken by someone whose mouth is numb from a visit to the dentist. Guthrie realized the light had stiffened its jaw.

In answer, Guthrie twitched the flashlight beam in the troll's direction again, and the creature immediately flinched back and held up its hands to protect its face. After a moment, the hands and portions of its chest looked gray.

"No!" it howled, though it didn't try to lunge forward.

"Stop!" Thorvald wailed, pushing down Guthrie's arm. "Turn it off! You're hurting him!"

Ignoring Thorvald, Guthrie switched off the light.

"Don't lie to me, Halvor," he said. "Thorvald already hinted that you don't like powerful light. That's why you're hiding down here in the dark."

"I have delicate skin," the troll admitted. "So what?"

"So, this," Guthrie said, giving it another brief blast with the flashlight that sent it cowering back and turning away.

"Enough, enough!" Thorvald implored, clutching at Guthrie's arm. "I'll tell you. You aren't getting out of here, anyway. Trolls are strictly nocturnal."

Guthrie turned the light away from the troll, who continued to crouch against the far wall.

"Seem's like a little more than that."

"Okay," the troll muttered like a guilty ten-year-old being forced to tell the truth. "We're allergic to sunlight."

"All corrupt things are."

"Corrupt?" The troll turned then and laughed. "Not at all. I'm destined for great things."

"I'm sure you have something in mind," Guthrie replied, and the monster looked at him almost shyly.

"Oh, yes. Definitely. Come a little closer, won't you? Let me whisper it in your ear."

The hands on the ends of the long, knotty arms clutched but were still too stiff to grab anything. Even so, Guthrie kept the renegade priest in front of him.

"Stay back," Guthrie warned, then he glanced behind him.

He had to get out. Moran was presently unarmed, but there still was another pistol belted to Paige's corpse.

"Go get Paige's pistol. Careful, now."

Moran, obviously reluctant, did.

"Field strip it," Guthrie said, "And toss the parts."

The magazine, slide, barrel, and spring went off into the dimness, leaving Moran holding a paperweight shaped like a pistol butt. Essentially unarmed, Moran would have to rely on the troll to take care of Guthrie. That didn't bode well for Guthrie, but the fact that the light had stiffened the creature a little might give him a chance to get to the entrance without dragging Thorvald along.

Once there, though, he couldn't actually let the thing chase him out. Not with the guards outside. But wait…. Maybe he could use the thing's own power against itself. It all hinged on how much Thorvald had told the Bugle Boys about the troll. He was betting not much. Would-be dictators don't reveal their hidden sources of power, they just wield it.

So, there was a good chance that the men outside didn't know the troll couldn't stand direct sunlight. If they thought the troll was hot on his heels when he came out of the mine, maybe they'd be more concerned about it and themselves than about him. And he had Paige's rifle and two handguns. Maybe he could escape, and if he did, maybe he could find Gil.

A lot of maybes, he thought. Might as well get on with them.

Realizing that Thorvald would now be more of a burden than a benefit, Guthrie hit the troll in the hands again with the flashlight beam, shoved the renegade priest toward it, and fled. The last thing he saw was the troll catching up Thorvald and carefully enfolding him in its grayed and stoney embrace.

"Don't scream, Daddy," it said, holding the renegade priest up to its bloody face. "You called this my room, but I like to think of it as my womb. It's time to think about a family."

26

AHEAD OF GUTHRIE WAS THE rough oval of the adit. Fresh air. The light at the end of the tunnel. But not yet. Aiming Paige's AR toward the opening, he slid down the wall, keeping back in the shadows. None of the guards were visible, but any number of them could be waiting around the toe of the mountain that masked the adit from the house. The ones who hadn't gone down the troll's gullet, that was.

Guthrie knew one thing for certain: He couldn't stay here. It wouldn't be long before the troll or Moran came up behind him. And even if the troll couldn't go outside the mine right now, surely it would be able to snatch Guthrie if he stayed in the shadows close to the opening. And if it couldn't, night would fall all too soon.

Guthrie considered his options. The remaining Bugle Boys outside had no idea of what had just transpired in the mine. As far as they were concerned, Guthrie was literally dead meat. But if Thorvald, Moran, and Paige didn't come strolling out within a reasonable amount of time, they might get suspicious and investigate.

With at least three of them, there was no way Guthrie could confront them head-on. They had him outgunned, and they had plenty of reserve ammo. All Guthrie had was a single magazine in the AR and one in each of the two pistols in his belt. Not to mention the troll and Moran at his back and the coming darkness. Which, he noted, glancing at the sky, wasn't more than an hour away, at least here in the shadowed lee of the ridge above. Two or three hours longer before true darkness settled in.

He briefly thought about going down the creek bed that led down the western slope of the mountains. Even if he was spotted, he'd have some cover from the piles of spoils deposited in that direction. But escaping that way was no escape at all, even if he eluded the Bugle Boys. There was nothing to the west but miles of downslope and rugged desert and, finally, seven miles distant as the crow flies, a lone truck stop on I-10. Which he'd never reach in the time he had. Not across the kind of terrain that lay out there, where the actual walking distance was probably three times farther. Besides, it would be a fool's errand to try to outrun the troll in the dark. It was a creature of darkness. The darkness was its domain and friend. Plus it already had demonstrated it could follow his scent.

The closest thing to civilization was the rail line to the east—five miles as the crow flies. But the place where the rail crew was working was at least a several-hour walk from the ranch house: across the shallow but very rugged trough of the valley, up the far rim of mountains, then down to the desert floor, with another four miles across rough ground after that. It would be impossible for him to make it there before dark, and by then, the crew would have left for the night.

He had to do something. All too soon, Halvor would be hot on his trail. He'd gotten under the troll's skin, and he was a threat to it. The only real threat. And he'd escaped, sort of, and neither it nor Thorvald could afford to let him go. And now Moran had a personal beef with him, too.

But Guthrie had no intention of running. At least no farther than he was forced to. His only focus was on escaping the troll then killing it, and he had to effect the escape part immediately. There was no time to waste engaging in a probably futile gunfight with any of the guards who remained. Instead, he had to look at them not as enemies but as impediments. You didn't have to kill impediments, just remove them.

First, he had to assess the situation, and he couldn't do that from here. Besides, he was beginning to hear thick scuffling sounds from deeper in the mine. It sounded like Halvor might be crawling through the narrow shaft toward the adit, and Moran wouldn't be far behind.

Guthrie had to take the chance that none of the guards were on the slope above the adit. Cautiously, he edged out of the opening, looking up as the slope above gradually became visible. Finally, he could see that the slope was empty. Moran didn't have the manpower to mount a guard up there, and probably none of the Bugle Boys would take it on their own initiative to station themselves that close to the adit, especially after the incidents of last night. It's one thing to have a monster locked in a steel box and tethered to a slab of stone and quite another to have it chasing after you.

Keeping close to the rock wall flanking the left side of the adit, Guthrie crept to the shoulder of rock and peeked around it. He could see three guards patrolling the compound—if you could call it patrolling. One was lounging against a pile of discarded and rusting mine machinery, and the second was near the barn, and the third was about fifty feet away, pissing against a boulder. None of them were looking toward the mine. Kelly sat in the shade of the front porch, gradually scanning the compound, though at the moment, thankfully, his attention wasn't on the mine.

Guthrie didn't know how many men Thorvald originally had, but he'd never seen more than ten at one time besides Moran and Fleming. One was in a hospital with a broken knee, and three others were now troll food. That left two unaccounted for. Most likely, they were down at the depot, guarding the boxcar and railcar mover. That was borne out by the fact that only one of the Suburbans was parked in front of the bunkhouse, next to the Ford dually, now un-tethered from its trailer. Guthrie wondered how long any of the Bugle Boys would stay once they knew that Paige had followed their companions down the troll's gullet. Not long, he thought, especially if they believed it had eaten Thorvald and Moran, too.

More scuffling came from the mine, louder this time, accompanied by a thick grunt of effort and a clatter of stone-on-stone. The monster had grown almost too large to squirm its way through the narrower stretches of the tunnel, and for the moment at least, its hands were still partly ossified.

I'll have to remember that, Guthrie thought. Apparently trolls can suffer stress and maybe even get tired. He almost chuckled, but what was coming up the shaft was no laughing matter.

From behind the noise, came Moran's muffled yell.

"If you get out of the way, I can get the motherfucker!"

"Forget it, Moran," the troll snarled. "He's mine. You stay back."

In that moment, Halvor's face appeared from the gloom, and the troll spotted him.

"Guthrie!" it bellowed, lunging forward. But it couldn't let its flesh pass from the dark side of the shadow line into the direct sunlight. It brought itself up short, face twisted into a horrible cross between a grimace and a grin. "Tonight, Guthrie! As soon as the sun goes down!"

Moran's face appeared in a gap between the troll's side and the stone wall.

"Get out of the way!" Moran yelled as he spotted Guthrie and tried to stick the barrel of a pistol through the crack. He must have had a second backup somewhere. Or maybe Paige had.

But now was not the time for contemplation. Guthrie had to act, knowing that sometimes the actions of one enemy can be used against another. He had to play his hand perfectly, making the remaining guards more afraid of the troll than of him. He sent a burst of rifle fire in the troll's direction, sweeping the barrel toward Moran, who fell back behind the safety of the troll's bulk. Guthrie knew the bullets wouldn't hurt the troll much, but they'd annoy it, and he did it as much for dramatic effect as to thwart Moran. The troll roared, and Guthrie darted around the shoulder of rock, turning and firing back at the troll.

The Bugle Boys outside were instantly on the alert, raising their weapons. Kelly came off the porch in a crouch and the others turned and leveled their rifles, but before they had a chance to do more than that, Guthrie fired again. The bullets sent chips flying from the shoulder of rock in a cloud of dirt and dust.

"It ate them!" he screamed as he ran. "It ate them all! It's coming right now!"

As if on cue, Halvor bellowed again.

"I'll get you, Guthrie!"

If the guards thought they might take cover and shoot at Guthrie, the troll's enraged voice right at the mine entrance changed their minds. In seconds, they were dashing toward the vehicles parked near the front of the bunkhouse. The two who'd been patrolling reached the vehicles first, jumped into the Suburban, and panicked, sped off, leaving Kelly and the other to take the dually, which quickly vanished in the Suburban's dust, raising a pall of its own. Inside a minute, both vehicles were out of sight along the winding dirt road.

Guthrie wondered how far they'd go, and if they'd come back. They might believe their paycheck, Thorvald, was dead, and the only future for them at the ranch was to become troll shit. If so, they wouldn't be back. Considering how fast they'd left, they could probably be in El Paso within the hour. But the stronger possibility was that they'd turn around once they realized they'd been tricked. No doubt Moran would contact them after he realized they were gone. That could be sooner than later, but it wouldn't be much later, in any case. Guthrie was glad he'd smashed Moran and Thorvald's phones, but they might have others in the ranch house.

Guthrie glanced at the sun, which was beginning its descent. He had about an hour before the sun dropped below the rim of mountains above the house and mine, casting the entire valley and the land beyond into shadow. He doubted that Halvor could go far before full nightfall, but the shadow cast by the mountains might be sufficient for it to roam the ranch compound. It had come out of the mine, into the shadows, to try to snatch Guthrie, only halting at the line of direct sunlight. It was time Guthrie worried about himself, and he didn't have a lot of options.

Or time. Halvor was still howling from the adit, sometimes in wordless rage, sometimes with culinary references, both punctuated by curses with Guthrie's name attached. Guthrie turned that way and saw Moran peer around the shoulder of rock. A quick burst of rifle fire sent the man ducking back, but Guthrie couldn't afford to spend the rest of the day—the rest of his life—keeping Moran at bay. Not with the seriously depleted magazine in the AR and the troll just waiting for darkness.

The only vehicle the Bugle Boys had left when they fled was Thorvald's Mercedes, but that was as useless as the abandoned and rusting mine equipment. A Mercedes of this caliber couldn't be hot-wired. He'd need the key. If he was lucky, it would be in Thorvald's desk, along with Guthrie's phone, gun, and other possessions, but could he get to what he needed before Moran came after him?

At least there'd be more ammo inside. Taking the chance since there was no other option, he dashed to the house and burst through the door. Keeping an eye on the sweep of outside visible through the open doorway and the front windows, he searched Thorvald's desk, but the Mercedes key wasn't there. Thorvald must have it on him, and there was no way Guthrie was going back into that mine to ask for it.

But Guthrie's phone was there, along with the other items he'd carried on him, including his pistol and spare magazines. The phone battery had been dead before he'd been captured. Nor did he find any other phones, and now he kicked himself for not confiscating Moran and Thorvald's instead of destroying them.

Guthrie was stuck. He couldn't drive out, he couldn't call Espinoza, and Sierra Blanca was too far to walk in the remaining daylight. The troll would surely catch him out in the open, and that would not bode well for Guthrie. Plus, he had Moran to worry about. The house, bunkhouse, and barn were too flimsy to provide shelter. Halvor could tear any of them apart in minutes. That left only the boxcar and railcar mover down at the ranch depot, about a mile and a half as the crow flies. but the rugged ridges and hills in the valley and the high, steep slopes above the rail line made direct travel impossible.

Going by the road, the only feasible route, was nearly a five-mile jaunt, most of it in darkness. He seriously questioned his ability to make it to the ranch depot in time, even if he could find adequate shelter there.

Guthrie wasn't very worried that Halvor might try to leave the area during the night, believing it could find enough shelter before daybreak. Now he understood Thorvald's cleverness in locating the troll here. It might be a monster, but it was canny. It could roam around, get the lie of the mountain valley and the lowlands around the small range, but it had everything it needed for the moment: the mine for a home, plenty of cattle in the nearby corral, and the Bugle Boys to take care of it. And it had hinted at some sort of plan that sounded more long-range than a short and ultimately unsatisfying rampage across a pretty barren countryside.

It also had Thorvald. At least Guthrie assumed it still had him since Moran was alive. Halvor wouldn't eat either of them. Without Thorvald and his financial resources, the troll was effectively trapped, and without Moran's muscle, Thorvald was hamstrung. As soon as the troll's food supply—men and cattle alike—was gone, it would be forced to leave, make its presence known, and be too-soon destroyed.

Besides, the troll called Thorvald Daddy, and Guthrie supposed that was technically true. Maybe Thorvald's paternal affiliation with the troll, no matter how sick it was, might save him, assuming trolls felt anything but desire for mayhem, destruction, and human flesh.

A movement down the slope attracted his attention. It was Moran, dashing from the shoulder of the mountain toward the corner of the barn. The distance was too far for a good shot at a moving target, but Guthrie sent the final rounds in his magazine in the direction of the barn to let Moran know he was watching. Lead splintered the old wood as the bullets gouged through, and Moran fired back, just as futilely, and then stopped. It was possible that he was out of ammo, but Guthrie wasn't taking chances.

Keeping a sporadic eye through the open door, he gave the house a quick search and found a closet with weapons and ammo. He swapped out his empty magazine for a full one and went back to the front of the house and fired the entire mag into the barn. Hoping the threat would keep Moran pinned for at least a little while, Guthrie darted back to the closet, rearmed his AR, donned a tac vest, jammed several more magazines for the AR into its pockets, then grabbed a daypack, into which he stuffed half a dozen more magazines for the AR and several for Moran's .45, too.

In the front room, he emptied another magazine into the barn then made a quick stop in the kitchen, where he found a case of water. He put five bottles into the pack just before the contents of a sixth went down his throat. While he drank, he surveyed the larder and filled the remaining space in the pack with food that wouldn't require cooking. He wished he could cook something since he hadn't eaten a real meal in several days, but there just wasn't time. On his way through the front room to the front door, he noticed the case of flashlights. Four were still inside, and he stuck three into external loops in the the pack, while the fourth went into the appropriate pocket of his tac vest.

The last thing he did was snatch Brother Fidelio's manuscript from Thorvald's desk and slip it into the pack with everything else.

He glanced at the sky through the door. He'd better hustle. In the kitchen, he'd found several bottles of whiskey, and he used one to make a Molotov cocktail. After firing another long burst at the barn, he ducked out the back door, lit the Molotov, and threw it through down the hall toward the living room. It shattered about three quarters of the way there, splashing liquid fire on the floor and walls.

That should occupy Moran and eliminate a lot of his resources, Guthrie thought as he ran around the back of the bunkhouse and barn, hoping Moran's attention remained on the front of the house, Already tendrils of black smoke were leaking out of the structure. Guthrie scurried toward the dirt road, keeping features of the lumpy terrain between him and the barn. Glancing back, he spotted Moran running from the barn toward the house. Flames licked out of one of the front windows, followed by more.

Guthrie found the road at a spot just over a shallow rise from the ranch compound. There, out of sight of the burning ranch house, he set off at a moderate trot. He had a long way to go. Time was of the essence, but so was endurance. If he bogged down from exhaustion before he reached the ranch depot, it was all over. Unpleasantly.

Smoke from the ranch house now cast a pall over the central valley, bringing a sort of premature dusk. Guthrie could hear ammo going off like a huge 4th of July celebration. He hoped Moran would be hit by a stray round or two, but he knew the man was too smart to stay near while the fire burned his arsenal.

Guthrie couldn't celebrate just yet, though. By the time he reached the trough of the valley, it already was in shadow, with the peaks of the valley's hills and ridges sticking above the shadow line like islands of light about to be completely inundated in a tide of darkness.

Behind him came a distant roar that must have been ear-shattering up close.

"Guthrie! Ready or not, here I come!"

Guthrie threw a look over his shoulder, but an intervening hillock blocked sight of the ranch compound. He saw all too clearly in his mind's eye, though, the ungainly but quick and powerful body of the troll striding down the road behind him, occasionally bending low, perhaps, to sniff the scent of his track.

Guthrie quickened his pace. Ahead, the up-curved inner slope of the mountains on the east side of the valley was nearly twice as high as its western counterpart and so remained bathed in light. If he could just reach that light before the troll reached him. He glanced back and no longer had to imagine the troll in pursuit. His real eyes saw it, and he started to run. The heavy pack slammed angularly against his back, the AR felt like lead in his hands, and his lungs and legs complained. In moments, he could hear the troll's heavy tread pounding the road behind him, closer and closer.

Just ahead was the line between shadow and light, death and life. Just ahead. He wanted to run faster, but he couldn't risk stumbling. Then, there it was, and with the horrendous breath of the troll washing over him, he half lunged, half dove across the line, into the light. The troll took a swiping grab that just missed, its outstretched fingers brushing Guthrie's right foot, sending him tumbling.

Staggering to his feet, Guthrie backed off a dozen paces then faced Halvor. One of its hands clutched a huge club. Guthrie saw it was a discarded mine timber with a handle crudely carved into one end.

"That was close, Guthrie," it said, raising the fingers that had touched Guthrie to its nose and sniffing. "My. Is that fear I smell?" It grinned its horrible grin and took another sniff. "Yes, I do believe so. How nice. All those fearomones make flesh tender and tasty."

Ignoring its laughter, Guthrie turned and hurried on. He knew the troll wouldn't be able to cross the mountains ahead until near full darkness, but he still had a couple of miles of winding road to go down on the far side of the mountains to make it to the ranch depot. And that whole distance would be in darkness. Guthrie's only break was that the eastern slopes of the mountains were too steep for the troll to try to travel cross-country. It would have to stick to the road, too, though there was nothing to stop it from cutting across the twists, bends, and switchbacks.

Guthrie raced over the pass and down the road toward the bottom. He'd gotten about three-quarters of the way to the ranch depot when true darkness descended. Behind him sound a huge guffaw of laughter, and he threw a quick glance over his shoulder to see the troll, silhouetted against the dying sky as it crossed the pass, arms swinging loosely with its slow lope, the club dragging along after it.

"Fear me!" came the distant shout.

Guthrie ran full out.

While he ran, he considered the options ahead. There were only two: the boxcar or the Trackmobile. Undoubtedly, the troll could tear into either one. On the surface, the boxcar seemed a better shelter in that it had no windows, while the Trackmobile had them on all sides of the small cab. But in the boxcar, he'd simply be a fish in a barrel waiting to be caught and unable to see attacks when they came. Not only that, if it chose, the troll could lock him inside, which it couldn't do with the Trackmobile.

Also, Guthrie doubted that Halvor would do much damage to the Trackmobile. Not only was it built of heavy-gauge steel, it was a more essential and expensive piece of equipment and would be more difficult to replace than the boxcar. Whatever Halvor's plan, it needed the little engine, and while it might superficially damage it, it wouldn't completely destroy it, even to get at Guthrie. He hoped.

Guthrie also realized that the Trackmobile's windows could be an advantage. The vehicle's cab sat to one side of the deck and the large engine block protruded from the other. On the side of the cab opposite the engine, the windows were protected by heavy steel rails, which also ran all the way around the deck, enclosing the side with the engine. The windows might be vulnerable to blows by the troll, but giving a full panoramic view, they also would allow Guthrie to shine his flashlights in all directions. He didn't know if that would be enough to beat back the troll, but it was all he had.

So the railcar mover was where he went, though he barely made it inside and slammed the door before the troll swarmed over the cab. Guthrie was shocked to see how big it had grown. It was now nearly thirty feet tall, though it walked with a pronounced simian stoop that made it seem shorter. It leaned close to the windows and leered at Guthrie.

He didn't think that Halvor, big as it was, could overturn such a heavy piece of equipment as the railcar mover. The troll's heavy club might do some damage to the cab, but eventually, even it would break against the Trackmobile's steel body. He wished he could drive the mover away, but even if he had the key, the little locomotive was on the wrong side of the boxcar, pointing down the decrepit and incomplete southbound tracks. Nor could he unmount the railcar mover from the tracks and drive the damn thing off down the road. Thanks to Espinoza's tutelage, he could have done it with the Hi-Rail, but the railcar mover was a much heavier and more complex piece of equipment, and he had no idea what the various switches and levers did. And he had no time. All he could do was hunker down and hope he made it through the night.

"I can see you're going to make this difficult," Halvor growled. "I think we can sacrifice a window."

The troll jammed the end of the club through the big, unpro-tected side window, showering Guthrie with a heavy glitter of safety glass. It pulled the club out of the hole to jam it in again and smash out the remaining glass, but Guthrie had already jerked the flashlight from its pouch in the tac vest, and he shined it right into Halvor's face. The reaction was almost instantaneous as the troll yelled in consternation and heaved itself backward.

Keeping the light trained on the troll, who scuttled back into the growing gloom, Guthrie groped the other three flashlights from the pack loops and switched them on, carefully avoiding shining them onto himself. He set one on the instrument panel, pointing through a window on the engine side, and fastened another to shine through the second-largest window, which faced the front of the mover and was unprotected by railing. He kept hold of the remaining two, using them to guard the small, railing-protected back windows and the large, now broken side window. That was the most vulnerable because it was the only one large enough for the troll to reach through to pull Guthrie out.

The dim form of the troll, some hundred yards away, was barely etched against the deepening darkness by the powerful lights. Guthrie knew by now that the flashlights were only a temporary expedient. They might keep the troll at bay—as long as the batteries held out—but they couldn't do it any serious or lasting damage. When the troll had leaned forward to leer at him through the glass, Guthrie had noticed that the places he'd ossified on its hands and face during his escape from the mine had already healed and returned to their usual color and flexibility. Obviously, it would take full sunlight to permanently freeze the damn thing.

If Guthrie didn't bake first. After a few minutes, the interior of the cab began to heat up, and Guthrie was thankful for the breath of air coming through the broken window. He cracked the door to give a little cross ventilation.

"You can't escape me," the troll called out, in a friendly manner. "I admit you've done pretty well for yourself. Almost as well as that little fucker, Jack. He managed to rid a whole region of us. For a time. But it seems that some guys just can't resist whacking-off underneath bridges or in dark corners, and there you have it. More of us. An endless supply of us. And with Daddy's help, I'll make that a reality, and there's nothing you can do to stop me."

Just for the heck of it, Guthrie set the AR to full auto, stuck the barrel through the hole in the window, and emptied a full magazine at the troll. He knew that the rounds wouldn't be fatal, but they might annoy it. It jeered in response, but there was pain in its voice, and it crouched behind a clump of boulders. Then, as Guthrie jammed another magazine into the AR, he could hear large rocks clattering in a confused scramble. He tried to followed the sound, but the troll too quickly melted into the darkness. But it wasn't gone.

"You'll suffer for that, you bastard," it yelled.

An instant later, a large rock shattered the windows on the engine side of the cab and wedged itself in the remains of the frame.

"Keep it up, Halvor, and this machine will be useless. One more rock, and I'll fuck it up permanently. You'll never get it to pull that boxcar anywhere.

"I can get another."

"Who's going to do that for you? There's nobody left but Thorvald and Moran."

"How did you drive everyone off?"

"Wasn't me, you oaf. It was you. They already know they can't trust you not to eat them when you find it convenient. The promise of pay doesn't count much if you're troll shit."

Halvor laughed.

"You might be right. Along with my new plan, I must adopt new attitudes. I'll have Brian call them back, and I'll promise not to eat any of them who don't die at your hands. Thank you, once again, Guthrie, for giving me ideas."

Guthrie cracked the door and emptied another magazine toward the sound of the troll's voice. The troll grunted and moved farther away.

"The Bugle Boys will come back, Guthrie, and when they do, I'll send them for you. You're all alone out here, and you have no transportation. If I don't get you tonight, there's always another."

The troll didn't attack again, but that didn't make the remainder of the time til dawn any less nightmarish. Just knowing that the troll was close and waiting kept him sleepless and alert. At last, the eastern sky began to lighten the landscape. Guthrie didn't actually see the troll depart but he knew it must have in order to make it to the mine before daylight. He emerged from the battered railcar mover and stood on the deck. Soon after, the troll's misshapen slouch was silhouetted against the lightening sky as the monster crested the pass.

27

THE FIRST THING GUTHRIE DID before leaving the depot was to cut every wire he could find on the Trackmobile and pour sand in its fuel tank. If it was ever going to be useful again, it would need a lot of work. Then he breathed a sigh of relief as he turned toward the east, the first rays of the sun feeling better on his face than he ever remembered. He'd managed to survive, but now there was much to do. The first thing was to contact Espinoza, but with his phone dead, it looked like he was going to have to walk somewhere to make a call and hope he didn't run into any of the Bugle Boys he'd driven off the day before.

Sierra Blanca was an obvious destination, but the work crew he and Espinoza had talked to were only four miles away and in the same direction, near the spot where the long southern leg of the ranch line swung closest to the main line—a two-hour walk. Maybe he could used one of their phones or even ride out with them. If they were still working on the siding.

Guthrie descended from the Trackmobile and struck out along the decrepit line south of the ranch depot. He hadn't gone more than a hundred yards when he heard a subdued roar and clatter of gravel on metal. He ducked behind a creosote bush, realizing it might be cover but no protection. But that didn't matter. The Mercedes was careening down the dirt road from the mountains above. It spun across the open area beside the corral, then was temporarily lost to sight behind the Trackmobile and boxcar before coming into sight again as it raced down the dirt road beside the ranch tracks, toward the main line.

That has to be Moran at the wheel, Guthrie thought. Thorvald wouldn't know how to drive like that.

Turning back to the decrepit ranch line, he continued walking southeast. As he walked, he opened and ate a couple of the energy bars he'd brought in the pack. They didn't do a lot to assuage the deeper hunger he felt after not having eaten much for several days, but at least his stomach quit growling. At last he saw the crew's vehicles sitting on the siding a couple of thousand feet away. He left the ranch line and cut overland, crossed the main dirt road running north–south, and dipped into a broad dry arroyo—the same one that eventually, joined by the dozens of other gullies and dry washes, formed the major creek that circled the northern end of the mountains. When he climbed out, only a couple of hundred feet of flat, scrubby ground separated him from the crew.

They'd already spotted him coming out of the desert and had stopped working and stood around, staring as he approached. No wonder, he thought, acutely conscious of the pack and AR.

"Hey," he said, smiling, as he stepped up to the foreman, Edgar. Donnie and another of the crew came over to listen. "My phone battery's dead. I wonder if one of you gentlemen would loan me his phone to make a quick call."

"You're that fellow that was with the safety inspector. What's his name?"

"Espinoza."

"That's him. Is he who you're calling?"

"Yes."

The foreman chuckled and shook his head.

"You're half an hour late. Your buddy just went by here in his Hi-Rail, heading toward El Paso. Here." He passed his phone to Guthrie.

Guthrie quickly dialed Espinoza's number, and a moment later, the trainman answered.

"It's Guthrie. Where are you?"

"I'm on the siding near the switch for the ranch line, waiting to hear from you. I tried calling, but nothing. You're not on your own phone. What happened?"

"Go on to the depot. It's clear for now. I'll meet you there and tell you."

Guthrie disconnected and handed the phone back to the foreman.

"Thanks."

"Pretty strange goings on out here," the foreman commented dryly as he slipped the phone back into its holster. "First, that other safety inspector goes back and forth like a bat outta hell. Then you two guys come along, chasing after some railcar missing in Houston, and we see you driving around out there." He waved toward the ranch line. "Then yesterday afternoon, two carloads of guys tear down the road like more bats outta hell." He indicated the dirt road across the wash. "Looks like they was headed for the interstate. Then first thing this morning, some fancy Mercedes comes tearing down the road, too. And right after, your buddy drives by, and you walk out of the desert half an hour later looking like you just came out of a war zone but acting like everything's normal. Which I know it ain't."

"Sorry," Guthrie said with a rueful smile. "I can't enlighten you."

"You going back out there?" The foreman nodded in the direction from which Guthrie had come.

"I am."

"I tell you, there's some crazy shit going on out here on this line, and I seen some crazy shit out here."

Donnie and the man with him nodded.

You have no idea, Guthrie thought.

"Alls I can say is, I hope *somebody* around here has a handle on things," Edgar said. "Anything you *can* tell me?"

"Don't be out here after dark."

Guthrie turned and headed back out into the desert. This time, the four miles back to the ranch depot passed at a snail's pace, which was about how fast Guthrie seemed to be moving over the rough ground. Finally, he arrived at the ranch depot to find Espinoza already there, sitting in the HiRail.

"Clay!" Espinoza exclaimed as Guthrie laid the AR on the floor of the cab's back compartment and dropped the daypack next to it. He clapped Guthrie on the back as he climbed onto the seat. "Where the fuck did you get all that stuff? Where are the guards? The troll?"

Guthrie gave him a brief rundown of events since the trainman had left.

"So," Espinoza said. "The troll's up in the mine, and all the guards are gone."

"Bugle Boys."

"Huh?"

"Bugle Boys. That what they call themselves. They say they're the ones who blow the Trumpet of Faith. I guess they blow something. But, yeah. Nobody's up there right now but Thorvald and Halvor."

"I still can't get over the idea that that ugly motherfucker has a name."

He chuckled, and Guthrie followed suit, but their mirth was short lived.

"We'd better get cracking," Guthrie said. "We have a lot to do before the sun goes down and Halvor starts roaming around."

"Why doesn't it just come after us now?"

"I learned that trolls freeze or turn to stone or something like that in direct sunlight."

"Stone?" Espinoza asked incredulously. "Roger that, but you must be joking."

"I've seen it happen on a small scale with these flashlights." He tapped the one in the loop in his tac vest.

"Yeah, you know, it flinched back in Houston when I shined my flashlight in its face. That was a pretty powerful one, but not anything close to these."

"I'd say we're okay as long as there's full daylight, but it can freely move around in the shadows. The only way we'll be safe at night is to be too far away for it to travel there and back before dawn."

"You don't think it'll just leave one night?"

"I'm not worried about that. Yet. Thorvald's right. We're too far from anywhere for it to try to randomly leave the mine. Even for Sierra Blanca. Going there would only expose it to people, and I don't think it wants that yet. But it and Thorvald are hatching some sort of long-range plan, and it'll leave eventually. I think we're okay for the moment, but we have to stop it before it's ready to act."

"What about that?" Espinoza said, point to two crates in the corner of the HiRail's back compartment. They were labeled "Caution—Dynamite" in large black letters on a red background. "Why don't we just go up to the mine, blow the entrance, and trap the troll inside? There's more than enough here to do the job, and I brought several remote detonators."

"I don't think that'll work. That thing was made to dig its way through a rockfall. It might take it a little while, but it would get out eventually. Blowing the mine would only delay the inevitable by a few days. And there's another consideration. The explosion might kill Thorvald, and I want to take him alive if possible. No." He shook his head. "The way I see it, we have to rig the boxcar to explode and lure the troll inside."

"How? With *you* as bait?"

"Who better?" Guthrie grinned.

"Well, you'd better hope it becomes complacent."

"I doubt that trolls are ever complacent. But maybe we can distract it."

"How?"

"I've been thinking about our strategy. The first thing is to give Halvor something to worry about besides us. Something it can't ignore."

"What's that?"

"So far, it's had its meals delivered. It's time to make it work for its food. Right now, there's only one body in the mine, so it'll need more food soon. It's gotten huge, and from what I can tell, it's hungry all the time. There are a bunch of cattle in a pen next to the barn. A dozen. Easy pickings for it, but if we free the cows, it'll have to chase after them every time it wants to eat. That'll preoccupy it at least part of the time it's on the loose."

"I'm a trainman," Espinoza laughed. "Not a cowboy. I've never even been on a horse."

"We don't have to lasso them. We just have to let open the gate and drive them away."

"And after that?"

"We fix our trap and go troll baiting." Guthrie glanced around Espinoza's HiRail. "Let's get this off the tracks. It's five miles to the ranch and five miles back, and I've had a rough night and already walked ten miles this morning. I'd rather ride."

What he didn't say was that he didn't want to be without a vehicle and be forced to repeat the terror of the night before.

Espinoza did as he asked, then the two men conferred as the truck made its way along the dirt road to the ranch, its big tires and four-wheel drive easily taking the ruts and potholes.

At the ranch, they discovered that the Molotov cocktail Guthrie had tossed into the house to preoccupy Moran had done its job. The structure had burned to the ground. After more than a century in the hot, dry climate, the wood it had been built of must have gone up like cardboard. All that remained were smoldering timbers and ash. The rust-mottled tin roof, now warped and further discolored by heat and char, lay collapsed over the ruins like a sheet over a dead body. An uncoiled hose testified that Moran had tried to stifle the flames, but the melted residue of PVC pipes meant that any water pressure to the hose had soon died. Guthrie was glad he hadn't been around when all that ammo inside had gone off.

Driving off the cattle proved more difficult than Guthrie imagined. There were eleven cows, so obviously Halvor had consumed one since the last time Guthrie had looked. The bovines bolted from the pen readily enough, but they all stopped within a hundred-yard radius to munch on the thin sparse grasses. The two men had to race up to them, firing rounds into the ground to scare the beasts away. Eventually, all but a couple were out of sight of the ranch compound. They'd run for sure when they saw the troll coming, Guthrie thought, but probably not fast enough. From what Guthrie had seen, Halvor, despite its size and ungainly limbs, was as quick on its feet as it was at snatching prey, and that was pretty quick.

The bunkhouse was intact, though the wall facing the erstwhile ranch house was riddled with holes. Inside, they found food, water, and more weapons and ammo. While Espinoza donned a tac vest and armed himself with an AR, Guthrie, still famished, searched the kitchen for something to eat. There, he discovered that all the food that didn't need to be refrigerated or cooked was missing. Taken by Thorvald and Moran into the mine, no doubt. After that, they began carrying all the weapons, ammo, and remaining food out to the HiRail and stacked it in the bed.

They were nearly done when Guthrie noticed a furtive movement at the shoulder of rock that masked the adit. It was Thorvald, watching them.

Guthrie slowly walked toward the mine. Thorvald ducked down, but then he stood, realizing he'd been seen. He looked nervous as hell and ready to bolt back into the mine and Halvor's embrace.

"Wait!" Guthrie said, raising his hands. "I won't hurt you."

Thorvald hesitated. He looked dirty and disheveled, and his face, fleshy and florid just days earlier, had taken on a tinge of gray gauntness. The ducktail had sagged, and now the thin orange hair drooped down from the renegade priest's cranium like dead grass.

"I can't. He won't let me."

"Come out here in the sunlight," Guthrie said as he walked closer. "It can't reach you out here."

"There's nowhere he can't reach me," Thorvald said.

"Nonsense. Espinoza and I are still here." Guthrie stopped about thirty feet away. "We've driven off your men. Even Moran has abandoned you."

"Not so. He's gone to bring his men back. And Fleming, too. He's just gone to San Antonio to pick up something I purchased, but he'll bring others with him."

"You need help," Guthrie insisted. "Let us help you."

"You can run and be safe enough," Thorvald said. "He can't find you if he can't follow your scent. But I'm different. He always knows where I am. It's some kind of psychic connection. I could be in Siberia, and he'd find me. There's nowhere I can hide. Now I understand why Brother Fidelio's shaman was unable to kill the troll he created. He simply could not because he and his son were spiritually linked."

As Thorvald spoke, Espinoza came up behind Guthrie.

"Come with us," Guthrie urged. "We can get you far enough away that it can't get to you without revealing itself, and when it does, it'll be all over. But I get the idea that it's not ready for that— at least not yet."

"I don't know what he's going to do," Thorvald said with a furtive defensiveness that made Guthrie think he was lying.

From what Guthrie could tell, Halvor was as loquacious as they came. Maybe that was because, for most of its existence, it lived in a netherworld, cut off from all interpersonal associations. That isolation made it talkative when it had the chance, but the talk was all one way. All ego. All warped. It didn't care what Thorvald or anybody else thought. It didn't care about the reality of the situation or truth or honor. It cared only about itself and its own desires, which too often were simply impulses rather than needs. People were just objects to it, forced to satisfy its desires, impulses, and needs and to be consumed. It was impossible that Halvor hadn't bragged to Thorvald—its own father and sole spiritual connection—about its intentions.

"You know," Guthrie said. "You can't help but know. Whatever it is, you have to help us stop it, or whatever happens is on your head."

"So be it," Thorvald said. "I've always accepted my place in the plan, but Halvor has opened my eyes to larger possibilities. Our offspring ought to outdo us, don't you think? I can see now that my own ideas were small-minded, limited by the notion of revenge. My son's aspirations are much higher and broader because he has no ax to grind. He *is* the ax, and his hewing will be highly public, long lasting, and very calculated without the impediment of emotions. He will bring about the results I wanted all along, but on a grander scale. Much grander. They'll be the grandest."

With that, Thorvald ducked behind the shoulder of rock and was gone. Guthrie, raising his AR, ran to the shoulder and cautiously peered around it, Espinoza on his heels. Thorvald was standing in the shadows just inside the adit, looking steadfastly at him, while Halvor filled the gloom behind him, face attentive. Seeing Guthrie, the troll's visage twisted into a snaggletoothed, sneering grin. Guthrie was glad he wasn't close enough to catch more than a faint wisp of its rotten breath.

"Well, Guthrie. I wondered when we'd have a chance to chat again. You and Expinoza." It hissed out the name. Then it snuffed the air and wrinkled its nose. "You know, Guthrie, there's something unpleasant about your odor. I can't quite place it, but there's something about you that's different."

"That's not my odor," Guthrie retorted. "That's the smell of your defeat."

"What are you and Expinoza doing out there? I know you've driven off Daddy's Bugle Boys." The troll chuckled. "What a stupid name, don't you think? Buglers eagerly playing reveille to herald the day of their own demise. Ah, well, no matter. They'll be back, lured by the lights of wealth and power. Daddy pays them handsomely to dream dreams larger than their lives, and he has an endless supply of money to hire stupid men who have nothing to offer but aggression and violence." It grinned. "Just my kind of people. So go ahead and stick around. It'll make capturing you so much easier. And then...." It smacked its lips then frowned. "But I wonder why you're still here."

"Let's just say I'm doing you the kind favor of watching over you while Moran and his men are gone."

"Somehow I doubt that you will ever do me a kind favor."

"We can agree on that."

"So why *are* you hanging around?"

"Duty."

"To the Catholic Church? Somehow I can't see you in the role of religious savior."

"I'm not. I already told Thorvald I have nothing to do with the Church. My boss has a lot more going for him than they do."

"Daddy thinks he's some mystic seer sending you out to do his dirty work."

"You're dirty enough."

"You'll see just how dirty if I catch you around here after dark."

With that, the troll backed down the tunnel, Thorvald slinking after it. In a few moments, they'd faded into the gloom, though Guthrie could hear Halvor's heavy grunts as he squirmed backward through the shaft.

Guthrie turned and looked at Espinoza.

"We gotta eliminate that fucker," the trainman said.

While Espinoza returned to the bunkhouse to finish loading the HiRail, Guthrie walked to the barn. Inside a tool storage room, he grabbed a pick, an ax, and a four-foot pry bar and took them to the HiRail. By then, Espinoza had carried out the last of the food and weapons, and the two men got into the truck. Espinoza steered it across the valley and down the mountains' flank to the ranch depot. There, he remounted it on the tracks.

Then he went to the boxcar, where he closed and latched the door on the opposite side from the corral and rigged the cases of dynamite on the floor in front of it. He slid the door on the corral-side almost shut, leaving it open just enough to give Guthrie quick entry.

"Since the dynamite is near the open side of a steel box," Espinoza said, "the car should act to direct most of the blast right at the troll after it opens the door."

"A giant shaped-charge," Guthrie nodded.

He was in one of the back corners, using the tools from the barn to hack a hole in the car's plywood floor. He planned to let the troll chase him into the car, while Espinoza hid in a clump of rocks a safe distance away. Once the troll was inside and Guthrie had dropped through the hole, Espinoza would switch on three of the flashlights aimed to shine right at the door. Hopefully, the light would be enough to drive the troll into the protection of the boxcar while Guthrie got clear. Even if it was only partially inside when Espinoza detonated the dynamite, the explosion should be enough to blow it apart.

"What if your timing's wrong?" Espinoza asked. "What if it gets you before you get out?"

"I'll have one of the flashlights. That should help keep it back, but if it doesn't and it gets me, blow the charge."

"Let's hope it doesn't come to that." Espinoza paused, then waved at the boxcar. "Won't it be suspicious of you going in there?"

Guthrie shrugged.

"It might. But I'm hoping it'll be too focused to think. It does well enough with sneak attacks at night, but it doesn't think clearly when it gets mad and tends to lash out. It'll just be trailing me like a blood-hound with nothing but my blood on its mind. In the heat of the moment, believing it's got me, maybe it'll lower its guard." He shrugged again. "I don't know what else to try in the short time we have."

Outside, they arranged two of the flashlights so their beams were trained on the door, and each of the men kept one for personal protection. They hoped. They finished about three.

"Now what?" Espinoza asked.

"I guess I'll have to go up there." Guthrie nodded toward the pass. "If I'm bait, I need to give the predator a whiff of me. Until then, let's eat something. I'm starved."

Since all the food they'd brought from the bunkhouse needed to be cooked, they simply ate the remainder of the food Guthrie had in the daypack and chased it with bottles of water.

"I'll be happy to sleep in a bed again," Guthrie said when they were done.

"I'll be happy to sleep again, period," Espinoza said. After a pause, he said, "Mind if I ask you something?"

"Go ahead."

"You seem pretty...I don't know...okay with what's going on. I mean, like you're used to this sort of thing."

"This is the first time I've faced a troll," Guthrie chuckled. "But it's not my first rodeo with the weird."

"It's that old man. Mr. Terry, isn't it? I was so mired in my own problems that I didn't really notice at the time, but he's got some kind of power, doesn't he?"

"Yeah," Guthrie said reflectively. "Some kind of power." He glanced at his watch, then at the sun. Four, and the sun was nearly behind the mountains.

"It won't be long, now," he said. "You ready for this?"

"No. But I'll have to be."

"You don't have to be here."

"Yeah. I do. I owe it to Buddy, at the very least. And to you. You didn't know me from Adam two weeks ago, but you've stepped up to the plate for me. Hell, I might be dead now if it wasn't for you. And if you work for a guy like that Mr. Terry, well, what can I say?"

He shrugged.

"Fuck," Guthrie said.

"I can say, 'fuck'?"

"No. Sorry. Look."

Guthrie, who'd been warily watching the landscape to the north and east, spotted a glitter of sunlight spark off a windshield as it emerged over the top of the rise about a mile away, just this side of the large arroyo. A second glitter followed the first, then a third and fourth. Moran had come back with his men. And others.

"Yeah, I'll say fuck," Espinoza said as the approaching vehicles dipped out out of sight behind a low ridge. "What do you want to do?"

"They'll be here in a couple of minutes, so I don't think we're going to have much choice."

He picked up his AR, checked and charged it. Espinoza followed suit.

"There's no way we can stop them here," Guthrie said. "Not with so many. Our only edge is surprise. Thank goodness we're on the rails. Get this thing going as fast as you can," he said. He got out of the cab and clambered into the bed, where he'd have a better range of fire. The piles of boxes and crates they'd taken from the bunkhouse would provide some cover. He made sure the cases of ammo were even better protected than himself.

Espinoza sent the truck rolling forward on the rails, and it was moving almost as fast as the tracks permitted when the Bugle Boys' vehicles came into view around a bend, the Mercedes in the lead. Guthrie sighted his rifle.

No mercy, he thought. He didn't know if Moran was at the wheel—distance and glare on the windshield masked the driver's face. Guthrie waited until it was nearly on them then stitched a burst across the hood and windshield.

The car immediately swerved off the road and plowed into the hillside next to the road. The door fell open, and the driver—not Moran, unfortunately—sprawled halfway out of the seat, blood splashed over his torso. Guthrie ignored him as the other vehicles ground to a stop in a clatter of rocks and clouds of dust, occupants spilling out, guns blasting. Two of their bursts sent glass flying from the HiRail's rear window.

Guthrie returned fire, but with little effect, as the Bugle Boys took cover. The HiRail passed the vehicles, and Guthrie kept firing continuously, joined by Espinoza, who leaned awkwardly out of the window with his own AR. Between the two of them, they managed to keep their enemies at bay long enough to roll past them and out of sight around a bend.

"Are they coming?" Espinoza yelled through the shattered rear window.

"Not yet. I don't think they will" Guthrie answered. "Moran'll want to see what's going up at the ranch. Stop and let me in."

"Want to go back?" Espinoza asked when Guthrie was settled in the cab. He didn't look particularly anxious to do that.

"No. Moran might have left a couple of men to guard the depot. If he did, they'll be watching for us. Besides, I've had enough shooting for one day."

"Shit. Do you think they'll find the dynamite?"

"I don't know. Maybe they won't see it. It's inside the boxcar, and someone would have to deliberately look to find it. Since we were in the truck, not near the car, there's no reason for them to suspect we did anything to it." He paused reflectively. "All the same, I wish we didn't have to leave it." He made a sour face and shook his head. "Let's just go to Sierra Blanca. We need to regroup."

28

ESPINOZA DROVE WITHOUT INCIDENT THE couple of miles to the junction to the main line, and Guthrie jumped out to throw the switch. A few minutes later, as the HiRail sailed down the tracks, the rail repair crew stared at them with half-raised waves and puzzled expressions. They waved back.

"Do you think they'll be all right?" Espinoza asked, staring at the sideview mirror and seeing the crew diminished in the distance.

"They'll be off duty and long gone by dark," Guthrie said. "They'll be safe enough, and so will we once we reach Sierra Blanca."

"I hope you're right. I'll bet that thing can probably make pretty good time across open terrain."

"Maybe, but even if it is a troll, it just got loose from its crack, and it's barefoot. While it was attacking me last night, I noticed it avoided rough ground. It's only been walking around for a couple of days, so it's feet probably aren't tough enough yet to take the terrain out here. Not for long distances, anyway. I doubt it'll walk all the way to Sierra Blanca, especially since it can't be sure we went there."

"I hope you're right, but Sierra Blanca is the only town around. Where else would we go?"

"Good point, but trust me. Halvor has some plan, and it's not going to screw things up by making its presence known prematurely."

The miles passed swiftly beneath the HiRail's wheels, and before long, Espinoza maneuvered the truck onto the same siding in Sierra Blanca they'd used before.

"The ladies in the railroad museum mentioned a motel just off I-10," Espinoza said as he parked and shut off the engine. "The Americana. Want to stay there?"

"When we were here before, I noticed several motels just a couple of blocks from here, closer to the rail line. Let's try one of them. They look homier and less conspicuous."

Espinoza chuckled.

"I imagine you're ready for both of those after the past couple of days."

He drove over to Sierra Blanca's main commercial street. A few minutes later, they'd chosen the SB Historic Lodge, which was practically across the street from the railroad museum. The lodge consisted of two parallel rows of small, one-story stone buildings facing a common parking lot. Each side was subdivided into eight or so separate units. The place looked quaint but well-kept.

The clerk in the office enlightened Guthrie about the presence of so many small motels in a town that seemed to be drying up.

"Deer and javelina hunters, mostly," the clerk said. "We make enough during the season to last out the summer."

"It must not be the season right now."

"Nope. Right now 'bout all we got among us are a few temporary Border Patrol agents. Smith, in the other nice motel down the road, has a rail crew right now. So we get by. But in another month, this place and most of the others—even the trailer park, will be full up. Even the Americana."

The man's tone was slightly disparaging.

"The one over on the interstate?" Guthrie said. "Anything wrong with it?"

"Not if you like sleeping in a cardboard box. It's out on the highway, and mostly caters to travelers." He chuckled. "Desperate travelers. It's so noisy in there, it's a miracle anybody can get a decent night sleep. Not like here." He patted the stone wall next to him. "Solid makes the best insulation for sound and temperatures."

And bullets, Guthrie thought.

After they checked in, renting two rooms for a week, they went to the HiRail and grabbed their kits. Heading for their rooms, they agreed to meet outside in an hour to eat and make plans.

Guthrie's room really wasn't much different than any small, independently owned motel, though all the rooms in the row seemed to be slightly different in shape and size, as if they'd been built one at a time, each one tacked onto the previous one. His was quaintly Western themed. Inside, the first thing he did after locking the door was to head straight for the shower. An hour later, dressed in fresh clothes and feeling a hell of a lot better, he went out the door. He'd even charged his phone. Espinoza was already outside when he emerged.

"Got a place in mind to eat?" the trainman asked.

"That same cafe we ate at before."

As they walked, Guthrie couldn't help but stare around him and try to imagine the troll rampaging down this street, tearing into the buildings and homes, extracting the occupants, and eating them or tucking them, screaming and squirming under its arm. It was like a vision from some 1950s atomic monster movie, only this was no monster accidentally created by radiation, but one deliberately and maliciously created to kill, destroy, and terrorize in the name of an ideology. Worse, that ideology was based on nothing but hatred for another ideology that was, itself, false. Mass murder in the service of a lie told about another lie.

Fuck Thorvald and all his ilk, Guthrie thought, then shoved the thought aside as they strode up to the cafe door. After they seated themselves, they didn't say much, and the waitress—Irene—the same slender woman with the poofed hairstyle, brought water and menus. This time the barrette in her hair was green. She left for a few minutes, and Guthrie scanned the menu, mouth watering at everything he saw. Irene returned, took their orders, and went to the kitchen. Even then, with her out of earshot, Guthrie was just too tired and hungry to talk.

The food came quickly enough, and Guthrie ate his salad, steak, and potato almost as fast as the waitress put the plates on the table. It was the first decent food he'd had in several stressful days. He didn't say anything until he was finished eating, but his brain was working.

"What now?" Espinoza asked, wiping his mouth and tossing the napkin onto the table.

"I don't know." Guthrie leaned back in his chair, feeling energy from the food begin to course through him. "We have a lot of empty afternoon ahead of us. I think I'll visit the county clerk's office and check out the property records for the Dunton Ranch."

"That sounds like detective work," Espinoza said, smiling. "I'll do train work. Maybe walk over to the sidings behind the railroad museum and see what's what."

"Okay. Meet you back at the lodge."

"Want a ride?"

"That's okay. This town isn't that big. I'll walk."

Indeed, he reached the county courthouse in less than five minutes—it was just three long blocks across the railroad tracks. With walls of what looked like rough-dressed brown stone, the building was one of the most substantial structures in town, attesting to the value assigned to property in these parts, where wealth was measured in tens of thousands of acres. It faced the city park the women at the railroad museum had mentioned.

Inside, he asked if he could do a property search, and the woman behind the desk asked him if he had a specific property in mind.

"I heard there's a place for sale just west of here. The Dunton Ranch. Do you have anything on that?"

"I do," she said, "but I can tell you it's probably not for sale now."

"Why's that?"

"Someone else just bought it . Earlier this year."

"Who would that be?" Guthrie asked, expecting her to turn to her computer. But she surprised him.

"Some company called the Trumpet of Faith," she said without hesitation.

"You know that off the top of your head?" Guthrie asked, smiling.

"Well," she admitted. "I couldn't do that with every property in the county, but you have to admit that name sure stands out. Besides, it just happened, and we don't have a lot of big property transfers like that very often."

"Is it some kind of religious organization?"

"Could be," she said with a small shrug, though her brow looked troubled.

"You have doubts about them?"

"Not doubts. I really don't know anything about them. I just hope they aren't going to start some sort of religious cult up there. I mean, I'm a Christian and all, but I'm old enough to remember Waco, and we don't need anything like that around here." She shrugged again. "But like I said, I don't really know anything about them. So far, they don't seem to be doing anything but ranching. All I do know is they must have a big pocketbook since they paid cash."

"I suppose that was a pretty penny," Guthrie said.

"Pretty enough," she replied. "But I hear the old ranch houses and barn up there are in serious need of repairs."

"Did you ever meet the new owners?"

"Nope. They did all their dealings through a lawyer. Kinda peculiar." She shrugged. "Oh, well. To each his own."

"I heard that the place was originally owned by someone named Dunton."

"That would be Silas Dunton."

"You know anything about him?"

"Plenty," she said. "Or at least as plenty as anybody. He was kind of famous in these parts. My daddy was county clerk before me, and he knew Dunton's son who took over after his father died, and his son after that."

"How'd he end up here?"

"It's said he rode into Sierra Blanca on the train fifteen or twenty years after the transcontinental line met here. The train was just stopping to take on water and fuel and to give the passengers a break. Dunton was on his way to Nevada or California or some such place to try his hand at prospecting. He came down to the platform and went into the station—that same station that's a museum now. After he came out a little while later, he noticed an old Apache woman who was selling Indian pots off the end of the depot platform. Probably to kill time, he went over to talk to her and look at her pots, though the station master said he didn't seem to be the sort to be interested in Indian pots.

"But he sure was interested in something after he looked at her pots and talked to her. Interested enough to go into the train, get his belongings, and come back out onto the platform. And quite a collection it was, too, including everything you'd need for prospecting except a horse and mule. Or, more likely, a burro out in these parts. The conductor and station master were both baffled because Dunton's ticket was all the way through El Paso. But he said he wanted off here.

"He found himself a place to stay—which was the only boarding house in town, and not much of a boarding house at that. A couple people said they saw him talking to the old Apache woman later on, and she drew something in the dirt for him to look at and pointed out into the desert. The next day, he bought a horse and a mule—or was it a burro? I never can remember. If Dad was alive, he could tell you.

"Anyway, he also bought supplies, and the day after that, he went off into the desert. Nobody knew which way he went since he left before dawn. A couple of fellows went over to the dirt where the old Apache woman had drawn something for him, but whatever it was was all scuffed over. And the old woman was gone, too.

"Wasn't much to talk about in town back then—heck, not now, either—so you can imagine that Dunton's sudden appearance and disappearance, so to speak, got everybody talking and wondering. Well, wasn't but a few of weeks later that the wondering about what had happened to him stopped. That was because the wondering about where he'd been started. He came back to town, dirty, tired, and with his clothes all torn to heck. But he still had the horse and burro—I guess it was a burro. But messed up as he was, he didn't go to the boarding house but came straight here. Or, rather, to the old county courthouse that was here before they built this one. Did you know this is the only adobe courthouse left in the state?"

"I didn't know that," Guthrie said, recalling the handsome rough-dressed stone look of the building's exterior.

"Sure is. Well, the land Dunton wanted was government-owned, and back then, he could pay for it and register it all at the same time. Not like now, with all the legal rigamarole when you buy and sell property.

"Only after he had the deed did he go to the boarding house to clean up. Even before he was done with his bath, the whole town knew he'd bought that small, supposedly worthless range of mountains northwest of town past the Quitman Mountains. People thought he was crazy until he started bringing in wagonloads of galena that assayed out at nearly five percent silver. Then everybody thought he was crazy as a fox.

"Seems that old Indian woman was using powdered galena to color her pots, and Dunton picked up on that right off. He got her to show him where she got the galena. Seems she was digging it out of a crack in one of the mountains up there that was caused by some earthquake in the past. All Dunton had to do was enlarge the crack, dig out the galena, and get rich—or at least rich for around here—before the mine played out. That's an old story in this county. We have nearly a hundred old mines just like the one Dunton dug."

"I had no idea there were so many."

"Most are small and played out and shut down. The only one that's a real going concern is Texas Ores and Minerals. But it's not like most of the mines I'm talking about. Most of them are holes in the ground, but Texas Ores and Minerals is an open-pit operation."

"I saw it a couple of days ago," Guthrie said. "Pretty impressive."

"I don't know," the clerk said with a small shake of her head. "Seems to me that one or two men digging a hole deep into the ground to find something they're not sure is there is a pretty impressive thing. Out at the TO and M mine, they just blow up the ground, scoop it up into railroad cars, and haul off the dirt."

"I read it's pretty valuable dirt."

"Special dirt," she laughed. "But don't ask me why. I can talk all day about the property around here, but I'm ignorant as a new-born calf when it comes to knowing about newfangled technology. Or what people do with their property."

"Well, thanks for your help," Guthrie said.

"You're not interested in some place else? We got a lot of places where you can buy a chunk of property. Like the Sunset Ranches over on the east side of town. I can put you in touch with them, if you like."

"Maybe. Let me look around a little. I'll be back if I find something."

After Guthrie left the county clerk's office, he went to the SB Lodge to think and wait for Espinoza. The return of Thorvald's men was a complication but not really unexpected. He'd just have to figure some way around, over, or through them.

When Espinoza showed up, Guthrie asked if he'd learned anything of value.

"Nothing," Espinoza replied. "Nobody knows nothin'. You?"

Guthrie told him what he'd learned about the Dunton Ranch, which, he had to admit at the conclusion of his briefing, didn't bring them any closer to their goal of ridding the Earth of the troll. They went to the cafe to eat.

Inside, Irene waved at them like old friends.

They sat, she brought water and menus.

"You fella's have become regular customers," she smiled. "Irv and I sure appreciate it."

"Irv?"

"My husband. We own this place."

"No wonder you're always here," Guthrie said.

"Heck, this is like my living room. I barely do anything at home but watch TV and sleep."

"I've never seen Irv," Guthrie said.

"You probably won't," she said with a smile. "He's not much for socializing. He converses through food, you might say." She smiled again.

"Well, you can tell him he's very well-spoken," Guthrie said.

Irene smiled even wider.

"He'll like that," she said. "And if you fellas are still here tomorrow, he's baking an apple pie. You won't want to miss a piece of that. 'Specially when it's fresh."

After they ate and returned to the SB, they retired to Guthrie's room to discuss their next moves.

"If we plan to trap the troll in the boxcar, we'd better hope it doesn't bring any of those Bugle Boys along," Espinoza said. "Our flashlights might be able to keep the troll back long enough for us to blow the fucker up, but they won't stand up to bullets."

"I'm thinking the troll will come down from the mountain on its own, without any Bugle Boys. That thing is just too temperamental and capricious, and I can't see Moran putting his troops in harm's way for no reason. Not after it's eaten several of them. Another one or two, and the rest are likely to abandon the cause. No, it'll come alone. Besides, it's hungry for my blood. And yours. It'll want to take care of us personally."

"So, we're still going to try to lure it into the boxcar and blow it up instead of running like hell as fast and as far as we can?" Espinoza gave a wry grin.

"That's right."

"There's still a lot of Bugle Boys up there if we encounter them," Espinoza pointed out.

"We're going to have a head start on that," Guthrie said.

"How do you figure?"

"One or more of them are going to come down from the ranch first thing tomorrow."

"The guy you wounded yesterday?"

"If he's still alive. It won't look good to the rest of them if Moran just feeds him to the troll. But even if he's dead and already troll food, someone will come down."

"Why?"

"Don't forget, we took all their food. The troll can eat the cattle, but there are six guys up there—eight counting Moran and Thorvald. That's a lot of mouths, and I'll bet they soon tire of eating nothing but steak that they have to butcher themselves. Besides," he chuckled, "they'll be running out of toilet paper pretty quick. They'll need supplies right away."

Espinoza stood. "We'd better hit the hay if we're going to be there by dawn."

Guthrie wished he could have slept better. Every little noise that woke him during the night was magnified to troll size. Every time, he imagined he was wrong and that Halvor wouldn't wait but would storm into Sierra Blanca, nose to the winds for a hint of Guthrie's scent. As he slept, he kept his guns close, but the flashlights closer.

29

RESTLESS AS HIS NIGHT WAS, at least he slept a little. He woke a couple of hours before dawn, and after cleaning up, he met Espinoza in the parking lot. With the light not yet tingeing the eastern sky, they were off. Once again, they were still too early for the rail line crew to be there when they rolled past the work site, but Guthrie could tell they'd made significant progress on the new siding.

They shunted the HiRail onto the ranch line and drove toward the depot. Thankfully, the rails guided the truck, so they didn't have to turn on the headlights. Certainly the troll had retreated to the mine by now, but there was no way to tell if the depot was guarded or if one of the Bugle Boys was somewhere along the way, waiting in ambush.

Guthrie thought either unlikely. Moran had just returned and had only six men. Five subtracting the one Guthrie'd shot in the Mercedes. He wouldn't want to spread them too thin. Plus, they were scared, now. Scared of the troll and scared of Guthrie and Espinoza. Moran would want to make them feel safer before he entered the fray again. And he needed to secure the ranch compound. Most likely, he'd use his remaining forces to guard it.

But unless Moran had fed the wounded man to Halvor, which wouldn't do much to reassure the remaining Bugle Boys, someone would bring him down. And if Moran had fed him to Halvor, the troll was the only one eating. Someone would come, if only to stock up on supplies. But however many men Moran sent, they'd come soon. The Bugle Boys had been without food for nearly two days, and Guthrie's recent ordeal demonstrated that was long enough to get pretty hungry.

Even so, he and Espinoza were careful. Experience had shown they could drive as far as the big dry wash without being seen or heard from the depot, so Espinoza derailed the truck, drove it down the dip into the arid watercourse, and stopped. Within minutes, they were on foot, rapidly making their way cross-country in the still-dim but growing light, toward the ranch depot. Keeping concealed in this country wasn't too hard, but the same was true for Moran's men, so they remained wary and moved cautiously.

They arrived at the ranch depot about half an hour before sunrise, circling the depot and coming up from the south. It was unguarded. Obviously, Moran, desperate to regain and consolidate his control over the compound, had left none of the Bugle Boys to guard the depot. Guthrie suspected that wouldn't last long.

While Espinoza went back for the HiRail, Guthrie watched the road coming down from the mountains and went to check their arrangements to trap and kill the troll. They hadn't been tampered with. Most important, the dynamite was still there.

"Sloppy," he muttered. "I suspect Moran's a little too distracted by Halvor and our attacks to think about checking a supposedly empty boxcar."

He glanced around the site. Only eighty feet up the road to the ranch, the dirt track crossed a small arroyo. It wasn't much more than a shallow trough, but if the road were to be blocked there, the walls of the arroyo were steep and rugged enough to prevent a normal vehicle from climbing them to drive around the blockage. Also, shallow as it was, it would still put anyone in it at a disadvantage to shooters hidden by rock and scrub brush on the banks above.

"Up there," he pointed when Espinoza arrived. "Just on this side of the arroyo."

Espinoza drove the HiRail up the road to where Guthrie indicated, blocking the way out of the arroyo. He parked it, shut off the engine, and hopped down to join Guthrie.

"It won't be long," Guthrie said. "Let's get into position."

They hid off to the road's high side, where they could catch an approaching vehicle downward and from two angles.

Not half an hour later, one of the Suburbans rounded the pass and began to descend. The driver was driving fast but not recklessly, as if he was in a hurry. But that hurry stopped as he steered the vehicle down into the arroyo and looked up to see the HiRail squatting on the road just above him. After a few moments, the driver opened the door, cautiously got out, and crouched there, well covered by the car and open door. He held up his hands to show they were empty and slowly stood. Guthrie recognized him as the guard who'd been stationed outside the window of his room after the troll freed itself.

"I have a wounded man here!" he yelled. "You shot him up real bad! Let me pass! I need to get him to a doctor!"

"Throw out your weapons, and we can talk," Guthrie called back.

"How do I know you won't just shoot me?"

"I haven't shot you yet, but I'm going to if you don't throw out your weapons right now!" The man tossed out an AR and a pistol. "Come out here, away from the car."

The man shut the door and stepped forward ten paces.

"Stay there," Guthrie ordered.

He kept his rifle trained on the man while he and Espinoza came down the slope. Espinoza, weapon also at the ready, approached the car from behind and looked into it.

"He's wounded, all right," he called out. To the wounded man, he said, "You play your cards right, and you'll be seeing a doctor inside of two hours. I suggest you play them right."

Meanwhile, Guthrie approached the driver.

"Give me your phone." The man did. "Your wallet, too."

The man handed it over, and Guthrie stepped back, opened the wallet, extracted the driver's license, and glanced at the name. While he did, Espinoza relieved the wounded man of his phone and wallet. Guthrie used the phone to snap a photo of the driver's license, then tossed the license and wallet back to their owner.

"Let him keep his wallet but not his phone," Guthrie said to Espinoza without taking his eyes from the man in front of him. "He'll need identification for the hospital. But take a photo of his driver's license." While Espinoza did, Guthrie said to the man in front of him, "Okay, William Baines, tell me the situation at the ranch."

"You already know Moran's up there with four other guys not counting Thorvald and the troll, though the troll don't let Thorvald out of the mine anymore. They both come to the entrance whenever Thorvald needs to give us orders." Baines snorted. "Looks to me more like the troll is the one giving the orders, now."

"You come down for food as well as a doctor?"

"Yeah. How did you know?" Then understanding lit his eyes. "It was you who burned down the house and took the food." He smiled appreciatively and nodded. "Smart."

"What were your plans after taking him to the hospital?" Guthrie nodded in the direction of the car with the wounded man.

"I'm supposed to buy supplies and bring 'em back in the morning."

"What I want to know," Espinoza said, "is why did you come back? Why are you staying and helping Thorvald and that fucking monster?"

"A lot of those guys are in it because they believe in Thorvald and his cause. I mean, it's time to take back this country. Know what I mean? From…." He suddenly realized what he was saying and who he was saying it to, and turned to Guthrie with a last side-long glance at Espinoza. "Well, you know. I gotta admit I'm down with that one hundred percent, but I'm just a plumber. They hired me to update all the plumbing and then offered me a different job. I said 'yes' for the money, as much as anything." He shook his head. "I didn't know it was playing servant to some fucking troll, fer Christ's sake. But Thorvald's still paying, even if it's the troll giving the orders now. His original offer was a million per man, with the survivors taking equal shares of the wages of any guys who don't make it. Then Moran called Kelly after we left and doubled the of-fer, so we came back. Fuck, man, between you and the troll, you've set me up for life."

"If you get out of this alive."

"Yeah," Baines said dolefully, glancing at the muzzle of Guthries AR-15. "Looks like I won't be seeing any of it. So now what?"

"You gotta let us past," the wounded man called out, voice weak and pained. "Please. You send me back up there, they'll feed me to that fucking monster. You can't do that to me. Please."

"I ought to shoot both of you," Guthrie snarled. "You were willing enough for me to be troll food. But right now, the only thing I want to kill is that fucking monster. And I'm going to do just that. Anybody who gets in my way goes down hard. Get me?"

Baines nodded.

"Can I have my phone back?"

"So you can call Moran?" Guthrie shook his head. "I'll keep it."

"You can't do that."

"I can do anything I want. Now get the fuck out of here, before my mood changes. I suggest you drive safely and at the speed limit.

You won't want to get stopped by the cops with a shot-up man in the car. I-10 is due south of here, but there's a big Border Patrol checkpoint to the east, so I suggest you turn west and keep going until you reach El Paso. You can drop your buddy at a hospital, and after that, you should just keep going west. Or north. Far away, until you can't go any farther. The next time I see you, I'll kill you on sight. And don't think about calling your buddies from some gas station. I know who you are and where you are, and even if you move, I'll track you down. And if I don't, my associates will. Understand?"

The man nodded, gratitude in his eyes.

"I won't be back. That fucking troll is too scary and dangerous. And freaky." Baines shuddered. "I didn't tell you before, but that fucking thing came out last night, and we had to gather around and hear him make a stupid speech about how great he is and what great plans he has. Half of what he said don't make a bit of fucking sense and the other half sounded like bullshit, but he seems to have a lotta confidence. But even if he don't make sense, we gotta clap and cheer anyway. I'm glad to be outta here."

"Does it ever say what those plans are?"

"Not that I ever heard. It's all pretty vague. It's hard to tell what's real or not with that thing."

"All right," Guthrie said. "Remember what I said. Get going."

Needing no further urging, Baines hurried to the Suburban. Espinoza backed the HiRail down to the depot, letting the Chevy pass.

"We just eliminated two more men and cut their vehicles from four to three," Guthrie said as he watched the SUV drive around a bend and out of sight.

"Think he'll come back or call Moran?" Espinoza asked.

"No, but either way, it won't really matter. Moran's working with just a handful of men, now, and he won't want to spread them too thin. I don't think he'll send anybody down here today, even if Baines warns him about us. And he'll rely on the troll to secure the area at night. And if Baines comes back, well," Guthrie shrugged. "He won't be back before morning."

"I don't like that look in your eyes," Espinoza said. "You want to blow it up tonight."

"I don't see any point in waiting. This might be our only chance to kill the fucker. The dynamite is rigged, the hole's in the floor, and the night is free."

"Free," Espinoza muttered, as if the concept was something very distant.

They settled in, constantly keeping watch on both the pass above and the rail line to the north. But nothing human stirred in either direction, and not much that wasn't human either except for the scrub brush, which swayed and rustled in the occasional light breeze. Occasionally, they talked, sometimes about their pasts, sometimes about what was going on in their lives right now or their futures. Or rather, Espinoza talked about his future since he had someone to share a future with. About all Guthrie could muster was a future just like the present, with normal cases occasionally punctuated by some sort of weirdness Tereba directed his way.

By afternoon, the conversation had died out in direct proportion to the sinking of the sun. For the last half hour, they sat in silence until the sun touched the rim of the mountains then was gradually consumed by their ragged, toothy silhouette. The HiRail was pointed down the tracks, away from the depot. In four hours, they would either be victorious or Halvor's dinner. Finally, the last glimmer of the sun was swallowed by the mountains, though the trough of the valley above would be patchily lit for another hour. After that, the troll would come.

30

WHILE THEY WAITED, GUTHRIE MIGHT not have said much, but his mind and body were gearing up for the stress to come, and he assumed Espinoza was doing the same. As soon as the sun was gone, his eyes fastened almost unbidden on the distant indent where the road crested the pass. He supposed that the troll could travel overland easily enough in more regular terrain, but the slopes of the mountains directly above the ranch depot were some of the highest and steepest in the whole small range. They were probably too steep even for the troll to assail unless it was desperate. No, it would come by the road.

And it did.

Guthrie spotted its head, hunched shoulders, and lanky arms as it slouched over the pass then descended, dragging its club. Even though full darkness hadn't yet fallen, it was obscured by distance and shadow. But it would be present all too soon. Guthrie turned to warn Espinoza but saw that the trainman had been watching the pass, too.

"I'll get into position," Espinoza said.

He moved off into the growing darkness toward his hiding spot while Guthrie stood about fifty feet from the boxcar and made himself obvious. In one hand was a flashlight, but he'd left the AR in the boxcar next to the hole in the floor. The weapon was almost useless against the troll, and he'd learned the hard way during his race down the road a few nights before that its slapping, awkward weight would only slow him down.

Not ten minutes later, there came a distant yell.

"Is that you I smell, Guthrie? And Expinoza, too. Yum. I hope you're shaking like leaves."

Guthrie braced himself, and scant minutes later, Halvor came into view as a hulking shadow against the slightly lighter terrain.

"Ah, Guthrie!" it said, spotting him. "Just the man I wanted to see."

Guthrie turned and ran for the boxcar. Almost instantly, he could hear the troll's huge feet thudding against the ground behind him, spaced in frighteningly long strides. Damn, had he positioned himself too far from the car? His thumb sought the switch of the flashlight in his hand.

He scrambled up and through the opened boxcar door and scrabbled toward the back corner where he'd broken the hole. He hovered there, waiting for the troll to fully open the door and chase in after him, but there was nothing.

"Ah, I see you'd like me to come in there with you." Halvor chortled mockingly. "But you must realize I've been sequestered all day in my mine, so I have no desire to crawl back into that rolling cell. Maybe you'd like to come out. No?" There was a pause. "What about Expinoza? Maybe he has an idea. Hey, Expinoza! Where are you, my friend?"

The troll began sniffing the air and turned toward the rocks where Espinoza hid. But it barely took one step before the trainman switched on two of the flashlights and washed the beams over the troll. It reared back, bawling with surprise, and Guthrie darted to the door and hit it from behind with his own flashlight, aiming at its feet.

The troll staggered away, out into the desert, its feet clattering like stone on stone as it stumbled off. Guthrie could still see it in the wash of the powerful beams, some hundred yards out, but now it must have been far enough away to dilute the lights' negative effects. He saw it bend and pick up a large stone and throw it at Espinoza. Then another.

But the trainman was already moving. Scooping up the third light, he managed to make it to the boxcar before Halvor could hit him. The two men wrestled the door shut, and for a moment, they were almost blinded by the glare from their own lights until Espinoza switched off his. Even as he did, the troll came up and started pounding on the boxcar's side with its club, the booming inside as tortuous to their ears as the lights had been to their eyes.

The booming stopped, and the car rocked back and forth a little as the troll climbed on top, its feet clattering on the metal roof. Swinging its club, it smashed off the housing for the ventilation hatch, and the battered hatch clattered and clanged as it tumbled away across the ground. A second later, a huge hand and arm reached through, groping. Espinoza staggered back from the clutching hand and instinctively shot it with a burst from his AR. The hand jerked out as the troll howled in angry pain.

"You fucks!" it screamed.

The troll resumed its attacks on the car, pounding the walls and taunting them, but Guthrie noticed that the pounding wasn't as vigorous as before. The .223 rounds might not have permanently injured the troll's hand, but they'd have hurt like hell.

"Better watch it, Halvor!" Guthrie shouted. "You don't want to damage your boxcar. If you do, Espinoza will have to decommission it. You know he's a railroad safety and compliance officer, don't you?"

Halvor stopped pounding.

"Do those taste as good as detectives?"

"Look at it this way," Guthrie replied. "Even if you do break in here, we have four of these flashlights. We might not be able to freeze all of you, but we can start with your hands and feet. Maybe that one that's all shot up and probably hurting you pretty bad right about now."

"You're a smart ass bastard, Guthrie," the troll spat. "But maybe not smart enough."

They heard it move away then come back and climb onto the top of the car, where it dropped a small boulder over the hatch opening to keep them from escaping that way. Then came the sound of it hopping to the ground and going to the door through which the two men had entered. It fumbled at the latch with its big fingers for a moment then locked it and went around to the car's side, only to see that it was already locked.

"Well, thank you, gents, for delivering yourselves to this little prison you had in mind for me. I'll leave you two now. Daddy's men will come for you in the morning. In the meantime, have a pleasant evening. Before I leave, I'd like to invite you up to the house for dinner tomorrow evening. We'll be serving, well, you."

Laughing at its own joke, it strode off in the direction of the road to the ranch house, the sound of its voice and heavy footfalls fading in the distance. One of its feet still clattered while it walked.

"That didn't work too well," Guthrie said sourly.

"What now?"

"We wait til we can safely leave the car. Then we set a trap for Moran. He's sure to show up in force first thing in the morning thinking we're locked in here. We need to be ready."

They gave the troll a couple of hours to get long gone before dropping through the hole in the floor. They collected the dynamite and tools, and loaded everything in the HiRail.

"It won't be long," Guthrie said, glancing toward the east. The sky at the horizon was just beginning to lighten. "I want you to rig up an IED. Big enough to blow up one of their vehicles."

"What do you have in mind?"

"Baines stopped down in the dip, but he was non-confrontational and desperate to leave. I don't think Moran and the rest will be that accommodating. They'll stop at the top of the opposite side where it's tactically safer. If we can convince them to leave, fine. If we can't, that's where the fight's going to happen. I'm going over there and dig a hole in the road while you fix up an IED."

Guthrie retrieved the pick he'd used to chop the hole in the boxcar's floor and carried it up the road to the top of the short rise on the other side of the arroyo. There he carved out a hole big enough for the IED Espinoza cobbled together from dynamite and a remote detonator. While Espinoza planted the IED in the hole Guthrie'd dug and smoothed over the ground as best he could, Guthrie drove the HiRail to the same pinch point on the lip of the arroyo they'd used to halt Baines and parked, the HiRail hovering over the dip into the arroyo. The only difference was that this time, he backed up the truck.

He gathered a couple of big rocks that he set behind the rear tires to help deflect bullets. In the bed, he rearranged the goods they'd confiscated from the bunkhouse in a protective wall lining the inside of the tailgate. A couple of large steel tool boxes and a compressor unit added to the strength of the little fortress. The cases of dynamite went into the back of the cab, where they had the most protection.

By the time they were finished, the eastern flanks of the mountains were bathed in golden light. The two men stood at the rear of the HiRail, propped against the fender, to wait. The wait wasn't long. A glint of sunlight on a windshield, then a second following the first, said the time was down to mere minutes.

31

GUTHRIE AND ESPINOZA WATCHED AS the dually pickup, followed by the second Suburban, worked their way down the mountainside, occasionally disappearing from sight into a dip or behind a rise.

Two vehicles, Guthrie thought. Moran isn't fucking around. It'll be all four of them. And they'll have plenty of ammo. Plus, none of them were wounded, which meant they had no incentive to be compliant, especially with numbers on their side. Not only that, they hadn't eaten in two days, which would make anybody hangry as hell.

The scenario was different this time, so Guthrie and Espinoza didn't take positions in the rocks but crouched inside the HiRail's bed, one on either side, protected by the barricade Guthrie had assembled. Guthrie was a righty, but because of his hip, injured on his last day as an active police officer, he found it awkward to shoot a rifle right-handed. Thus his crouching left-handed stance complemented Espinoza's right-handed one on the other side of the bed.

As Guthrie predicted, the first vehicle—the pickup—didn't drive down into the shallow arroyo but braked at the top of the far side. As the truck stopped, the guy riding shotgun emerged, keeping low, the snout of his rifle aiming through the V between the pickup's windshield and open door. Guthrie had heard him called Thompson. The driver, whose name Guthrie didn't know, did likewise on the other side. The Suburban halted fifty or sixty feet behind the pickup. For several long moments, the scene was in stasis, then the Suburban's front doors opened and Moran climbed from the shotgun side while Kelly slid out of the driver's seat. Both bore ARs held at the ready. Moran stepped slowly away from the Suburban, toward the dually, dropping his muzzle slightly, though none of his men lowered theirs.

"Guthrie!" he yelled as he came abreast of the pickup. "You there?"

"I'm here," Guthrie called back without exposing himself.

"Step out where I can see you."

Guthrie raised up just far enough for Moran to see that he had his own carbine.

"What are you after?" Moran asked.

"I'm here to make you an offer," Guthrie said.

"It better be a damn good one."

"I'd say living the rest of your life is a pretty good one."

"Oh," Moran sneered. "You let me live. Me and my men who have you outgunned."

"That's right. All you have to do is disarm, give me your phones, and leave with the promise never to come back, and we'll let you drive out of here."

"Is that the best you can do?"

"Better than the alternative. Baines took me up on the same offer. That's why he and the guy with him are long gone and safe."

"That fucker. I'll kill him for this."

"Not if you don't leave here alive," Guthrie called out. "You can go back up there and starve and maybe become the troll's next meal, or you can try to get past us, and that's not happening. Take my offer and leave here intact."

"Yeah, and leave you two alone with Thorvald? I can see how this is going. The two of you step in and reap all the rewards after we've done all the work. Well, fuck that. I suggest you and your friend get gone and don't come back."

"Yeah, fuck that," said Thompson. He raised himself up, face belligerent. "I'm not giving up my millions just to give you jokers a break."

"I'm here for the troll."

"Sure," the pickup's driver sneered. "You're not interested in all that money?"

"I'm paid well enough," Guthrie responded.

"Yeah, I heard it all before," Moran said. "I don't give a shit who you work for. If you fuckers don't move that thing outta our way, we'll just take you out and move it ourselves."

"Throw down your weapons and come out with your hands up," Guthrie commanded. He used to love saying that when he'd been a cop.

"All right," Moran said. "We give up. Come and get us." He swung the muzzle of his rifle upward and sent a sustained burst at the HiRail.

Guthrie ducked back as rounds gouged through the tailgate and embedded in the protective wall. He poked his rifle barrel around the end of the wall and sent off his own burst. Moran dove off to his left, taking cover on the rocky slope below the road.

By now, everyone was firing, and bullets slammed through the tailgate and screamed across metal and rock on both sides of the HiRail.

"Blow it!" Guthrie yelled to Espinoza.

Espinoza hesitated.

"I don't think I can," he said. "I was trained to prevent something like that."

"I wasn't," Guthrie said, holding out his hand. "Give it to me."

Espinoza handed him the detonator, and Guthrie immediately fingered the switch.

A slamming blast shook the air, but Guthrie and Espinoza were shielded by the truck and wall from all but a scattered shower of pebbles. As the air turned preternaturally still, Guthrie popped up and scanned the scene, AR barrel ranging back and forth, seeking a target. The seeing was hard. Dust and black smoke obscured the arroyo and the rise on the other side, but Guthrie could see the shadow of the dually Ford burning fiercely.

He spotted a darting movement on the low side of the road, heading toward the Suburban. It was Moran, fleeing the scene.

Guthrie shot at him, but by the time the rounds left his gun, Moran already had disappeared into the dust and smoke. A moment later, past the pall, the Suburban backed rapidly up the road. After a quarter of a mile, Kelly found a place to turn around, and a few minutes later, the vehicle crested the pass and was gone.

Guthrie hopped to the ground and turned his eyes to the Ford. What had been the Ford. The little that Espinoza's IED hadn't destroyed had been taken care of by the exploding gas tank and subsequent fire. The vehicle was utterly destroyed. All that remained was a still-burning shell on collapsed, flaming tires, a charred corpse lying on either side.

"Fuck," Espinoza said, following Guthrie down and taking in the scene. He shook his head and turned sorrowful eyes on Guthrie.

Guthrie gestured toward the bullet holes in the HiRail's tailgate and scars on its fenders.

"They didn't give us much choice."

"Good thing you backed up. Otherwise the whole front of the truck would be fucked." Espinoza bent and glanced at the rear tires. "Good thinking about the rocks, too." The he straightened and stared up at the pass. "Do you think they'll be back?"

"I doubt it. Not today. But the troll will be down as soon as possible. It has no choice. It has to eliminate us, or Thorvald and what's left of his crew will starve. It'll be down here every night, keeping us clear of the depot, and at least one of them—Kelly, probably—will keep tabs on the depot during the day. Maybe even drive into town for supplies. If he does, maybe we can waylay him. But right now, we don't have many options. We probably ought to go back to town."

Before long, they were rolling down the track toward Sierra Blanca.

Guthrie was in a quandary. He knew they'd have to deal with Moran and Kelly before they could eliminate the troll. With their original plan defunct, they needed a new strategy. But end-game there must be. Guthrie couldn't let the troll carry out whatever plan it was hatching.

At present, though, they were in a vulnerable position, facing the possibility of constant predation by the troll at night and danger from Moran and Kelly during the day. Or both at night, which would spell certain death. At least they'd rescued the dynamite.

"What now?" Espinoza asked as the HiRail reached town.

"We need to keep tabs on places Kelly might go for supplies. There are only two grocery stores, the smaller of them over by the gas station on I-10, and the bigger one right next to the cafe. Why don't you drive me over to the interstate, and I'll watch that area, and you can come back and watch the big store. Go on and eat at the cafe without me. There's a taqueria next to the small grocery, and I'll eat there. Call if you see anything."

Espinoza dropped him off at the small grocery store then headed toward the larger one. The small store and the taqueria shared a house-sized, ramshackle building positioned between the Americana Inn to the east and the gas station on the west. It was the kind of place that catered to people on the road. Desperate people, since there wasn't much in it, all overpriced. Guthrie had lost the boonie hat to the Bugle Boys, and he didn't want to be without a hat too long out here in the desert sun. He picked a nondescript medium brown baseball cap from one rack, a pair of sunglasses from another, and a couple of bottles of water from the cooler, paid for his items, and went out into the sunshine. The hat and sunglasses made that a lot more tolerable once he donned them.

Almost anybody traveling to Sierra Blanca from any distance would come by the interstate, and he wanted to watch the comings and goings. The Americana, gas station, and store cum taqueria couldn't have been better situated for that. Most people stopping for lodging, gas, or food would likely show up here. And if Moran or Kelly came for food, maybe Guthrie and Espinoza would be able to dissuade him from returning to the ranch.

He strolled around the area to see where he might most profitably keep watch, but there was no single good place he could comfortably stay all day. Behind and next to the store and gas station was a scattering of about a dozen or more poor houses, and he couldn't conspicuously hang out in someone's yard all afternoon.

The only reliable place was the taqueria, whose front and side windows opened a clear view of the gas station and intersection where the main road into town ran beneath the interstate. Anybody stopping at the store or gas station would instantly be obvious. The only question was, how long would the taqueria staff let him occupy one of its few tables? He could eat meals there, but he couldn't stay all day. The only place he could do that was the Americana Inn, whose long, shallow veranda overlooked the area. But to stay there, he'd have to check in.

He called Espinoza, who said he was sitting in the truck down the block from the larger grocery.

"I'm checking into the Americana for the night," Guthrie said. "If you see Moran or Kelly, call, but otherwise, watch for as long as you can, then get some sleep. We'll get in touch in the morning."

He checked into the Americana, taking a room in the middle of the long shaft of the motel's L-shape for a week. No telling when he and Espinoza might need a safe house.

After the clerk handed him the key, he asked, "How's the food at the taqueria over there?"

"Pretty decent if you stick to the basics. The enchiladas and tacos are pretty good, but forget the burritos unless you got a gas mask." The clerk wrinkled his nose and waved a hand in front of his face.

Guthrie went to his room, pulled the desk chair onto the veranda, and sat for a couple of hours, watching the area. But eventually the sun, descending from its zenith, bathed the veranda in heat and blasting light. Guthrie discovered he could just see the gas station pumps from the end of the long branch of the Americana's L-shape, which was closest to the interstate's feeder road and on-ramp. That was where the motel's office was, so he hung out there for an hour, pretending to read the four magazines that sat on the side table between two chairs. One of the magazines was so dirty and dog eared, Guthrie wondered if the motel management had picked it up off the street outside. He wanted to wash his hands after handling it. The clerk looked questioningly at him, as if wondering what could be so interesting about years-old gossip that hadn't been all that interesting to begin with.

"I hate TV," Guthrie said with a shrug, ignoring the fact that the magazine cover featured TV personalities, as did most of the articles.

At five-thirty, he left the office, walked over to the taqueria. The interior was small, but it wasn't as shabby as its facade implied. The booth in the window corner was taken by an Hispanic family of five, but the one to the left of it was vacant. Guthrie told the waitress, a short, dumpy woman in too-tight jeans and a blousy white top filled nearly to overflowing, that he wanted to sit there. When he was seated, she put a menu and silverware rolled in a paper napkin on the table and asked if he wanted a margarita.

"Just water," he said, wishing he could have one. His nerves had been jangled, and a drink not only would soothe them, it would give him an excuse to linger at the table. But he'd long-ago reconciled himself to necessary abstinence. He couldn't go back to the way things had been before Tereba had offered him a way out more immediate and viscerally effective than drink—or counseling—could ever be.

She left, and he looked over the scanty menu, thinking that the TexMex combo probably was safe enough. She came back, he ordered, and she left. Guthrie watched the gas station and the few cars exiting the interstate. Most of the drivers seemed to be locals, though a few pulled into the gas station, gassed up, then got back onto the highway.

The waitress brought his meal, and he lingered over it for as long as he could. The food was decent enough. Afterward, he thanked the waitress, paid his check, and went back to the American's veranda to sit in his chair and watch. While the gas station was largely obscured by the store and taqueria, beyond it in the near distance, Guthrie could see the east-bound off-ramp.

He watched the headlights of several cars exit from that direction, but all just drove up to the overpass, turned left under it toward town, and moseyed on—obviously locals. Another few exited on the opposite side of the highway, but not many. Things in Sierra Blanca were slow, and they lapsed into sluggishness after dark. Even the interstate traffic grew sparser.

Just before eight, his phone rang. It was Espinoza.

"Anybody coming down from the ranch probably won't be doing it now," he said. "Not with everything closed, and not until dawn when the troll quits roaming around. I'm packing it in. You gonna be all right over there?"

"Yeah. I'm going to watch for a little longer. See you in the morning."

He hung up, wondering if continuing to watch would be a waste of time. But it wasn't any worse than watching motel TV or four boxy walls.

At last, at ten o'clock, he called it quits, went into his room, and hit the sack. The clerk at the SB Lodge was right. Even with the traffic on the interstate reduced by nightfall, the sounds of tires roaring down the pavement reverberated right through the motel's flimsy walls. In his dreams, the roaring was coming from the troll's mouth as it chased him down the highway.

32

GUTHRIE WAS UP BEFORE THE sun, thinking that something had to shake loose today. He grabbed his first cup of coffee in the Americana's office, not sure what continent offered coffee and store-bought cinnamon buns for breakfast besides North America. At least the coffee was decent, and with it in hand, he settled in his chair on the veranda and resumed his watch over the area.

The morning had a dull start, but after the events of the past few days, that didn't bother Guthrie a bit as he sipped his coffee and kept surveillance over the intersection and gas station. It was kind of interesting, he thought, watching the life of the remote town from this small slice that interfaced the world at large.

About the time he finished the coffee, his phone rang.

"Hey, Gil. Anything shaking over there?"

"Nada. We following the same procedure?"

"One of them has to come into town eventually. They gotta be starving up there."

They agreed to keep in touch regularly during the day, and after they hung up, Guthrie managed to do a set of tai chi in the empty parking lot, though he was constantly distracted by the traffic. Around ten, he moseyed over to the taqueria for a real breakfast.

He sat near the windows, and when the waitress came, he ordered something called huevos á la Mexicana. It turned out to be a hefty portion of eggs scrambled with pico de gallo, served with sides of refried beans and chunky fried potato. It looked great, but Guthrie didn't have a chance to do more than take his first couple of bites before a dark gray Ford cargo van riding low on its tires exited on the far side of the interstate, drove beneath the underpass, and wallowed into the gas station and up to the pumps.

A large, trim, tough-looking man in tan slacks and a light blue polo shirt emerged from the driver's door, went to the pump, and began filling the van's tank. Meanwhile, a similarly dressed, tall, leanly muscular man slid out of the shotgun seat like an upright snake. He stretched then strode into the sunlight. A moment later, a dark blue, mid-sized Ford sedan pulled up at the pumps behind the van, and four other rough-looking men got out. They greeted the man in the sun, who seemed to be the leader, then a couple of them headed toward the back of the gas station building, where the men's room was, while the driver gassed up the car.

The leader, trailed by the other two, walked to the side street and stared across at the taqueria. One of them pointed at it and said something to the leader.

"Yes," Guthrie breathed.

The taqueria was so small that any conversation could be overheard, and since Guthrie was already inside and eating, his presence wouldn't be questioned. But the leader shook his head, held up his phone, pointed to something on the screen, and spoke. Then he pointed to the north, across the interstate. The men with him nodded, and they all walked back toward the van, where they were joined by the first guy out of the men's room. He was replaced by another.

Guthrie tossed a twenty on the table and hurried out the door. The driver was still gassing up, and the leader was heading toward the men's room. Five minutes, max, he figured, and they'd be gone, but he knew where they were going. The leader had pointed straight at the cafe where Espinoza kept watch only three-and-a-half blocks away. Guthrie was across the feeder and walking under the highway overpass in under a minute.

As soon as he was out of sight, he pulled out his phone and called Espinoza.

"Where are you?" he asked as he cleared the overpass and, immediately on the other side, cut to the right, up a dirt road. It was the back way to the cafe. Two hundred feet up, the dirt road intersected another dirt road to the left, and this road ran, after a short distance, beside the cafe's parking lot.

"Parked down the street from the cafe and grocery."

"Have you eaten?"

"Not yet. What's up?"

"Get over to the cafe," he said. "But don't drive the truck. Park out of sight, and come on foot. If you get there before me, sit a couple of tables away from that big circular table at the back, near the restrooms."

He knew the small restaurant had only one table capable seating the six new Bugle Boys. No doubt that was who they were. Reinforcements. And a lot more professional looking than the ragtag bunch who'd been removed, one way or another, from the equation. Only two of them—Moran and Kelly—were as professional as this bunch, and that was why they were still alive and present. Now joined by six more just like them.

"I'll be there inside two minutes," he said. "Hurry. We both have to be inside before company shows up."

"Company?"

"You'll see, but don't act like you're checking them out."

Just ahead was the parking lot. It was surrounded by a wooden fence, but that was only four-feet tall. Guthrie quickly vaulted it, then darted toward the entrance. As he reached it, he straightened and nonchalantly walked through the door. Since breakfast was over and lunchtime not yet begun, the place was empty.

"Hi, hon," the waitress said when he came in. "Sit anywhere. I'll be right over."

He guessed that he'd become familiar enough to rate the "hon."

"Thanks, Irene," he replied.

He chose the table he'd suggested to Espinoza, about fifteen feet from the big circular table—close enough to overhear snatches of conversation but not close enough to arouse suspicion. Plus, he and Espinoza would already be in place when the new Bugle Boys entered the cafe. A moment later, Irene was there, glass of water and menu in hand, an orange barrette in her hair.

"Coffee?"

"Great." Guthrie nodded and smiled.

"Where's your friend?"

"He's right behind me."

"Well, bless him," Irene said. "You look this over, hon, and I'll be right back with your coffee and some tea for him."

She left the menu and went behind the counter for the beverages just as Espinoza came in and over to the table.

"Hi, hon," she said to him. "Your friend's over there." She nodded toward Guthrie.

Espinoza came over and sat across the table. No sooner was he settled in his seat than, through the windows, they saw the gray van lumber into the parking lot, followed by the Ford sedan.

Irene came over with water, coffee, tea, silverware, and menus.

"Thanks, Irene," he said. Just like he belonged.

"How are you gentlemen, today?" She asked brightly. Just like they were longtime customers. Regular customers, at least.

"I'll have the Number Three," Guthrie said, not bothering with the menu.

"Same for me," Espinoza said.

"Coming right up," she said and started for the kitchen.

The newcomers came into the cafe, blinking from the change of light. Irene looked at them, a slightly startled look in her eyes. They were a startling group—obviously mercenary types though dressed for the golf course. Uniformed, no matter what they wore.

"The big table's over there, gentlemen," she said, pointing. "I'll be right with you."

The scene was so domestic that it seemed to allay any suspicions the six men might have had about Guthrie and Espinoza. They walked past Irene to the table, all fit and tattooed and sporting close-cropped hair. Guthrie could feel their presence as they passed. Apparently Irene could, too. As soon as they were by her, she turned a glance at Guthrie and Espinoza and rolled her eyes.

Guthrie smiled back, but he wasn't smiling inside.

As the men settled in, Guthrie and Espinoza sat in silence, hoping to overhear any conversation, but there wasn't much of that. These men weren't the talkative sort, and they'd been riding together for hours, at least, and maybe days. What little talk they had in them would be all used up by now.

Irene came back with a large tray bearing water and coffee, a sheaf of menus under the other arm. After she placed the Bugle Boys' orders with Irv, the unseen cook, she sat at a table across the room and started wrapping silverware in paper napkins.

While Irv was occupied with what was probably the busiest mid-morning of the month, the leader of the newcomers laid his phone on the table and the others bent forward, peering at it. Guthrie smiled to himself. Though they all looked attentively at the phone, clearly only those directly on either side of the leader could see what was on the screen. They seemed to be discussing whatever was there, and the leader and one of the others kept pointing at it. Unfortunately, Guthrie couldn't see it, either, and he really wanted to. He developed a sudden urge to pee.

"I'll be right back," he told Espinoza and got up and headed toward the restrooms, walking right by the big table.

Only two of the men bothered to look up as he passed. He didn't hear much and didn't get a clear look at the phone, but one glimpse of the screen told all. He'd been perusing that same satellite image on and off for days, now. He stayed in the restroom for two minutes, flushed the urinal, rinsed his hands, then went back out to his table.

The six men were still bent over a phone, talking quietly, but as soon as Guthrie came abreast of the table, the leader straightened.

"Say, buddy," he said. "Got a minute?"

"Sure," Guthrie said, turning and putting a touch of drawl to his voice. "What can I help you fellas with?"

"You from around here?"

"Been here a little while," Guthrie said, nodding. That was true enough.

"I hear there's something called the Dunton Ranch around here. You know anything about that?"

"Why, sure. The original Dunton bought that whole little mountain range out there and found silver on it. I should be so lucky. Anyway, he mined it until he was rich, then he turned to cattle ranching. He lived out there until he died, and his sons took over, and theirs after that, but the last ones liked the big city life and finally sold out. I hear some other outfit's running it, now."

"What's it like out there?"

"Ain't diddly squat. Dirt, rocks, scrub brush, and wild cows."

"No people?"

"Not unless you count the Dunton hands. The railroad line's out there, and sometimes they have crews working it. Don't know about now. Ain't been out there for some time."

"Thank's for your help," the leader said.

"Sure. Anytime."

Guthrie went back to the table where Espinoza waited and contemplated the future. The six men were definitely replacements for the dead Bugle Boys at the ranch. But unlike the first shift, who'd been construction workers hyped up on the opportunity to do violence without reprisal, these men were a different breed: tough and competent looking. They were the sort who knew a lot about violence and reprisal and were only too willing to deal both. Guthrie had to admit that Moran knew how to pick them. But now, they were no surprise, though Guthrie and Espinoza were more heavily out-gunned than ever.

Since they finished their breakfast before Moran's reinforcements, they paid up and left, Guthrie directing Espinoza toward the side parking lot. The van's driver had parked the vehicle fairly close to the front, and the Ford was right next to it, so it was easy for Guthrie and Espinoza to walk between them. Both wore Montana license plates.

Unfortunately, what little Guthrie could glimpse through the van's rear windows consisted of a full load of unlabeled boxes, crates, large black plastic cases, and duffles. Surely they contained supplies, weapons, and ammo. No wonder neither Moran nor Kelly had bothered coming to town for supplies. The sedan's passenger compartment just held scattered personal effects, but from the sag of its rear springs, its trunk probably was filled with more weapons or supplies.

They climbed the fence and dropped to the dirt road.

"Damn," Espinoza said. "The first bunch were like a disorganized militia group, but these guys look like professional mercenaries. What the fuck are we going to do about them?"

"I'm not sure," Guthrie said. "But it'll get hairy if we're not careful. We need to scout the area around here. Maybe something will pop up."

Espinoza had left the HiRail hidden behind a defunct store a couple of blocks east of the cafe, and he and Guthrie were in it and driving away minutes later. Guthrie directed Espinoza to drive slowly around town while he kept tabs on their whereabouts on his map app. They didn't have to think much about which direction to go. The phone's screen showed that the only things south of the interstate besides open ranch land were a big Texas Department of Transportation facility and a federal detention center—probably tied to the Border Patrol checkpoint down I-10, just west of Marfa.

The rest of the town, which consisted of three distinct districts, lay on the north side of the interstate. Wedged between the interstate and the railroad line was the the half-mile-long strip of the main business district. The SB Historic Lodge and railroad museum were within its borders. Also on the street were a gas station, the post office, the newish bank, an auto mechanic, and the row of buildings housing the cafe and the larger grocery store, which wasn't much larger than an urban convenience store. Other typical but shabby small-town businesses occupied the single-block-long adjacent streets that were dirt more often than paved.

North of the railroad tracks was a mixed-usage district, with small poor to middling neighborhoods surrounding several square blocks of government buildings. The one that stood out the most was the adobe county courthouse where Guthrie had met the county clerk. Nearby were the public school and the sheriff's office and jail. The city park across the street from the courthouse was bounded on the east by a road and a bridge over the broad manmade wash that had been created to channel the area's infrequent rains into the New York slurry pit. That lay less than a quarter of a mile to the southeast. The wash marked the southern boundary of the city park. No wonder the citizenry had objected to New York sewage being dumped literally in their backyards and that close to their only park.

The park occupied two-thirds of a large block of mostly barren land. The main pavilion sat almost dead center, a basketball court and a pair of tennis courts occupying its eastern side. The whole was surrounded by paved walking paths, and the area between the pavilion and the ball courts was shaded by a scattering of skimpy trees. Nobody was in the park when they passed. In a climate like this, Guthrie mused, it was probably used less than half the year.

The eastern third of the block was taken up by a VFW post and a large, empty parking lot. Only about ten cars were lined up in front of the building at the moment, but the parking lot said that the small hall was the scene of at least some of Sierra Blanca's public gatherings.

Many of the small businesses on the stark, dusty streets were vacant and quickly turning into decrepit remnants of dreams abandoned by their dreamers. Sierra Blanca was half ghost town, and Guthrie wondered what kept the other half alive besides the county offices, the Border Patrol, and seasonal hunters.

One answer came when they drove by what seemed to be the most thriving company in town—Texas Ores and Minerals—the mining company whose open-pit operation they'd checked out several days ago.

A lifetime ago, Guthrie mused.

The company occupied a cluster of three medium- to large-size metal buildings just off the northeast corner of the mixed use district. From what Guthrie could tell, it was by far the largest non-governmental business in town.

To the northeast, beyond the mining company buildings lay the town's fourth district, which was less of a reality than a hopeful dream, itself. It consisted of a network of roads laid out like any city's residential suburb, though these roads were dirt and stretched and curved across a flat to gently rolling and nearly barren landscape. It was a lot like the phantom neighborhood they'd seen just north of the Texas Ores and Minerals mine, the only difference being that, here, a scattering of houses crouched low on the desert landscape.

Espinoza stopped at the old-fashioned ranch entrance whose tall crossbar bore the words, "Sunset Ranches." The county clerk had mentioned the place. But this sunset dream came with a blatant warning. Next to the entrance was a large sign that prohibited trespassing, hunting, and firearms and promised full prosecution under the law for violators. The sign was flanked by a Spanish-language version. Guthrie guessed that the restriction on firearms pertained only to visitors who were also trespassing since he couldn't imagine anybody out here not owning guns. In fact, they'd seen a large free public shooting range tucked between two toes of a large hill on the north side of town.

From where Espinoza stopped, Guthrie could spot the company offices and maintenance facility about a mile away, and beyond that and to the south was a scattering of seven roofs. A quick look on his map app showed that the whole area was about five square miles, but the satellite image showed only fourteen domiciles. Apparently, not many had bought into this sunset dream.

Looking at the maze of roads, Guthrie had to wonder if there was even enough water out here to support such a neighborhood if it were filled with a thousand homes. And if it were, the residents would certainly need their own slurry pit. And maybe a new dream.

Figuring there was no point in ignoring the warning signs and driving all those empty and probably pointless dirt roads, Guthrie directed Espinoza to head back to the main part of town.

33

THE DRIVE HAD TAKEN MOST of the afternoon.

"What now?" Espinoza asked as he steered toward the main drag.

"Dinner."

Espinoza turned toward the cafe. They were barely inside when Irene appeared, two menus tucked under one arm, a glass of water in each hand, and a smile on her face.

"Good evening, gentlemen," she said as she set the glasses on the table. "Can I get you coffee or tea?" She handed over the menus and pulled two sets of silverware wrapped in paper from a pocket in her apron and set them on the table.

"Too late for me," Guthrie said. "I'd be up all night." Maybe I *ought* to have a cup, he reflected. "Just water."

"I'll have iced tea." Espinoza said.

"Unsweetened, right?" Irene asked, and Espinoza nodded. "I'll be right back for your order."

She headed toward the kitchen, and Guthrie noticed that her attention was attracted toward the front door. At the same time, he heard it open. He looked at it and saw a tall man with a roundish but not unhandsome face come in and glance over at Irene.

He was maybe fifty-five, and his temples were a light gray. It was hard to see the rest of his hair since it was beneath a finely modeled, buff-colored Western hat. He wore tan slacks and a white, long-sleeve, Western-cut shirt with an open collar, a modestly sized but quite obvious star pinned over his heart.

"Afternoon, Sheriff," Irene said as she headed behind the counter. "Can I get you anything? Irv baked an apple pie."

"Thanks, Irene. I'm fine." he told her as she went through the door into the kitchen. Then he looked at Guthrie and Espinoza and came over to them. Guthrie saw confidence on his face and in his walk.

"Mind if I join you?"

"Our pleasure," Guthrie said, nodding to one of the vacant chairs. The sheriff sat, removing his hat and setting it on the table behind him. The hair beneath it was dark brown streaked with gray.

"Sheriff Jim Conroy," he said.

"Clay Guthrie," Guthrie said.

Conroy turned to Espinoza, who told him his name.

"As you can see," Conroy said, leaning back in his chair, "I'm the county sheriff. "Which means you know more about me than I do about you. And I'm sheriff. I'm supposed to know things. Besides, folks tell me you've been driving all over, looking at everything in town, and that makes me curious."

"We can resolve that," Guthrie said, nodding toward his hip pocket so Conroy wouldn't be spooked by him reaching for his wallet. Conroy nodded without moving a muscle, and Guthrie took out his wallet, extracted his drivers license, PI credentials, and concealed carry license and passed them over the table. Espinoza did likewise with his credentials.

Conroy perused them for only a few seconds, but as he handed them back, Guthrie had the impression he'd taken a mental photo of all of them and would be able to recall any detail any time he wanted. He also noticed that Irene had stationed herself behind the counter where she could hear the entire conversation.

"A railroad safety and compliance officer and a private investigator," Conroy said in a musing tone. He looked at Guthrie. "That's an interesting business, though I guess it could get kind of sordid at times. Divorce cases, and all. How did you get into that line of work?"

"I don't do divorce cases," Guthrie said. "If I had to, I'd find another job. No, I have a couple of corporate clients who keep me busy with more rewarding and interesting work. How I got into this line was the result of misfortune. I was Houston PD, but my hip was shot up in a drug raid gone bad. After that, no more street duty. I could grow a fat ass behind a desk or take early retirement with disability and find something else to do. So I did that, but the trouble was, being a cop was what I wanted to do. This was the next best thing."

Guthrie didn't mind telling Conroy the story, and he didn't even feel manipulative, though the story was designed to give Guthrie a place in the hearts of law enforcement officers who might otherwise be colder. It worked this time as it had in the past, and Guthrie saw Conroy relax a little. But only a little.

"So now you're out here in Sierra Blanca on a case? With you, Mr. Espinoza. Janie over at the train museum says you were asking about a missing railcar."

"News really does get around, doesn't it?" Espinoza chuckled. "That's right. I was sent out by my supervisor in Houston, Daniel Beaman. We're looking for a boxcar that went missing last week. Possibly it was hijacked."

"If he's the official investigator, Mr. Guthrie, what's your part?"

"One of my corporate clients owns a major interest in the contents of the boxcar and sent me to assist Mr. Espinoza in the investigation."

"Mind telling me what's inside?"

"Specialized electronics," Guthrie lied. "Really valuable stuff. The shipment came into the Port of Houston and was headed for a computer assembly plant in Arizona."

"And you think this boxcar is somewhere around here?"

"Not so far." Guthrie shook his head, convincingly, he hoped. He was lying through his teeth to someone experienced in seeing through people lying through their teeth. "We still need to check all the sidings and spurs in the area, so we'll probably be hanging around for a few days to a week. If we don't find anything, we'll move on toward El Paso. Plenty of places between here and there to ditch a railcar."

Conroy peered at him, then at Espinoza.

"And you're sure that's it?"

"That's it, Sheriff," Espinoza said. "I can promise you one thing, though. If we come across anything your office needs to deal with, we'll let you know ASAP."

Conroy squinted an eye and stared at him for several seconds, then he snorted and smiled.

"I'll bet you will." He even sounded like he believed it. "You fellows been through the Border Patrol checkpoint down the interstate?"

"Not yet," Guthrie said. "We probably won't if we keep on the rails. But I noticed there's a federal detention center south of town."

"That's for the illegals who get caught. Everybody else winds up in my jail."

"Everybody else?" Guthrie asked.

"Folks with outstanding warrants, stolen vehicles, and that sort of thing. Most are drug offenders. It makes for a lot of cooperation between the sheriff's office and the Border Patrol. Do you know how many arrests are made at that checkpoint? They inspect something like fifteen to twenty thousand vehicles a day, and every year, thousands of passengers end up in my jail."

"Sounds like an industry."

Conroy laughed.

"It basically is. We've even had famous people locked up here. Usually musicians. Willie Nelson was one, but that's not hard to believe. Most of the famous are here only overnight, and their lawyers spring them next morning. As for the rest, and I hate to say it," he shook his head, "the truth is, we let ninety percent of them go anyway. We just don't have the resources to prosecute all the minor offenders." He shrugged. "What can you do?"

"Lock them up overnight, I suppose. Most of them are just average people who want to get high and made the mistake of not knowing about the checkpoint."

"You're right about that." Conroy looked at Espinoza. "Janie said you rode in here on one of those trucks that go on the tracks."

"We did," Espinoza said. "A HiRail."

"A HiRail," the sheriff mused. "Must be fun. Kinda like your own private train."

"It's peaceful and quiet, all right, but it's also a lot of work. You constantly have to get off the main line to avoid trains going both directions. Still…." Espinoza nodded. "It's pretty nice."

"Peaceful and quiet," Conroy mused. "Just like I like it." He eased out of the chair, lifted his hat to his head, and nodded to them. "It was nice talking to you, gentlemen. Good hunting."

He turned and headed toward the door.

"Afternoon, Irene," he said as he passed by the waitress where she stood behind the cash register.

"Afternoon, Sheriff," she replied with a smile, handing him a small plate covered in aluminum foil and a styrofoam coffee cup. "Piece if Irv's apple pie."

Conroy nodded and smiled at her then went out the door. She came over to the table, note pad and pen in hand.

"Sheriff Conroy sure is a nice man," she said, looking through the window as the sheriff got into a white SUV with a gold five-pointed star above the word "Sheriff" on the front doors. A moment later, he drove out of the parking lot.

"Yes. Sheriff Conroy is a nice man," Guthrie answered. When he can afford to be, he thought.

"And you gentlemen." Irene cocked her head back and smiled, looking back and forth between them. "Look at you with such interesting jobs. Private detectives. Just like in the movies."

"It can be interesting," Guthrie admitted, "But not much like the movies."

If you only knew, he thought.

"What'll you have this afternoon?" she asked.

She took their order and disappeared into the kitchen.

"Now the sheriff's checking us out," Espinoza said.

Guthrie chuckled, nodding after her.

"She listened to the whole conversation," he whispered. "Now the whole town is going to know about us, not just the sheriff. As for him, I'm glad he checked us out. He'll soon see we're legit, and that's good, because having an ally in local law enforcement is never a bad thing."

"Any ideas on what to do now?"

Guthrie nodded.

"I have something in mind, but I don't want to tell you here," he whispered. "As soon as Irene comes out, she's going to listen to everything we say. Wait til we're back at the lodge."

"You're not going to tell Conroy about Thorvald and the troll, are you?"

"No. He'd never believe us, and his disbelief would only slow us down. Besides, Mr. Terry sent me here to deal with it, and that's exactly what I'm going to do. I'll call in the authorities only if it's absolutely necessary."

Irene came back and took a stool behind the cash register. Guthrie glanced up at her and smiled, and she smiled back. At last, she went back into the kitchen and came out with their food. After they ate, they were surprised when Irene brought each of them a slice of apple pie.

"Irv says it's on the house," she said, smiling as she set the plates in front of them. "He says it's because you've been such good customers, but tell the truth...." She leaned over and whispered, "Nobody around here ever compliments him on his cooking, so you fellas rank highly with him."

They all had a chuckle over that, subdued so Irv wouldn't hear.

"Tell him thanks," Guthrie said.

They ate their pie, paid their bills, and asked Irene to compliment Irv on the pie. Then they stepped out into the growing dusk.

Moran was out there, leaning casually on the HiRail, legs and arms crossed. He uncrossed them and stood erect as soon as he saw them approaching.

"Have a good meal, boys?" he asked.

"Fair enough," Guthrie answered.

"Good. Then all you have to do is fuel up this monstrosity of a truck, and you're good to go first thing in the morning."

"Go?" Espinoza asked.

"Out of town. Away from our operation. Get, and don't come back."

"Or?" Guthrie asked.

"You won't be leaving at all."

"So far, that's been your experience, not mine," Guthrie said. "A lot of your boys are already in the hospital, in the ground, or in the troll's belly, and we're still here. I'm wondering, did Halvor eat the two guys we blew up?"

Moran actually smiled.

"He wouldn't. Said they were overcooked and tasted funny. Probably from being cooked in gasoline."

"So, I guess it's hungrier than ever, now." Guthrie shook his head. "If we don't get you, the troll will. Looks like you're the ones who need to clear out. Now would be a good time."

Moran gave a sarcastic snort.

"The dynamite was a nice trick, but don't expect a replay. And fuck leaving. Thorvald and that troll are going to make me rich and powerful. We're going to rule the fucking world. I have more reinforcements coming. Lots more. My Bugle Boys are everywhere. Remember what I said. Leave and don't come back."

He turned, went to his vehicle—the remaining Suburban—and drove out of the parking lot, up the street, and out of sight.

"You think they'll come for us?" Espinoza asked.

"Almost certainly. Until now, we've taken the fight to them, and they're suffering for it. Moran knows that, and he's not going to let it happen again. If he can help it." Guthrie glanced around at what he could see of the small town from the parking lot. "But I think we're okay at the lodge for today and tonight. Moran'll give us the chance to leave without a fuss. He's not going to start something in town that'll draw attention to what's going on at the ranch. Not with the county sheriff's office and jail here. Not to mention the Border Patrol and federal detention center. There's just too much law enforcement around for him to try something here. Besides, he probably doesn't have a fix on where we're staying. But they'll be watching now, waiting for the first opportunity to catch us in the open."

Espinoza eyed Guthrie sidelong and chuckled.

"Knowing you, you want to give them that opportunity."

"It's only the polite thing to do." Guthrie smiled. "But not when or where they expect it. And I think I know just the place and time. We should be able to eliminate all the ones who come for us without firing a shot. Or many shots."

"Must be some plan. I gotta hear this."

"I'll tell you at the lodge."

The drive to the SB took them by the motel where the rail crew was staying, and they saw their two HiRails and larger truck pull into its parking lot. Espinoza trailed them in, parked, and got out along with Guthrie. The foreman, Jim Edgar, emerged from one of the HiRails, and Guthrie and Espinoza waved and walked over. Donnie came up behind Edgar, but the other men just trudged to their rooms.

"How's your work going?" Espinoza asked.

"Finished up this evening," Edgar said, his voice weary. "In the morning, we're on our way to Sanderson. They need some work on one of their sidings, and they got a boxcar with a messed-up truck. Gotta fix it before it can roll outta there. Can't say as I'm sorry. Usually I don't mind working the Sierra Blanca area, but not this time. Too much weird shit going on out there."

"Something new?" Guthrie asked.

"Yep." Donnie nodded. "A whole train."

"A whole train?" Guthrie repeated.

"What Donnie means," Edgar said, "is, a short train came by us from the east, stopped at the ranch junction, and backed up into the ranch spur."

"What kind of rolling stock?" Espinoza asked.

"An older locomotive pulling thirty boxcars. That was what was strange. I might expect a line of cattle cars, but not regular boxcars."

"How many on board?"

"We only saw an engineer and one other guy. I didn't get a good look at him, but he kinda looked like that safety and compliance officer who was driving that other HiRail. You think your missing car is one of them with the train?"

"Not likely." Espinoza shook his head. "Our car came through here almost two weeks ago, and is probably long gone to the west by now. But thanks for the tip. By the way, I saw that boxcar in Sanderson. It shouldn't be too hard to repair."

"Thanks. Hope you fellows find your car," Edgar said, and he and Donnie went toward their rooms.

Espinoza turned to head back to the HiRail, but Guthrie stopped him.

"Let's leave the truck here." He waved around the lot. "If Moran does try to zero in on us tonight, he'll have a hard time telling ours from theirs."

Espinoza nodded and locked the HiRail, and he and Guthrie walked toward the SB.

"Thorvald said he sent Fleming to San Antonio to pick up something he bought," Guthrie said. "I guess it was a train. Can he do that?"

"Sure. If he has the money. Which you say he does. All he has to do is pay his rail fees, and he can roll anywhere he wants around the country." He shook his head doubtfully. "So, now, with the two new guys—Fleming and an engineer—we have ten against us, most of them pros. That's not good odds, and I'm not anxious to get killed."

"Me, either, but I'm not leaving without eliminating the troll. Moran and his men can either stand with humanity or fall with the evil they support. It's their choice. But two against ten guys like that is tough odds. I won't blame you if you want to go back to Houston."

"And make the odds ten-to-one? The hell with that. Besides, that thing ate Buddy right in front of me. And then I had to look at that pile of shit in the rail yard. I want that thing dead as much as you do. Maybe more. For you, it's business, but for me, it's personal." He paused and shook his head. "But it's still tough odds."

They reached the lodge and went into Guthrie's room.

"So far, our plans to kill that fucking thing haven't worked out too well," Espinoza said after they sat down, Guthrie on the bed and Espinoza on the room's lone chair. "And there are still just as many Bugle Boys as ever. The only weapon we have to our advantage is the dynamite, but now they know we have it, it'll be impossible to get the troll close enough to blow it up."

"Which we never will, anyway, if we keep trying to work our way across ground littered with enemies," Guthrie said. "We need to eliminate as many of them as possible as fast as possible."

"You have any ideas?" Espinoza asked. "I'm fresh out."

"Maybe we've been going about this wrong," Guthrie said. "We've been attacking the Bugle Boys guarding Thorvald and the troll, but no matter how many we cut down, more crawl out of the woodwork. We should be attacking the troll. Taking the fight directly to it, not the Bugle Boys, before Moran calls in even more reinforcements."

"They're still ten of them between it and us."

"I might have a way to lower the odds," Guthrie said, and he told Espinoza what he had in mind.

"But it'll only work on Sunday," he concluded.

"Still, it's a good plan," the trainman said, nodding. "But tomorrow is Saturday. How are we going to kill it?"

"We need to do a little more recon so we know how Moran's deploying his men."

"We can scope out the train easy enough," Espinoza said. "But there's no way we can get up to the house for a look."

"Maybe there is. We keep barging in the front door, where the train is. What if we sneak around and come in from the back?"

"You mean climb up the mountains from the other side? But there's nothing out there. No roads or anything."

"That's exactly what Moran will think. But while you were gone, I did a lot of looking at the terrain around the ranch, and the sat maps show a lot of detail of the other side of the mountains. It was too far for me to escape from the troll that way in the time I had, but now we have the HiRail. Look at this."

Guthrie pulled up the the map app image of the Dunton Mountains on his phone.

"I wish we had a real computer with a larger screen, but this'll have to do. Okay, the mountains run roughly from the south, where they're highest, to the north, where the central valley slopes down to the general level of the surrounding plains. See this big creek that starts on the plains on the east side of the mountains? It's that wide arroyo and feeders we've crossed several times on the east side. Like the main rail line, it skirts the north end of the mountains, then it runs almost due south for about six miles until it goes under I-10. Right where that truck stop is." He pointed.

"Your truck is four-wheel drive, and a lot of these dry creek beds out here are wide and level enough to drive up. We can take the truck up to here, where this feeder creek comes in. You can see it begins as runoff from both ends of the mountain right behind the ranch house. The mine is right here, around the mountain's northern end."

"So we're going to climb up behind them and look down?"

"The map image is good enough for preliminary planning," Guthrie said, "but I need to see exactly what the valley looks like from the perspective of the ranch house. There just might be more than one way to skin a cat—or a troll."

"I hope so. What time tomorrow?"

"Before dawn."

Espinoza went back to his room to checking over his weapons, and grab what little sleep he could, leaving Guthrie to do the same. Before hitting the sack, Guthrie went over his plan to whittle the Bugle Boys down to more manageable size. Finally, he fell into a sleep troubled by large shadows looming out of an enveloping darkness.

34

GUTHRIE PROPOSED THEY ASCEND THE mountains' western slopes well after noon. He wanted the sun at their backs, partly to dazzle the men below if any glanced up at the ridge. More important, he needed a better idea of how the shadows from the western rim and from the hills and ridges along the valley floor fell as afternoon progressed. But he also wanted to see the train Jim Edgar had reported and how many men were guarding it, both at night and during the day. So he and Espinoza left Sierra Blanca before sunup and rode the rails toward the ranch. That was the quickest way, and it kept them off the nearby main dirt road, which might now be watched.

Espinoza drove the HiRail to the spot where the rail crew had been working, derailed the truck, and parked it on the right-of-way. Between here and the ranch depot lay four miles of only slightly rugged terrain that rose gradually toward the mountains, with several intervening low ridges and small hills to help mask their approach. The land sloped slightly downward toward the north and was crossed by the many small arroyos that fed the main channel just before it circled around the north end of the mountains. They'd ascend that from its lower reaches to the west before the day was done.

The light was still dim when Guthrie and Espinoza armed up and headed out, down into and out of the big arroyo, across the dirt road and ranch line, and toward the mountains. After a mile of trudging the gradually brightening landscape, they hadn't encountered any of the opposition. It was possible that some of the Bugle Boys were out there, but Guthrie thought not. Moran's newly arrived reinforcements had been on site for less than twenty-four hours and hadn't had time to become familiar with the terrain. Besides there still weren't enough of them to guard every approach. Even if some of Moran's men patrolled the area around the ranch depot, it was unlikely he'd spread them too thin by sending them too far into the desert. Any outliers would be within a mile of the depot.

If any were actually out here this early. By Guthrie's calculations, Halvor was returning to his den right about now, and he suspected that Moran, who'd seen too many of his men go down the troll's maw, might be reluctant to put any more in Halvor's way no matter what the troll promised. It was just too impulsive, with negative consequences for any human within arm's reach. Besides, the troll was guard enough at night.

They moved quickly for the first two or three miles. Guthrie had traversed this same territory several times, so he had a vague familiarity with it and knew where potential danger points might be. But they were unmolested as they trudged the rough and tumbled ground, which was rising steadily toward the steeper slopes ahead.

"Shit," Espinoza said as they took a brief halt on a low rise to rest and scan the terrain ahead. "I feel like I'm back on patrol in Afghanistan, only not in as good shape."

Another cautious mile brought them to a spot where they could see the depot and the road to the mountain crest, which was now crowned in golden light that was growing brighter as it edged down the slope.

Parked on the tracks was the train Edgar had mentioned. As he'd said, it consisted of thirty boxcars, with a caboose hooked to the end of the line.

The bombed and burned dually pickup had been pushed off the road and rolled down the slope. By the troll, no doubt. The Ford sedan was parked next to the locomotive, and two men were just emerging from the the cab, into the brightening dawn. They were two of the new arrivals, and both now wore tan desert fatigues, tac vests, and side arms and carried assault rifles. They climbed down from the loco and stretched. Having spent a recent night in a similar cab, Guthrie could sympathize with their discomfort, even if they'd had a much easier night than he'd had. Both wandered off in different directions to urinate, and by the time they'd finished and returned to the loco, a glint of light from the mountain pass said company was on the way.

Sure enough, a few minutes later, the remaining Suburban rolled to a stop at the depot. As the cloud of dust it raised lazily drifted off, the occupants emerged—five in all. Through the binoculars, Guthrie saw that two were new arrivals commanded by Kelly. One of the remaining two was dressed like an engineer—except for the assault rifle slung over his shoulder and the sidearm on his belt. The other, similarly armed, was Fleming.

They and Kelly conferred with the two who'd kept night watch at the train, then the two night guards went to the Suburban, got in, and drove up the road to the house. Before they'd disappeared around the first bend, Kelly signaled to his two soldiers to start patrolling the perimeter, while he, Fleming, and the engineer took up stations at the depot and on the train.

"There's too many of them to tangle with," Espinoza said."

"But now we know how Moran is deploying his men: five down here and four, plus himself, at the ranch."

"You ready to drive around and try to go up the back side of the mountains?"

"You go on back to the truck. I'll be a few minutes behind you."

Espinoza gave him a hard look.

"What are you going to do?"

"Annoy Moran."

"Don't do anything stupid."

"I'll try not to."

"I'll put the truck back on the rails," Espinoza said, then he hurried off in the direction of the HiRail.

After he was gone, Guthrie crept off on a course that would intercept one of the men on patrol—the one farthest south, who also was angling generally in the direction of the distant HiRail. A few minutes later, he crouched down behind a rocky outcrop, watching the man, rifle at the ready, cautiously move across the bottom of the slope below and to Guthrie's right. Taking careful aim, Guthrie sent a single round through the man's left knee. The man went down with a loud cry, his rifle clattering off to the side.

Guthrie barely saw it. Even before the man hit the ground, he was hurrying toward the truck. Behind him came the chatter of the man's AR. He wasn't shooting at Guthrie, only alerting his comrades that he was in trouble. Guthrie reached the truck an hour later, and as promised, Espinoza had it on the rails, pointing south.

"I thought I heard shooting," he said as Guthrie got in and slammed the door.

"One down."

"Did you kill him?"

"No. If someone's trying to take me out, I'll do what I have to. But even with someone like that, it's hard to commit cold-blooded murder. I took out his knee. He'll be out of action for some time. Maybe permanently."

"If they don't feed him to the troll instead of taking him to the hospital."

Guthrie shrugged.

"That's on them. But at least they'll think all the action is still down here." He waved forward. "Okay," he said. "Let's go down to I-10 and see what we can see from the back door."

They rode the rails until the tracks were at their closest point to the interstate. A dirt road crossed the tracks there, and Espinoza derailed the truck. A few minutes later, they were on the highway, heading west. The spot they entered the interstate was west of the Border Patrol checkpoint, so they had a clear shot to the truck stop. Fifteen minutes later, Espinoza took the exit.

It was still too early to go up the backside of the mountains, and Guthrie didn't want to linger. The longer they were there, the greater chance of discovery. All he wanted was to survey the rough-floored valley when the sun was a third to halfway down from its zenith and shadows were starting to pool and crawl across the rough-floored valley. He wasn't worried that the troll might catch them up there once the sun was behind the western rim, casting the valley in complete shadow and releasing it. The entire outer western slope would be bathed in direct sunlight for at least two hours longer before the sun dropped behind the true horizon. That should be plenty of time to drive down from the mountains to I-10.

"Let's grab a bite," he suggested, waving toward the truck stop. "And we'll need some bottles of water."

Espinoza nodded and steered the truck across the overpass to the truck stop parking lot. In another three minutes, they were seated at the counter, water and menus in front of them. They didn't say much while they waited for their food. They'd pretty much said everything for the moment. All that remained was the task at hand. After they finished eating, Guthrie paid and bought four bottles of water while

Espinoza went outside to gas up the truck. When Guthrie came outside, he walked over to the big wash to scout for a way down into its wide, relatively flat surface. It wouldn't be hard. A small maze of dirt tracks lay between the truck stop parking lot and the creek bed, and one led down a low spot in the bank, into the wash.

Espinoza was just putting the gas pump nozzle into its bracket when Guthrie joined him, and a couple of minutes later, the truck was sitting on the dirt track just above the bank. There, Espinoza paused for a few moments to survey the ramp, then he edged down the slope. As he turned north, Guthrie saw they weren't the only ones who'd driven down here. The wide, relatively level surface of the sometimes watercourse was torn up in every direction by tire tracks. Four-wheeling fun, he guessed. But as they drove north along the broad but sinuous wash, the other tracks quickly died out until the HiRail was leaving the only set.

Eight-foot bluffs were carved into the outside curves along this stretch, which was at least eighty feet across at this point. A short distance later, the creek bed narrowed slightly, but the sandy and pebbly bottom laid over hard, dry clay made for good driving, and the way ahead was clear.

Looking at the creek bed's width at this point, Guthrie could easily imagine a flash flood coursing down it, toward the south. It had taken such floods to gouge those low bluffs along the banks. Involuntarily, his eyes scanned the skies ahead. Rain ten miles north or on the opposite side of the Dunton Mountains could send a deadly torrent down this channel in minutes, even if the sky above was cloudless.

The junction where the spill-off from the west side of the mountains channeled down from the two smaller creeks was about four miles away as the crow flies, but the serpentine course of the stream and rising elevation more than tripled the driving distance. The bluffs alternated on the right and left as the creek wound across the sandy flatlands before they fell to nothing about half way to the mouth of the feeder creek they sought. There, the land began to rise more as it made a long, slow climb up the mountains' western slopes. They could have followed the big creek all the way to and around the north end of the mountains had they wished and ended up at the junction of the main rail line and the ranch line. But it wasn't long after the land began to rise that they found the branch that drained the western slopes behind the ranch house.

The first section of the branch spread out across a flat nearly a mile and a half wide. It was much sandier than the lower portion of the creek bed they'd just left, but the HiRail's weight and four-wheel drive took them across it. After that, the terrain rose more, gradually at first, then rapidly increasing in roughness and slope. Another mile and a half brought them to the first branching, each branch half the size of the channel they'd just come up. The right-hand one came from the range's southern highlands, several miles south of the ranch compound. The one to the left ran to the base of the mountain directly behind the compound. There, it, too, branched, the one to the right coming in from the south end of the mountain and the larger coming around the north end, up where the mine was.

They had to park the HiRail there. The northern branch was still wide enough to fit the truck, at least for a ways, but now it was too steep, and there didn't appear to be a place ahead to turn around.

Espinoza parked the HiRail pointing down the creek for a quick getaway should they need it. They got out, and Guthrie's first instinct was to look westward across the terrain they'd just crossed. Seeing how rugged it was and knowing how far away the now-invisible truck stop was, he was glad he hadn't tried to flee that way after escaping from the mine. He'd never have made it. Then he gazed at the slope above them.

On its east side, the mountain ridge loomed slightly less than two hundred feet over the ranch compound like an almost-peaking wave, its inward-curving scree slope topped with a ten-foot-high escarpment of harder stone jutting slightly over the slope. From below, it would present a challenging though not impossible climb, though anyone trying to do that in the face of gunfire would have to be suicidal.

The western slopes though, were much more benign, being the back side of the wave. Making the climb easier, the gully ahead provided a convenient trail that was like a rough staircase, and they were soon cautiously walking up it, rifles at the ready. They'd assumed this side of the mountain wouldn't be watched, but that didn't mean a guard wasn't up there right now, just waiting for someone to pop up. Guthrie hoped not. Any gunfire would alert the men below, spoiling his opportunity to adequately surveil the scene.

Their caution might have been warranted, especially since there wasn't a lot of foliage for concealment, but it was unnecessary. The top of the mountain was clear of Moran's men. In a few moments, they were lying on their bellies, peering over the edge at the rugged-bottomed trench of the central valley.

Since the Molotov cocktail Guthrie had thrown into the ranch house had destroyed the structure, Bugle Boy activity now centered on the bunkhouse, though he could see a couple patrolling the compound.

Moran had ten men, including himself. Five had been down at the train, but it was obvious that someone had brought up the injured man in the Ford, which was parked in front of the bunkhouse, along with the Suburban, the gray van, and the ruined Mercedes.

A few minutes later, Moran emerged, and behind him came Kelly and one of the two men who'd spent the night at the depot, supporting the man Guthrie'd shot between them. Fleming trailed behind. The wounded man's knee was wrapped in bloody bandages. His bearers got him into the Ford's front seat, and Fleming got behind the wheel.

A few moments later, the car was lost behind a rise caused by the tail end of the closest and narrow ridge wrinkling the central valley—the same ridge from which Guthrie had initially surveyed the compound. Even from this elevation, it was out of sight, for many moments before reappearing as the road meandered toward a distant rise about a mile away. The same rise, with its island of light, that had saved Guthrie's ass when the troll was chasing him. After that, the road was lost to sight as it ran toward the gap to the depot.

"El Paso's about an hour and a half," Espinoza mused. "Fleming'll be back before dark if he hustles."

Guthrie barely heard him. He was thinking about how the car had been out of sight of the ranch for at least twenty seconds. Maybe a little longer from down there in the compound. And his memory of the islands of light ahead was sparking an idea.

By the time the Ford had crested the distant ridge, Kelly and the other bearer had gotten into the Suburban and followed the sedan's dust—presumably back to the depot. Moran pivoted, surveying his three remaining Bugle Boys. The leader of the newcomers took up a station by the barn, one of the others positioned himself in the shade of the piles of junk lining the western creek, and the third meandered toward the adit. Moran stayed close to the bunkhouse, where he commenced pacing back and forth, occasionally checking his watch.

Guthrie briefly considered sniping either Moran or one of the others. Except for the man walking toward the mine, they were all static targets. He could easily do it. Any counteroffensive would have to come around the ends of the mountains, and if anyone did that, it would take five to ten minutes for them to get to Guthrie and Espinoza's position. By then, they'd be long gone down the creek bed.

But like he told Espinoza, while he'd do his best in a firefight— even instigate one, if necessary—he wasn't into cold-blooded murder without a damn good reason. He was here to scope out the terrain, not snipe. Eliminating the troll was more important than eliminating the Bugle Boys. Those types probably couldn't be eliminated, anyway, only subdued and suppressed. And moved aside.

By now, the man walking toward the adit had disappeared beneath the curve of the mountain.

"I'll check on him while you're looking over the real estate," Espinoza said. "Make sure he doesn't come up on us from behind."

Guthrie nodded, and Espinoza crept down the slope until he couldn't be seen from below then began to work his way into position a hundred yards to the north, around the curve of the mountain and right above the adit. Guthrie watched him until he disappeared from view then turned to survey the scene below. From his position, he had a good view of the entire valley. This was land where you didn't bury people; you just covered them over with rocks. Except at the Dunton Ranch. With the troll on-site, there was no need for a cemetery.

For several minutes, he watched the patterns of shadow crawl across the land. As he did, he had to take hold of himself, remembering all too clearly fleeing the troll on foot across that same darkening landscape just days before. But as he looked, a plan began to form in his mind. They did have a weapon, he realized. A weapon more powerful than dynamite. The sun.

But the dynamite would help.

What he was considering would be risky. But, he thought with a twisted smile, what wasn't risky about killing a troll?

Viewing the ranch from above and behind made Guthrie realize that they really had been going about things all wrong. They'd tried blowing up the troll, but that hadn't worked. They'd thought about blowing up the mine shaft while it was inside, which wouldn't work either. It would dig itself out in a couple of days at the most. But what if they blew up the shaft and collapsed it just moments before sunrise, trapping the troll outside?

The terrain below would help immensely. Because the dirt road dipped around the toe of the long ridge and was masked for a short distance before becoming largely visible again as it ran over the ruggedly undulating ground toward the last, low ridge, that interval, short as it was, presented an opportunity.

If Guthrie could get the troll to pursue him down the road at dusk, it would be forced to wait until the ground ahead was in shadow. From there, for at least twenty seconds, it couldn't see what was happening on the other side of the ridge's toe, giving Guthrie a few precious seconds to stop, exit the vehicle, and let Espinoza continue on, pretending to be Guthrie. Meanwhile, Guthrie could hide up the arroyo at the base of the ridge. Hopefully, the troll wouldn't realize he was no longer driving the vehicle and would go on past, Espinoza driving just slowly enough to encourage it to keep chasing. The one element Guthrie worried about was Halvor's sense of smell, and he could only hope that it wouldn't sniff out his actual trail.

The timing had to be just right to keep from arousing the troll's suspicions, but if it worked, Guthrie could approach the mine, take Thorvald into custody, plant the explosives, and seal Halvor's fate. If it didn't work....

All of that was predicated on Guthrie being able to get to and remain at the ranch compound while the troll pursued Espinoza, and that meant dealing with Moran and his men first. Nine, now.

The scheme for tomorrow, he thought, should help with that.

Guthrie's contemplation was interrupted by a volley of gunfire from around the curve of the mountain—first a three-round burst, then the chatter of bursts exchanged. The sound of the first shots galvanized the men below. Moran stepped away from the bunkhouse, and since the shots had come from the general direction of the mine, his attention was directed that way. He dashed toward the adit.

Guthrie gritted his teeth, aimed at Moran, and squeezed the trigger, but the distance was too great for such a fast-moving target. He missed, and Moran flung himself behind one of the mounds of rusting mining and ranching equipment jumbled in the small creek at the foot of the mountain. Then the dirt and rock around Guthrie erupted as the other Bugle Boys raked the top of the ridge with fire.

By now, the shooting from Guthrie's left had stopped. He sent a burst at the leader of the newcomers, forcing him behind the barn, and other bursts into the mounds of junk Moran and the third Bugle Boy hid behind, warning them to stay back. Then he ducked down and jogged toward the shoulder of the mountain, rifle ready. He'd only gone about a hundred and fifty feet before he saw Espinoza hurrying toward him.

"I couldn't help it," the trainman said. He looked a little pale. "I came around the side, and he was climbing up here. I tried to back off, but he shot first. I had no choice."

"Is he dead?"

"I don't know. But I hit him at least twice."

Moran and the others fired from below, peppering the rim of the ridge, mostly back at Guthrie's original position. Guthrie risked a glance and saw Moran working his way down the piles of rusting machinery toward the adit. Guthrie shot at him, not really aiming but wanting to slow him down, but Moran ducked around the shoulder of the mountain toward the adit. As he did, the third Bugle Boy darted after him. Guthrie calculated it would take them at least three minutes to reach a position where they'd be a danger. Certain danger, he revised as the leader of the newcomers ran across the space between the barn and the mine.

Guthrie and Espinoza still held the high ground if it came to a fight, but Guthrie didn't want it to come to that. The whole point was to recon, and if they'd managed to whittle down the enemy a little, fine. But he didn't want to get into a firefight where they might be wounded or killed.

"They'll be on us before long," he said. "We'd better leave."

The two men beat a retreat to the truck and drove in silence down the creek beds to I-10.

"At least we took care of another of them," Espinoza said as he steered the truck onto the interstate. "What now?"

Guthrie related his plan.

"It might be possible." Espinoza nodded. "After we get rid of Moran and his men. We have dynamite. More than enough to collapse the mineshaft." He gave Guthrie a sidelong glance. "One of us has to be up there all night while the troll is loose to set off the charges just before dawn." He shook his head and sighed. "You, I suppose."

Guthrie smiled.

"It won't be easy to stay alive," Espinoza warned.

Guthrie shrugged.

"I won't have to worry about that if I can't get up to the ranch in one piece. Let's hope tomorrow helps with that."

They arrived in town just at dusk and stopped at the cafe for dinner. It was in the parking lot afterward that they picked up the tail. He was one of the men who'd arrived in the Ford sedan, and he was in that same car.

"I guess Fleming's back," Guthrie noted.

"What do we do?" Espinoza asked.

"I don't want to be fidgeting all night," Guthrie said. "I don't think they know exactly where we're staying, so let's go over to the Americana. I kept the room for a week. Our tail will see us here and tell Moran. After a couple of hours, we'll sneak out and walk back to the SB Lodge. We'll leave the truck at the Americana, so they'll think we're there. If they decide to break in and try to kill us, they'll find only an empty room and will tip their hand to Sheriff Conroy. If they follow us out of town in the morning, hopefully that'll work according to plan. The room's in the middle of the long leg of the L, but make sure you park head-out out at the short end. That'll make it difficult for them to watch the room and the truck at the same time. If anybody shows up."

Espinoza shot him a jaundiced look.

"If?"

35

SUNDAY OPENED WITH ANOTHER BRIGHT and clear dawn, which probably was about the only way it did in these parts. Guthrie exited his room and met Espinoza in the parking lot. They'd made their plans and readied their weapons the night before, though Guthrie hoped they wouldn't need the latter. They'd also carted the dynamite and all the cases of food, weapons, and ammo they'd taken from the bunkhouse into the Americana room, after which, Guthrie re-arranged the compressor and tool boxes in the front of the pickup's bed so they would help shield the cab.

But even if they'd risen early, Guthrie had no intention of leaving yet. He wanted to make sure all the actors in the little drama he hoped would soon unfold were all awake, breakfasted, and ready to face the day. It was going to be a big one for a lot of people.

As he'd hoped, none of Moran's men were watching the lodge. They might already have showed up at the Americana, drawn to the bait of the HiRail. If so, let them stew for a while.

"Let's get something to eat," Guthrie suggested. "We're going to need it."

They walked to the cafe, arriving around nine. Today, Irene's barrette was bright yellow with sparkles.

There was still no sign of Moran's men when they finished forty minutes later, so they left the cafe and walked the dirt back streets to the interstate. From beneath the overpass, they could clearly see the front of the Americana and the parking lot. Besides the HiRail, only half a dozen other vehicles sat there—a couple of them green and white Border Patrol SUVs. All the vehicles were empty except one, parked right in front of the single room Guthrie had rented. It was the Ford, and it held four men.

Four men, Guthrie thought, both wary and pleased. Wary because it was four against two, and the four were undoubtedly well armed and trained. Pleased because the numbers showed how fearful Moran had become of Guthrie and Espinoza. But there was another important reason for Guthrie to like the odds. The more men Moran sent after them, the more men would be subtracted from the equation of the final confrontation—if Guthrie's plan succeeded—and the men in the car comprised the lion's share of his forces.

Guthrie was glad they'd parked the HiRail head-out and at the end of the short leg of the motel's L, away from the room. The men in the car would be focused on the room door, not the truck, which was off to their right and behind them. He wondered if the Bugle Boys would actually open fire if anyone came out of their room. He thought it possible. The assailants could be on the interstate going east in just seconds. Any law enforcement pursuit, which would be minutes behind at best, might try to track them on the highway, but Guthrie knew they could be off the main roads and hidden in the Dunton Mountains inside of half an hour.

But he doubted the Bugle Boys would try to shoot it out right here. The presence of several Border Patrol officers in the motel would dampen their enthusiasm for creating a scene in town. No, they'd wait to catch Guthrie and Espinoza out in the open with no witnesses and no pursuit.

Guthrie led the way across the feeder road and around and behind the gas station. From there, they were largely masked from the watchers by the little grocery store and taqueria, and after that, the angle was wrong for the watchers to easily spot them as they made their way toward the HiRail. In a few minutes, they crouched beside the driver's side of the truck, the Bugle Boys in the Ford none the wiser. Guthrie opened the door and let Espinoza in then slid in behind the wheel. For what was to come, Espinoza had to have his hands and attention free.

Guthrie knew that the moment he started the engine, the men waiting in ambush would know they'd been flanked. He had to get out of the parking lot and headed west along I-10 before the ambushers could easily catch up. Out on the open road, the HiRail's speed was limited by the weight of the track gear, but the ambushers'

Ford, with a lesser engine, also was burdened by four big, heavily armed men. Anyway, they didn't have far to go, so any speed advantage their pursuers might have wouldn't be a problem. He hoped.

"Ready?" he asked.

"I better be."

Guthrie cranked the engine to life, threw the gearshift into drive, and slammed the door as he pulled off. As he drove toward and behind the grocery store and taqueria, Espinoza craned around to look at the ambushers.

"Here they come," he said.

Ignoring the stop signs at the interstate, Guthrie sped beneath the overpass, turned left just beyond, and stomped on the gas. Instead of entering the highway ramp, he stayed on the access road. To their left, I-10 was already fairly crowded with weekend traffic, but Guthrie was quickly traveling faster than most of the passenger cars and semis. He had only three miles to go to The Boulevard, and he couldn't let the ambushers catch up before then.

They didn't, though it was a close call. With the Bugle Boys only an eighth of a mile behind but still refraining from firing due to the proximity of the interstate, its dozens of witnesses, and limited access, Guthrie spun the HiRail onto The Boulevard and pushed the truck's speed as high as the road surface allowed. Being unpaved, the road was rougher than the access road, and the HiRail's weight, big tires, and four-wheel drive were assets, while the attackers' smaller, lower vehicle, loaded down as it was and made for smooth streets, bottomed out on the heavier dips and bumps.

"Go on and call!" Guthrie shouted over the roar of the engine.

During their reconnaissance of Sierra Blanca, Guthrie had realized that the town had only three major employers: the county government, which included the sheriff's office, the Border Patrol, and Texas Ores and Minerals. He was willing to bet big that the first two would do whatever it took to protect the third.

Espinoza, phone already in hand, punched a button and lifted the phone to his ear.

"Yeah," he said excitedly into the phone. "County sheriff? This is Gilbert Espinoza. I'm a safety and compliance officer with Union Pacific Railroad. I met Sheriff Conroy a couple of days ago. I'm up here at the Texas Ores and Minerals mine, and there's a car-load of men armed with automatic rifles. Yeah. Four of them. Looks to me like they might be trying to sabotage the mine equipment up here. Yeah. No, they haven't seen us yet. Oh, shit! They're coming after us and shooting! Send help, quick!"

He thumbed off the phone and gave Guthrie a grin.

"Sound okay?"

"Yeah, I couldn't have done be…."

A burst of automatic fire from their pursuers ended the conversation, though none of the rounds connected. At the next bend in the road, Espinoza returned fire with his pistol, and the pursuing vehicle dropped back a little. But not much, and not for long.

"You have to keep them off for another couple of minutes," Guthrie said.

Espinoza managed to, though half a dozen rounds from the attackers pierced the HiRail's tailgate and lodged in the equipment and tool boxes in the bed.

Ahead, Guthrie could see the intersection where the dirt road to the mine led off to the left. It was rutted by heavy traffic, and the pursers' vehicle was forced to a crawl while the HiRail jolted onto the road, over the tracks, then to the right. A little less than a mile ahead sat the engine at the head of the line of gondola cars. When they reached it, it was obvious, as Guthrie figured, that the mine operation was closed down on Sunday.

He drove about halfway up the line of cars and ground the truck to a halt in a billow of dense white dust. He and Espinoza bailed out, turned toward the tail end of the train, and ran the length of three gondola cars, where they climbed the ladder on the end of the fourth.

The rare earth inside was mounded along the center of the car but didn't completely fill the bin. Along the gondola's sides, the tarp cover, held by ropes looped around tie-offs along the gondola's upper edge, was pulled taut as a trampoline, leaving no room for them to hide. But beneath the tarp's taut surface remained a two-foot height of metal wall where the dirt had yet to settle. Espinoza pulled out a large pocket knife and slashed the ropes, letting the tarp sag, leaving just enough space to lie lengthwise and not be exposed to anyone below.

"Down," he said, and Guthrie went prone, feeling the loose, dry dirt beneath the tarp settle under his weight.

Espinoza moved quickly to the other side of the car, cut the ropes there, and threw himself down. The two of them were armed only with the pistols. They didn't want to have to explain to the sheriff why they were in possession of illegal arms, so they'd left their stolen assault rifles back at the SB Lodge. Besides, they couldn't very well have carried them into the cafe or across town to the Americana without arousing unwanted interest and possible alarm. Their sidearms would just have to suffice for the short time it would take the sheriff to get here.

The pursuers' vehicle pulled up behind the HiRail and the four Bugle Boys got out. They were the four remaining newcomers, led by the man who'd asked Guthrie about the ranch. They started scouting the train, two on each side, one moving forward, one back. In less than a minute, two of them would pass the car on which Guthrie and his companion hid.

Unfortunately, the dusty ground beside the train plainly showed their tracks and where they'd climbed onto the car.

"There up here!" yelled the Bugle Boy who'd followed them up Guthrie's side of the train. "On top!"

To prove his point, he backed off a few paces and raked the top edge of the gondola car with automatic fire. Lead spattered the air above Guthrie, but the gondola's heavy steel walls would stave off any rounds this crew could throw at it. Eventually, though, one or more of them was going to risk climbing up, and to make clear the risk involved, Guthrie poked the snout of his pistol over the edge of the steel wall and sent three rounds in the direction from which the automatic fire had come. The only response was more fire. Espinoza, taking the cue, peered over the other side of the gondola then jerked back as rounds sprayed the steel wall. He, too, fired over the side to no avail.

"Watch the north end," Guthrie called softly. "They're bound to climb up. Don't shoot any unless you have to."

He turned his attention to the south end of the car. A moment later, he heard a faint clank of metal on metal, and almost immediately after, a head poked up for a quick look. Guthrie, knowing where the ladder came up, was ready and shot carefully. The bullet sparked off the metal wall just below the head, which jerked down. Guthrie had deliberately missed, but just enough to make the guy think twice about attacking from that direction. He didn't want to kill any of their attackers. That would entail too many legal ramifications that he and Espinoza didn't have time for. If anybody was going to kill any of them, let it be the sheriff and his deputies.

Speaking of the sheriff, where the hell was he?

He heard Espinoza fire toward the north end of the car, but he didn't turn to look, and it was well he didn't. He could see another of their attackers climb up onto the second car back. What the guy hadn't realized was that there was no way he could slog across even one of these carloads of soft, sinking dirt or bouncy tarp close to the sidewalls, much less two, without being taken out. Guthrie raised himself slightly and shot at him, and he scrambled back down his ladder. Guthrie almost took a face-full of lead for his trouble, but in the brief moment he'd been up, he'd seen salvation in the distance.

"The sheriff's coming," he called to Espinoza. "I saw his lights."

The lights were atop three small white SUVs in a row, all marked with a star and the word "Sheriff" on their forward doors. They were just turning off the main road and onto the mine road. A fourth vehicle, this one an unmarked black Dodge Challenger, followed a quarter of a mile back, and a state police cruiser and two Border Patrol pickups hove into view a short distance behind.

The two Bugle Boys on Guthrie's side of the train hadn't yet seen the approaching law enforcement vehicles, but the faint sounds of the sirens now reached through the dry desert air to the two on Espinoza's side.

"Fuck!" yelled one of them. "It's the cops!"

That got the attention of the Bugle Boys on Guthrie's side, who climbed beneath the car to join their companions. The sirens grew louder, and Guthrie used the opportunity to crawl over to Espinoza and peer over the gondola's sidewall. All four attackers were running toward the Ford, but they were too late. There was nowhere to go, anyway. Guthrie and Espinoza had driven all over this area, and Guthrie knew that seven vehicles were more than sufficient to trap any single vehicle on its dirt roads. And the locals knew the territory.

The Bugle Boys briefly huddled behind the Ford, which was instantly shrouded in a tsunami of dust as the law enforcement vehicles circled them and came to a halt. Guthrie saw that the attackers could have tried to use the dust as a smoke screen in an attempt to flee, but they must have realized that flight on foot was futile.

"Throw down your weapons and come out with your hands up!" Sheriff Conroy called into the mic of a loud-hailer. An experienced West Texas lawman, he'd used the dust screen to emerge from his car, crouch behind the door, draw his sidearm with one hand, and lift the bullhorn to his mouth with the other. "Don't make us shoot."

"All right," yelled the leader of the Bugle Boys. "We're coming out."

His compliance might have been encouraged by the approach of two additional State Police SUVs.

The Bugle Boys dropped their carbines and sidearms in the dirt, lifted their hands, and emerged from behind the Ford. The sheriff ordered them to walk forward about thirty feet from the car.

"Down on your knees! Lock your fingers behind your heads!"

The prisoners complied, and one by one, they were cuffed.

"Mr. Espinoza! Mr. Guthrie!" the sheriff called out. "You all right?"

"Over here, Sheriff!"

Espinoza holstered his pistol and slowly stood up, hands raised. Guthrie followed suit. They padded across the spongy tarp to the end of the car, climbed down the ladder, and walked over to the sheriff.

"I see you kept your promise," Conroy said to Espinoza.

"Promise?"

"To inform me if there was anything I needed to know about."

"Oh, yeah. Right," Espinoza chuckled. "I guess we did, at that."

Conroy gestured toward their holstered sidearms. "Good thing you fellows were armed, otherwise we might not have gotten here on time."

"The boxcar we're looking for holds valuable electronics," Espinoza said. "Any time a theft of that magnitude occurs, violence might, too."

"Well, I'm glad you didn't actually shoot any of them. That would have meant a lot more paperwork." Conroy scrutinized them for a moment. "So, what brought you up here to the mine on a Sunday?"

"It might be Sunday," Guthrie said with a chuckle, "but investigations don't stop until they're over."

"I hear that," the sheriff said, nodding his Stetson. "I guess I'm up here on Sunday, too. So you were checking this spur, and you just happened to run into these boys? They have anything to do with your missing railcar?"

"Not as far as we can tell," Guthrie said.

"What happened?"

"We drove up here and got out to walk the train to made sure the car wasn't here," Espinoza explained. "We also wanted to get a look at the mine. Looks like an interesting operation. Anyway, we were here just a few minutes when those guys showed up. We thought they might have something to do with the mine operation, so we started to go over to ask if they'd seen the missing car, but they just pulled out those assault rifles and started shooting. They shot up my truck, so we took cover on top of that car and held them off until you arrived."

"That's it? You didn't see them do anything else?"

"Nothing. But I guess they didn't have a chance. They had to take care of us first, and you showed up before they could."

"You're sure they don't have anything to do with the railcar you're looking for."

"Well, it isn't here and there's no sign it ever was," Espinoza said. "So probably not."

"There's not many spurs out here besides this on, but there is one other. Belongs to a ranch up in the mountains over that way." Conroy waved carelessly toward the west.

"The one about ten miles up the track?"

"That's the one. I hear there's new owners up there."

"Yeah, that's our next stop."

"Go check it out," the sheriff nodded. "But other than that, I'm going to have to ask you fellows to stay in town for a few days while we get them sorted out." He waved toward the law enforcement vehicles, where the handcuffed men had all been interred.

"No problem, Sheriff," Guthrie said. "We were planning to stay here for a few more days, anyway to check out that ranch spur you mentioned and maybe take in a little more sightseeing. We're at the SB Lodge."

"Isn't much out here to sightsee," the sheriff said. "Dirt and rock and scrub brush."

"Enough to keep some folks here," Guthrie said.

The sheriff dipped his hat in a little sideways nod of acknowledgment and gave a little smile.

"I guess it's true enough there's a certain charm out here."

One of the sheriff's deputies left the vehicles and walked toward them.

"I called Ben Jacobs to bring out his tow truck and haul the car back to town," the deputy told Conroy, who nodded.

"Tell him he better not touch one damn thing inside," the sheriff said. "If he does and screws up this investigation, I'll have his ass."

"Yes, sir." The deputy returned to the vehicles.

Conroy turned back to Guthrie and Espinoza. "Why don't you fellows drive back to town with us. It'll be a lot more comfortable taking your statement in an office than out here in the sun and wind. Besides, I need another cup of coffee after all this."

Mercifully, the visit to the sheriff's office was relatively brief. Since their breakfast meeting with Conroy, the sheriff had done a background check on both of them, and their credentials and legitimacy cemented their story in place. Even Beaman backed them up —on Thorvald's orders, no doubt. Guthrie wondered how Moran was taking *that*.

"You fellas did our town a great service," Conroy told them after they'd given their statements. "Sierra Blanca depends on that mine, but we never thought it might be attacked. Hell, it's nothing but a big pile of dirt to most folks."

"Are the prisoners saying anything?" Guthrie asked.

"Not a peep except that they were just out at the mine for target practice. After I pointed out there's a big free range on the north side of town where they can shoot holes in paper to their hearts' content instead of doing it on private property with illegal weapons, they called their lawyers. Or maybe one lawyer, since only one of them made a call."

Not to a lawyer, Guthrie thought, though Thorvald had at least one on his payroll. He wondered if Moran might mount an attack on the jail to break out his men, but he decided that wouldn't happen. Neither he nor Thorvald would want to draw undue law enforcement attention to their operation, especially with so many law enforcement agencies and officers in the vicinity.

"Any chance they'll get out tomorrow?"

"Not a whisper. We're holding them on attempted murder—of you two, that is—weapons violations, and criminal trespass. The DA is doing his best to figure out if any other charges might stick. Their auto registration isn't exactly legit. The arraignment isn't until Tuesday. Even if somebody posts bail, nothing can happen til after that."

Then, the sheriff let them go. It was now about four in the afternoon, and hungry, they went straight to the cafe to eat and discuss their plans for tomorrow.

When they left the cafe, they found Moran outside, again leaning on the HiRail.

"We're going to have to stop meeting like this," Guthrie said as he and Espinoza approached.

"Very neat play, Guthrie. But I'll have my men out by the end of the week, and more are on their way. You haven't a chance."

"Excuse us," Guthrie said, brushing by Moran and opening the HiRail's passenger door.

"Have it your way," Moran hissed before Guthrie closed the door. "Halvor's been itching for your blood, and he'll get it if I don't first."

That was all. Espinoza slid into the driver's seat, started the truck, and backed out of the parking space. Moran had to step quickly to the side to avoid being struck by the swinging bumper.

"Do you think he'll try anything tonight?" Espinoza asked.

"No. We just trapped most of his hard-core soldiers in jail. All he has left are Kelly, Fleming, and the engineer."

"And the troll," Espinoza reminded him.

"No matter," Guthrie shrugged. "He doesn't know what we have in mind, so he'll keep his few forces close."

Espinoza nodded.

"All the better for tomorrow."

36

MONDAY MORNING, ESPINOZA PUT THE truck on the tracks and drove toward the ranch line. At about the same spot they'd parked a couple of days before, he stopped and dropped off Guthrie, who wanted them to approach from more than one direction. Espinoza continued on toward the junction of the ranch line while Guthrie headed overland. They figured they'd each reach the ranch depot at about the same time, but Guthrie, now familiar with the terrain, hurried and arrived first.

The Suburban was parked at the foot of the road to the pass. Scanning the train, he saw Fleming and the engineer. That made sense. Moran was low on forces, and he wouldn't squander Kelly, his sole remaining warrior, on the train if he had Fleming and the engineer to watch it. Kelly would be up at the ranch with Moran, waiting for something to happen. Watching for it. Knowing it would come today.

Guthrie called Espinoza.

"I just parked in the arroyo," the trainman said. "I didn't want to go too close or someone might hear me. I'll be in position in ten minutes."

While Espinoza moved closer, Guthrie let him know about Fleming and the engineer.

"The engineer is hanging around the engine," he said, "but Fleming is patrolling the line of cars. I'm going to try to talk them into surrendering, but if it comes to a fight, let me start it if you can. You're coming up from the engine end, but the engineer's attention will be in my direction, away from you, so you take care of him while I handle Fleming."

As Espinoza finished his approach, Guthrie worked his way through a series of gullies and rock outcrops toward the tail end of the train. Because of the way the track curved through three-quarters of a circle, Guthrie was loath to try to get close on the east side of the train, the entire length of which was visible from the engine on back to the caboose. He had no intention of getting caught in enfilading fire from the engineer while he tried to brace Fleming.

Guthrie watched as Fleming walked the cars along the inside of the curve toward the end of the train then went around the caboose and disappeared up the outside flank of the curve. As soon as he was out of sight, Guthrie crouched and scrambled through the gullies until he was masked from the engine by the caboose. There he stood and hurried in Fleming's wake, being careful not to move faster than his quarry, letting the curve of cars mask his presence.

About six cars up, he climbed onto the coupling, swung to the other side, and leaned against the boxcar's end wall. From here, he could surprise Fleming as he walked by and stay out of sight of the engineer. Not wanting to speak, he texted Espinoza that he was in position, and the trainman texted the same back.

"Going ASAP," Guthrie texted then stuffed the phone in his pocket and pressed back against the boxcar.

A short time later, footfalls crunched on the gravelly ground as Fleming approached. Guthrie lifted the barrel of his carbine. Fleming strode past the end of the car, his attention so focused on the curving line of cars and the open terrain to the east that he didn't notice Guthrie at all.

"That's far enough," Guthrie said in a quiet, flat voice.

Fleming froze almost in mid-step, but his hands tightened on the stock and handguard.

"If you move," Guthrie said, "my first shot might not kill you. Then I'd have to shoot you again and again until there won't be enough left for Halvor to bother with. That would be painful for you, so I suggest you remain perfectly still except for dropping that rifle. And your pistol. Carefully."

Fleming complied.

"Kick them down the embankment.

Fleming's kicks were desultory, but the two weapons skittered far enough that they weren't an immediate threat.

"Turn around. Keep your hands where I can see them."

"Now what?" the trainman asked as he turned toward Guthrie, who remained up on the coupling. He might have been facing Guthrie, but his eyes twitched to the right before looking steadfastly ahead.

The engineer, Guthrie thought. He couldn't see Guthrie, but he could tell that Fleming had surrendered. He must be on his way.

At that instant, a sudden argument broke out at the head of the train, with two carbines shouting at each other on full auto. Fleming flinched and crouched down, eyes nervously scanning the encounter. A spatter of bullets whanged off the side of the boxcar, and as Guthrie ducked back, Fleming dove down the embankment toward his guns.

Guthrie hopped to the tracks on the opposite side of the train from Fleming, crouched, and peered beneath the car. More gunfire from the front of the train raked the air, but no rounds came close to Guthrie. He heard Fleming shooting his own rifle—not at him, but giving enfilading fire toward Espinoza's position. He couldn't see Fleming, so he dashed to the other end of the second car back, climbed onto the coupling, and peered up the tracks.

Fleming was crouched in the gully down the slope of the rail berm, still shooting toward Espinoza, but keeping half his attention on the train for any sign of Guthrie. He was partly covered by the edge of the gully, but he had to pop up to shoot at Espinoza, and on the second time Guthrie saw him do that, he sent a burst at him. Fleming spasmed, dropped his rifle, and spilled out of sight into the gully.

Guthrie peered along the length of the train and saw that Fleming's enfilading fire had forced Espinoza to hole up in the train's engine, and the engineer was edging closer by the second. Guthrie sprayed lead across the lip of the gully where Fleming lay, warning him to stay down if he was still alive. Then he sent more slugs toward the engineer, catching him in his own enfilading hell. The engineer flinched and ducked, his attention distracted from the engine. The distraction was fatal. Hearing Guthrie's gunfire, Espinoza leaned out and sent two short bursts of his own at the engineer, who was desperately turning from one of his attackers to the other. Espinoza's second burst caught him, and he tumbled against one of the engine's wheels and sank to the ground, chest a churn of red.

Guthrie hurried toward the gully, finger hovering over the trigger, and peered cautiously over the edge. Fleming lay in a crouched position on one hip, pressing a wadded up handkerchief, already soaked red, against his outer thigh. It looked like the bullet had gone clean through, and the wound was bleeding profusely. Probably a lot of torn muscle in there, Guthrie thought, but no serious damage.

Fleming glanced at his fallen rifle.

"Don't think about it," Guthrie warned.

"Don't shoot me," Fleming pleaded. "I'm already fucked up."

"That you are," Guthrie affirmed. "Get up."

"I don't think I can."

"You'd better if you expect to live."

"You're not thinking about feeding me to that monster, are you?" Fleming asked as, groaning, he struggled to his feet.

He started staring wildly around as if Halvor might jump out from between two of the boxcars. His dancing eyes caught sight of Espinoza standing over the body of the engineer, then turned back to Guthrie, glazed with fear.

"That's up to you," Guthrie said.

"What do you mean?"

"It means, how much trouble are you going to give me?"

"None. I told you I give up. My leg's all fucked up. You gotta take me to the hospital."

"I only have to do one thing," Guthrie said, "and that's kill that fucking monster you helped turn into a serious danger. Get moving." Guthrie jerked the muzzle of his rifle in clear command.

"I can't walk," Fleming whined, wincing and groaning.

Guthrie retrieved the man's AR, dropped the magazine, and ejected the round in its chamber. Then he jammed the muzzle into the ground, fouling the barrel, and sifted a handful of grit into the receiver.

"Here," he said, tossing the useless weapon to Fleming. "Now you have a crutch. Over there."

He pointed toward where Espinoza stood over the fallen engineer, staring down at the body and followed as Fleming hobbled toward them.

"What about him?" Fleming asked, nodding at the dead engineer when they arrived.

"I think Halvor will take care of him, don't you? Get up there." Guthrie indicated the cab of the locomotive.

"What the fuck for?"

"I'm tying you up and leaving you in there for a few hours."

"You can't do that! What about that fucking monster?"

"We'll be back before dark. Now get up there or I'll have to shoot you again. I don't have the time or patience to fuck around."

"I get the picture."

Fleming climbed up into the cab, Guthrie following.

"What now?" Espinoza asked after Guthrie had secured the prisoner and climbed to the ground. "What about the two left up there? Moran doesn't know we just took out these guys, but even if he thinks they're still operational, he's not going to take any chances. He said reinforcements are on the way, and he knows we have only a narrow window of opportunity to try to control the situation."

"Like you say, there are only two of them, now," Guthrie pointed out, "and they've got a lot of territory to cover around the ranch compound. I'm betting Moran will patrol the compound and mine entrance. He'll want to be near the mine if things go haywire so he can hole up in there with Thorvald and the troll until nightfall when the troll can come out. Kelly, though...." He shook his head. "Moran knows we can take advantage of the ridge above the compound, and certainly he'll want to cover the mine entrance. I'm betting Kelly will be on the ridge. From there, he'll have full view of the compound and the last stretch of the road to the mine, not to mention control of the approach from the west. And he'll be no push-over."

"It's going to be difficult."

"Maybe not."

Guthrie outlined his plan. Espinoza would drive him up the creek beds on the west side and drop him off on the near side of the large, flat sandy area. From there, it was only about an hour and a half's hearty walk to the top of the last of the gullies that climbed the mountain's western flank. While Guthrie was doing that, Espinoza would head back around the mountains to the ranch depot. There, he'd exchange the HiRail for the Suburban, which would be less cumbersome to drive over the ranch's dirt roads.

He'd then proceed up the dirt road to the pass and across the valley until he was as close to the compound as he could get without being detected—about a mile distance. Because the dirt road actually continued down the creek bed to the mine, Espinoza would be able to drive right up to the adit when the time came to attack. By then, Guthrie should have reached the top of the western ridge and spotted Kelly. If the Bugle Boy was up there.

"As soon as Moran knows we're active," Guthrie said, "he's going to run for the mine. We have to stop him before he gets to it. If he gets inside, it'll be more difficult to finish this thing. If Kelly's up there, I'll take him out if I can. As soon as I signal, you haul ass to the mine. I know that'll take a couple of minutes, and I'll do my best to keep Moran away from the entrance, but you'll have to hurry. If I'm lucky, I'll be able to take him out, too."

It might work, Guthrie thought, though he knew that battles couldn't always be planned out in advance. Once the fray was joined, it was anybody's guess what would happen.

Three hours later, Guthrie was peeking over the edge of the gully where it shallowed out within ten yards of the top of the ridge. He'd already spotted Kelly, who was steadily and alertly patrolling back and forth along the ridge and down toward the adit. But Guthrie didn't fire just yet. He was waiting for the text that said Espinoza was in position. He had to wait another half hour, and while he did, the just-descending sun washed this side of the mountains with baking heat.

At last, his phone vibrated. It was the text he'd been waiting for.

37

KELLY WAS PATROLLING THE RIDGE from north to south, sweeping his gaze and the empty eye of his carbine back and forth, down the slope to the west then over the valley and the ranch compound below. His path took him about eighty yards south of Guthrie's position, and Guthrie waited in the gully until he turned around and stalked back toward the head of the mountain, where he disappeared around the downslope. Guthrie couldn't see how far he went down toward the adit, but he timed him from the point he disappeared to the point he reappeared. A little more than four minutes.

Kelly was wearing a bulletproof vest but no other armor, perhaps to prevent hinderance to his movements, which were lithe and expert. No wonder he was the sole surviving member of Moran's Bugle Boys. That very expertise would be his demise, Guthrie thought sadly but without remorse for what he had to do. Like Thorvald and Moran, Kelly had made his choices, and they'd been the wrong ones.

Even so, a sling of magazines hanging over the vest implied he was ready to defend those wrong choices to someone's death. But he also looked tired, and tired men make mistakes and are less keenly observant. Plus one man—even an alert one—can't watch everywhere. Guthrie waited for Kelly to make another pass, and the moment he disappeared down the slope toward the adit, Guthrie darted toward the ridge's rim, and peeked over.

It took a moment to spot Moran. He was standing in the shade and cover of a jumble of old mine equipment lying in the gully at the foot of the mountain. From his position, he could survey the entire ranch compound and any approach, and at about half way between the bunkhouse and the mine, it would take him but moments to run to the safety of the adit once the firing started. If he made it, Guthrie's plan would be shot.

On the plus side, Moran was facing away from the mountain, watching the approach to the mine, no doubt relying on Kelly to take care of any issues at the back door. Guthrie eased over the lip of the ridge. The escarpment just below him would be largely unclimbable from below without equipment, but from above, parts of the ragged rock substrate shelved out far enough for him to crouch on and have his head below the rim. He had to be extra careful not to dislodge any loose stones as he eased over the edge. Even a small pebble impacting the scree-covered slope below might cause other rocks to tumble in a mini landslide, attracting Moran's attention.

He'd just made it when Kelly returned. Guthrie was low enough that Kelly didn't notice him as he passed by, went on for a couple of minutes, then turned around and came back, heading toward the adit. Once again, he failed to see Guthrie, and as soon as he disappeared around the curve of the mountain, Guthrie composed a text that read, "Come now." Then he waited, finger hovering over the send button.

As soon as Kelly reappeared a few minutes later, Guthrie pressed the send button. Then, while Kelly was still relatively distant and wouldn't notice the top of Guthrie's head barely poking above the rim, Guthrie watched him swing his attention back and forth, clocking the rhythm of his movements. Guthrie would have to act quickly but from a blind position once Kelly was almost close enough to spot him. Guthrie ducked down and counted in his head. When he reached the appropriate number, he abruptly stood erect.

His calculations were just about right. The Bugle Boy was in the midst of turning to the west, but he caught Guthrie's movement out of the corner of his eye and whirled, swinging his weapon. Too late. Guthrie's burst caught him across the thighs, and with a sudden surprised shout, he went down, rounds from his rifle ripping the air as his finger convulsed on the trigger. But Guthrie paid him no mind as he spun and aimed downward.

Moran was already a quarter of the way to the curve of the big wash around the mountain's head, and Guthrie fired at him. And kept firing. The rounds sparked and spattered off the rocky ground and piles of rusting machinery, and Moran threw himself behind one. Guthrie couldn't tell if he'd hit him, but it didn't matter as long as he was pinned down. He could see the Suburban, trailing dust, tearing and jouncing down the creek bed as fast as Espinoza dared drive and knew he'd get to the mine before Moran. Just to be on the safe side, Guthrie swapped magazines and rained more fire down onto the tangled metal mass that hid the head of the Bugle Boy snake. Then he called Espinoza, who'd stopped the truck just out of sight around the shoulder of the mountain.

"I took out Kelly," he said. "Moran's pinned down behind a pile of junk just below me, about half way to the bunkhouse. Keep him away from the mine. I'll be down there in three minutes."

Before he joined Espinoza, he checked on Kelly. He was still alive, but just barely and wouldn't be for long. Guthrie's rounds had torn through the inside of his thigh, and his femoral artery was quickly and weakly pulsing the last of his life into the rocky soil. He'd be drained within another minute. Pushing down feelings of guilt, Guthrie stripped off Kelly's sling of magazines, picked up his carbine, and went to join Espinoza.

No sooner had he started hurrying toward the head of the mountain than the air was ripped by gunfire from Espinoza's position, though there was no return fire from Moran. Guthrie scrambled down the side of the head of the mountain to the creek bed, then followed it past the adit to where the Suburban sat. Just beyond, Espinoza crouched behind the last of the mountain's shoulder, watching up the slope.

"It's me," Guthrie called out so Espinoza wouldn't be surprised.

"He's in the bunkhouse," Espinoza said when Guthrie was beside him. "I tried to get him, but there's too much junk out there for cover."

"We can assume he's rearming himself," Guthrie said. "We need to flush him out."

"That's going to be tough. He's on slightly higher ground, and most of the area in front of the bunkhouse is open. He's protected on the right by that steep slope, though we could use those piles of junk in the creek for cover like he did. But all that stops a good eighty feet away. We'd never get across that open ground without getting shot down."

"I have an idea. You go on up there as far as you can and still stay hidden. Here, take these." He handed over Kelly's rifle and magazine sling. "When you get there, shoot at the house with both rifles."

"Both? Oh, yeah." Espinoza's eyes lit. "Two rifles, two shooters. And meanwhile, I suppose you'll be sneaking around the back."

"Not the back, exactly. I'll have to go in the front door. But as long as Moran thinks we're both down here, he'll concentrate his attention on you. With the creek beds, corral, and barn, I've got plenty of cover until I get right beside the bunkhouse. Once I'm there, he won't look for me if he thinks we're both hiding behind those piles."

"Okay. Let's do it. But don't let that bastard get the better of you. I can't deal with him and that fucking monster by myself."

"I have no intention of not going home in the next day or two," Guthrie said. "You just have to make sure all his attention is down here until I'm ready to go in. I'll text you when I'm in position."

Guthrie watched Espinoza edge around the side of the piles of junk closest to the mountain slope and start working his way up the nearly choked creek bed, then he set off on his own journey. The first part was to crouch up the main creek bed until he was at the junction of the dirt track that angled away from the creek and behind the barn. Once there, the barn masked him from the bunkhouse, and he ran beside the corral, toward the far corner of the building and peeked around it.

The bunkhouse sat sixty or so feet away. He couldn't see any movement behind the windows, but surely Moran was there, watching not only down the gentle slope toward the mine, but also the terrain on either side of the building. Crossing that distance unseen was critical, but Moran would have a good view through the east windows. If his attention wasn't directed toward Espinoza, he was sure to see Guthrie dashing toward the bunkhouse. Guthrie pulled out his phone and texted Espinoza to begin firing.

The trainman must have already had his finger on the trigger. A couple of ragged bursts spattered the front of the bunkhouse, breaking two windows. Then more bursts from a slightly different spot followed. Moran, well hidden in the dimness of the living room, returned fire through one of the broken windows, his rounds spanging off twisted metal near the place the second set of bursts came from. But the first rifle was already speaking again as Espinoza sprayed an entire magazine at the house.

That's it, Guthrie thought, and even before the magazine was empty, he sprinted toward the rear corner of the bunkhouse. Espinoza could easily see him, so there was no danger he'd be hit, and he hoped that Moran, ducking from Espinoza's fire, wouldn't see him either. He rounded the back corner and stopped, now out of Moran's sight. Unfortunately, the bunkhouse didn't have a back door, so Guthrie would have to go in through the front.

He listened for footsteps inside. He needn't have bothered as Moran again fired from the front room toward Espinoza.

"Shoot again," he texted. "Stop when I get on the porch."

Espinoza complied as Guthrie, crouching, ducked beneath the bunkhouse's side windows and hunkered down at the front corner as the front wall and windows erupted with Espinoza's gunfire. It was amazing Moran wasn't hit.

But apparently he wasn't. The instant Espinoza stopped firing, the muzzle of Moran's gun appeared through a broken window, spitting fire and bullets at the trainman's location. Guthrie hoped Espinoza was well protected.

His only cover the blasting racket of Moran's AR, Guthrie raced down the front porch and slammed through the front door just as Moran's gun ran dry. Moran, crouching behind three mattresses leaned against the front wall, was ejecting an empty magazine and reaching for another from a case on the floor behind him. Apparently the racket of his own firing had temporarily deafened him because he seemed surprised when Guthrie burst into the room.

Guthrie raised the barrel of his carbine, but Moran was too quick, throwing his empty rifle at Guthrie's head and lunging in its wake. In an instant, he was grappling for Guthrie's rifle.

Moran was a big man. Bigger than Guthrie. And maybe even better trained. They struggled over the gun for a moment, and as Guthrie tried to get his right hand on the weapon to twist it away, Moran swung a left hook at his temple. Guthrie managed to twist his head enough to take the blow on the rear quarter panel of his cranium. It hurt, and lights flashed briefly in his head, but Moran's knuckles landed awkwardly, and he'd hurt himself, too.

Moran grunted and jerked his hand back, and the interlude was all Guthrie needed to tighten his grip on the gun and pull the trigger. The muzzle wasn't directed at Moran's head, but his face was next to it, and he turned violently away as prolonged muzzle debris ravaged his cheek and ear.

Then the gun went empty, and with Moran momentarily stunned and blinded by the debris and blasting racket right beside his head, Guthrie let go of the weapon and, in the same instant, delivered a knuckle strike to the hollow beneath Moran's jawline, right where the adenoids were. It was a vicious move designed to incapacitate or kill, but he was a little off. Even so, Moran gave a choking gasp and staggered back. The rifle fell to the floor between them, but Moran didn't make a move toward it. Instead, his hand groped for his sidearm. He was moving sluggishly, off hand at his throat as he drew a ragged breath.

Guthrie threw himself to the side, snatched at his own pistol, and fired four times into Moran's torso.

The man stumbled backward against a wall and tried to raise his Glock, but dropped it instead. He wilted to the floor.

"I had it all, you bastard," he snarled. "You fucking bastard."

He slumped, and that was all.

At that moment, Espinoza rushed in through the front door, carbine raised.

"Fuck," he said, staring at Moran.

Guthrie holstered his pistol.

"Come on," he said, patting Espinoza on the shoulder as he passed by on his way to the front door. "We have work to do."

38

AFTER THEY DRAGGED MORAN'S BODY into one of the two bunk rooms, Guthrie went through his pockets and found a ring of keys to the Bugle Boys' vehicles. All that remained were the Mercedes, the gray van, and the Suburban. Espinoza would need the latter during the chase. The Mercedes' front end was mashed in and bumper askew from plowing into the mountain, and its bullet-riddled windshield and engine made it unserviceable. Guthrie was disappointed. He'd like to have driven an expensive car like that at least once in his life, but if he'd ever have the chance, this wasn't it. No matter. The gray van would do as a temporary paddy wagon.

He drove the Suburban down to the ranch depot and down the dirt road beside the track to the HiRail, Espinoza riding shotgun. There, Guthrie retrieved the tools he'd used to break the hole in the floor of the boxcar, while Espinoza collected the dynamite. Guthrie also picked up the HiRail's first-aid kit. Back at the depot, Guthrie untied Fleming from the engine's cab and handed him the kit.

"Fuck," the man snarled as he snatched the kit from Guthrie's hand. "That's it? Fuck. You gotta take me to a hospital."

"Don't be repetitious," Guthrie said. "When this is all over, we'll take you, and not before, so shut up about it, or I'll leave you tied up at the mine entrance."

That shut Fleming up.

"Bandage yourself, then come down," Guthrie said. "We'll be waiting."

Guthrie climbed down from the engine and joined Espinoza next to the Suburban. Many minutes later, Fleming, pant leg torn open and thigh thickly bandaged, eased himself, wincing and groaning, to the ground. Leaning on his AR crutch, he hobbled over to the Suburban.

Guthrie drove them back up to the compound, and while Espinoza went to work in the bunkhouse, putting together the IEDs for the mine, Guthrie took Fleming into the second bunk room and trussed him to one of the wood-frame bunks. Then he went out to get the tools. He had some work to do if he was to endure another night with the troll.

Inside the bunkhouse, he attacked the floor in the corner of the room closest to the barn. The room where they'd put Moran. In short order, he'd made a hole in the floor big enough to fit through if the troll came after him. As an added precaution, he dragged Moran's body close so he could pull it over the hole after he dropped into the crawlspace. Hopefully, from there, he'd be able to escape, maybe into the barn. There wasn't much of anywhere else to go except for the mine, and that wasn't a viable option.

Finished, he went to the front room, where Espinoza was working on the IEDs. He was ready to take a break, too, so they sat for a few minutes, drank some water, and finalized their plans.

"I don't like it," Espinoza said. "If the timing is off just a little bit...."

Guthrie just shrugged as he trailed off.

"No choice. Moran might be gone, but his reinforcements are still coming. They could be here tomorrow. We have to finish this by morning, or *we're* finished."

"Hell, I don't think I can take much more of this, anyway."

Espinoza went back to work on the IEDs, and Guthrie went to the kitchen, found a bottle of water, and took it into the room where Fleming sat against the bunk post.

"Thirsty?"

Fleming nodded, though the hatred and fear in his eyes didn't diminish. Guthrie squatted and tilted the bottle so the captive could drink.

"Okay," he said as he stood after Fleming was done. "Tell me what you know."

"They don't tell me squat," Fleming spat. "Thorvald and Moran. They're the ones you need to talk to."

"They're not here. You are."

"Moran? Is he dead?"

"He's dead."

"And Thorvald?"

"You tell me."

"Down in the mine, I guess. He's always down in the mine with that fucking monster. Shit," Fleming shook his head. "I wish Beaman hadn't gotten me mixed up in this mess."

"Don't blame others for your own bad choices," Guthrie said. "Tell me about Thorvald. You said he's always down in the mine. What about food and water? How did he communicate with Moran?"

"They bring him everything he needs. A couple of times each day, he and Moran meet at the mine entrance. That's when he gives orders and gets supplies. Usually right after Halvor retreats for the day and again not long before he comes out after sundown."

So it was possible, Guthrie thought, that Thorvald and his monster might not be aware that the remnants of their support team had been eliminated. Halvor's cavern was deep, and maybe neither it nor its father had heard the gunfire. Even if they had, gunfire wasn't unusual around the ranch the last few days.

Maybe they were waiting for Moran's evening report, when the troll emerged for the night. But by then, it would be too late to alter the track of events. Guthrie only wished he could be sure that track led to a favorable outcome—for the sake of the world as well as himself.

He took hold of himself. No matter. The tactics of stealth were past their prime, anyway. Direct confrontation had always been inevitable.

"All right" Guthrie said. "Keep quiet, and we all might get out of this. Raise a ruckus, and…. Well, like I said, I'd hate to have to shoot a bound man—again—or see another eaten by that thing. Relax. You won't be here for long."

He left the room, shut the door, and went to the living room.

"How are the IEDs going?"

"Just finishing up."

"When you're done, hide them inside that overturned mine cart right beside the mine entrance."

"What about you?"

"I have to go down there to retrieve Thorvald, whether he likes it or not."

"Why the fuck would you want to do that?" Espinoza asked. "Look at the misery he's caused. He needs to be punished. Besides, he wants to stay with the troll, so let him die with it."

"Yes. He needs to be punished, but we don't. He's not only the cause of what's happened, he's our only proof of our innocence. I don't want the Catholic Church on my ass for the rest of my life over this, and neither do you. We have to rescue him and turn him over to them. Only they have the power—and the need—to cover up everything that's happened here."

Those were all good reasons, Guthrie told himself, but personally, he wanted to see what the hell was going on down in that mine.

Leaving Espinoza to move the explosive charges, Guthrie walked to adit, hesitated a moment at the choking atmosphere wafting from its depths, then stepped into the dim interior.

It stank of rot and the troll's foul body odors. With him, Guthrie had three of the powerful flashlights, one taped on either side of the barrel of his rifle. Those two were off for the moment, but the one in his right hand was casting its shocking glare ahead of him.

Guthrie proceeded with caution, and all too soon, the shaft turned and the adit disappeared from view. The air grew greasy with stench. After he'd gone another hundred feet, a huge voice boomed down the tunnel.

"Ah, Guthrie! So nice of you to visit. Would you be so kind as to extinguish your flashlight?"

Guthrie had to wonder how the troll could smell him through its own BO and halitosis and the more pervasive and powerful stench of decaying flesh.

A few moments later and keeping his flashlight trained directly on the floor, he came to the spot where the shaft opened into the larger cavern. The troll reclined against the far wall, and Guthrie could see that a fresh body lay on the charnel pile—the man Espinoza had shot above the adit. Guthrie decided he wouldn't mention it to Espinoza.

Thorvald, completely naked, stood beside the troll's right knee. The last few days had wrought a drastic change over the renegade priest. Thorvald looked terrible: filthy, haggard, and worn. His once fleshy face and body were turning gaunt beneath sagging flesh and pallid skin, and the look in his eyes combined terror and fascination with feral caution. But he obviously was still attentive.

The troll flinched from the light and tensed up.

"Ouch," it said, shrinking back and drawing a large tarp over its body and head like a blanket to keep the rays from striking it directly. It looked like the tarp that had covered the adit to protect the troll before it freed itself from its slab. "I hope you aren't going to shine that beastly light right on me," came its slightly muffled voice. "You know it isn't really powerful enough to do me permanent harm, and we're very resilient, aren't we, Daddy?" It didn't bother waiting for Thorvald's confirmation. "But if you annoy me with it too much, I might have to do something about it. Please turn it off so we can talk like civilized…. Well, not men, exactly. Beings."

It probably *could* do something, Guthrie reflected. The light might stiffen the monster where it struck, but the cavern wasn't all that large, and Guthrie knew just how fast the troll could move. And now it had the tarp for protection.

"I have three flashlights, which is probably more than you can tolerate," Guthrie said. "I won't do anything if you don't, but I'll kill Thorvald the instant you move toward me."

"Fair enough."

Guthrie switched off the light. The scattered electric lights strung around illuminated the space well enough, and Guthrie could deploy the flashlights in a second and shoot Thorvald even faster. Halvor lowered the tarp enough that its head stuck out.

It blinked and said, " How nice to see you again. I hope you'll stay a little longer this time." It grinned.

"I'll stay long enough."

"Who is it, Brother?"

The squeaking voice came from Guthrie's right, and he spun that direction, barrel of his rifle rising.

"No!" Roared the troll, nearly deafening him.

Guthrie heard the sound of the tarp being flung back, and he swung back toward the troll, fingers of one hand flipping on the flashlights. The entire cavern lit with blinding light.

"No!" Halvor shrieked in a panic Guthrie had not yet seen from it.

Almost instantaneously, Thorvald wailed, "The buds!" He scrambled toward Guthrie, his bare feet stumbling over the stones littering the cavern floor. He crashed down then scrambled to his feet, oblivious to the blood leaking from cuts and abrasions on his shins, knees, and hands. Then he was knocked aside as the troll, grunting with desperate anger, lunged toward Guthrie, raising a forearm across its eyes but otherwise heedless of the light that grayed and stiffened any flesh it swept across.

Guthrie, surprised by the troll's sudden angry surge, instinctively leapt back but still was jolted as the thing's massive fingers clipped his shoulder, sending him reeling backward up the tunnel. Staggering around the first bend, out of sight of the troll, he managed to lift the barrel of his AR. The .223 rounds might not do a lot of damage to the troll's body, but a face full of them might hold it off or even permanently blind it. They'd certainly shred Thorvald.

A movement at the bend in the tunnel sent Guthrie's forefinger hovering over the trigger.

"Guthrie!" It was Thorvald. "Don't shoot." He eased into the wash of light, protecting himself from their raw energy with the tarp. "Please stop," he called. "You don't understand. Turn off those beastly lights and come back. Halvor's sitting down again. Just don't shine those lights in here."

"Don't fuck with me, Thorvald."

"Nobody is fucking with you. Come back. Let's talk."

Guthrie switched off the flashlights and slowly approached the mouth of the tunnel. As he did, Thorvald backed up to the troll and dragged the tarp into its hand. Halvor again reclined against the back wall, regarding Guthrie with an expression that could have been amusement, anger, or curiosity, or a bit of all three. Guthrie made sure the man and his monster were in place before he poked his head into the cavern and looked to the right, in the direction the squeaking voice had come from.

At first he didn't see anything in the subdued light, but then, when it moved, he did. Or *was* that the one he'd heard? Maybe the voice had come from one of the others. There were dozens in various stages of growth. Polyps. Troll polyps. The largest were entire and fully-formed troll heads from the size of bowling balls to basketballs, while the smallest were mere glistening bumps with tiny faces pulsating in some of the cracks from which they grew.

Oozed.

The chest and shoulders of some of the larger were emerging beneath their already hairy chins and brutal features. He cast his eyes toward the opposite wall and saw dozens more, squirming in the dim light like sentient pustules. No wonder Halvor needed lots of cattle, Guthrie thought. And lots of boxcars.

"You are Guthrie," said one of the largest polyps. "Big Brother told us all about you."

"Yes," shouted another large polyp. "Guthrie!"

"Will he do it, Brother?" piped in one of the small voices. "Is he a patriot to our cause?"

Suddenly all the polyps were writhing and yelling Guthrie's name, though a few said they'd rather eat him right then and there. Most were so small that their voices were mere squeaks, but the larger sounded like unruly teenagers.

"They're big," Guthrie commented.

"Thanks to you, they've been eating well," Thorvald said, satisfaction in his voice. "The more food—especially human—the quicker they grow. Look at Halvor. Only a year old and already almost full grown."

Because most of the mouths were small, the cacophony quickly rose into the treble with a tenor undertone, and Guthrie stared, a little taken aback. He wondered if he ought to feel nauseous at the sight of the walls now writhing with troll polyps all yelling and piping his name, but all he felt was sarcastic disgust.

A bass shout from Halvor cut across the racket, and Guthrie jerked in its direction, thumb on the flashlight's switch. But the troll remained sitting against the back wall. The cacophony, suddenly silenced.

"Yes, little brothers. This is Guthrie. Guthrie, this is my brood of brothers. Our father chose well. The walls of this cavern are lined with just the sort of cracks we need. What do you think?"

Instead of looking at the troll, Guthrie stared at Thorvald.

"I think you must be getting kinda sore," he commented. "Or did Moran bring you a bottle of baby oil?"

The renegade priest made no effort to appear embarrassed.

"You think this is some sort of joke?" he demanded. "No man has ever had a family such as mine, and I intend to make it an army. An army of my own flesh and blood and no other's. When I'm done, it won't be just the Church that suffers, but everyone involved who tries to thwart my will with modern corruptions and falsehoods. I'll show them all."

"Why is it that petty dictators like you are so predictable?" Guthrie asked. "Is it because you all possess shallow personalities? It seems like you have to hurt all mankind just to feel alive."

The cacophony erupted again, this time with more of the voices expressing a desire to eat Guthrie.

"Quiet, little ones," Halvor yelled, and the buds went silent. "How about it, Guthrie? Perhaps you would like to participate alongside Father Thorvald? I hate to admit it, but Daddy is just a little too old for what I have in mind. He's only good for a couple of squirts a day. Sometimes only one. At this rate, it's going to take well more than a year to get my army together. And eventually, he'll no longer be productive at all." It smiled invitingly. "Things would go much more rapidly if you'd join us. You're younger than Daddy. You probably could create three or four comrades a day. Just think, Guthrie: an instant dynasty of your own. We'll even call you Father Guthrie, if you like, and enshrine you in our pantheon of remarkable progenitors."

"Do I get my own cave? This one's getting crowded."

"There's always room for one more," Halvor said. "Besides, once a brother has broken free, the cunt crack is good for another. And another. This cave is plenty big enough."

"Just what I always aspired to," Guthrie said. "Being the father of a clan of inbred assholes with no cojones and over-productive pituitaries and amygdalas."

"I think it's preferable to being eaten alive. Besides, the smarter the human, the smarter his trolls. Isn't that right, Daddy?" The troll grinned at Thorvald, who smiled back weakly, then it looked at Guthrie, amusement in its eyes.

"Seeing how exhausted Daddy has become, I'm beginning to wonder if artificial insemination would work. I could have the Bugle Boys raid a sperm bank...."

"Stop," Guthrie said, holding up his hand. "Enough of your thwarted sex life. If you're asking me to join Thorvald's pathetic inseminary, the answer is, no thanks."

Halvor laughed.

"Ah, well, no matter. If he," the troll nodded at Thorvald without taking his eyes from Guthrie, "gives out, I can always find another to take his place. I think you are more valuable than as a stud or a snack."

"So you think you have a use for me, after all."

"You are here," Halvor said. "Moran is not, and he would be if he were able. That means you bested him. And," the monster held out its hands, palm up, and shrugged, "you must have eliminated all his men. How many was that? Twenty, perhaps?"

"I wasn't counting. Besides, I think you ate a few of them."

"Well, yes. I did. And tasty they were, being fairly young and, shall we say, meaty examples of your species. But enough of gustatory pleasures, and down to business. You eliminated my army. I know more are on the way, but they will be leaderless now. I'd have settled for Kelly, but you took him from me, too, I suppose. That leaves only you. Our previous offer stands, but now you will replace Moran. *You* will be in charge and reap all the benefits."

"Me? To lead your troops in decimating the world? How could that benefit me?"

"It's not like that," Thorvald said. "We're saving the world. Cleansing it of the corruption and lies that have ruled it all along."

"Not a bad goal on the face of it," Guthrie said. "But who do you consider to be the corrupt, and how do you plan to change things?"

"Forget all that." Halvor snapped. "Wealth, Guthrie, and the power to do whatever you want to whomever you want. That's what's in it for you. As you can see, I'll soon have an army of my own brethren." The monster, focused on Guthrie, didn't notice the hurt look Thorvald shot it at the use of the singular pronoun. "When enough of us have broken free from their mother cracks, I will send them out into the world. Finally, we will conquer and rule, just as we have always been destined to do. It will be Ragnarök for all of humanity, with no Valhalla in sight. I'm sure you've noticed my own personal train. Thirty cars and an engine. Oh, yes, and a caboose, too. Can't have a train without a caboose."

"I noticed the caboose. You must be planning to export a lot of beef."

"No, Guthrie. A lot of grief. I even have a name for it." Halvor beamed. "Many trains have names, such as the *Texas Eagle* and the *Sunset Limited*. I would have liked to use that one, but since it's taken, I've settled on another I like very much. Want to hear it?"

"Why not?"

"*The Texas Troll Unlimited*. Like it?"

"Nice double entendre."

"Thanks. And do you know what we're going to do with my little train?"

"Don't tell me."

Halvor chuckled.

"We're going to ride in boxcars right into the hearts of cities. There, we can find homes in subway tunnels, service tunnels, drain pipes, sewers, basements, subbasements. Even abandoned shopping malls. Anywhere we can prosper, thrive, and multiply."

"I thought you wanted to rampage across the countryside. Hiding out in the shadows isn't logical."

"I'm a troll, Guthrie. Trolls don't have to make logical sense. They just have to rampage. And rampage we will, just in a different way. We will settle near wi-fi hotspots so we can use your marvelous Internet to communicate in secret and sow seeds of destruction. We'll bring down your economy, then the social structure will fail, displacing millions. The more homeless people on the streets, the more they'll venture into underground spaces, seeking shelter, only to stock our larders. Eventually, more and more brethren will go overseas to do the same everywhere. And when the time is ripe, there will be rampage galore without facing our own deaths. Then we, not humans, will rule the Earth, and your species will become our cattle. It's a win-win."

"A win for you, maybe," Guthrie said. "Who's the other win for?"

"Me, of course," Halvor grinned. "I'm the leader. And for you, too, if you choose. You sure you won't join the cause? We can seal the deal right now—just a few squirts into cracks here and there, and you'll be an integral part of the family. You can take over Moran's position and run the operation as you see fit, and I can call you uncle. I wouldn't eat an uncle." It paused reflectively, then said. "At least, I think I can resist."

"Uncle Guthrie," shouted one of the larger polyps squirming on the cavern wall nearby, and the cry was taken up by the whole horde. Halvor managed to quiet them after a full minute of raucous outcry.

"You sure you won't?" it asked. Guthrie just stared back. "Ah, well. To tell the truth, I thought not. You are irredeemably recalcitrant. But no matter. There's nothing you can do to stop me, and when the time is ripe, we're gonna boogaloo! Isn't that right, Brothers?" It shouted this last.

"Boogaloo!" screamed the polyps in a chaotic rage, their shrill voices reverberating painfully around the cavern walls. "Take it down! Take it down!"

Halvor tried to silence them again, but by now they were too worked up to listen to anyone, even their leader. Guthrie was glad they were nothing but voices at the moment, but his mind readily envisioned hundreds, thousands of trolls rampaging across the countryside and through cities and towns, multiplying everywhere thanks to those willing to masturbate their lives away in dim spaces for a pocketful of tarnished silver.

At last the polyp cacophony mostly fell silent, with just a few chirps and peeps here and there.

"I have you pegged, now," Guthrie said to Halvor. "You want to control people because you can't control yourself. And you want to do it from the shadows so you don't have to reveal your corrupt monstrosity. Your inherent impotence. But in the end, you're nothing but a coward banking on the violence of others to enforce your will. Rampage? Ha! You do nothing but attack those weaker than you, yet you have to act in secret until there are enough like you to hide among them in plain sight. No wonder you can't stand the light of day."

"You're either with us or against us," Thorvald said.

"Funny," Guthrie said, looking the renegade priest straight in the eyes. "I came down here to say the same thing to you."

"These are my children," Thorvald said. "I'm going to ensure that they inherit the Earth."

Seeing there was nothing he could say to persuade Thorvald to leave, and unable to extricate him because of the troll, Guthrie just backed into the tunnel.

"Work with me, Guthrie!" the troll called down the shaft after him. "Think about it. I'll even take in Expinoza. I can use good trainmen as well as warriors!"

As Guthrie emerged from the dank, fetid air of the mine, the bright sunshine and gentle, dry breeze washed him with welcome warmth and freshness, but he knew he'd need a long shower to feel clean again. Maybe two. But all he could do now was wait for darkness to replace the safety of daylight.

39

FAILING TO LURE THORVALD OUT of the mine, Guthrie and Espinoza took care of the final preparations. After they again drove down to the HiRail—this time to move it to the siding on the main line—Espinoza positioned the Suburban on the creek bed leading away from the compound, leaving the vehicle where it would be in full sunlight and in full view of the troll when it emerged from the mine. Meanwhile, Guthrie went into the bunkhouse and untied Fleming. He let him eat, drink, and relieve himself then tied his wrists.

"The house isn't going to be safe after dark," Guthrie said. "Come on."

Guthrie led the hobbling prisoner out to the van, which he'd parked nose toward the road running behind the barn, ready for a quick getaway if he needed it. He opened the side door, and gestured for Fleming to climb inside. Fleming did, complaining the whole time.

"How long you gonna keep me in here?" he demanded. "My fucking leg's killing me. I think it's getting infected. I gotta a fever."

"Keep quiet," Guthrie warned, ignoring the complaints. "You're going to be in here all night. I suggest you don't try to run. You won't make it far on that bum leg, and Halvor will be lurking around after dark. It's not going to be very happy, and the smell of blood might make it forget who you are."

He shut the door, pocketed the key, then joined Espinoza in front of the bunkhouse. The trainman had pulled a couple of chairs onto the plank porch. After that, there was little for them to do but wait for dark and the troll to emerge and their plan to play out. Hopefully, the troll wouldn't catch on to the switch when Guthrie exited the Suburban and would follow Espinoza down the mountainside to the rugged plains below, thinking he was Guthrie. If it didn't and realized Guthrie was actually hiding up the side canyon.... Guthrie tried not to think about that.

At last, with the sun less than half an hour above the mountain rim, they decided it was time to get into position. Before they did, Guthrie went to the van.

"It's nearly dark," he told Fleming. "We're leaving, but you're staying here."

"Why the fuck don't you take me with you?" Fleming snarled. "That fucking thing gets hold of me, I'm dead."

"You'll only be in the way, and I don't trust you. I anticipate the troll will be pretty occupied, and if you're quiet, it probably won't realize you're here. So I suggest you keep your mouth shut. I'll be back before morning."

"*Before* morning? Like hell!"

Guthrie's lifted a forefinger to his lips and said, "Shhh. And remember: Don't try to run."

He closed the door and walked down to the Suburban. Espinoza was already seated shotgun, and Guthrie got behind the wheel. Gradually, the shadows crept across the area where the Suburban was parked as the sun edged behind the western ridge. Then Guthrie saw movement at the shoulder of the mountain, just around from the adit.

"Here it comes," he said. "Better get down."

Espinoza crouched into the footwell just as the troll spotted the vehicle. Guthrie pulled ahead another hundred feet into the sunshine, stopped, then got out.

"What the fuck are you doing?" Espinoza hissed.

"Making sure it's pissed off," Guthrie said.

Halvor slouched just on the other side of the shadow line, muscular shoulders aggressively hunched, its timber club dragging from its right hand. Guthrie approached the shadow line as closely as he dared.

"Well," he jeered. "Here we are again. Man versus monster, each in its appropriate element."

"You won't laugh long, Guthrie. You had your chance to join me, but that's over. All that's left is to catch you."

"I'll try to be as unpalatable as possible."

"Oh, you're not for me. Once, maybe, but not now. I think I'll feed you to my brethren. Share you among them one bitty bite at a time. One way or another, you're going to be part of my family."

"Gotta do that catching first," Guthrie said. "So far, your team is way down. Just like you—the lowest of the low. Hell, you can't even reproduce yourself but have to rely on some onanist jerking off into a crack in a stone. You're nothing but an overgrown virus. Pathetic."

"I'll show you who's pathetic," Halvor snarled, raising his club in a one-handed swing backward then flinging it at Guthrie like a spinning baseball bat.

Guthrie didn't know what to expect, but he expected something, and as soon as Halvor cocked back the club, he dove behind a large rock beside the road just as the butt end of the club slammed across the top of the rock, scattering fragments. The timber spun off into the desert behind Guthrie.

Guthrie stood, stepped back onto the road, and laughed sarcastically.

"Oops. Strike two. Your batting average is pretty low, Halvor. Why don't you just step out here in the light and end it all?"

"I'm just beginning, you bastard," it snarled.

Guthrie wanted to further enrage the troll, but he noticed the thing glancing at the advancing shadow line and edging forward with it. Time to move.

"I'm not going away," Guthrie called out. "You'll have to kill me to stop me. I'm going to kill you and all your brethren."

He turned to go back to the car. Behind him, the troll yelled, "You'll be dead by dawn."

Already been there, Guthrie thought.

He got into the Suburban and drove through the dying day. Neither he nor Espinoza said anything. There was nothing to say. After the vehicle rolled around the first bend and out of the troll's sight, Guthrie slowed to a little less than ten miles per hour but didn't stop.

"It's all your's," he said as he opened the door and hopped out, taking a stumbling roll.

He quickly regained his feet and saw that Espinoza was already in the driver's seat. After the vehicle passed, speeding up slightly, he dashed across the road and ran up the sluice between the hill and ridge. Espinoza drove on, out of sight, pretending to be Guthrie to lure the troll for as far and long as he was able. When he had the troll close to the road that ran roughly parallel to the main line, he'd just drive south as fast as he could, out of the troll's range. After dawn broke, he'd come back to see the outcome.

Guthrie could only pray he'd be there to see it, too.

Gripping the AR with the flashlights taped to it in one hand and the third flashlight in the other, he ran up the gully for about a hundred yards, then hunkered down behind a boulder flanked by a pair of creosote bushes. He hoped he was far enough away from the road that Halvor wouldn't catch a whiff of his scent. If he wasn't, he had the flashlights, though he doubted they alone would stave off the troll for a whole night. Not out in the open, where it could stone him from a safe distance.

He poked his head barely above the rock, relying on the surrounding brush for extra concealment, and could see a narrow slice of road, still lit by the waning light. He waited breathlessly, heart pounding in his chest. Abruptly, several minutes later, all direct sunlight to the valley sagged into dusk as the last of the sun fell below the mountains' western rim.

But enough light remained to see the troll lope down the road in pursuit of the Suburban. The thing didn't even pause at the mouth of the arroyo. All its attention was focused ahead, and Guthrie noticed it had retrieved the club. Then it was gone from sight, though a minute after it passed, he heard it yell his name attached to a string of threatening curses. Guthrie waited two minutes longer to make sure it was well along in its pursuit, then he trotted down the gully to the road and up to the ranch compound.

First things first, he thought, as he hurried through the fading twilight toward the mine. A moment later, he was moving down the tunnel.

He heard the insane gabbling of the dozens of troll polyps well before he reached the entrance to the natural cavern, and the sound of their own voices kept them from noticing his stealthy approach. At last, he peeked around the edge of the opening, into the space. The walls were writhing with the polyps as they noisily chattered among themselves. The talk was mostly inane and disconnected babbling about victory, blood, rampage, and revenge, peppered with snarls, growls, and joyful laughter. Troll nursery school, Guthrie thought.

Guthrie ignored the sounds as his eyes searched the dim space for Thorvald. At first he didn't see him, but then he spotted him, still naked, facing the left wall, hand jerking spasmodically at his groin. The renegade priest stiffened, groaned, and slumped against the rock.

"You keep that up, you're going to grown hair on your palms," Guthrie said dryly.

Thorvald spun, eyes wide, and for just an instant, the chattering polyps went silent. Then a single voice from the polyps screamed, "It's him, Daddy! He's here! Do something!"

Suddenly the air was filled with raucous cries of babbling panic.

"How…?" Thorvald began, but Guthrie cut him off by switching on all three flashlights and playing their beams across the polyps, which proved much more delicate than their full-grown brother.

The first thumbnail monster, about the size of a soccer ball, screamed as it grayed.

"No!" Thorvald shrieked, and he threw himself at Guthrie, but Guthrie just swung the flat of the rifle butt against the side of his head.

Stunned, Thorvald fell to the cave floor while Guthrie continued to shine the lights over the polyp. Its writhing and screaming quickly stopped as it ossified. Just to make sure, Guthrie lifted a large stone from the floor and smashed it down on the frozen polyp, which shattered.

Yep, he thought with satisfaction, picking up the flashlights and turning to the others. He discovered that it was more efficient to target one polyp at a time with all three lights. They ossified in just moments, except for a few of the largest, which took a minute or so.

"Can't stand the light of day, can you?" Guthrie ground out as he turned the biggest one to stone.

Thorvald was stirring, so Guthrie bound him with the remains of his own clothing then turned back to his work.

For half an hour, the cries of the polyps diminished one by one until, the walls of the cave were still and silent, the features of the lumpen stone heads frozen in pain, fear, and rage. He also made sure to douse Thorvald's latest effort. Then he turned to the renegade priest who lay there, twisting in his bonds, glowering at him.

"You'll pay for that," Thorvald spat. "As soon as my boy comes back, he'll make you pay."

"Well, it's not back. Let's go."

He tried to force Thorvald to his feet, but the priest just lashed out with a vicious kick.

"You either get up and leave here on your own," Guthrie said, "or I'll knock you out and drag you out. Since you're naked, that'll be mighty uncomfortable."

"All right," Thorvald said, getting to his feet. "But it won't do you any good. Halvor will be back soon, and when he sees what you've done, he'll rip you apart."

Guthrie made no answer but just shoved Thorvald toward the mouth of the tunnel. Outside, he took the priest to the van, where he tied him to the spare tire bracket inside the cargo hold.

"I know I can't trust you," he said as he gagged Thorvald. "But I can fuck you up if you do anything to thwart me. And maybe Fleming here will have something to say if you don't keep quiet. You got that, Fleming. If Thorvald lets Halvor know where it is, it'll know where you are. Keep him quiet, and stay in the van. I'll be back."

Guthrie returned to the mine to retrieve the IEDs hidden in the overturned mine cart. There were five of them, each consisting of a bundle of five sticks wrapped in brown wax paper. All had radio-controlled blasting caps linked to the detonator hidden with them. Espinoza had assured him the charges would do the trick, and Guthrie was betting his life on that.

He spent the next twenty minutes placing and disguising the charges: two just inside the adit and the other three fastened to the first three timber bridges holding up the tunnel's ceiling. But he couldn't blow them. Not yet. He had to wait until dawn. If he blew them too early, Halvor might have a chance to dig out enough rubble to stay out of direct sunlight. And a chance to seize Guthrie, which it was sure to try to do after it discovered Guthrie had petrified its brothers and taken its father. It would be out for his blood more than ever.

He went to the kitchen and grabbed a bottle of water. His mouth was unusually dry, but the hand holding the bottle was steady. Drinking, he went outside and down to the barn. The moon wasn't yet full, but it was big enough to cast dim light over the compound and the creek bed, and he took a vantage point at the juncture of the corral and barn. From there, he could see when Halvor approached from the road but be masked by the shadows at the corner of the structure. The same shadows that had hidden Moran when he'd captured Guthrie. The corral was still empty after its inhabitants have been driven off.

He perched on the top rail, leaned against the barn, and watched the now nearly full moon rise in the east as he wondered just how the hell he was going to stay alive until the sun replaced it. It was hard to figure since there was no way to know how long he'd need to elude the monster. It could be that it wouldn't suspect he was around, but he doubted that. One look in the mine would tell it Guthrie was near.

Half an hour later, his phone buzzed. It was Espinoza.

"Where are you?" Guthrie asked.

"Just coming up on I-10," the trainman said. "The fucker almost got me. Twice. I can't believe how fast it is. But I made it to the main road in time."

"How long ago?"

"Couple of minutes. I called as soon as I was sure it stopped chasing me."

"What did it do, then?"

"I only saw it for a few seconds as it faded into the darkness, but it looked pretty disappointed, and it yelled, 'I'll be waiting, Guthrie. I'm still hungry for your blood.' Or something like that."

"It's always the same shit from that thing," Guthrie snorted. "I guess trolls have no real aspirations higher than satisfying their appetite for the destruction of others and hiding in a hole in the ground while controlling the local population through intimidation, fear, and violence. But at least it still thought you were me. It didn't hurry back this way?"

"Not that I could tell."

"All right. Stay safe. See you in the morning."

"I'm not the one who needs to stay safe or be seen in the morning," Espinoza said, and he hung up.

Guthrie waited a little longer, reluctant to leave the clean night air but knowing he had to hide. The bunkhouse was his first line of retreat. He'd already broken the hole in the floor of the bedroom for an escape hatch, though he hoped it wouldn't come to that. Halvor could tear the place apart in minutes, but that might be all Guthrie needed. And since he'd spent time inside and in the area in front, his scent already was present, so maybe Halvor wouldn't notice that some of it was fresher than before. And Guthrie could watch through the shattered windows to observe the troll's movements up close. If he had to fall back, there was a chance—a small one—that he could make it to the barn. That was a more substantial structure and might thwart the troll for critical minutes.

Suddenly, he heard a distant bleating scream of bovine panic. The sound came from less than half a mile away. Halvor was on the move back to the compound. Time to hide. He hurried into the bunkhouse, shut the door, and stepped to one of the front windows but kept to one side. A few minutes later, the troll lumbered into view, clearly visible in the nearly full moonlight.

40

HALVOR HAD A COW TUCKED under the arm holding the club. The animal was ineffectually writhing, kicking and crying out in mortal panic. The troll's other hand gripped the body of the engineer, half-eaten. It raised the corpse and took another bite like it was eating a candy bar. Guthrie realized it was headed toward the corral, and when it reached it, the troll casually dropped the club and the engineer's body, and used both hands to put the cow into the pen. The animal staggered as the monster let it go then raced across the enclosure, blowing loud breaths of terror. Halvor ignored it, and leaving the club and the engineer's body lying where they were, it turned and disappeared into the darkness.

Over most of the remainder of the night, Guthrie watched the troll retrieve five more cows. During the process, Guthrie heard the troll loudly grousing about having to do all the work itself and not being able to trust anybody human. It would have been amusing if it wasn't coming from a mouth that would eat him alive if Halvor caught him. It finished an hour and a half before dawn, and after its last trip, it looked worn out as well as pissed off. Catching a bunch of terrified and desperate cows in the rugged terrain of the central valley must be pretty hard work, even for a troll.

Even the orange hair on top of its head wasn't coiffed in its usual oversized ducktail that blended in with the yellow hair sprouting in profusion down its spine. Instead, it was frazzled into a pointed peak that looked a little like a big, orange candle flame. It picked up the engineer's body and sat on a boulder to finish consuming it, clothes, bones, and all. It must have been hungry because it was sucking blood from its fingers just ten minutes later. Then it started picking and squeezing at spots in its flesh with its big, clumsy fingers, like it was popping pimples.

"You fucking bastard, Guthrie," it snarled as it squeezed a bullet out of its flesh like a leaden blackhead and let it drop to the ground. It extracted half a dozen more then stood, grabbed one of the cows, killed it with a single blow of its fist, and started dragging the carcass toward the adit.

"Ready to eat, little ones?" it called out.

Guthrie didn't want it to go into the mine just yet. The eastern sky was tingeing with light, and if the monster crawled back into the darkness where it lived, it would see the frozen pustules of its brethren, it would see that Thorvald was gone, and it would know that Guthrie was responsible—and close. With dawn approaching, it might have second thoughts about coming out again and stay inside the mine, though Guthrie knew he also could bank on the monster's blind, unthinking rage.

Unfortunately, it was still too early to blow the charges. There was still nearly half an hour before sunlight would wash the ranch compound, and he didn't want to give Halvor even the remotest chance to dig enough debris from the adit to make a cubby large enough to protect it. The only thing Guthrie could do to keep it outside was to distract it. He moved to the doorway.

"Why don't you bring some of that over here?" he yelled. "I could use a nice steak right about now!"

Halvor whirled, a stunned look on its face. It let go of the cow's legs, and the bovine body flopped to the ground as the monster muscled its way through the air toward the bunkhouse. Guthrie kept well back from the door as it stopped, knelt down on all fours, and peered through the opening at him.

"You gotta lot of fucking gall, Guthrie," it snarled.

"I also have these."

Guthrie aimed his rifle at the troll's face and switched on the flashlights taped to the barrel. Halvor bellowed and jerked back, almost stumbling. But it recovered quickly, stood, stepped forward, and started smashing at the building with its club. Guthrie fled to the room where he'd chopped the hole in the floor and dropped into the crawlspace, pulling Moran's body over the opening and switching off the flashlights. He was just in time as the troll cast its club aside and, grunting with effort, began peeling back the tin roof like it was opening a can of sardines—Guthrie being the sardine.

There was no way, no direction Guthrie could flee. Even enraged, the troll would see him running away from the demolished bunkhouse, and it could take one step for Guthrie's five. Guthrie could blow the mine. That would distract the monster and surely draw it away. But it was still too early. He had to drag this out as long as possible, so he just cowered under the floor as, within a handful of minutes, the last of the roof came away, revealing the interior of the building like it was a troll's dollhouse. The monster saw Moran's body. The penultimate sardine, Guthrie supposed.

"There you are, you fuck!" Halvor screamed. "You can't hide from me!" It snatched up the body, lifted it, and stared at its dead face. A growl of disappointment rumbled across its lips.

"Guthrie, you bastard!" it yelled even louder than before. It twisted off Moran's head and popped it into its mouth.

"Nutty," it commented with a smile, and it was about to take a bite of the corpse when it suddenly jerked erect—as erect as it was able—and threw a panicked gaze toward the mine. Fear and rage washed away the thing's gustatory pleasure. It flung Moran aside like so much trash. The body flew fifty or sixty feet before it hit the ground with a solid thump and tumbled stiffly and awkwardly for a dozen feet farther before lying still.

Screaming threats and curses at Guthrie, The troll loped toward the mine and disappeared around the shoulder of the mountain.

While it was inside, Guthrie raced to the van, got in, and started the engine.

"What the fuck is going on?" Fleming moaned.

"Shut up."

Guthrie didn't put the vehicle in gear yet. He wasn't finished. He twisted around and climbed into the back of the van, where he leaned over the fallen priest, grabbed him by the collar, and jerked him close.

"I'm going out there and kill your boy. You do anything to try to stop me, I'll kill you, too." He looked at Fleming. "You, too."

Time was short. Maybe too short. Guthrie slammed the doors and raced to the barn. He barely made it through the back door and over to the main barn door before Halvor emerged into the still dim but growing light. Opening the door a crack, Guthrie watched a line of light begin creeping down the face of the ridge above the compound.

The troll's shoulders were slumped in defeat. Then they bunched with rage, it's body hunching with murderous vitality and intent.

"You motherfucker!" it shrieked, raging and slamming its club onto the ground. "All you humans are motherfucking bastards! I'll kill every last one of you!"

It raced back to the ruins of the bunkhouse and resumed its demolition, but it spotted the hole in the floor in moments and realized Guthrie wasn't inside. It ripped at the hole, pulling at the floor and tearing it off its foundation piers. Water spurted from broken pipes, spattering the dry ground. When the troll didn't find its quarry beneath, it raised up and cast around, unthinking rage smeared across its face.

Guthrie was just about to step out of the barn door, when the sound of the van pulling off came through the wooden walls. Guthrie raced across the barn and opened the back door to see Fleming at the wheel of the van, gunning it toward the dirt road off this mountain range. Somehow he's gotten free, but the freedom didn't last long.

Guthrie stepped out of the door as the van jounce into the creek bed, and as it did, Halvor lunged into view and after the escaping vehicle.

"Not so fucking fast," it snarled and hurled its club at the van.

The heavy timber caught the van on its back upper right corner just as the van came down the bank into the stream bed at an awkward angle. The impact sent the van skewing and skidding, and it careened across the creek and ran part way up the bank before toppling onto its driver's side and sliding to a stop.

As dust enveloped the van, the passenger door burst open and Fleming crawled out, dropped to the ground, and began hobbling down the creek, away from the wreck. Of Thorvald, there was no sign. Maybe he was injured or unconscious. Guthrie hoped he was still tied to the spare tire mount. Whatever the reason, there was no sign of him as Fleming fled.

"There you are, you little fucker!" The troll shrieked, spotting Fleming. The man screamed and tried to run faster, but the troll was too quick. In five massive strides, it snatched up the writhing man, held him up, and finally saw who it was. The look of glee on its features writhed into an expression of frustrated rage.

"Fleming?" It looked up and stared into lightening sky. "How many fucking surrogates do I have to smash to get to you, Guthrie? Maybe Expinoza's out there with you. Expinoza! I'm coming for you, little man!"

"Don't hurt me!" Fleming screamed. "I helped you! I helped you!"

"You did," the troll snarled at the trainman. "But that was yesterday. You're all used up, now."

Fleming's drawn out "No!" was drowned in the thunder of the troll's rage.

The monster raised the shrieking man high, then threw down, bashing his body against the ground. Without a second glance at Fleming, who looked like a man who'd taken a dive off a twenty-story building, the troll turned to the van.

It must have thought Guthrie was still in there, and Guthrie sure couldn't let it get to the vehicle and find its daddy tied up inside.

"Right here, big boy," he called, stepping a few feet from the barn.

Halvor gathered its huge, powerful body and lunged forward, and Guthrie darted back into the dimness of the barn, preparing for an onslaught. But Halvor suddenly halted before it reached the barn and stared the brightening sky and at the line of light creeping down the face of the mountain ridges, consternation clear on its face.

"You win once again, Guthrie," it snarled. "But there's always tomorrow night."

It turned and ran for the mine.

If there was any right time to blow the charges, it was now.

No more tomorrow nights for you, Halvor, Guthrie thought as he fingered the detonator.

A thick explosion belched from the direction of the mine. The ground shook, rock debris spewed out and showered down in a cloud of dust, and a hundred feet of the slope above and behind the adit collapsed inward.

Halvor skidded to a halt as the explosion rocked the ground, ignoring the rocks and gravel pelting it. Guthrie couldn't see its face, but its body language spelled defeat even as it gathered itself and ran toward the shattered mine. At least Guthrie hoped it was shattered. He ran through the barn to the other side just as Halvor disappeared around the shoulder of the mountain.

It reappeared moments later, frothing with rage.

Waves of relief surged through Guthrie, knowing that the troll was trapped outside. But things weren't over yet. Not if he was to survive. He stepped through the door, into the growing light.

"Two for one, Halvor!" he yelled. "Me and shelter! It's a win-win!"

Rage, hatred, and madness distorted the troll's face more than ever as it stormed toward him, bellowing and shrieking curses, lips writhing across its horrible teeth in a fearsome grimace of blood-lust, its club leaving a furrow across the harsh ground.

Indeed, the barn was the only place Halvor could hide, and by now, the line of sunlight was just grazing its roof line.

Guthrie darted across the floor to the back door. He reached it just as Halvor rolled the main door aside and crawled into the interior, casting around for Guthrie. But Guthrie was already backing outside, into the sunshine, leaving the troll in the cavernous space. He wondered how beams of sunlight piercing holes in the old structure would feel crawling across the troll's flesh, leaving ossified streaks. Not nice, but he didn't plan on giving Halvor long to suffer it.

Guthrie's only question was whether or not to wait for Espinoza. He would, he decided. The man deserved that much. He called him on the phone.

"You're still alive," Espinoza said, joy obvious in his voice.

"Yes. And so is the troll. I thought you'd like to be here for its demise."

"I'll be there as soon as I can."

"Bring gasoline. And a lighter."

They hung up, and Guthrie stepped close to the barn.

"Any last words, Halvor?" he called out.

"You got me, Guthrie. But you know I'll be back. There are always men who will create those such as me for their own ends without ever realizing that I *am* their own ends. They will always seek to use me, only to be used themselves."

"I don't think so, Halvor. You see, before I burned up the ranch house, I snatched Brother Fidelio's manuscript. Now, only you, Thorvald, and I know the secret of creating more aberrations like you. I'll never tell, and Thorvald is going where he won't be able to tell anybody anything—and they wouldn't believe him, anyway. And you…, well, you'll be Ozymandias. This is the end, Halvor. The real end. People don't live in caves anymore, and all the bridges are cement now. No more dank cracks to ooze out of. No more rampaging across the countryside, terrorizing and eating people and livestock. You'll be stuck in that netherworld for eternity, and I won't have to smell any more of your foul odor."

"You condescending motherfucker," Halvor roared. "I'll smash you!"

"Come on out in the light of day, then, and do it," Guthrie called back.

There was no answer to that, and Guthrie didn't want to keep talking with the thing. There was nothing it might say to alter the facts of its corruption despite its denials. To help pass the time until Espinoza arrived, Guthrie did some chores around the ranch. First, he went down to the pump house, shut off the pump, and watched the low fountains of water jetting from broken pipes in the bunkhouse ruins peter out. Next, he visited the corral, where he drove the cows through the gate. This time, with the troll in the barn right next door, they couldn't bolt and leave the vicinity fast enough. Then he went up to the ruins of the bunkhouse and scavenged through them for a couple of bottles of water and some clothes.

Down at the overturned van, he loosened Thorvald from the spare tire mount, dragged him out into the sunlight, and took off the gag. The man was groggy from having his head banged against the inside of the van when it toppled, but he remained hostile. Even so, he looked grateful for the clothes and water.

"Halvor is still alive right now, but it's all over for it. And for you," Guthrie said as Thorvald dressed.

"I tell you you've got it wrong. I'm the only one who can save the world. Halvor and I. And you. You must join us or let us go. You must."

"Shut up, and finish dressing."

Thorvald's lips tightened in anger and his eyes flared, but he didn't speak as he put on the clothes. Guthrie retied his hands.

"I'll gag you again if you start talking," Guthrie warned. "I've had enough of your bullshit. More water?"

Thorvald shook his head, and they sat in silence until Espinoza drove up in the Suburban. The trainman emerged and hauled two five gallon gas cans out of the back seat as Guthrie walked up.

"It's in the barn," Guthrie said, taking the lighter and cans from Espinoza. "Watch him." He indicated Thorvald, then he hefted the cans over to the barn and started splashing the liquid on the dried out old wood along the bottom of the structure.

"Is that you, Guthrie?" Halvor asked. "What are you doing out there? What's that smell?"

"It's gasoline," Guthrie replied as he dumped the rest of the second can's contents on the wall. "Which do you prefer, Halvor? Burning or turning to stone?"

He pulled out the lighter and lit a final tail of gasoline. With a long, throaty whoosh, flames crawled across the building. Black smoke billowed into the air, and Halvor, realizing that its only source of shadow was burning around it, bellowed and screamed, first in frustration then in pain as the building, essentially dry tinder, went up like a house of cards, searing its flesh. Inside of five minutes, the entire structure was blazing, and the tin roof was about to cave in.

"I'll kill you, you fuck!" the troll shrieked, surging to its feet through the writhing flames and swirling smoke, lifting the barn roof, and shouldering it aside with a crash. The orange hair on its body flared with greasy smoke and crisped away. The flame-shaped orange peak of thin hair atop its cranium wafted and waved in the updraft into true flames that wavered a few moments before turning to smoke.

Halvor swung its club up to smash Guthrie—or maybe anyone or anything it could—but the club, too, was aflame, and the sun said there was no time—only just enough for the troll to rise up and raise the club.

Halvor grunted, unable to smash the burning club down as its arms froze into gray stone. An almost wistful sigh escaped its lips as its head solidified in a permanent expression of pain, fear, rage, and frustration. Its chest and torso were next, and the huge stone troll wobbled a little on still flexible legs, as if whatever remained of the creature's vitality still struggled for a toehold, for equilibrium in this world. But in a moment, they too, solidified. In less than a minute, the troll had become a huge and terrible statue standing amid the barn's final flames and smoldering ashes, holding the still flaring club.

"It looked like it was going out in a blaze of glory," Espinoza said. "But it kind of died with a whimper, didn't it?"

Nearby, Thorvald stood, weeping.

41

GUTHRIE TURNED FROM HALVOR'S STATUE and looked at Thorvald.

"It's not my place to punish you," he said ignoring the man's grief. Better his than the whole world's. "But I'm turning you over to those who will." He turned to Espinoza. "Watch him. I have to make a phone call."

Leaving the trainman to guard their prisoner, Guthrie strode away, pulled out his phone and punched in the number on the business card Gerald Croft had given him in Ninfa's parking lot. Croft answered on the second ring, and he sounded surprised.

"Guthrie?"

"Thought I'd run out on you, eh?"

"That had crossed my mind. You have news for me?"

"Not news. I have your boy."

There was silence from the other end of the line for a few seconds, then Croft said, "Come again."

"You heard me. I have Thorvald in custody."

"When can we come get him?"

"Not so fast. I want a few things in exchange."

"You want to be paid off?"

"You could say that, but it's not for me. More than forty people are dead because of your priest...."

"You can't blame the entire Church for the actions of one man."

"I'm not. I'm blaming the Church, period. Get it? And for your information, the money Thorvald stole was ill-gotten gains from a criminal cabal ensconced within the Church hierarchy. Were you aware of that?"

"Sweet Jesus," Croft said nervously. "Why did you have to tell me that?"

"So you'll understand and listen carefully."

"I'm listening."

"Innocent people have been caught up in this mess and had their lives destroyed. You're going to make that as right as possible."

"I'll have to consult with my superiors."

"You do that, but make it quick. Thorvald has the account numbers containing all those stolen funds you're looking for, and if your bosses don't agree to my terms, I'll take what I want, anyway, and force him to give the rest to charity. You'll never get a cent of it back. That's millions of dollars, Croft. Multiple multiple millions."

"What are your terms?"

"First, there's an ongoing investigation into the disappearance of a Houston railroad employee named Benjamin Horton. Thorvald caused him to be killed. I need you to make the investigation disappear."

"How are we supposed to do that?"

"I don't know, nor do I care as long as it's convincing and passes muster with the authorities. Maybe you can tie it in with my second term. Thorvald employed an international smuggling ring during the time he was on the loose with your money. It's also used by the Church cabal. I want the smuggling network brought down. You can even say that they murdered Horton. Unfortunately, Horton's body was destroyed."

"Where are we going to get a body on such short notice?" the enforcer asked.

"I can supply you with another," Guthrie said, knowing there were several candidates lying around the ranch, though not all were intact. But that shouldn't matter. "There are three up here, and you can take your pick. But you have to take them all, and Horton's funeral has to be closed casket."

"Okay. What else?"

"A railroad worker named Gilbert Espinoza is currently and erroneously the focus of the investigation. Make him the hero who brings down the smugglers. He's even got respectable reputation as a hero around the area where we discovered Thorvald and has a shot-up work truck to help bolster the story. After that, he deserves a nice promotion and raise, so make sure he's put in charge of the Englewood Rail Yard in Houston. The position will be open after the smuggling ring is broken. And don't forget to start off with a hefty reward for uncovering the smugglers."

"You aren't asking much," Croft said sarcastically.

"No, I'm not, considering the damage Thorvald and your Church have done. Could have continued to do if Thorvald had his way. What I'm asking is a drop in the bucket of what Thorvald stole. I'm giving almost all that back to you in the person of Thorvald. He can tell you where it's all hidden. Next...."

"So there's more?"

"Much more. Horton left a family that is now destitute. You're going to magically come up with an insurance policy or inheritance that sets his wife up for life and puts her kids through college. It doesn't have to be extravagant, but it has to be more than just sufficient."

"That'll be easier than the other stuff. Anything else? Nothing for you?"

"Only this: Espinoza provided invaluable aid to me in capturing Thorvald. You will give him and me complete immunity from any sort of retaliation by the Church for this affair. You leave us alone, and we forget Thorvald ever existed."

Unfortunately, that was a promise Guthrie didn't think he'd be able to keep. The thirty-foot troll chasing him across a darkening West Texas landscape was an indelible memory.

Croft said he'd call back as soon as he could, and Guthrie hung up. He walked back to where Espinoza and Thorvald stood, both still staring up at Halvor. Thorvald had stopped weeping, and his face had set into lines of loss and resignation.

"I called the Catholic enforcers. They'll call back soon." He didn't tell Espinoza about the terms of the handover. He'd find out soon enough.

The wait for Croft's call wasn't long.

"Guthrie?" Croft said after Guthrie thumbed the answer button.

"I'm here."

"They agreed."

"There better be no double-cross."

"Who do you think we are?" Croft demanded. "We're the Catholic Church."

"That's what bothers me," Guthrie responded. "Okay, come and get him."

He and Espinoza had already decided not to meet the enforcers at either the ranch or the lodge.

"Drive to Sierra Blanca and find the cafe on the main drag. Call me when you get there. If you start now, we can meet for breakfast. Just you and Miller. Drive a van."

He hung up and looked at Espinoza.

"They'll be here in the morning. Until then, we probably ought to stay up here. If we take Thorvald to town, somebody might notice that he's our prisoner."

"We have the Suburban," Espinoza said. "And there's probably something in the ruins over there to eat and drink. We'll survive." He laughed suddenly and brightly. "Have survived!"

Survive, they had, but it was still a long day. Leaving Thorvald tied to a pile of rusting mine equipment in the western stream bed, they filled up some of the time bringing up the HiRail and scavenging for food and water. They also performed the distasteful task of gathering the bodies of Moran, Fleming, and Kelly.

"The enforcers will take them all," Guthrie said.

"Not all," Espinoza said.

Guthrie looked at him quizzically, and he lifted his eyes and bobbed his chin upward toward the threatening-looking but harmless statue looming over the ruins of the compound.

"Yeah," Guthrie said. "We should leave no stone unturned. Do we still have any of that dynamite?"

They did. Plenty. Half an hour later, they put Thorvald in the Suburban's back seat and drove a hundred yards from the compound. There, Espinoza pulled out the detonator.

"This is one charge I'm happy to set off," he said.

"Blow it," Guthrie said.

Espinoza's explosives were attached to the statue's ankles and lower legs, the higher portions of the body being out of reach. The explosion blasted out in a donut-shaped billow all around, and for a split instant, the upper body seemed balanced on top of the cloud, then it crashed down into the dust and debris of its own legs, torso and arms shattering and head sailing upward for a moment before crashing to the ground and rolling off across the compound.

Thorvald simply sat stoically on the back seat, staring at the cloud of dust dissipating over the debris of his dream.

Over the next hour, Espinoza set charges that systematically destroyed any part of the statue that might be identifiable, starting with the head. The fall had broken off the end of its nose and its ear tips, making it uglier than ever. But it was soon gravel and fist-sized chunks of rock.

The night that followed was long but curiously peaceful. At seven-thirty AM, Guthrie's phone rang. It was Croft.

"We're here."

"You made good time. I'll be at the cafe in half an hour."

The two enforcers were already inside at one of the tables when Guthrie showed up. Both were looking a little tired from the long drive. Guthrie wondered how *he* looked. Not too well, judging by the sympathetic look Irene gave him.

"Hi, Irene," he said as he sat at the table and she came over. Today's barrette was purple. "These are a couple of my colleagues."

"Any friend of Mr. Guthrie is welcome here," she said. "Will Mr. Espinoza be joining you?"

"Not right now," Guthrie told her.

"Well, can I get you gentlemen some coffee?"

"No, thanks…," Croft began, but Guthrie stopped him.

"Three breakfast specials, Irene. And coffee."

"Three breakfast specials, coming right up," she said.

"We don't have time for this," Miller said as Irene went into the kitchen.

"Of course you do," Guthrie said. "You've driven all night, and you're going to turn right back around and drive for another twelve hours. Let's eat. I'm starved. That'll give us enough time to make sure our deal is still straight."

"It's still straight," Croft said. "As long as you really have Thorvald."

"We'll go get him after breakfast."

Despite Miller' complaint, both men ate like they were hungry.

"My friends are paying the tab," he told Irene when they finished. "Make sure you leave her at least twenty percent," he told Croft after she went to tally the bill.

He got up and went outside to wait. There, he texted Espinoza: "We're on our way."

The enforcers emerged.

"That yours?" Guthrie asked, waving toward a white Chevy cargo van.

In response, Miller pulled out a key fob, thumbed a button, and the van beeped and its lights flashed.

Guthrie nodded.

"Follow me."

He got into the Suburban and led them out of town, toward the sidings out on the main line near the ranch. Espinoza was already there in the HiRail, Thorvald tied up on the seat next to him. The three bodies lay in the bed, covered with a tarp.

As soon as the Suburban and the enforcers' van arrived, they all transferred the bodies to the van. The enforcers had even brought body bags.

"What the fuck happened to them?" Miller asked. "Damn, one of them doesn't have a head, and another is smashed all to hell."

"That information isn't part of the deal," Guthrie said. "But you might know the headless one. His name was Brian Moran."

"Moran?" Miller said. He and Croft both looked uneasy. "Yeah, I knew him. He worked for some high-level group…. Oh, the cabal. How'd he get mixed up in that?"

"Not my story to tell," Guthrie said. "Let's bag them."

They did, and Croft shut the back doors.

"You better drive carefully. You don't want to get stopped with that load."

"Not to worry," Croft said. "We have credentials to transport corpses." He smiled. "We're priests, after all."

Then it was time to hand over Thorvald.

"I guess you took care of what you needed to take care of," Croft said.

"I think you could say that once we exposed the problem to the light of day, it gelled into something we could deal with."

Then Thorvald, stoically inert, was loaded into the back of the van with the bodies.

"You still not going to tell us what he was up to out here in bumfuck nowhere?" Croft asked as he shut the door.

"You wouldn't believe me if I did," Guthrie said. "But make sure he gives you the deed to the Dunton Ranch and his little train as well as the money."

"What?"

"The Dunton Ranch." Guthrie waved. "That whole mountain range over there. There's a train on it, too. Maybe he'll tell you all about it." He shrugged. "Maybe not. Makes no difference to me. So, we all good here?"

"You'll text me the details on the smuggling ring and the rest?" Croft asked as they walked toward the van.

"Tomorrow." Guthrie leaned close as Croft climbed up into the passenger seat and said in a low voice that Espinoza couldn't hear. "You make sure Espinoza is the hero of everything, and leave my name out of it. Understand?"

"Sounds like a plan."

Then the enforcers were gone, taking Thorvald out of the ken of anybody outside the highest levels of the Catholic Church. As the van disappeared down the road, Espinoza turned to Guthrie.

"I can't believe it's over," he said, looking almost disappointed.

"It's not," Guthrie said. "Now there's the rest of your life."

"I'm not sure there'll be much of that. The HiRail is shot to shit, and Dan Beaman will have it in for me more than ever."

"Cheer up," Guthrie said, smiling to himself. "It might not be as bad as that. You never know what's around the corner."

"Let's just hope it's not another troll."

They both laughed

"It think you should just go back to work like nothing happened," Guthrie suggested. "The HiRail isn't an issue since it got shot up while you were playing the hero of Sierra Blanca. Sheriff Conroy will back you up. Besides, I think you'll find things much changed around the office when you get back."

"Maybe," Espinoza said. "But it's sure going to be dull after all this."

Then there was nothing left for them to do at the ranch, so they drove back to Sierra Blanca, taking both the HiRail and the Suburban. In town, they retrieved the supplies and ordnance they'd stolen from the bunkhouse and loaded it all into the Suburban. Guthrie would drive that back to Houston and add it all to the growing arsenal he was collecting from various cretins and other bad guys. Espinoza would return the HiRail to the Englewood Yard.

But they couldn't depart Sierra Blanca just yet. Leaving the Suburban in the Americana's parking lot, they drove the HiRail over to the sheriff's headquarters. As soon as the desk sergeant saw who they were, he called the sheriff on the intercom.

"Send them on back," Conroy's voice said, and the sergeant smiled and waved them down the hall.

Conroy was sitting behind his desk when they came in, and he gestured to two chairs in front of it.

"Well, sirs, what's on your mind."

"It looks like our job is finished," Espinoza said.

"Yes?"

"Yep. They found the car in El Paso. Empty. For us it was a big chase with little reward."

"I wouldn't say that." Conroy smiled. "You did this town a big favor the other day."

"What's happened with those guys?" Guthrie asked.

Conroy shook his head.

"They got bailed out right after the arraignment. They claimed you shot first, and they were just defending themselves."

"You believe that?"

"Not on your lives. You two check out fine, but those clowns...." He shook his head slightly. "They don't check out at all. My guess is, they won't show up for the trial."

"You might be right, there, Sheriff. So we're free to go?"

"As long as you say you'll come back for a trial. If there is one."

"You can count on it," Guthrie said.

"Well, then," Conroy said, rising and coming around the desk.

"Pleasure meeting you, Sheriff." Guthrie stuck out his hand, and Conroy shook it.

"You fellows are welcome here, anytime." He turned and shook with Espinoza. "Next time, let's hope things are a little less interesting in our usually quiet little town."

"We'll be going, then," Guthrie said, and the sheriff nodded as they headed for the door.

"One more stop," Guthrie said. "We can't leave town without saying goodbye to Irene."

After their final meal at the cafe, Espinoza drove Guthrie to the Suburban.

"I guess this is it," Espinoza said as Guthrie gathered his kit from the back of the cab.

"Not on your life, Gil. I'll call you next week to see how things are going."

"That would be great," Espinoza said brightly.

They shook, and Guthrie waved as the trainman drove off toward the main line. Then he got into the Suburban and drove over to the gas station to fill up. Just as he finished and was hanging up the pump nozzle, two carloads of rough-looking men pulled up to the pumps. Eight of them. Several went toward the restroom, while one approached Guthrie.

"Any good place to eat around here?" he asked.

"The best place in town is the cafe just across the highway." Guthrie pointed. "Tell 'em Guthrie sent you."

"How about the Dunton Ranch. You ever hear of that?"

"I sure have," Guthrie said, smiling. "It's out west of here about fifteen miles. But I can tell you for a solid fact that there isn't shit out there."

He opened the Suburban's door, got behind the wheel, and pulled out of the gas station. Just ahead was the entrance ramp to the interstate and the long drive back to the everyday.

42

"YOU'LL NEVER BELIEVE WHAT HAPPENED," Espinoza said excitedly, almost as soon as he sat.

"Good news, it looks like."

They were in Dot Coffeeshop. It was mid morning—dinnertime for Espinoza—and Guthrie lingered over a second cup of breakfast coffee. Kay, the waitress, arrived before Espinoza could answer and left water, silverware, and a menu.

"Couldn't be better," Espinoza said after she left, ignoring the menu. "Dan Beaman's gone."

"Gone?"

"As in fired. And arrested. Ray Hudson, too. Somebody ratted out their smuggling operation sometime before I got back, and both of them are in jail right now."

"That is great news," Guthrie said nonchalantly, taking a sip of coffee to hide the faint smile growing on his lips.

"Yeah, but there's something weird about it. The authorities say I'm the one who called in the tip, but I know I didn't. Did you do that for me?"

"Not me," Guthrie said. "Must be the Catholic Church needed someone to hang the heroism on. It might as well be you. The ring is smashed because of you."

"Heck, I even got a reward for it. On top of the one from the mine company in Sierra Blanca." Espinoza's brows lowered as he peered at Guthrie. "I feel guilty about getting all that reward money and you getting nothing."

"Don't worry about me. "I was amply rewarded."

"Mr. Terry?"

Guthrie nodded. Tereba had paid him well, but for him, the real reward was less tangible. He was gradually recovering a sense of himself, a recovery he owed to Tereba. Each time he helped the old man, his debt to himself diminished. But even so, Guthrie figured that if he ever paid off the account, he'd still help out if Tereba needed him.

"That's not the only good thing," Espinoza said. "Guess who they hired to replace Beaman?"

"That would have to be you. Not only the hero of Sierra Blanca, but for UP, too. So, with all that newfound responsibility and pay raise, how about that ring for your girlfriend's finger?"

"Tomorrow night. I'm taking her to our favorite restaurant and proposing there."

"That's wonderful. Be sure to invite me to the wedding."

"I was hoping you'd be my best man," Espinoza said.

Guthrie had to chuckle.

"Something funny?"

"Yeah. The day you first called me I'd just served as best man in another wedding."

"No kidding?"

"I'll be happy to. Just let me know when."

And when, he thought, would *he* find time to find a woman to spend time with?

Not today, apparently. Just after Guthrie arrived home, his phone rang. Sheriff Conroy was on the other end.

"I'm calling to let you and Mr. Espinoza know that you all can relax about coming back out here for a trial," Conroy said. "Looks like those four boys skipped out. Heck, close as we are to the border, they could've been out of the country an hour after they posted bail."

"I'm sorry to hear that, Sheriff. That was probably one case your judge would like to have heard."

"He would. Well, thanks again for your help, and if you ever get out this way again, be sure to look me up."

"I'll do that."

Guthrie had two more things to do that afternoon, and to prepare for the second, he called Li Wu.

"Finished with the case?"

"Finished. Would you let Master Tereba know I need to debrief. Preferably this afternoon so I can put this all behind me."

"I'll let him know. Shall we resume our regular practice?"

"We shall."

Before Guthrie drove to Bellaire to talk to the old man, he headed toward the Horton house.

Emily Horton, herself, opened the door. There was no sign of her mother.

"Mr. Guthrie," she said, letting him into the house. "I didn't know if I'd see you again. I guess you know about Buddy."

She still looked careworn, but something about her was lighter, somehow, and a spark of hope was in her eyes.

"I do, Mrs. Horton, and I'm terribly sorry."

They sat.

"Buddy was a good man, and he got killed trying to stop some criminals. I can't bring him back, but I'm proud of what he tried to do."

"*Did*, Mrs. Horton. Without Buddy, the whole smuggling operation would have stayed hidden. If anyone brought it down, it was him. It was a worldwide organization, and it hurt and killed a lot of people."

"At least I have that consolation."

"I heard that there was some sort of settlement? Are you going to be okay financially?"

"More than okay," she said, looking a bit bewildered. "The insurance money is more than I ever imagined, and they're setting me up with a financial advisor to help me understand how to deal with it. What am I going to do with a financial advisor?"

"Follow his advice," Guthrie said.

"They even recommended an experimental treatment for Mom's cancer and got her into the program."

"I noticed she's not here."

"She's in M.D. Anderson Cancer Institute. The insurance is paying for everything. They say the treatment is promising." She shook her head. "I can't believe that I'm feeling glad. It's all because Buddy's dead."

She hung her head, weeping for a moment. At last she straightened and wiped her eyes on a tissue from a box on the end table.

"Yes," Guthrie soothed. "It's terrible your good fortune was at the expense of your husband's death. That can't be changed. But life always progresses through death. Think of it like this: Now you have the opportunity to completely change your children's future, and the future is what life is all about."

After he left the Horton house, he steered the Xterra toward Bellaire. Thankfully, the door to Tereba's lair was in place. He got out of the car, picked up the plastic grocery sack that was lying on the passenger seat next to him, and went to the door. Inside, he found the old man perched as usual, like some low-key genie, atop his stool. Guthrie pulled over another stool and sat across the counter.

"Hello, Mr. Guthrie," Tereba said jovially. "I'm glad to see you've returned intact. Did you take care of the monster man? What was it, exactly?"

"A troll."

"Really?" The old man seemed surprised. "I always thought those creatures were myth."

"This one wasn't."

"What happened to it?"

"I forced it into the sunlight, and it froze into stone."

"Ah." Tereba nodded. "Sunlight."

"Here," Guthrie said, handing over the grocery sack.

"What have you brought me?" Tereba asked, opening the sack and pulling out a a thin sheaf of papers and the manilla bubble-wrap envelope containing Brother Fidelio's letter to the pope.

"The pages are a report on what happened. I thought that would be simpler than telling you every single detail. The other is an interesting historical document about the Christianization of Scandinavia. It's really old. Ancient, even. From about the time you were born." Tereba shot him an offended look that Guthrie pointedly ignored. "At least I'm told it's interesting, but I can't read Latin."

"Where did you get it?"

"Donner Thorvald. He stole it from the secret Vatican archives."

"Why would a simple historical document be kept secret unless it contained something damning. Since your monster was a troll and the letter regards Scandinavia, I presume there's a connection."

"The manuscript describes how to create trolls."

"Oh, my. I guess the method is accurate."

"Oh, yeah. At the moment, only Thorvald and I know the secret, and you will, too, if you read the manuscript. I thought about destroying it, but I can't bring myself to. So I'm giving it to you because I know you'll either destroy it yourself or keep it safe. Whatever you decide, I can assure you that we don't want a bunch of trolls running around, preying on humanity. They're a little harder to get rid of than you might imagine. And clever in a nasty sort of way."

"I imagine," Tereba responded with a smile.

Guthrie briefly related the story of trapping the troll and eliminating it. He didn't say "kill."

"Life is a school from which you graduate, sooner or later, whether you've learned your lessons or not," Tereba commented when Guthrie finished. "The precipice is the price of understanding as well as a symbol of the order of knowledge gained."

"I don't know about that, but at least it was going to eat me instead of melt me alive like Aswad Mar," Guthrie said dryly. "Is it still alive, do you think, trapped with all its brethren in some amorphous netherworld?"

"Perhaps," Tereba said. "Monstrosities like that usually find ways to reemerge despite our best efforts."

"Speaking of monsters, what did you do with Bertrando Galtero?"

"Why, I put him on my payroll, of course." Tereba smiled. "There's no use in wasting obvious talent. But you needn't worry about him, Mr. Guthrie. He understands that he is now your ally for life, so if you see him again, don't hurt him."

"He's seen the light, is that it?" Guthrie asked doubtfully

"Something like that. You have to learn about gravity in order to stand up. As you have."

"I don't know that I've seen the light. Or stood up. Right now, I'd rather see the insides of my eyelids for two or three days straight."

"I'll try not to disturb you for at least another week."

"What I don't get is why some people have to be like Thorvald. Not to mention the cabal he was trying to destroy."

"The minds of people like Thorvald and his ilk are like mazes," Tereba said a little sadly. "To serve its function, a maze must be enclosed and limited. If its parameters become too open and broad, a maze ceases to be a maze and becomes too much its own reality."

"Unfortunately," Guthrie said, "we can't see the maze from above, only the passageways right in front of us. In the end, we take the turns we take and do what we do, and that's what we do. What more could there be?"

"Bravo, Mr. Guthrie," Tereba said with seeming sincerity. "You have justly but kindly put an old man in his place. Age, it seems, does not always confer wisdom."

"Be seeing you, Master Tereba," Guthrie said, sliding off the stool and heading for the door.

"Yes, Mr. Guthrie. You will."

For the further adventures of Clay Guthrie, check out these titles.

THE DEAD DETECTIVE

Teetering on the edge of the gutter, ex-cop Clay Guthrie is offered a way out of his bitter isolation. All he has to do is locate a stolen sculpture. The task seems simple enough until Guthrie finds himself enmeshed in a series of surreal events that push him to the breaking point. His disturbingly dangerous employers threaten him with pain and death if he fails, and the mysterious old man who is their antagonist forces Guthrie to act on his behalf, warning that worse horrors will greet his success. The only way Guthrie can survive is to find the sculpture and help the old man destroy the terrible power that lives within it. But first, he must endure a series of trials that test his endurance and drive him into the core of his own corruption.

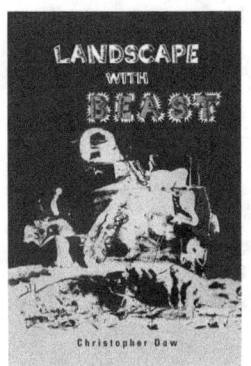

LANDSCAPE WITH BEAST

"Who better to send into a grave situation to find out what lies buried there than one who has known death? Such as you." With those words, mysterious old Tereba sends Guthrie on the trail of a missing artist. Having to deal with a witch from an ancient lineage and the ultimate hunter seeking the ultimate prey didn't bother him, but the doorway to another world was a different matter. Out there an unknowable predator waited, and it wanted nothing more than to lay waste to everything in its path. But Guthrie couldn't refuse. He knew that anythingTereba directed his way would be as interesting and important as it might be dangerous, and those were lures he couldn't resist. Besides, when he set a trap for his nemesis, the bait wasn't the only thing that disappeared into the unknown along with the artist. Now Guthrie's client had vanished, too.

THE TEXAS TROLL UNLIMITED

When a frightened railroad employee tells Clay Guthrie that a monster in a boxcar ate his co-worker, Guthrie finds himself drawn into a web of corrupt and warped ambition and wanton violence. Traveling to far West Texas in search of the monster, Guthrie and the trainman encounter an organization whose goal is the total destruction of social order and whose weapon is an abomination from the past. Waging a guerrilla war against their enemies beneath the harsh Texas sun, they quickly discover that the nights hold a mortal danger more terrible than their human enemies. With the fate of civilization in the balance, they must eliminate the humans who stand in their way before they can root out and confront a canny and clever inhuman foe.

DARKNESS INSATIABLE

Clay Guthrie is sent by his mysterious employer to track down a missing man, but finding the objet of his search in an unnatural place and in an impossible condition provides no easy answers. Far worse, he encounters a town the grip of an unknown, unseeable, and malevolent force that thrives on turmoil and destruction and has left the utter annihilation of three other towns in its wake. What will it take to learn the cause and remedy it before it's too late? And who—or what—will get in the way?

Phosphene Publishing Company
publishes books and DVDs relating to literature,
history, the paranormal, film, spirituality, and the
martial arts.

For other great titles, visit
phosphenepublishing.com